Valhalla Found
By
Christopher Cartwright

Copyright 2021 by Christopher Cartwright
This book is protected under the copyright laws of the United
States of America. Any reproduction or other unauthorized
use of the material or artwork herein is prohibited. This book
is a work of fiction. Names, characters, places, brands, media
and incidents either are the product of the author's
imagination or are used fictitiously. All rights reserved.

Prologue

Atlantic Ocean, Newfoundland, 980 A.D.

It was a good day to die.

Ragnarök gripped the silver amulet depicting his gods, and made a silent prayer to Thor and Odin. In his other hand, his fingers clasped over the hilt of his sword, *Gunnlogi* – which meant battle flame – holding so tight the whites of his knuckles developed an angry glow like fire. If the Gods had ordained this as the last day of his life, he wanted to be sure to fight his way to Valhalla – that majestic hall for those who died in combat to feast alongside other legendary Viking heroes and kings. He grinned sardonically as he stared out at the darkened sky and the evil that approached from the distant horizon.

A moment later, the wave crashed over the prow of *Íslendingur*, his longship, little more than a toy in the tempestuous seas, sending a spray of saltwater rushing across the open deck. The ship's prow rose out of the trough, and for a split second, all that could be seen was the dark sky above. When the Viking ship righted again, they were greeted by a second wave.

Ragnarok braced for the onslaught.

A wall of water slammed into the hull with jarring ferocity. The force and momentum of the wave, undisturbed by the warship, kept going with the casual indifference of a master's boot upon a dead slave.

The crest of the wave ripped across the deck, taking with it several of his crew, who disappeared overboard in the violent wake. A series of popping sounds echoed throughout the hull as more than a dozen planks of oak broke free of their caulking and began to splinter.

The sixteen rows of oars began to move in unison.

It was a valiant display of
looked down upon their plight
what remained of his crew. Ra{
saltwater spray from his eyes, a
managing to crawl its way out of the turbid waters.

For a few minutes, the seas appeared to settle, and the longship built up momentum once more, its sleek lines ploughing through the sea, slicing at the waves. Ragnarök ran his eyes across the swell, toward the imposing dark clouds that raced to greet his fleet. There was a deep haze over the water, and the skies were now dark gray. There was something sinister about the giant spirals that rose hundreds of feet into the air, as they whipped the sea into a deadly frenzy.

There was no sign of the rest of his fleet. Not even any flotsam or evidence those once proud Viking ships ever existed.

The ocean had simply swallowed them all whole.

Ragnarök's eyes were wide. His regal face animated, his strong jawline, beneath which stood a plaited beard that tapered at the center of his chest, was set with the fatalistic confidence that came from knowing within his veins flowed the royal blood of the warriors who came before him. His sea-green eyes remained defiant and determined.

A fierce wind began to whistle through the longship, sounding almost ghostlike, a spectral flute playing the tune of a melancholy dirge. Its rhythm and pace rising to a staccato, whipping his long, flowing, red hair into a flurry as the tune turned to a violent howl, as though it too suddenly sensed the need for battle.

Like the wind, Ragnarök felt the urge to scream his battle cry against his deadly enemy. As he ran his eyes across the turbulent seas, before landing on the fast-approaching storm, he knew that he and his crew were the last. The remainder of his fleet were at rest at the bottom of the ocean. It was unfortunate, given all that they had found in the new and fertile lands, but it was the will of the gods.

It was the third wave that finally caused *Íslendingur* to capsize.

The wave lifted the longship up and over, turning it around in a barrage of raging white-water. Ragnarök held his breath and gripped the tiller, keeping it straight, as though his will alone might be capable of steering the vessel out of the dark confines beneath the sea, to rise free to the surface once more.

The next few seconds passed slowly.

Ragnarök had no idea what happened after that. He was nothing more than a passenger on his own upturned vessel.

Once they had gone over, the gods deemed it necessary to save his ship.

A fourth wave turned *Íslendingur* onto her keel once more.

Ragnarök kissed his amulet and thanked the gods. His eyes traced what was left of *Íslendingur*. Part of the ornamental, carved dragon head on the bow had been cracked, leaving two distinct pieces – or one ugly looking double headed dragon. Following the lines of the hull backward, he saw that the ship was still sound, her hull straight and intact, with no catastrophic breaches. His gaze landed on the remnants of the mast, which had snapped where it was mounted to the deck, leaving giant shards of splintered oak that formed a deadly array of spear like edges – upon which, one of his men had been impaled.

He drew a sharp breath. His men. Brave men. They should have died in battle, not at sea.

Ragnarök counted the men left aboard. There were just twelve in total. Two were badly injured and would most likely be dead before the end of the day. One was dead, impaled on the remnants of the mast. That left nine able-bodied men on board… ten once he included himself. The mast and sails were gone, along with some of the oars, but there would be enough to limp back to land.

If the storm didn't finish them all.

Ragnarök worked to rally his men at the oars. *Íslendingur* was full of water, making her ride low. It seemed futile to try and empty her flooded bowels, and besides, the additional weight was actually making her more stable in the sea. She was cumbersome to steer and slow, but his men were strong and each one rowed with the knowledge that his life depended upon it. Soon, the Viking ship was ploughing through the water.

He set a course back to the strange lands from which they had set out eight days earlier. A quick evaluation of his sunstone confirmed that *Íslendingur* had settled into a westerly course.

The worst of the storm seemed to abate and Ragnarök lay back and rested on the tiller.

For the first time since the storm had struck, his mind was free to wander. He thought about the fleet he'd lost. The battles that they had fought and won together. The strange new land and the wealth that it had brought them.

Íslendingur limped westerly at a snail's pace despite her crew's best efforts. Ragnarök studied his sunstone, trying to mark basic reference on his navigational chart, etching small runic marks in stone. And what he saw disturbed him. Without a full crew on oars, they were powerless to make adequate headway, and were being dragged into the northern currents.

He tried to make navigational adjustments using a type of guessing game called dead-reckoning, but without any land references to go by, it was nearly impossible to predict whether they were being dragged too far north, or if they had overcorrected and were now heading too far south.

Only time would tell.

And that time, it turned out, would be nearly three weeks, long after his two injured men had died, and another two had succumbed to the hostilities of the elements.

They spotted land.

It was a different land. Instead of a world filled with lush meadows, they came upon giant cliffs that barred their entrance to the shore.

After following the coastline for two days, they reached an opening, and entered the vast fjord. *Íslendingur* traveled down the long, narrow, deep inlet of the sea between the high cliffs. Something about the land brought the calmness of familiarity to Ragnarök. Snow caps covered the crests of the nearby peaks, as they sailed inland, passing several majestic glaciers. They traced the river through the fjord for a further three days, before reaching the first opening in the mountains.

The mouth of the opening was guarded by two giant rocks, which had fallen on each other to form a natural arch. The gateway was big enough for the largest of longships to enter, and the stilled water seemed to continue a long way inside.

Ragnarök eased *Íslendingur* to a standstill at the opening, allowing a clear view of the inside. His eyes followed the darkness of the cavern, tracing the vast void, before drawing a sharp breath, as his vision landed on something so strikingly beautiful as it was surreal.

A natural fissure in the cavern's ceiling allowed sunlight to filter down into the massive grotto. The crepuscular beams fixed upon a small island at the center. There, massive butterflies as large as a grown man's hand, danced in the warmth of the rays.

Their wings were a dark purple, and the butterflies congregated in such large numbers that the formation produced a sort of flowing velvety purple drape. The butterflies turned and Ragnarök noticed that the creatures' wings produced a prismatic rainbow on the other side, which now caused the drape to turn into a river of color, beneath which, stood a vivid mass of dark green vegetation.

The solitary island was shrouded in a carpet of plants that Ragnarök didn't recognize. The strange, foreign plants had a sort of primordial look about them, with their over-sized leaves that were several feet in diameter, and had most likely evolved to extract as much energy from what little sun reached their subterranean world. The plants had grown prolifically, overtaking the small confines of their underground island, and stretching out like lily pads overlapping the water's edge.

Ragnarök was spellbound.

It was the most magical thing he'd ever witnessed.

More priceless than any amount of gold.

He said, "Let's beach *Íslendingur* inside."

Bjørn, a tall man with a barrel chest that seemed to match well with the origins of his name, which meant *bear*, said, "Are you sure you want to go in there?"

"No," Ragnarök admitted. "But there's an island there. Some dry land. We need to bring *Íslendingur* out of the water, drain her, and make repairs."

Bjørn touched his amulet, in an attempt to ward off the evil he was certain was present. "There might be a place to do so deeper inside the fjord?"

"And there might not be. The fjord may end with an impenetrable cliff and we will be forced to retreat back out into the ocean." Ragnarök took a deep breath, sighed, and said, "No, we'll enter here. Making the ship seaworthy is the priority."

"It will be dangerous."

"Yes, but without the *Íslendingur*, the threat is even more certain."

Bjørn nodded. "The gods will decide our fate."

There was no more debating, no challenges. The men trusted Ragnarök with their lives, and would follow him in the depths of battle, even if it took them to Valhalla itself.

Ragnarök took a reading on his sunstone, making a note in his navigation chart. He stared at it. Until recently, the chart looked sound and he was proud of the detailed maps of the Newfoundland that he'd developed. But since the storm, and losing his fleet, the map was filled with gaps. Even so, he made a note of the strange grotto, referencing it to what he'd seen through the sunstone.

To the aft of the longboat, Ragnarök opened a secret locker. It had been built into the ship's hull. The only fixed, and therefore permanent locker on the boat, which otherwise was an open hull. Inside were his most valuable treasures. He retrieved *Gunnlogi*, feeling better with the glistening, gold encrusted hilt of his sword in his hand, and replaced the sunstone and navigational runestone inside, securely locking the hidden mechanism, and sealing it.

At his command, the men eased *Íslendingur* into the deep chamber. She had a rounded belly, like most Viking ships, giving her a shallow draft. It meant she was unlikely to get beached, and even if she did, they would be able to drag her out again. But that didn't mean she was immune to the jagged rocks that might lay beneath the dark waters.

It was dangerous.

But it was a risk that must be taken.

His men gently pulled on the oars and *Íslendingur* slowly rounded the entrance, providing Ragnarök with his first glimpses of the full underground chamber. He gasped at what he saw – more than thirty ships lay wrecked, strewn throughout the ancient grotto. Spears and swords littered their decks, the only visible remnants of a battle that took place long before.

Bjørn said, "Where have you taken us?"

Ragnarök grinned. "Why Bjørn, I believe we've just entered Valhalla."

*

They dragged *Íslendingur* up onto the leafy shore of the island.

Ragnarök stepped across the giant leaves of the strange plants, heaving the longship out of the water, until at last they were standing on the island's solid ground. With the ship out of the water, he was able to examine her hull. His lips curled with pleasure as he found her in good shape. Despite some of her planks being de-caulked, for the most part, she had come out of her ordeal intact.

His crew went to work, cutting up parts of the strange leafy plants to re-caulk the ship. No wooden boat can claim to be entirely watertight, but the Vikings did their best. The caulking was generally made from animal hair, such as sheep's wool, dipped in a sticky pitch made from pine resin. They carried the pine resin, but would need to use the fibrous tissue of the strange leaves in place of the animal hair to make any viable caulking.

Ragnarök watched as the men set about their work.

Satisfied that all was being done for his ship, he decided to take a stroll and explore the small island. The weight of command sat heavily on his broad shoulders. He had to think. He needed space to be as alone as a god. Using his sword, he cut his way through the thick vegetation, hacking his way as he headed toward the inner section of the island.

About thirty feet off the center of the island, where the beam of light struck, a single butterfly caught Ragnarök's eye. The magnificent creature gracefully flapped its wings, making short bursts of flight between the giant leaves of individual plants. Ragnarök's eyes narrowed, the edges of his mouth curling upward, as he watched, mystified.

He was hit by a wave of curiosity.

The butterfly was testing the leaves.

He followed the butterfly until it finally landed on a leaf that met its desires. Ragnarök stepped closer, careful not to disturb the delicate and beautiful creature. The butterfly appeared to be oblivious, or at the very least, unconcerned by his appearance. He studied the large wings. They were royal purple with a double set of eyes on its back. Up close, he could just make out the four individual images that looked like eyes, but from any distance, they looked like a pair of eyes.

The double set of eyes gave the butterfly's wings the unique effect that no matter where you were, the eyes appeared to be tracking you, following your every movement. It was obviously a natural response to predatory attacks, but like so many things found in nature, the design was flawless.

The butterfly took off again, revealing the prismatic colors of the other side of its wings, and returned to the warmth alongside the flowing drape of purple velvet, basking in the rays of sun. Ragnarök returned his gaze to the spot where the butterfly had been resting. In its place, he noticed there were about a hundred tiny eggs on the enormous leaf.

He turned to leave and noticed the outline of the vessel beneath the plants.

Ragnarök made short work of it, cutting and hacking away at the giant plants until the outline of the old vessel came alive. It was much larger than any Viking ship. It had a high freeboard – the distance between the waterline and the deck – from which three sets of oars originated. It was a design he'd never seen or even heard of previously.

On the deck, he found a locked storage chest made of wood, wrapped in a shell of iron bands, with a locking mechanism at the center. Unknown years of exposure had rendered the box dilapidated, the iron rusted, and the lock sealed permanently.

Ragnarök lifted his sword, ready to use the blade to fracture the lock.

But stopped short.

Because something caught his attention.

It was a long spear known as a Gungnir. Beside it was an iron hammer with a noticeably short handle. It was called a Mjölnir. He would have identified it instantly. In fact, he recognized both weapons.

And why shouldn't he?

One was the *Spear of Odin*.

The other the *Hammer of Thor*.

Ragnarök drew a reverent breath at what appeared to be the final resting place of his gods. His eyes narrowed.

Could it be that Odin and Thor fought – to their deaths?

The thought wasn't entirely implausible. The Viking gods were notoriously violent and barbaric. It seemed not only possible, but fitting, that they should have killed one another.

But over what?

Ragnarök's eyes locked on the treasure chest.

He stuck the tip of his sword into the lock and pushed. The tough steel of the sword ripped through the brittle metal of the ancient locking mechanism with a satisfactory *crunch*. He lowered the angle of the blade and forced it through the top of the chest. Pleased that he was developing enough leverage to do something with it, Ragnarök pulled on the hilt, and the sword pried the chest wide open.

Inside was a rich hoard of treasure.

There were golden trinkets, ornaments, and masks depicting the face of monsters. Beside these were several pieces of jewelry made from jade. At the center of the chest was a single clay pot with two handles and a neck that was considerably narrower than the body. Painted on the side of the pot was a depiction of two warriors fighting.

He turned the pot around.

And felt a shadow of fear cross over him like a ghost.

Painted on the side of the pot was a butterfly. It was identical to the purple ones that filled the island. Even without the purple color in the paint, he could tell they were the same. Those double sets of eyes on the back of the wings seemed to track his movements as he turned the jar around. He popped open the clay lid. Inside, were thousands of seeds. He dug his hands into them, expecting to find some other treasure, but there was none.

Ragnarök replaced the lid. Something about it felt wrong. He couldn't justify his sense at a rational level. After all, a butterfly is a magnificent creature. There was nothing intrinsically evil about a butterfly. Yet, somehow, in his gut he had a foreboding sense that these butterflies had been the source and the reason of the ill winds that came and slaughtered his gods – Odin and Thor.

Panic reared its ugly head in an instant.

Ragnarök knew they needed to leave this mysterious cavern – immediately.

He ran back to his ship, where the men were working to make the vessel seaworthy. His thumping heart had settled. There was something evil within this dark underground chamber, but the rational side of him – the warrior side of him – still lusted after treasure. He and his men returned to the shipwreck and retrieved the ancient treasure chest. They carried it, along with the *Spear of Odin* and the *Hammer of Thor* – storing their cache between the thwarts – the rowing seats-cum-chests.

With greed taking hold of his men, Ragnarök agreed to return to the ancient wreck once more to search for any more treasure.

They reached the dilapidated vessel.

But never entered its hull.

Instead, a crack of thunder snapped outside, echoing throughout the cavern. Seconds later, a wave more than ten feet high filled the grotto.

Ragnarök and his men raced toward *Íslendingur.*

But they were too late.

The water receded, as the wave returned, having bounced off the edges of the cavern walls, taking with it *Íslendingur*. Ragnarök and his men ran through the shore of the cavern trying to keep pace. It was an impossible task, and in the end, they watched impotently as their ship disappeared out the mouth of the grotto.

A moment later, there was a second crack of thunder.

This one was followed by the crumble of the mountain, as thousands of tons of rock and ice suddenly filled the opening, sealing them inside, to be entombed forever in Valhalla.

While outside…

Íslendingur sailed free.

Her hull filled with a priceless cargo of ancient origin, the ghost ship sailed blithely out into the unnamed fjord – to a fate unknown.

*

Battle of Fish Creek – Saskatchewan – 1885

It was an unusually cold April morning.

The sky was a rich cerulean blue, with only a few cumulus clouds scattered across the horizon. The air was crisp and, in the distance, the landscape still white with overnight frost, which had failed to thaw.

Felix Tremblay pulled the top of his fur coat in tight across his neck. The balloonist met the piercing gaze of his observer, Major General Frederick Middleton, as the man stepped into the basket. Middleton gave him a single curt nod, confirming he was ready to take flight. Felix released the first 100-pound sandbag and the Intrepid balloon – a remnant from the American Civil War – rose eagerly into the air.

The balloon was tethered to a landing platform, via a cable, and was taken up into the air a full thousand feet. Major General Frederick Middleton wore the confident smile of a leader who knew the outcome of a battle before it had been fought. And why shouldn't he? Felix knew that they were ahead of their enemy in every measurable means.

Felix thought about their enemies. The Canadian forces were expected to quell the North-West Rebellion, headed by rebel Métis leader, Louis Riel. It would be a decisive victory.

The Métis traced their descent to both Indigenous North Americans and European settlers. Not all people of mixed Indigenous and Settler descent were Métis, as the Métis were a distinct group of people with a distinct culture and language. The indigenous group's homeland encompassed parts of Canada and the United States between the Great Lakes region and the Rocky Mountains.

General Middleton stared down at the battle unfolding with startling speed at the coulée – where the large, steep-walled, trench-like trough formed part of the flood channel along Fish Creek and basalt created a natural plateau. His militia began advancing with more than two hundred men when approximately forty Métis soldiers ambushed them.

Middleton asked Tremblay to take them down to 500 feet, so they could get a better view of the battle, including their certain triumph. He gave a knowing grin at the sight. His men outnumbered the enemy five to one. It would be a bloodbath of their own making.

But war was never that simple.

Tremblay watched as the battle unfolded. The two uneven armies clashed. The Canadian soldiers were mostly equipped with Snider Enfield rifles. The weapons were somewhat antiquated, with fat, stubby cartridges that held soft lead bullets plugged with clay. Some marksmen were equipped with the more accurate and deadly, Martini Henry rifles. The army had four nine-pound field guns, and a brand-new weapon known as a Gatling gun, on loan from the American Army to see how it performed in actual battle.

In comparison, the Métis used repeating, lever-action Winchesters, double-barreled shotguns, and muskets, as well as some previously captured army carbines. The muskets were a type of muzzle-loading shoulder gun with a long barrel, formerly used by infantrymen. Carbines were rifles with a relatively short barrel. When the Métis ran out of ammunition for their guns, they used nails and made bullets from spent bullets.

The Métis pounded Middleton's men with one devastating fusillade before withdrawing into cover and restricting themselves to sniper fire in order to conserve ammunition. Their position was strategically selected and enabled a simple and effective strategy of defense. The Métis were positioned in the coulée, meaning that the Métis soldiers were restricted to shooting up toward the Canadian army in which many of the casualties and wounds were mainly in the upper body and head area. It looked like the Métis were about to be slaughtered.

Strung out along the coulée's edge, silhouetted against the sky, the militia fired a vast amount of ammunition at the resistance, succeeding mostly in showering tree branches across the ravine, but when the artillerymen pushed their guns to the coulée's edge to try to fire down at the concealed Métis, they suffered heavy casualties. The only targets the militia could clearly see were the Métis' tethered horses.

It would have been a massacre if it hadn't been for the five strange Métis soldiers.

Tremblay watched on in horror.

It was like nothing he'd ever seen. The men appeared to go crazy. Frustrated by being pinned down with enemy fire, something apparently snapped inside them, and the men broke free of the safety of their cover, and attacked. In the full view of the enemy the Métis soldiers raged.

They fired shots.

A group of five Métis soldiers broke off from the main army. It looked like a series of lone-wolf style fighters – unsupported by the rest of the resistance. They were armed with repeating, lever-action Winchesters, double-barreled shotguns, and the violent determination and tenacity of battle-hardened men, whose psyche had been forged with pain and suffering so that they no longer feared death.

They were lone-wolves.

Felix Tremblay watched, expecting the incredibly outnumbered attackers to be picked off like ducks lined up in a row. Yet, against all odds, the approaching men – psychopaths with death wishes as far as he could tell – seemed to be advancing with speed, firing with deadly accuracy as they ran up the coulee.

The men made a beeline for the American Gatling gun.

It seemed an unlikely target. Tremblay knew that the Métis made fun of the weapon, nicknaming it *"le Rababou,"* which meant noisemaker, because it made a lot of noise, but its unwieldly nature made it difficult to target, and the weapon rarely inflicted much damage.

Yet, five Métis appeared to be willing to risk their lives to gain control of it.

The Canadian gunners turned their sights on the lone-wolves. The Canadian high ground filled with smoke from the discharged Snider Enfield rifles.

Two of the Métis fell to the ground, after sustaining shots, but the other three kept going for the Gatling. The two soldiers who had been wounded, stood up, like men rising from the dead, and continued to fight.

The soldiers ran up the coulee.

A team of Canadian gunners fired at them, and Tremblay watched as the advancing men were picked off, one after the other, until they all lay dead on the ground. The insane attack. A forlorn hope by desperate men, had finally reached its inevitably, and grizzly end.

Middleton placed his hands together, steepling his fingers. A grin formed on his thin lips. "Well, at least that's over now."

"Crazy!" Tremblay agreed.

But then, a moment later, the five men, appeared to spring back to life. They stood up simultaneously and continued their brazen attack on the Canadian forces. The attackers moved quickly, without any sort of coordinated focus. Emptying rounds from their shotguns, before dropping them, and firing with a second or third weapon.

Through a combination of luck and sheer surprise, the attackers took control of the Gatling gun. The lone-wolves turned the cumbersome weapon, and opened up into the Canadian force.

To Middleton's horror, the Canadian militia began their retreat and up in the balloon he was powerless to stop it. The dangerous team of Métis soldiers fired upon the retreating soldiers, turning the Gatling gun on its 360-degree arc along its swivel, shooting at anything and everything. To Tremblay, the attack seemed discombobulated at best. More like a child enjoying shooting than any sort of targeted attack.

But coordinated or not, the Métis suddenly took control of the battlefield.

The Canadian militia turned and ran despite their superior numbers. The American Gatling gun, which had been reserved up until this point, now fired up to a thousand shots per minute. As hundreds of rounds flew across the battlefield, every living person who hadn't found adequate cover was slaughtered.

When it was all over, and the Gatling gun's barrel spun with an empty ammunition belt still feeding into the weapon, the strange Métis soldiers turned their weapons on each other. Violent anger swelled until it could no longer be suppressed, and rage poured out like molten lava. The men began shooting one another with the short-barreled carbines, which were the only weapons still available to them.

Some of the men fell.

The others rose, and kept fighting.

It was brutal. The most horrific style of fighting, used by desperate men, driven wild with blood lust, and no longer capable of being responsible for their own actions. They struck out at each other with whatever weapons they could find, until they eventually resorted to clubbing each other with rocks picked up from the ground beneath their feet – until eventually, all five of the Métis soldiers finally lay dead on the ice-cold battlefield.

"What the hell did we just witness?" Felix Tremblay asked, his eyes wide and his mouth open. "I mean, they just successfully stormed an impossible defensive point, guarded by at least a hundred Canadian soldiers. Then they attacked each other!"

Middleton shook his head, having watched his Canadian army's bitter defeat. There was a fine tremor in his hands, his piercing eyes solemn and incredulous. "I have no idea."

Chapter One

Deer Island – Bay of Fundy, Canada – Present Day
Sam Reilly was on a RED vacation.

That stood for Reading, Eating, and Diving.

He had just solo dived *The Drift*, a world-renowned SCUBA diving site off Deer Island and was on board the *Abnaki II* on his way back to the mainland with his dog, a golden retriever named Caliburn, by his side. They had prime position on the bow of the ferry despite the cold. Caliburn was nestled on Sam's lap, his large brown eyes, staring vacantly at the sea, lost in whatever thoughts might overcome a lovable dog. In Sam's case, his mind, left to wander, returned to the dive he'd just enjoyed.

It was considered a mixture of danger and negligence, and almost certainly the height of arrogant stupidity to SCUBA dive without a buddy, but then again, Sam Reilly dived a way few people dived. And diving on his own offered him a unique sense of solace. Besides, Tom and Genevieve, the two other people he regularly dived with, were off on their own vacation, trying to do anything except SCUBA dive for a few days.

The Drift had been an enjoyable dive. It began at the small pebbled beach area behind the Deer Island campground and, as the name suggested, the dive consisted of drifting along the boulder shoreline until reaching the lighthouse, at the point of the island. It was a shallow dive, no more than 50 feet at any point, but its boulder and rocky bottom were home to a splendid array of marine fauna that called the crevices home, including a series of wolf fish, crabs, tube anemone, star fish, and scallops.

At the end of the dive, he spotted the sandy ledge that marked the exit of *The Drift*. He had to work hard for a good twenty minutes to overcome the dangerously strong current, pulling him toward the dive's greatest danger...

Old Sow.

It was the horrifying thought of becoming trapped in *Old Sow*, which made him look up now.

Located amid the ferocious tides of the Bay of Fundy, Deer Island New Brunswick was a disconcerting place for divers. Two times a day the largest tides in the world roared in and out of the bay, moving billions of gallons of water in and then back out to sea. If that wasn't unsettling enough; the largest tidal whirlpool in the Western Hemisphere, second largest in the world, could be found just off the tip of Deer Island.

Sam thought of the world's most powerful system of whirlpools. The Moskstraumen, or Maelstrom, near the Lofoten archipelago in Norway, followed by three other large whirlpools located at Saltstraumen, Norway; Corryvreckan, Scotland; and Naruto, Japan – and then there was *Old Sow*.

When conditions were right, it could open a hole in the sea some 40 feet deep in a swirling area hundreds of feet wide. The *Old Sow* and smaller surrounding whirlpools, or "piglets," created deadly navigational hazards for boats, let alone divers. The *Old Sow* was caused by fierce seawater currents running through Passamaquoddy Bay. The whirlpool is created when the regular flood tide, which can rise to 22 feet high and flows northerly up the bay, and a similar tide that flows from the west, between Deer Island and Indian Island, rush into the confined Western Passage of Passamaquoddy Bay at right angles.

The *Old Sow's* name was thought to have been derived from the mispronunciation of "sough," which means "sucking noise" or "drain."

It's one thing to hear about this force of nature, it's another to witness the whirlpool effect taking form before your very eyes. Watching a large ferry struggle against the massive force, despite its engine on full throttle, might have been enough to turn Sam off diving nearby.

He drew a long exhale and smiled.

Once again, he'd gotten lucky.

It had been a great dive and well worth the trip.

The ferry's twin C12 engines that each drove a Voith Schneider Propeller fought against the pull of the *Old Sow*, finally overcoming the extreme current, and heading toward the mainland. Twenty minutes later, *Abnaki II's* engines roared as her skipper pulled her to a stop at a rustic jetty at L'Etete.

Sam and Caliburn climbed into the Bricklin SV-1, a two-seater sports car made locally in 1974, and colored a bright harlequin green. The ferry lowered its gate, and Sam drove down the ramp, pulling north onto route 72 and releasing the reins, letting the sports car run free.

And onward, to Canada's wild northeast.

Chapter Two

The Bricklin SV-1 headed along route 72 as it wound northeast along the coast.

It was spring and the lush forest that hugged the road was rife with black bears, moose, and deer. In the passenger seat, Caliburn watched the world go by without a care in the world. Sam had been to most points on the globe, but Canada was still one of the greatest when it came to sheer natural beauty.

He drove on through St. John before pulling up at a campground overlooking St. Martins Sea Caves and the Bay of Fundy, which held the record for the greatest tidal range on earth. Achieving some 38 feet, the amount of water that flows in and out of the Bay of Fundy in a day was equal to all of the water pumped into all of the oceans by all of the rivers of the earth.

Sam noticed the tide had recently turned, and the beach along the sea caves was quickly flooding with what appeared to be something more akin to white-water river rapids than a tidal change.

It was an awesome sight to behold.

Caliburn gave a couple sharp, excited barks. There was something in his tone that caught Sam's attention.

His eyes turned to the dog. "What is it?"

The golden retriever's eyes stretched out toward the beach, where a woman was running to meet them. At a glance, Sam picked her as probably being in her early sixties. She kept running right up until she reached the car. Sam was already out of the Bricklin, ready to offer whatever assistance might be required.

"Hello," he said, meeting her panicked gaze.

She had blue eyes and gray hair, tied back in a neat plait around her shoulder. She wore glasses and might have been the grandmother from next door, but there was a hardness about her, too. Like someone who had been on her own long enough to know how to look after herself – in any situation.

The woman's eyes glanced between the sports car, the dog, before finally settling on him. "Quick, I need your help!"

Sam met the woman's gaze, and spoke with a soothing and confident voice. "What can I help you with, ma'am?"

"A young man just fell into the entrance to St Martin's Sea Cave." The woman shook her head. "The tide's coming in fast. He looked distracted by something... like he'd been chased by someone or something... I tried to warn him, but he entered the cave seeking refuge."

Sam looked at the incoming tide, racing like an unstoppable river, swallowing anything and everything in its way. He frowned. "Not the best choice with the incoming tide."

"Bad choice..." she said, shaking her head. "That cave reaches a dead end. He'll drown in there for sure."

Sam sighed. "You'd better call an ambulance."

The woman's face hardened. "Ambulance? I might as well call the coroner. There's nothing the paramedics are going to be able to do for him."

Sam listened to her in the background and opened the trunk of his car.

Inside, he reached for his dive tank. The dive gauge read just 80 bar left in the tank. A little under half empty, most of its content spent during his earlier dive off Deer Island. He was thankful he hadn't used more of it up on the dive. It wasn't much. But it would have to do.

A flash of fear ran up his spine as he glanced at the incoming tide. It was so powerful that it looked like one of those scenes where a flashflood had swept away everything in its path. There was no way he would be able to swim against it.

He paused a moment, reached back into the trunk, and retrieved his diver propulsion vehicle. The device was basically a caged propeller attached to a pair of handlebars. It weighed just eighteen pounds, but could propel him at six knots through the water. There was no telling whether or not it would be enough once he was towing an additional person.

But he had to try.

Caliburn locked eyes with him, and gave a defiant mewl. Sam had seen that look before. It was filled both with genuine concern and a mixture of admiration. And it meant, do you really have to do this?

"I have to try," Sam said, as he knelt down and gave Caliburn a quick pat. "You stay here and look after the car for me."

The woman stared at him, her face a mixture of confusion and incredulity, as though he must be stupid, insane, or the bravest man on earth – or just a horrible mixture of all three. "Where are you going?"

Sam began making his way toward the viewing platform just above the cave's entrance. "To see if I can save a life."

"Really?" The woman's voice rose a pitch with incredulity. "You want to dive into that?"

Sam stood directly above the arched entrance to St. Martins Sea Cave. "I don't want to do anything. I want to be on vacation. But sometimes fate just won't let go."

"Are you crazy?" she persisted. "You're really going to go through with this?"

Holding on to the sturdy branch of a beech tree, Sam glanced over the side. Fifteen feet below, turbid water flowed into the sea cave like a river. It was hard to imagine anyone still alive in there. And if they were, they wouldn't be for much longer.

He swallowed hard. "Yeah, why not?"

"You might die," she observed blandly.

"Maybe," Sam said, an air of fatality in his voice. "But we've all got to go someday."

And with that, he zipped up his dry suit, placed the regulator into his mouth, and, holding the sea-scooter in his left hand, stepped off the ridge...

Free-falling into the cold water far below.

Chapter Three

The icy water struck him like a sledgehammer.

Sam's head dipped several feet beneath the water before surfacing a few seconds later. He was immediately caught in the tendrils of the incoming tide, and dragged into St. Martins Cave. He gave the inflator button a quick burst, adding air to his BCD – buoyancy control device – which blew up like a balloon around his chest, propping his head out of the water. He shifted his position onto his back, held onto his DPV, and let the river do its job.

The tide was moving quickly. The water, already racing toward the top of the cavern wall, allowed just a foot of air to breathe between the surface of the flowing river and beneath the rocky ceiling. A small gap that was rapidly closing in on him, reminding him just how little time he had left to perform a miracle. A fine tremor teased his hands as a chill ripped through his eight mm neoprene dry suit like a razorblade.

Suddenly, Sam knew just how unlikely the success of his rescue mission really was. Even if the man hadn't drowned yet, he would almost certainly freeze to death within minutes if he wasn't removed from the water and warmed.

The dappled light from the entrance of the cave dissipated until darkness overtook their world. Sam reached down toward the large zipper pocket on the left side of his BCD and retrieved his flashlight. With a well-practiced and adept shift of his thumb and forefinger, he switched the light on. A beam shone through the murky water like a sabre, piercing the walls of the cave as it flickered side to side as he bobbed around with the motion of the river.

A few seconds later, the chaotic water appeared to change direction. The current that had been sucking him into the cave now appeared to circle back, creating a type of eddy at the end of the cave. With his head no more than a few inches above the water, he could barely make out his position in the cave. He considered putting the regulator back in his mouth and descending a few feet beneath the surface, but was loath to utilize any of his remaining air supply until it was absolutely necessary.

There was an abrupt change in the direction of the water's flow. The river turned into a narrow, spiraling whirlpool, Sam imagined he must have reached the end of the cavern.

A dead end.

Caught like a ragdoll in a washing machine, Sam worked to orient himself, and pick a way out of the sea cavern. His first attempt to swim across the current proved futile. His powerful kicks making no progress through the water whatsoever. On his third attempt, he hit his head on a rocky outcrop that hung low from the ceiling like a stalactite.

The impact to the side of his head concussed him, nearly knocking him out cold. His world kept spinning. The suction from the whirlpool dragging him lower and lower in the water until he was gasping for air, his mouth being drawn underwater.

Time passed slowly.

He felt the daze of someone awoken from a deep sleep. He tried to break through the misty haze of confusion, but the disorganized state held firm, and like sleep, its inertia kept tugging at him – until his head was finally fully submerged. The ice-cold water roused him before he accidentally drew a deep breath of water. With his right hand he fumbled for the regulator, placed it in his mouth and took a deep breath.

His world slowly returned to him. His head was still spinning, but the shroud of confusion lifted, and consciousness finally saw its way through.

Sam let himself float to the surface.

There wasn't a lot of air in the tank and, somewhere in the back of his mind, he knew he would need every last bar of it to reach dry land outside the sea cave. His head broke the surface. There wasn't much space between the water and ceiling at all now.

The force of the whirlpool had finally settled as the eddying water approached equilibrium. Sam sucked in a few cold breaths of air and then stopped.

He brushed up against something.

It was moving.

Not much, but moving all the same. Sam's confused mind couldn't quite place its origins. Still caught in the suction of the current, he made another lap, before brushing up against it again. His hands tried to catch it this time, but in the darkness, and numb from cold, they were unable to hold on.

On the third time around Sam caught it.

Whatever it was, it seemed cold and slippery. His other hand moved upward and caught a piece of stone jutting out from the cavern's roof. He latched on and didn't let go despite the current's best efforts to sweep him away. With his mouth just above the water he reached for his flashlight, lifting it upward until the beam shone through the water onto his rocky perch.

Next to it, he saw the white knuckles of another man's hand.

Sam lowered the beam of light until he could make out the stranger's face. The man's breathing was slow and labored. His eyes wide and unseeing. For a moment, Sam feared he was too late.

He touched the stranger's shoulder. "Are you alive?"

It seemed like a stupid thing to ask, but there wasn't much time and he needed to know. After all, he might try risking his life to save someone's life, but if that man was already dead, he would rather expend what was left of his energy to save himself. After all, there was no certainty that either of them were getting out of the sea caves alive.

The stranger turned his head with a jolt. Their eyes locked. He spoke slowly, as though in a trance. "Who the fuck are you?"

Sam drew another breath, his mouth just above the waterline. "I'm here to rescue you."

"Rescue?" The man was past being scared about dying. He'd reached the acceptance stage. "You're a bit late. I think we're about to drown together."

Sam shook his head. "Not if I have anything to do with it."

The next second, a final wave of water swept through the cavern, flooding it all the way to the ceiling. The stranger seemed to not only accept his fate, but welcomed it – letting go, the man began to sink toward the bottom.

Sam placed his regulator back in his mouth and dived after him.

Chapter Four

The stranger fell fast.

His lifeless body quickly disappearing as it drifted toward the bottom of the cavern. Sam released the air from his BCD, ducked his head under, and kicked his fins until he was heading straight for the bottom. Sam shifted the arc of his flashlight downward, and its beam flickered across the velvet blackness, as he frantically tracked the sinking body.

The man hit the sandy bottom of the cavern. There was no movement. Sam sped up, trying to reach him before it was too late.

The clock was ticking. Every second wasted meant his brain was being starved of oxygen, his brain cells dying. The ice-cold water would help. Hypothermia slowed the body's natural metabolic rate, but without oxygen, the brain damage would soon be irreversible.

Sam slowed his descent, becoming neutrally buoyant just above the stranger.

He reached forward.

His outstretched hand just about to catch hold of the victim...

Before a sudden change in the current grasped the stranger first, tearing both of them away in a turbid flow of disturbed water. Sam's world spun around wildly for the second time in as many minutes.

The sudden wash ended within a few seconds.

Sam took a breath, and fixed the flashlight around in a broad arc, trying to orient himself. The entire flooded cave looked identical irrespective of whether you were facing upward or down. Without moving and keeping track with a pressure gauge, it was impossible to tell.

And Sam didn't care.

All his focus and attention were on finding the victim, before he died.

He increased the arc of the flashlight, moving the beam in big, broad strokes across the cavern, slicing the dark environment into small parcels of light. It was in the sixth such allotment, that his beam finally landed on the stranger.

The body was still caught up in whatever undercurrent had originally pulled them apart, and was now moving swiftly away from Sam. His eyes fixed on the narrow beam of light, trying to prevent the body from disappearing a second time.

Sam switched on the electric DPV. Its single propeller whirred to life. He opened up the throttle and raced after the victim, catching up to him and locking hold of him by his belt roughly fifteen seconds later.

Sam shoved his secondary regulator into the man's mouth, and depressed the purge button, flooding the victim's mouth with air. Sam hoped as the victim sank, the icy cold water had prevented him from taking in a deep breath. If it hadn't, the man's lungs would already be full of water, and, while they remained underwater, there would be nothing Sam could do to save him.

Sam watched the man's face.

It looked lifeless…

The victim was unconscious and on that terrible edge between life and death, frozen and drowned. There was no response to the air. Sam depressed the purge button again, and the man's mouth filled with air. The man's body drifted toward that primitive state of life. Unconscious, the autonomic reflexes that drive a person to breathe, kicked into place – the man's chest rose and fell in a giant breath.

Sam didn't wait to see if he regained consciousness. He grabbed hold of him behind his torso, oriented the sea-scooter toward the entrance of the cave, and raced to greet it.

Two minutes later, Sam dragged the stranger up onto St Martins beach.

The man was freezing and without help, hypothermia would kill him just as fast as drowning – but he was breathing on his own. He took a couple deep breaths and regurgitated a large gush of seawater. His eyes opened, his pupils dilated and filled with terror. They locked on Sam's and the man tried to speak, but nothing came out.

Sam said, "Come on, we've got to get you warm."

Chapter Five

The melancholy sky broke.

The dark clouds that threatened rain earlier, gave way to large rain drops that quickly turned to sleet. The temperature dropped further, and sleet gave way to snow, before the clouds parted minutes later, and the sun came out once more.

Even in a dry suit, Sam had felt the chill of the ice-cold water, as it slowly sapped the heat and energy out of him. For the young kid, who wore nothing more than a pair of jeans and a woolen sweater, he would be lucky to survive without being warmed immediately.

Caliburn gave an excited bark.

Sam turned his gaze toward the golden retriever, where someone with good forward thinking, had already started a fire. It had been built well using porous driftwood, all lined up against each other in the shape of a small teepee, like a Scout might have been taught. The flames danced wildly, casting long, glowing shadows across the frigid beach in the dusk light.

Sam carried the stranger toward the fire. The woman who had alerted him of the man's misfortune came over to help. Together, they carried the man right up to the fire and laid him down before it.

Caliburn glanced at the ragged body, like a doll, lying strewn next to the fire. He gave a curt bark and nudged the man's white, frigid form.

Sam caught his meaning. "Quick, we need to get his clothes off."

The two of them worked to free the stranger from his soaked clothes, removing everything right down to his underwear, leaving them open on the ground to dry on the opposite side of the fire. The woman who'd alerted him of the kid's misfortune had the foresight to bring out a couple blankets and a towel. Together, they worked to quickly dry him.

Sam ran his eyes across the kid's body, looking for any injuries as he dried him. He was short. Somewhere around 5'2" he guessed. He had long auburn hair tied back and a scraggly beard, that looked like it had been grown to make him look older, rather than a decent fashion statement. He was skinny but muscular, like he'd probably blown some of his youth pumping iron and taking supplements. He didn't wear a watch or have any other jewelry. The only other noticeable thing about him was the appearance of a single tattoo displayed prominently on his left shoulder.

Sam paused, taking in the tattoo.

It depicted the face of a Viking warrior, protected by a steel helmet with horns. Beside which, were three filled in tear drops. That made him think. Tear drops on the cheeks were generally associated with gang members who had murdered someone. In this case, three people.

Sam shook his head. The kid looked too young to be caught up in such things. Then again, who knew what he was really involved in? Maybe he was reading into the tattoo a little too much? Maybe he was just a kid with a tattoo he picked because he wanted to look cool? Who knew?

After the rush, and with the worst of the life-threatening emergency over, Sam began to strip himself, removing his dry suit and keeping his shorts and woolen sweater underlay still on. He warmed himself by the fire for a few minutes before taking his dive gear and DPV back to the car and exchanging them for long pants, a thick jacket, and pair of leather boots.

Back at the fire the woman said, "Thank you. You saved his life."

Sam grinned and met her eyes. "No, he has you to thank for that. I never would have known that he'd fallen in if it wasn't for you, and he almost certainly would have frozen to death if you hadn't had the foresight to build a decent fire."

She gave a casual shrug, holding up her hands in a placating gesture. "We'll call it even and just say he was lucky."

"Yeah, he sure was."

"I'm Deb, by the way," she said, offering a candid hand. "Deb McClean."

Sam took it in his. Holding it for a few seconds, as they shared the enormity of what they had both just achieved. "Sam Reilly. Pleased to meet you, Mrs. McClean."

"You too." She smiled. "And you can call me Deb."

Something about the way she said it, made him feel like she'd been upset by the implied suggestion that she was married. He met her eye, holding her gaze for a beat. With a knowing smile, he asked, "Divorced?"

"Widowed. Twice actually."

Sam said, "I'm sorry…"

She shook off his apology with the wave of her hand. "Don't be. It was a long time ago and I was lucky to find true love twice. That's two more times than most people get in any lifetime."

Sam nodded, thinking back to his time with Aliana and Catarina with a similar sentiment. "Yeah, not everyone's so lucky." Sensing that she was ready for a change in topic, he asked, "Do you live around here?"

"No. Just visiting. I came to see the unique tides, actually." Her eyes drifted toward the water that still flowed more like a river than an ocean. Pre-empting his next question, she said, "I live on Vancouver Island."

"Vancouver Island," Sam said, his mind quickly retreating to fond memories of exploring the remote and wild wilderness as a kid. "Nice. It's a beautiful part of the world."

"Most of Canada is," she replied, not trying to hide any pride she held for her country. Her lips parted in a simple smile and she admitted, "But then, I may be biased. I've lived here all of my adult life."

Sam was about to ask where she was originally from, but was interrupted by the kid stirring. Sam looked at him. He opened his eyes, trying to blink away the fog that shrouded his memory. Confusion gave way to terror, and the kid jolted, trying to sit upright.

"It's all right, stay where you are and conserve your energy," Sam said, placing a reassuring hand on the boy's shoulder.

The kid tried to fight to sit up, but Sam's hand held him with a firm authority that dispelled any further attempt to move immediately. The kid looked around, his eyes finally landing on Sam. "Where am I?"

Sam said, "St. Martins beach."

The kid squeezed his eyes shut tight, as if to block out a painful memory. "There was an accident..."

"That's right," Sam said, "Do you remember what happened?"

He drew a deep breath and then exhaled slowly. He gave a curt nod. "I fell."

"That's right." Sam kept going. "Do you remember why you fell?"

The kid nodded. "I was being chased by someone."

"Chased?" Sam asked, "By who?"

The kid shook his head. "It doesn't matter. I needed to get away. The tide was coming in quick and I hoped that I could take refuge in the sea cave."

Sam nodded. "Except you didn't take into account the unbelievably large tides in the area, giving way to more than forty feet of seawater, flooding the entire cave system."

The kid blew out a long breath and licked his dry lips. "No. I didn't expect that," he said, sitting up, his eyes staring vacantly into the fire.

Sam's eyes fell on him, really seeing him for the first time. He looked to be in his late teens or possibly early twenties. There was an intelligence to his eyes, and a determination in the set of his jaw that seemed at odds with his age. Maybe he was a lot older than he looked? Just like one of those people with a baby face. You know the type? Or maybe, he'd just lived a full life despite his short years?

He gave the kid some space. "I'm Sam Reilly by the way."

The kid met him with piercing blue eyes. There was cunning and calculation in them, as well as a certain hardness, too – almost as though he was sizing Sam up in case they clashed violently. In the end, there must have been recognition in what the kid saw, because he broke his gaze with a suppressed smile, revealing a full set of pearly white teeth. "You were in the caves with me!"

Sam nodded.

The kid said, "I saw you right before I passed out. I thought you were a ghost, or perhaps an angel."

Sam spread his hands open. "It was just me."

"Either way, you risked your life to save mine." The kid's voice sounded solemn and honest, almost religious in its severity. "I owe you my life."

"Actually," Sam said, gesturing an open hand toward Deb, who was talking to the authorities on her cell phone to update them on the situation. "That accolade belongs to Deb over there. She was the one who saw you enter the sea cave and alerted me that you needed help. She also had the good foresight to start a fire in the off chance that I got lucky and pulled you out of the water before you drowned."

The kid's eyes fell toward Deb. "Thank you. Both of you. I really mean that. I owe both of you my life. If you ever need something, I will do my best to repay you."

"That's fine," Sam said, "I'm just glad you're okay."

Caliburn gave a curt bark, his tail wagging enthusiastically as he nudged his head onto Sam's lap.

Sam acknowledged him with an affectionate pat around his golden mane. He turned to the kid. "And this here is Caliburn."

"Nice to meet you Caliburn," the kid said with a grin, giving the dog a friendly pat. "Caliburn... like the famous sword initially built for King Arthur?"

"That's the one. You know your history," Sam said, surprised that the kid knew the difference between Excalibur and Caliburn.

"Well, I don't know about the history, but I've heard of the legend."

Sam was about to tell him what he knew to be fact about the Arthurian legend, when Deb ended the call and put her cell phone in her pocket, heading toward them. "That was the RCMP. There's been a major road accident on the highway near Tynemouth Creek. They said there was going to be a delay reaching you, and that they would have to bring in a helicopter from Nova Scotia, but I told them they could probably cancel it, because you seem to be all right. Just a bit cold. I hope that's all right?"

"Suits me," the kid agreed, with a voice sounding more like relief than regret. If Sam had to guess, a visit from the Royal Canadian Mounted Police was the last thing he needed. "I'm Miles Godkin by the way. I believe I owe you the gratitude of my life."

She blushed. "It's nothing. All I did was mention to this guy that it looked like you just got yourself killed. I never expected him to do anything about it. But then, he had his SCUBA gear out and was jumping in after you. Most foolish thing I've ever seen anyone do in my life, if you ask me."

Miles laughed. "I agree wholeheartedly. Sounds pretty reckless to me, even if I was the fortunate recipient of his stupidity."

Caliburn barked a few times again. His big brown eyes darting between Miles and Deb, before finally landing heavily with an accusatory blow on Sam.

Sam suppressed a grin. "Yeah, I've been known to do the occasional reckless thing over the years."

Caliburn barked again.

Sam shrugged. "Once or twice."

Miles turned and reached for his jeans pocket. A mixture of confusion and panic swept across his face. His wide, open mouth, turned downward on the edges, and his piercing blue eyes locked on Sam's with startling anger. "What have you done with it?"

"Your clothes?" Sam asked, his arms spread apart.

"My jeans. What have you done with them?"

"It's all right," Sam reassured him. "They're just over there, drying beside the fire."

The kid's eyes darted furtively toward the jeans, the fire, the dog, the woman who had raised the alarm, before landing defiantly on Sam without saying a word. He stood up, without wrapping the blanket around himself. The kid, wasn't quite a kid. Sam readjusted his age to be early twenties, and had the muscular physique of someone who led an intensely active life. His entire body was full of lithe muscles, without an ounce of fat on him. On second assessment, he didn't look like a gym junky. More like a fighter, not martial arts, probably more like a boxer, with that focused and defiant strength.

Miles retrieved something metallic from the left pocket of his jeans. It looked like it might have been a USB stick or memory card, but Sam couldn't be certain from the glance. Either way, it must have been valuable to the kid. He gripped it in his left hand, holding it tight. A moment later, he tried to put on his jeans. The pants were still obviously wet and he struggled.

Sam said, "Why don't you give it another twenty minutes or so. You must still be half freezing to death."

"I can't. I have somewhere to be."

Sam arched his eyebrows. "Really? You just about died."

Miles pulled up the wet pants, throwing the t-shirt over his head. "I have to get out of here."

There was something emphatic about the way the kid said it that made Sam take notice. In an instant, he wished he was closer to the car, where a loaded firearm was locked in a secret storage compartment between the driver and passenger's seat.

Sam's eyes looked around. As far as he could tell they were alone on the beach, with no one but the three of them and Caliburn for miles. "Why?"

"The people I was being chased by," Miles said, his voice trailing off into nothing. "They must have suspected I drowned or if not died of hypothermia, but there's a chance they stayed around long enough just to make sure. Maybe even a chance they're going to come back as the tide begins to recede. Either way, I plan to be long gone well before then."

Sam's eyes narrowed. "Who was chasing you?"

Miles grimaced as though certain he shouldn't be talking. Then something seemed to give way, as though he knew he could trust them, or maybe it was something else, something entirely different – as though he was already in all the trouble he could get in, and telling the truth couldn't place him in any greater danger.

He exhaled heavily. "They call themselves Berserkers."

Sam said, "Come again?"

"Berserkers… like the most ruthless Vikings."

"I've heard of Berserkers, I'm just not sure what they have to do with you being chased and then nearly killed. I mean, we're nowhere near Viking territory anymore, are we?"

Deb intervened. "Actually, there was a Viking settlement here in the 10th century, if my history serves me correct."

A flicker of a smile crossed Sam's lips. "That's right… L'Anse aux Meadows! It was discovered in the 1960s and is the only confirmed Norse site in or near North America outside of the settlements found in Greenland."

"Yes! That's the name," Deb agreed. "I've actually just come from a tour of the site a few days ago. The archeological site has always interested me and I finally got around to seeing it for myself. Some believe the place was found by Leif Erikson, the son of Erik the Red, the founder of the first Norse settlement in Greenland. According to the sagas of Icelanders, he established a Norse settlement at Vinland, which is usually interpreted as being coastal North America. There is ongoing speculation that the settlement made by Leif and his crew corresponds to the remains of a Norse settlement found in Newfoundland, Canada, called L'Anse aux Meadows and which was occupied somewhere between the 10th and 11th Century. Of course, later archaeological evidence suggests that Vinland may have been the areas around the Gulf of St. Lawrence and that the L'Anse aux Meadows site was a ship repair station."

"I don't mean to interrupt your archeological cum pre-Columbian discovery of America history lesson and all…" Miles said, frustration and intolerance plastered across his youthful face, "But I'm talking about a Viking gang…"

Sam's rolled his eyes. "Viking?"

The kid shrugged his shoulders. "They have red hair and long plaited beards. They say they were all descendants of the first Norsemen who visited the region in the 10th century."

"Really?"

"It's just one of the sagas they tell…"

Sam had heard about the Viking tendency toward sagas, the story-telling lore. He tilted his head. Bit his lower lip. "What's the other one?"

The kid swallowed hard, and exhaled deeply. His eyes darting furtively across the woodland, as though someone might still be watching him. "That they're all Berserkers, the most violent of all Vikings, and they've risen from Valhalla."

Sam spread his hands. "They sound like a bunch of punk kids. What's their real aim?"

Miles sighed. "Drugs. They're part of a syndicate of drug cartels… they have global links… and they're up and coming on the global drug market."

Sam said, "How do you know all this?"

Miles drew a deep breath, held it for a moment, and exhaled. Sam watched the relief fade away, as he finally decided to relinquish the truth. "To be honest, until a few hours ago, I was trying my best to join."

"You were in the process of an initiation thingy?"

"Uh-huh," the kid said, nodding his head.

"What went wrong?"

Miles shrugged. "I failed."

"Failed what?"

"My initiation test."

Sam continued. "And the price of failure?"

"Isn't it obvious?" Miles said. He folded his arms across his chest, breathed out. "Death."

Chapter Six

Sam glanced at the sky.

The setting sun was washing the azure sea with shades of pink across the Bay of Fundy. It had been a while since Sam had seen anything quite so beautiful, and he'd seen a lot of sunsets from the deck of his ship over the years. He doubted Miles had ever seen anything as beautiful in his short years, but the kid barely registered it – his mind, lost in the troubling memories of the past few hours.

Sam asked, "Where do you live?"

"I've been staying at a place called Sunny Corner."

Sam had never heard of it before. "Is it far from here?"

"Not far. Maybe twenty minutes by car."

Sam's mind returned to the place where he'd parked. He recalled seeing Deb's blue Toyota Camry Hybrid when he pulled up, but besides his own car, the place was empty. "Did you drive here?"

"No. I came with one of the other members of the gang."

"Right." Sam shrugged. "Okay, how about I give you a ride home?"

"That would be great. Thank you."

"No problem." Sam picked up his car keys. Hearing them jingle, Caliburn stood up, his tail beginning to wag enthusiastically.

Deb glanced at Miles, taking him in with the watchful eye of a mother. "Are you sure you're okay to go?"

"Yes, ma'am." Miles replied politely. "And thanks again for the part you played in saving my life."

She looked like she was going to challenge him on that again, but decided against it at the last minute with a shrug. "All right," she said, beginning to kick sand over the fire to put it out. "Well good luck with everything."

Sam said, "Thanks again for your help."

"You're welcome. It was nice to meet you." She handed him a note with her details. "If you're ever on the island, give me a call."

"Thank you, I will," Sam promised, taking the folded note and putting it in his pocket. "I was actually planning on taking a drive right across Canada, possibly ending my trip out on Vancouver Island… so we'll see, I might just take you up on the offer."

"Please do," she confirmed.

They headed toward the car, with Caliburn leading the way.

Sam unlocked the door to his Bricklin SV-1.

Miles swore excitedly. "You own a Bricklin SV-1!"

"Hey you know your cars?" Sam said, opening the gull-wing doors. Caliburn jumped up taking a seat in a small alcove behind the twin seats.

Miles ran his hand admiringly across the hood. "This is the 1974 model am I right?"

"That's right," Sam confirmed, suppressing a smile. "How could you tell?"

"The engine. That's the 360 cubic inch V8 from AMC, not the 354 cubic inch V8 from the Ford Windsor used in the later models."

Sam grinned, his eyes glancing at the AMC badge back to Miles. "You know a lot about the Bricklin. Tell me, are you a fan of batman or do you just know cars?"

The Bricklin had been used in the original Batman film as the bat mobile. It was the sort of thing that only a car enthusiast might know. Or Batman enthusiast, he guessed.

Miles climbed into the passenger seat through the open gull-wing door. "I might just be patriotic."

Sam's eyes narrowed. "Are you?"

"Patriotic?" The kid shrugged. "Sure."

Sam turned the key and the gravelly V8 engine awoke. "Your accent doesn't sound very Canadian to me."

Miles spread his hands in a *you got me there*, kind of gesture. "No, I was born in the good old US of A."

Sam tried to place the kid's accent. "Midwest?"

"Uh-huh. Originally from Minnesota. Been here two years."

Sam smiled as he released the handbrake and took off, quickly working his way up the 4-speed BorgWarner T-10 manual into top gear as he headed back toward the main highway. "So, which is it?"

Miles laughed. "You really want to know why I know so much about the Bricklin SV-1?"

Sam nodded. "Yeah, not many people do."

Miles slouched back into the old leather seat and laughed. "All right. The truth?"

Sam kept his eyes on the road. "Sure."

"The Bricklin SV-1 was produced in St. John – that's fifteen minutes south of here if you're wondering. The town still promotes the car as the height of its automotive manufacturing. I've been living nearby for two years, it's hard not to stop and learn a little about the Bricklin too."

It was Sam's turn to laugh.

Dusk turned to meet nighttime and Sam switched on the Bricklin's headlamps. They were those hidden, pop-up style lights that rose out of the hood, and were woefully under powered, providing two narrow beams of light. On the main highway, they would do, but he didn't like his odds of spotting wildlife up ahead before he hit it.

They drove on toward Sunny Corner in silence.

A few minutes out, Sam asked, "What are you going to do?"

The kid pulled his sweater up to cover part of his face. It reminded Sam of the sort of act a teenager might perform out of defiance, rather than trying to get warm. "I don't know. I'll think of something."

Sam said, "I mean, you know you can't stay where you are?"

"No. The Berserkers think I'm dead. I might be all right for a few days, but soon enough someone's going to realize I survived. I'll pack up my things and leave tonight."

"Good idea." Sam kept his eyes on the road. "Where will you go?"

"I don't know. I'll probably go see my brother in the US."

Sam shifted down a gear, slowing as he entered the small, rural township of Sunny Corner. He turned to Miles. "Where am I heading?"

"Take the second left and I'm the first house on the right."

"Okay."

Sam followed the directions and pulled into the driveway of a small wooden house, painted an odd shade of teal that really stood out like an eyesore against the other rural houses. He stopped the car and switched off the engine.

He asked, "Do you want me to wait for you?"

"I'm all right," Miles said. He shook his head, and then with a tone bordering on teenage bravado, he said, "I can look after myself."

Sam humored him. "Sure."

"What? I can. Or at least I normally can. I just got unlucky today, that's all."

"Okay," Sam said, thinking about that old adage, *you can lead a horse to water but can't make it drink*, and letting it go. "Best of luck."

"Thank you. Really. I mean that."

Sam watched Miles get out and walk toward the door. A moment later, he switched on the ignition and shifted the gear into reverse. He took his foot off the brake and began idling back up the driveway.

Caliburn gave a curt bark.

An icy shadow of fear washed over him.

Sam knew that bark. It wasn't playful. It was a warning. Something wasn't right and they sure as hell weren't alone. He jammed his foot on the brake, shifted back to neutral, and pulled up the handbrake – leaving the car to idle. Sam unlatched a secret compartment built into the subfloor between the Bricklin's twin-seats and retrieved his Glock. The weapon was already loaded with a 17-round magazine of 9mm parabellums. He gripped the weapon in his right hand, feeling it like a natural extension of his arm and stepped out of the car.

Miles was already unlocking the front door.

Sam shouted, "Wait!"

Miles opened the door and turned to face him. "What is it?"

A second later two shots were fired from inside the house.

Both struck Miles's gut.

And he fell backward.

An assailant stepped out of the house. Followed by a second person. At a glance, both looked remarkably like modern day Vikings – if Vikings were to ever become bikers – and both carried pistols.

Sam fired two shots back.

He was less than ten feet away and a decent marksman. Each shot landed directly on the chest of their intended targets.

Perfect kill shots.

The two wannabe Vikings hit the deck hard.

Sam raced forward and helped Miles stand. "You okay?"

"Never better," Miles replied. "Let's get out of here."

Running on adrenaline, Miles made his way quickly back to the Bricklin without Sam's help. The door to the house opened fully and another three bikers swarmed out to greet them.

Miles shouted, "Drive!"

Sam threw the gear stick into reverse and planted his foot on the accelerator.

The Bricklin SV-1 screamed backward along the driveway.

Sam swung the wheel around and the car skidded on the gravel driveway to a stop. He shifted the gear into first and accelerated hard.

In his rearview mirror, he spotted the three remaining bikers climbing onto Harley Davidsons.

Chapter Seven

Sam turned onto the main road and gunned the engine.

The car picked up speed along the rural road. It was long and straight and as the nearby pine trees whirred past there wasn't much for him to do once the car reached its top manageable speed. He risked a quick peep in his rearview mirror, and spotted the distinct flicker of three separate beams of light coming from their pursuers.

His eyes darted to the passenger seat, glancing at the kid. Miles's eyes were wide, his mouth pursed, and his breathing deep and erratic. His face was white. More like a ghost, and beneath his façade of stoicism, you didn't need much medical training to see he was dying. In his lap, the kid curled his arms across his gut, hugging himself tight, as though willing by sheer determination alone to keep his vital organs inside. Through the kid's fingers Sam watched a dark liquid overflow and spill out. It was moving so quickly, that for a second, his mind didn't even register that the kid was bleeding heavily from the bullet wounds to his gut.

Sam frowned. "You going to be okay?"

Miles grunted. "I'll live."

Sam shook his head. "Not with that sort of gut wound without help. Any idea where the nearest hospital is?"

"Yeah, Horizon's Miramichi Regional Hospital." The words came out in a single word at a time, labored response.

Sam tried to mentally picture a map of the area, but came up blank. "How far is that?"

"Ten minutes northeast of here…" Miles cracked the ghost of a smile. "Depending on how well you drive."

Sam kept his foot planted to the floor and the Bricklin's speed kept creeping upward. The underpowered headlamps providing minimal illumination, making it strenuous to keep track of the road.

Sam strained to see what was coming up in the distance.

His eyes narrowed.

"Oh shit!" he cursed, hitting the brakes hard, as he approached the T-intersection.

Beside him, Miles clenched to the edge of his seat.

Sam swung the wheel around hard to the left, heading south toward the main township. The Bricklin SV-1 shared its suspension's DNA with Datsun, including front suspension A-arms with coil springs and a Hotchkiss system of leaf springs on a live axle to the rear. It was the latter of these – despite once being ahead of its time – that struggled to accommodate for Sam's driving behavior.

Around the bend, the Bricklin hugged the road like it was ice. Its rear wheels fishtailed, and Sam had to use just about every ounce of skill, working the delicate balancing act between steering, brakes, and acceleration, to keep the car on the blacktop.

A moment later, what little control he had over the vehicle, was lost completely. The twin-seater spun off the road, its tires churning up the gravel, before the Bricklin came to a complete stop, facing the opposite direction.

Sam exchanged a quick glance with Miles. Neither were injured by the crash. Through the windshield, three beams of light punctured the thick shroud of dust.

The Berserkers had reached them.

Sam didn't wait to evaluate the damage to the car. He dropped back down to first, swung the wheel around and planted his foot on the accelerator once more – speeding off toward the main township. The Bricklin gathered speed at the sluggish pace of 10.1 seconds from zero to the sixty miles per hour mark. At that pace, the Harley Davidson's didn't even have to work to catch up.

The bikers quickly closed in on them, positioning themselves on either side of the Bricklin and one behind it, like police guarding a motorcade. Contrary to what Hollywood might have us believe, it was next to impossible to shoot – and hit anything with any sort of accuracy – while riding a bike. In this case, none of the riders attempted to draw a weapon, instead, they seemed content to follow – and why shouldn't they? There was no way Miles Godkin was getting away from them in an antique sports car.

Sam slowed his pace to a more manageable speed. No reason to get himself killed if they couldn't outrun their predators. Then again, he had no idea what he was going to do once they reached the hospital. If Miles didn't get surgical help soon, he would be as good as dead, with or without the biker's involvement.

They approached the main township of Sunny Corner. Sam asked, "Which way?"

"Cross the bridge and turn left," Miles replied in a whisper.

Sam shifted down a gear, turning onto the bridge, as he crossed over the Northwest Miramichi River. Up ahead, a beefed-up Kenworth T800 18-wheeler logging truck – massively overloaded – approached the bridge. Even without his escort of three Harley Davidsons, he would have struggled to squeeze past the truck while on the bridge. Ordinarily, he would have given way to the truck, stopping before he entered the bridge, but that was impossible given the circumstance.

While the truck turned to enter, it needed to use up the entire width of the bridge. Sam slowed the car to give him those precious few seconds to make it around the bend before both vehicles clashed – and any rudimentary study in Newton's Second Law of Motion revealed that the Bricklin was never going to come out of that equation very well.

The truck driver gave a sharp burst of the horn, either as a reproach or simply a warning. Sam made a silent apology, and kept driving. He could see it was going to be close, but the Bricklin was a small car and was reasonably confident he'd make it.

That's when the opportunity presented itself.

He suddenly switched from the brake to the accelerator and the V8 roared enthusiastically in a cacophony of gravelly exhaust sounds as the Bricklin lurched forward.

The truck driver spotted what Sam was trying to do and gave another sharp burst on the horn.

Beside him, Miles roused enough to say, "You're not gonna make it!"

Sam grinned sardonically as the oversized truck and tiny sports car raced toward a head-on collision. "Sure we will."

The biker to the right of them sped up, slipping through the gap.

In front, the truck tried to straighten up, leaving just enough gap for the Bricklin to squeeze through. But at the last moment, Sam jammed on the brakes, swerving to the left.

The biker to the left swerved to avoid the collision. But he overshot his mark. Realizing his mistake, the Berserker tried to swing back around to the right, but he was too late. He clipped the side of one of the Kenworth T800's 18 wheels. Even at a low speed, the massive wheel ripped straight through the Harley Davidson, swallowing up the rider with a gut-wrenching crunch – before the bike and rider were pulverized beneath the remaining wheels.

Sam swung as far to the right as possible, until the Bricklin scraped along the edge of the bridge, and squeezed through the gap. A second later, the driver of the truck jammed on the brakes, but it was a futile gesture, and the overloaded logging truck was incapable of stopping. Instead, its wheels locked up, and the entire rig jackknifed.

On the other side, Sam brought the Bricklin to a complete stop. The biker that had made it through was nowhere to be seen. He turned his head around to look at Caliburn. "Do you see the other one?"

Caliburn mewled in apology. His scent was exceptional, but his eyesight not as impressive. Sam stared at the destruction they had caused. The massive logging truck was jackknifed across the entire width of the bridge, and its main cab had broken through the railings, suspended in the air above the water. No one would be crossing the Northwest Miramichi River for hours. Behind the truck, the remaining Harley Davidson that had backed off earlier was now making one of the fastest U-turns in history, before speeding off on the opposite side of the river.

Sam drew a long breath.

Beside him, Miles began to cough blood.

Sam said, "Come on, let's get you to that hospital."

Chapter Eight

The Bricklin took off again.

Sam headed northeast, following the southern bank of the Northwest Miramichi River. He drove at a fast, but manageable speed. Up ahead, he spotted a flash out the corner of his eye. It was followed rapidly by a series of them, and the sound of gunshots. The bullets landed down the middle of his windshield in a small grouping of fragmented stars.

He ducked down, trying to reduce his exposure to the short barrage of pistol shots and within seconds he was past the biker who'd tried to shoot them. The biker emptied the rest of his magazine into the back of the Bricklin.

Sam kept driving. His eyes glanced in the rearview mirror. Behind them, he could see the biker feed another magazine into his pistol, before climbing back onto the bike and commencing pursuit. It looked like the rider was going to try and prove Hollywood right, and attempt to shoot them while he rode.

He glanced at his passenger. "You still with us?"

Miles put a single thumb up.

"Hang in there, I'm trying to get you to the hospital as quick as I can."

Sam kept edging the speed up until he was racing along at over 100 miles per hour. Behind him, he heard the crack of another shot being fired. The shot missed the car completely, and Sam had no way of knowing where it landed. He gently swerved across the lanes, trying to create a more difficult moving target.

When the second shot whizzed just past his head, Sam turned to Miles and asked, "I don't suppose in all that training to become a Viking member…"

"Berserker… you mean?" Miles asked, interrupting him with a forced grin.

"Whatever…" Sam said, jamming on the brakes with a skid, and swerving to miss a baby brown bear crossing the road, before hammering his foot on the gas once more. "Did you ever learn to shoot a firearm?"

"Can I shoot?" Miles asked, with a suppressed smile.

"Yeah, can you shoot?"

"I can shoot," Miles assured him. "You want to give me a gun?"

Sam pressed a red button on the dashboard. It was like something straight out of an old Bond film. Only, instead of producing a hood mounted rocket launcher, a secret compartment between the twin-seats opened up, revealing a small cache of weapons – no doubt highly illegal for civilians to carry in Canada – too varied and high powered to be used for hunting, far too complex for reasonable defense.

Miles's eyes widened, his mouth opened, and he swore. His eyes locked onto Sam with a unique blend of incredulity, awe, and concern. "Who the hell are you?"

"It's a long story." Sam swerved hard to the left, overtaking a car. "Can you just pick a weapon and start shooting!"

"All right, all right."

Miles retrieved a Heckler & Koch MP7 submachine gun and attached the 40 round detachable magazine. The kid, still covered in blood, appeared to come alive with the weapon in his hands, giving Sam the strange impression of Rambo.

"You sure you know what you're doing?" Sam asked. "I mean, I'd hate to get killed by friendly fire."

"Yeah, I'm sure!" The kid's eyes rolled across the doors, back toward the rear windshield. A puzzled frown appeared. "How the hell am I supposed to aim back there?"

"I have an idea," Sam said.

He pressed another button in the middle of the dashboard that controlled the gull-winged doors. Each door weighed 90 pounds, and were raised by hydraulic cylinders controlled by switches in the interior. The hydraulics began to crank over, and it took an obligatory twelve seconds to open both doors simultaneously.

The Bricklin looked like the epitome of everyone's impression of a futuristic flying car as it raced along at nearly 100 miles an hour, with its winged doors wide open. Miles tried to lean out the door far enough to shoot, but it was impossible with his injuries. He released a couple rounds, but the shots were wasted, falling nowhere near their intended target. While the biker on the Harley Davidson had a perfectly clear line of sight.

Miles cursed. "This won't do!"

Sam glanced at his passenger. The kid could barely hold the submachinegun without losing what blood remained from his gut. There was no chance he could lean far enough out of the open door to take a reasonable shot at their pursuer.

He drew a long breath. "I have an idea."

Miles said, "I'm listening."

Sam came around a corner, braking hard to avoid slamming into a truck moving slowly in the same lane. An oncoming car prevented him from crossing over to the other side of the road. He dropped down a gear, and kept the Bricklin's RPM's high as he was forced to slow down. As soon as the oncoming car had past, he planted his foot again, and overtook the truck.

His eyes darted between his passenger, who still wore an expression of curiosity as though it was an interesting matter rather than life and death whether or not Sam had a solution, and then back to the rear-view mirror – where the Harley Davidson was in the rapid process of closing the gap – reinforcing the whole life and death issue.

Impatient, Miles asked, "What's your plan?"

Sam licked his lips. "In a minute I'm going to swing the car around."

A perplexed look crossed Miles' face. "Okay?"

"When I do, you'll have a direct line of sight, but he'll have an equally direct line of sight on us. That means you get one shot at this. One chance to kill or be killed. Do you understand that?"

"I get it!" Miles confirmed.

"All right… here we go."

Sam jammed on the brakes.

His right hand instinctively and protectively fell over Caliburn, who gave a somber whine. The Bricklin's 10 inch, Kelsey-Hayes rear drum brakes locked up almost immediately, sending the Bricklin skidding around like it was on ice. Sam had over played his card, and, unable to correct it with steering, simply let the sports car ride it out, as its low-profile tires screeched, before the Bricklin finally skidded to a halt in a shroud of burnt rubber.

It had stopped perpendicular to the road.

And racing toward them, Miles had a perfectly straight line of sight with a Harley Davidson that roared toward them.

Miles didn't hesitate.

He squeezed the trigger and the Heckler & Koch MP7 submachine gun began to fire. It was a prolonged burst and a barrage of 4.6×30mm rounds exploded out of the 7.1-inch muzzle at a speed of 2,411 feet per second. The weapon had a rate of fire of 950 rounds per minute. All in total, it took just 2.53 seconds for him to release all 40 shots downrange. When the last chamber fell silent, Sam hoped to hell that Miles hadn't missed.

Sam didn't have to wait long to find out.

The polished chrome and metalwork that make Harley Davidsons so popular, erupted in a series of sparks that lit up the entire road like a flaming meteorite. An instant later, one of those sparks found its way inside the motorcycle's fuel tank and the entire thing exploded. The mangled remains of the motorcycle and the no-longer human remnants of the biker kept sliding, missing the Bricklin and slamming into a nearby traffic light pole.

Sam exhaled a long breath. "It's over."

"We did it," Miles agreed. Despite being weak, he wore the proud grin of one who'd overcome a great adversary. A second later, he swore, "Quick! Get down!"

Caliburn barked aggressively and Sam squished back into the seat, reaching for his Glock 17. He turned and looked directly at the incoming Harley Davidson, that now approached from the opposite direction – his side of the Bricklin.

The rider drew a weapon.

Sam moved quickly.

He fired three shots.

The first two missed. But the third one got the biker in the head, knocking him off the bike. The Harley Davidson, without anyone at the handlebars, teetered unbalanced for a split second, before wobbling uncontrollably until the side peg clipped the blacktop, sending a burst of sparks skyward. The bike rolled on its other side, before the steel peg dug deep into the blacktop, causing the entire motorcycle to flip and cartwheel on itself, before slamming into the guardrail. Its fuel tank ignited, and the entire thing erupted in a ball of fire.

Sam swallowed hard and then exhaled. "That was close."

Caliburn mewled.

Sam looked at Miles whose mouth was set in one of those *well, you win some you lose some* sort of smiles. He'd been hit by another bullet. This one had struck a vital organ... or more likely a major blood vessel like part of the abdominal aorta. Sam didn't know which. And it didn't matter. Even without much medical training, he knew the amount of blood Miles was losing made the wound mortal.

Godkin stopped trying to stem the blood with his hand. Instead, he concentrated his last, remaining strength on retrieving something from his pocket.

In a barely audible grunt, Miles said, "Take this."

It was the USB stick.

Sam said, "Where? To the police?"

"No," Godkin shook his head. "Can't trust the authorities."

"Which authorities?" Sam asked.

"All of them."

Sam said, "Someone from this Berserker gang has deep pockets with the local police?"

Miles frowned. "You think this has to do with some low-level drug cartel?"

"It doesn't?"

"Not a thing. This goes much higher."

"How high?"

Godkin said, "All the way to the top."

Sam asked, "What do you want me to do?"

"Find my brother. Give him the USB. He knows what needs to be done."

"Okay."

Miles was emphatic. "Promise me."

"Yes. I promise." Sam asked, "Where can I find your brother?"

"Minnesota. His address is on the USB stick. Get it to him. He's the only one who can stop this now."

Sam asked, "Stop what?"

Godkin didn't answer.

Sam cursed. "What am I supposed to stop?"

But Godkin didn't answer.

How could he?

He was already dead.

Chapter Nine

Horizon's Miramichi Regional Hospital

Sam decided against trying to perform CPR by himself.

There was no point. Godkin needed surgery and probably multiple blood transfusions. That was the only thing that might save his life. Besides, he wasn't even sure if he was really dead yet. Every now and again, he seemed to take a decent breath, albeit gurgling with blood. He searched for the nearest hospital on his cell phone and was relieved when one came up exactly three minutes away. He clicked the *Navigate To* button, and made it to the hospital in under two minutes, without ever bothering to lower the gull-wing doors.

The hospital was in the middle of a circular clearing of an otherwise mature forest of tall, straight, conifers. At the heart of which, stood a proud hospital – clad in red clay masonry. A large, glass annex protected the main entrance and emergency department from the elements.

Sam pulled into the Emergency Department, parking at one of the Ambulance Bays. Two paramedics restocking their rig approached him, ready to tell him off for parking in the wrong place. Their eyes landed on Miles's bloodied body, darting to Sam's grim face and hardened resolve. They turned in silence and grabbed their stretcher instead.

The older of the two paramedics, with a trim gray beard, placed a saline soaked gauze on the worst of the abdominal wounds, squeezing the combine dressing inside the wound. He turned to Sam and asked, "Is it just the two bullet wounds in his gut?"

"No. There's a third to his lower chest."

The paramedic's eyes glanced at the chest wound. It was sucking in with every breath Miles took, and there was the almost imperceptible sign of a pneumothorax, but it hadn't started tensioning yet.

"All right," the paramedic said, his demeanor calm, his resolve resolute, as he exhaled slowly. "We're not going to be doing him any favors staying out here. Let's get him inside where a surgical team can give him the best chance he's got."

"Agreed," Sam said. "What do you need me to do?"

"I need you to come here, and put as much pressure as you can on this pad, while we get your friend out of the car."

"Okay," Sam said, relieved to see someone else take control of the situation.

He shuffled into the middle space between the seats and kept pressure on Miles's wound. Now that he could see the injuries clearly in the light, Sam could see the same thing the paramedic had seen – the bullet had severed part of the large blood vessel in the abdomen and was bleeding out with every second.

Sam had seen his share of bullet wounds over the years. He didn't particularly like the sight or smell of blood, but he knew better than to be squeamish. He placed his hand on the combine dressing, gentle at first, before increasing the pressure as hard as he could manage. The blood just kept pouring out – until he realized that his hand was now buried inside the wound.

He swallowed hard, gritting his teeth, but kept the pressure on.

The paramedic controlling the lift, positioned himself around Miles's shoulders ready to lift him in a classic top and tail procedure. They worked in unison with the speed and efficiency of a well-greased machine.

Sam climbed out through the passenger side of the car, keeping his hand in the abdominal wound the whole time, as the two paramedics lifted Miles onto the stretcher and quickly wheeled him into the emergency department.

Caliburn jumped out of the car and tried to follow.

Sam said, "You'd better wait there, buddy."

The golden retriever laid down and placed its head on its front paws. A somber expression on his kind face, as his dark, melancholy eyes followed them until they were out of sight.

A triage nurse approached as Miles was wheeled through the doors. She took one look at him and said, "Go on through to the resus bay."

"Thanks," the paramedic in charge replied, politely and kept moving, as though this was an everyday activity, and good manners and general professionalism were still to be observed.

On the overhead PA, Sam heard her say in a calm voice that defied belief, "Resus team to resus one, we have a *Code Crimson*. Multiple gunshot wounds."

A second later, without even pausing for a beat, Sam heard the same woman lean forward, and say, "Next patient, please."

The paramedic rolled the stretcher into the resus room.

A not-so-small multidisciplinary team greeted them, including doctors, nurses, and orderlies. Their eyes flashed awake at the sight of Miles's lifeless body. Each of them being roused with a sudden surge of adrenaline, knowing that their work over the next few minutes would mean life and death to the stranger who had just arrived.

Sam watched as they were all still tying off the impervious trauma gowns that gave the whole experience a surreal feeling that shocked him to the core. Not only were these people about to deal with a traumatic experience that no one should have to deal with, but they did it so frequently, that they needed gowns to throw away when they were done, so they could go right back to doing it again, without changing their clothes.

The paramedic handed over what little he knew so far about the patient. Everyone paused for a few seconds and listened. When he'd finished, the entire scene changed. Everyone got to work. In a daze, Sam watched as they worked to orchestrate Miles's best chance of survival. The kid was still breathing on his own, he had a weak pulse, but he was still alive.

Intravenous lines were put in to both arms. An array of monitors were placed all over him, his blood pressure was taken, and the computer screens started to show his EKGs. An arterial line was inserted into his left radial artery, and a new line on the monitor showed his continuous blood pressure reading in real time.

Different people had different roles Sam observed. To him, it all looked like a discombobulated mess, but beneath that, there seemed to be purpose and procedures being followed. Everyone knew their role and what looked impossibly complicated to an outsider, appeared to just flow for the team.

In the background, Sam heard a scribe, continuously confirm what had been done or not done, taking notes and documenting everything as it happened, from assessment findings, history, procedures performed, drugs given, and their outcomes.

Miles's breathing quickly became erratic and an anesthesiologist at the head of the bed said, "It's time to intubate him."

The doctor had already been providing him 100% oxygen through a mask. When he was ready, he inserted a metal device called a laryngoscope into Miles's mouth, searching for the opening of the trachea – more commonly known as the windpipe.

The room went silent for a moment. Right now, Miles's chest had stopped rising and falling, which meant that he wasn't breathing at all. Every second counted.

The anesthesiologist pulled the laryngoscope out and kept manually ventilating using the mask and squeezing an attached balloon, like a pump. "He's a Mallampati grade four. Can I please have a bougie and some cricoid pressure."

Instantly, someone stepped forward, and placed pressure on Miles's throat – more specifically, his cricoid cartilage – changing the position of the windpipe and making it easier to insert a breathing tube. Next, an aluminum wire called a bougie was inserted into the endotracheal tube, where the anesthesiologist adjusted it, bending the tube into a slight curve, so that it could get around Miles's naturally awkward airway anatomy.

A few seconds later, the anesthesiologist tried again.

This time he was successful.

He began ventilating the patient. "Can I please get someone to listen to his chest and confirm my placement?"

Another doctor stepped in and placed her stethoscope on Miles's chest. After a few seconds, she confirmed that the tube's placement was correct and both lungs were being ventilated.

"Thank you," the anesthesiologist said, attaching the other end of the endotracheal tube onto a ventilator.

In the minutes that followed, Miles was given an array of different blood products, and clotting factors, designed to help his blood clot.

One of the nurses looked at Sam. "Are you gonna be all right?"

Sam nodded. "Yeah."

Her eyes narrowed, running from his eyes back to the wound on Mile's abdomen which he was still holding with a gauze combine. "You want me to take over that?"

Sam exhaled. "Yes, please."

He felt the nurse's gloved hands on his, taking over the pressure on the abdominal wound. After a couple seconds, she said, "It's okay, you can let go now."

"Thank you," he said, and he really meant it. He'd never been so happy to relinquish responsibility to someone else in all his life.

She said, "There's a basin over there for you to wash your hands."

One of the other doctors pulled Sam aside and tried to take a more detailed history of what had happened, as well as any other known medical conditions Miles might have. Sam filled him in as best he could, but didn't have much to tell, barring the obvious – he'd been shot three times.

A few minutes later, the resus room erupted with the sound of various alarms going off on all the monitoring equipment.

Sam turned his gaze to the main monitor display. He couldn't read the meaning of any of the alarms being displayed, but he didn't have to. He knew that despite their best efforts, Miles was deteriorating.

One of the doctors felt for a pulse. "He's just arrested. Let's get someone up on the chest to commence CPR."

The on-call trauma specialist walked through the door.

The emergency physician quickly brought her up to speed. When he was finished, he said, "It's your call now. What would you like to do?"

She nodded. "All right, let's set up for a clamshell thoracotomy."

Chapter Ten

It was the sort of thing that no one considered until you were dead.

You'd sure as hell hope to be before they even thought about attempting to perform a clamshell thoracotomy. If there ever was a procedure to leave to the very last case-scenario, this was it. If you were to Google the term, Wikipedia might tell you its survival rates were low – about 9 percent in penetrating trauma and just 1 percent in blunt trauma. And even in those cases, the mortality rate from infection and subsequent problems often killed you more often than it saved you.

But what did Miles have to lose?

The trauma specialist worked quickly. This wasn't the sort of procedure where you really focused on the finer details. This was meatball surgery at its finest. The sort of procedure doctors would have baulked at outside of a military hospital in a warzone not so long ago.

Sam should have left the room.

Hell, someone should have insisted on it. Who was he anyway to witness this? He only met the kid a few hours ago. He thought about standing up and leaving on his own accord, but now the giddiness made him think twice about that.

He should have looked the other way. Maybe even just closed his eyes until the worst had passed. But sometimes the more grotesque something is, the harder it is to resist. Sam didn't know what it was. Either way, he couldn't escape it now.

The trauma specialist took a scalpel and made four separate thoracostomies – little breaches in the intercostal muscles and parietal pleura – along the 5th intercostal space in the mid-axillary line. They were the same technique and landmarks as for conventional chest drains.

Each of those holes were connected with deep skin incisions, following the 5th intercostal space. The specialist moved quickly, her eyes focused, never wavering as she worked like a butcher, performing the unimaginable on another human being, in an attempt to save his life.

She inserted two fingers into one of the holes to hold the lung out of the way while she continued cutting through all layers of the intercostal muscles toward the sternum using heavy scissors. She worked both sides, leaving only a sternal bridge between the two openings, before severing the sternum.

A minute later, Sam's world went dizzy before turning completely dark, as the specialist used retractors to open the chest wall like a giant clamshell.

Sam didn't find out what happened next.

He didn't know that he hit his head giving himself a minor concussion in the process. Nor did he know how long he'd been out. But when he woke, his back was up against the wall on a pillow just outside the resuscitation room with no one else around.

Sometime later… he couldn't say how long, because he couldn't say how long he'd been unconscious for, one of the doctors – the trauma specialist – came and found him.

She gave him her name, looked him in the eye, and said, "I'm sorry. There's nothing we could do to save your friend. The damage was just too severe. Even had this happened right out the front of the hospital, we wouldn't have been able to do anything to save his life."

Sam nodded. His world still spinning. He knew better than anyone the lengths she'd gone to save the man's life.

Despite her best efforts, Miles was dead.

Chapter Eleven

Sam nursed a strong coffee.

He was sitting outside in front of the hospital. Next to him, Caliburn sat with his paws outstretched in front and his head resting on Sam's lap. His big, brown eyes, a mixture of melancholy and unconditional love, providing the sort of solace that only a dog can provide a wounded human being.

It had been a long day, and after all that Miles Godkin had been through today, Sam just couldn't believe that he had died. It was strange. Sam, more so than most people, knew the facts of life. Some injuries were just too great and can't be repaired. But for some reason, he just really felt as though the kid was going to pull through.

He finished his drink and returned it to the nurse who had kindly offered it to him in the first place. It was the triage nurse who had met them at the entrance when he'd first arrived with Miles. She had stepped away from her position of sieving out the health acuity of arriving patients and paused long enough to notice him.

She had light brown skin and long black hair, showing some sort of Asian heritage. She was fit and healthy looking. Dark eyes, long lashes, and a suppressed, mischievous smile. At a glance, he could tell she was quite beautiful. But it was more than that which drew him to her, there was an innate kindness about her that made him look twice. As a passing thought, he would have been happy to meet her in another place at another time.

She took the cup. Her eyes meeting his. "It's Sam Reilly, isn't it?"

"Yes."

"I'm Maricris by the way." She paused a beat, drew a breath. "You look like you've had one hell of a shitty day."

"Pleased to meet you, Maricris." Sam said, "Yeah, I've had better days. That said, I don't know how you do your job. You all seem amazing."

"It can be pretty crazy, but at the end of the day, it's what we do. The same as everyone else. We all have a role to play, and this just happens to be the thing that I can do." She paused a beat, really looking at him for a moment and seeing the shattered look in his eye. "Are you okay?"

She had an accent. It wasn't Asian. Instead, it was Australian. If he had to guess, she was second or even third generation Australian. He smiled. "Yeah, I'm okay. The truth is, I only just met him today. In fact, before he was shot, I rescued him from nearly drowning at St. Martins Sea Caves."

"The tide came in quicker than he expected?" she asked, her voice betraying that this wasn't the first time she'd heard of a tourist nearly getting killed by doing just that.

Sam nodded. "That's the one."

"Can I get you anything else?" Maricris asked.

Sam shook his head. "No. I'm just waiting for the police. Actually, I thought they would have been here by now. After all, how many shootings can the RCMP get in the area?"

"We don't do a lot," Maricris admitted. "How about I give the station at Sunny Corner a call, and I'll let you know what they want to do."

"If you could, that would be great, thank you."

Sam waited at the nurse's station.

A few minutes later, Maricris returned.

There was something about her expression that concerned him. The kindness that she'd shown him from before seemed to have been replaced by a mixture of confusion and something else, he couldn't quite place – possibly fear – was she afraid of him?

He asked, "Any news?"

"Some," she said, her voice level and coy, as though she was holding something back. It seemed strange. Sam already knew that Miles was dead. With the worst out of the way, what could she possibly want to hide? She bit her lower lip, playing over in her mind what to say and what to withhold. "Look, the RCMP are really busy tonight."

Sam's eyes narrowed. "They're not coming out for a shooting?"

"Yes, of course they will, it's just they can't get here for a while. I just spoke to the officer in charge at Sunny Corner, he's requested you to come and make a statement at the station."

Sam listened to what she said, but remained silent, letting it sink in. Nothing was quite adding up. They were in rural Canada and someone had been shot dead. How busy could the police be? Surely, everywhere else in the world, they would have jumped at this case, racing down to the hospital to grill the only person who had seen it happen.

Maricris interrupted his thoughts. "Did you hear what I said, sir?"

Sam nodded. "Sorry… I was just thinking. When was the last time you had a shooting here?"

"A shooting?"

"Yeah, when did you last have a shooting come in?"

She shrugged. "I don't know. It must have been six months ago. Why, what's this got to do with that?"

"Nothing. I'm sorry. I'm just surprised the police don't want to come here to question me. I mean, what's to say I didn't shoot Miles? I should at the very least be a cursory suspect."

Her eyes flashed wide, but she held his gaze. "Did you?"

"Did I shoot him?" Sam asked, shocked by the question. "No. Of course not."

"Good. So, they don't need to rush." Her voice was curt, and professional, without a trace of the kindness or friendliness he had previously enjoyed. "I assume I can tell the officer in charge you will meet him at the station in twenty minutes?"

Sam wanted to ask more, but figured the easiest way for him to get answers was to head down to the police station. He nodded. "Sure, I'll be there in twenty."

With that, Maricris walked away without even saying good-bye or good luck.

Chapter Twelve

At exactly 9:15 p.m. he stepped into the police station, once more leaving Caliburn alone in the Bricklin SV-1.

He was greeted by an officer at the desk as he stepped in. The gentleman wore the red dress uniform of the Royal Canadian Mounted Police and looked much too senior in rank to be managing a rural station.

"Sam Reilly?" The officer asked.

"That's me, sir," Sam replied, offering his hand.

"My name's Eric McMurran, you can call me Eric," the officer said, shaking his hand. He stood up and opened a door to the back of the station, and gestured for Sam to follow him through. "Come this way if you would, please."

Sam followed him.

Eric was a giant of a man. At least six-six at a guess, with a barrel chest, and big hands to match. He wore a large, graying mustache, but despite his size and position, he had the kind and polite demeanor that Sam had found almost uniquely Canadian.

Sam walked through the back of the station, before being offered a seat at a desk. It was in the middle of the station with other desks nearby, not like one of those interrogation rooms you tend to see in the cop shows.

Sam took a seat.

"You looked wrecked. Can I get you anything?" Eric asked, "A coffee, or a soft drink?"

Sam was about to decline, but something about the way the officer said it made him think that this wasn't going to be a quick interview. He smiled. "If you've got a diet coke, I'll take one please."

Eric arched an eyebrow. "Diet?"

"I don't know why. It's just the taste. I'm not kidding myself for an instant that it's any better for my health, but I do like the taste."

Eric shrugged as though it wasn't any of his business what sort of health vices Sam might or might not have. He withdrew a can of soft drink and handed it to Sam, before pulling up a chair and taking a seat opposite. He opened up a laptop and switched it on. He seemed to be taking his time. Every move he made was slow and deliberate.

"Okay, just bear with me for a minute, will you? While my laptop starts up," Eric said, as his massive frame hunched over his laptop. "I've been away for a few days, and it seems stuck on updating its software."

After a few minutes the sign-in tab finally came up on Eric's laptop. He typed his password, and smiled as he waited patiently for the computer to fully open. He was so deliberate with the process, almost theatrical, that Sam began to wonder if this was all part of the process – trying to place him in a position of casual comfort that lulled him into a sense of safety, before revealing one's guilt.

Who knows?

Eric sighed. "Ah, here we are, we're good to go. I just want to be able to type this up while I hear your story."

Sam said, "Okay."

"Now, the triage nurse at Horizon's Miramichi Regional Hospital told me that you were involved in some sort of incident tonight, is that right?"

Sam frowned. "An incident?"

"Yeah, the nurse said you wanted to have a talk to one of my officers, and wouldn't really take no for an answer, when she informed you that we were really busy."

Sam couldn't believe what he was hearing.

He'd expected an apology for not sending a squad car to the hospital earlier, along with some sort of report about the Berserker gang causing trouble in the area, but never in a million years did he imagine the police hadn't heard about the shooting.

Sam suppressed the anger that was building up quickly. He shook his head. "I'm sorry, Eric. Something must have been lost in the communication, did Maricris mention to you that someone had been shot?"

Eric's earlier vacant expression turned to one of genuine concern. "There was a shooting?"

"Yes," Sam confirmed, both relieved and mystified that Eric's blasé response was related to the fact that he honestly hadn't been informed of the shooting. "A man, Miles Godkin, was shot three times tonight. I took him to Horizon's Miramichi Regional Hospital, where their exceptional team worked to save his life for nearly forty minutes, before he died."

Eric tapped a pen on the table. His eyes darted between his laptop and Sam. Sam could see the man changing mental gears, trying to decide his next course of action. "I'm sorry. I don't know what's happened here. You had better start from the very beginning, and then I'll make some calls and bring some officers in tonight. By the sounds of things, this is about to blow up around here."

"I have no doubt," Sam said, "Particularly once you hear what I have to say."

Over the next hour and a half Sam retold the story commencing from his rescue of Miles Godkin at the St. Martins Sea Caves, all the way through to Miles getting shot at his own place by bikers who he'd identified as being part of the Berserker gang, the logging truck jackknifing on the bridge and killing one biker, shooting another, and finally Miles being fatally shot just three minutes out from the hospital. He told it hard and cold and straight, like one of those accident reports you read in the daily news. The only thing he left out was any reference to the USB stick that he'd promised to deliver to Miles's brother. His gut told him he could trust Eric, but somewhere, in the back of his mind he kept hearing Miles's voice…

You can't trust anyone.

This thing goes all the way to the top.

Intermittently, throughout the story, Eric made him pause at a point, while he called various people in to help investigate. Once the ball got rolling, Eric's phone kept on pinging with texts and ringing with calls from various officers. When Sam was finally finished, Eric asked him again to just relay the order of each shooting so that he could confirm it.

When Sam had told his story again, he looked at Eric and asked, "Well, what do you think, do you think you'll have enough to convict one of the Berserkers?"

Eric paused for a beat. His face unreadable. "Berserkers?"

"You know, the local gang?"

Eric spread his arms. "I'm sorry, you have me at a loss. Do you mean, like Vikings?"

"Yes, Berserkers, like Vikings. Dangerous ones. These ones in particular sell drugs to children and indoctrinate young kids into a life of violence."

"I'm afraid I've never heard of them." Eric gave an apologetic shrug. He held a hand as a warning. "Mind you, that doesn't mean they don't exist. I'm not a part of vice… so maybe if I make some phone calls, I can find out… but I must warn you, I'm really not prepared to do that just yet."

"You're not?"

Eric shook his head. "No, I'm not."

"Why?"

"Look, I appreciate you taking the time to make your statement," Eric said, his baritone drawl just a bit heavier than usual, his cadence a beat slower.

Sam arched his eyebrows. He didn't like where this was going. "What's going on here? Why wouldn't you look into a possible connection between a homicide – multiple homicides for that matter – and a known biker gang?"

Eric made a theatrical sigh. It almost looked like an apology in itself. "Because, so far, to be entirely honest… I don't believe a word that you've said tonight."

Rage boiled up in his chest, but Sam's voice stayed surprisingly even. "What are you talking about?"

"Look…" Eric met his gaze. "I sent some officers to the address you gave me where this man – Miles Godkin – was staying. They knocked on the door. The people who live there have never heard of him, and say they've been home all afternoon and all night and didn't hear the sound of any gunshots."

"Maybe they knocked on the wrong house?" Sam suggested.

"It's the address you gave me. Besides, even if you were off by one or two houses, it still doesn't explain the fact that no one heard the gunshots."

"Maybe they were inside watching a movie… or perhaps they're old and partially deaf?"

"That's not the case. In fact, the people my officers spoke to were a young couple with a baby. New parents have the best hearing in the world." Eric's tone took a didactic lilt to it, like a professor telling a story. "I think it's one of those evolutionary things, really, designed to keep babies safe. I don't know, but I do know that parents tend to hear everything."

Sam persisted. "All right, forget about his house... someone must have covered their tracks. What about the bridge?"

"What about it?"

"Surely the log trucker must have reported the incident?"

Eric glanced back at the laptop, checking his notes, before saying, "An 18-wheeler logging truck jackknifed on the Northwest Miramichi River bridge. In the process, it ran over one biker, before the cabin finally smashed through the railings, hanging precariously over the side. Is that right?"

"Yeah... that's the one." Sam swallowed.

Eric folded his arms across his chest. "It never happened."

Sam's heart stopped for a beat. "Never happened?"

"No. That's what I'm telling you. None of those things happened tonight."

Sam suppressed a grin. Incredulity plastered across his face. "How can that be? I mean, how can someone cover something up like that? You must have heard the crash from the station!"

"Exactly," Eric agreed, his voice cold and hard. "I was in the first few hours of my shift. If such a thing did happen, I almost certainly would have heard it – and yet I didn't."

"What about the railing?"

"It's completely intact."

"With all due respect, sir – I don't believe you."

Eric turned his palms upward. "Believe me or not, it still doesn't alter the facts."

"Okay, okay… so then I may as well guess that the bodies of the other two bikers haven't been found, either?"

"Afraid not."

Sam laughed… feeling like he knew what it was like to go crazy. Then he stopped. A wry grin played out on his lips.

I gotcha.

"Okay, I see what's happened here. He said this would be the case if we went to the authorities. Godkin said the Berserkers were well connected."

"Listen, I can assure you that I've worked for the RCMP my entire life. Honor and duty are built into my very being. There's no way I've been bought."

Sam held up a hand in a placating gesture. "Of course not. I'm not suggesting you are. But I believe the Berserkers went into protection mode after the events of tonight, quickly covering up their tracks, even any evidence of the deaths of their own people – but there's one piece of the puzzle that they couldn't cover up… one thing that exonerates me as not crazy, and telling the truth."

"And that is?"

Sam grinned. "Miles Godkin's body!"

"Who?"

Sam's eyes sparkled, like a condemned man who finally held the truth in the palm of his hand. "The kid I dropped off at the Horizon's Miramichi Regional Hospital emergency department."

Eric spread his hands outward. "I don't know what to tell you. I just spoke with the leading physician… he said there's no record of anyone coming into the hospital tonight with gunshot wounds."

Sam swallowed. "You're kidding, right?"

"Afraid not, son."

"What the hell's going on here?" Sam looked around, trying see if someone was recording him. Had it all been a horrible set up? His mind raced, shifting mental gears, and trying to make something compute, but no matter which way he tried, nothing seemed to jam together. "Wait…"

"Yes?"

"I spoke with a triage nurse. She said that she called you to notify you that I'd be coming. You said so yourself! That's why you knew my name as soon as I walked through the door to the station."

Eric loosely suppressed a wry smile. It was becoming obvious he now thought Sam was simply delusional. "Yes?"

"What did she say to you?"

"Who?"

"Maricris. The triage nurse!"

"I didn't catch her name."

"But someone from the hospital called?"

"Yes."

"So, what did she say?"

Eric made an apologetic smile. He sighed. "She said that there was a violent man out the front of the hospital, clearly delusional, yelling about how he'd been in a shootout with a biker gang – a gang in rural Canada that as far as we're concerned doesn't exist – and that they had tried to sedate you and bring you into the hospital for observation and treatment because you were clearly having some sort of psychiatric issue, but that you had left before they could restrain you, and had told them you were heading here."

Sam grinned again. "Wow! They're really good. They've gotten to everyone, haven't they? If I'm just a psychiatric patient, why have you talked to me so long? Why not just lock me up and bring me into the hospital right away?"

"To be honest, you don't present like a crazy person. I'm no doctor, but when you started talking, I genuinely believed your story. It was only after my officers started to check on the facts that I realized I was wrong about you. Also, we've looked you up. You have an amazing record and one I would rather not taint by calling you a liar."

"So what do you suggest?"

"Well, I believe you should get in your car, and head back to the hospital. In fact, I insist on it. I'm going to have one of my officers follow you there, just to be sure."

"Okay."

Eric's eyes narrowed. "We have a deal?"

Sam nodded. "Sure."

Sam thanked Eric for his patience and promised he'd seek help for whatever was going on with his memory.

He got into the Bricklin.

Caliburn nudged him with his wet nose.

Sam gave him an affectionate pat and said, "Yeah, it's been one of those nights."

The car still had bullet holes on the hood and both the front and rear windshield. Despite confirming he wasn't crazy, it was the last thing he needed. He didn't want to bring up anything more while in front of the police. Better to let them assume he too was starting to believe he'd had a nervous breakdown and was delusional. On the drive to the hospital, he noticed the bridge across the Northwest Miramichi River was perfectly intact. The guardrail completely sound. He squinted, and part of him wondered, if he could see the dark marks of recent welding work.

In his rearview mirror, he watched the police squad car trailing him, and kept going. He needed to maintain the impression that he had accepted his part in this story, as the crazy one. Fifteen minutes later, he pulled up at the hospital. He waved goodbye to his police escort, who appeared relieved that he'd returned to the hospital willingly, without any further altercations.

Sam walked into the emergency department.

It was 10:45 p.m.

Just after change of shift.

He looked around, casually trying to spot someone he recognized. He didn't. Not even the doctors. Everyone had left.

A nurse caught Sam wandering and asked, "Can I help you?"

Sam smiled. "Yes, please. I hope so, that is… I believe a friend of mine was admitted here tonight. He wasn't in a very good condition and I'm worried he might have died. If I give you his details, are you able to find out if this is the hospital he came to?"

She smiled kindly. "I'm afraid I can't help you, but if you go back out through that corridor, out the front there's the main inquiry desk – that's what you want. Someone will be able to help you there."

"Thank you very much."

Sam casually walked out toward the inquiry desk.

He spoke with an elderly lady who seemed very helpful. She typed Miles Godkin's name into her computer system and frowned. "Can you please confirm his spelling for me again?"

"Sure." Sam spelled Miles Godkin again. "Any luck?"

"No. I'm afraid not. What time did you say he might have arrived here?"

"Around 7 p.m."

"Hmm, I'm sorry, there's no record of Miles Godkin being seen anywhere in this hospital yesterday or tonight."

"You're sure?"

"Certain. Everyone who comes in here gets logged."

"What if they didn't know his name?"

"Then he will be identified as a John Doe and color coded."

"Color coded?"

"Yeah, sometimes… it's not very often, mind you, but sometimes, we get multiple John Does, and so we need to color code them to differentiate them."

"Really? That happens?"

"Not very often, but yeah, it does happen."

"Go figure."

"Yeah, crazy, huh?" The lady sighed apologetically. "I'm sorry I couldn't be of much assistance. What did your friend come in here with? Maybe I can point you in the right direction of a ward he would have gone to… in the off chance he used a different name."

"That's a good idea. Thanks for considering it. Miles was shot three times tonight."

The color drained from the woman's face. Her amicable demeanor suddenly replaced by fear. "If he was shot, I can tell you right now he didn't come to this hospital."

"You're certain?"

"I'm certain. We have mandatory reporting laws for all shootings. That means, irrespective of what your friend's name was, we would have had a record of his arrival."

"And you don't?"

"Son, we haven't had a shooting in here for at least six months."

"So if my friend didn't come here, where did he go?"

She wrote down the names, addresses, and phone numbers of the next three closest hospitals. "Try these. Good luck."

"Thank you."

Sam began to walk out of the hospital.

On his way, he spotted the trauma specialist who had been on-call earlier in the night.

He stopped the woman. "Excuse me, doctor…"

"Yes?" the doctor replied. "Can I help you?"

"I hope so." Sam held his breath. "Do you remember me?"

The doctor looked at him, meeting his eyes, and then taking him in whole, before shaking her head. "I'm afraid not, but I see a lot of patients during my shift. Where should I recognize you from?"

Sam said, "You looked after my friend earlier."

"What's your friend's name?"

"Miles Godkin."

The doctor repeated the name. Gave an apologetic shrug. "I'm sorry. Like I said, I see a lot of people throughout my shift, and can't always put names to faces or names to anything for that matter. Like most doctors, I'm afraid I'm better with conditions and injuries… what did your friend come in with?"

"He was shot multiple times. I believe you performed a clamshell thoracotomy."

A flicker of what might have been fear crossed her face. The doctor turned. "You must excuse me, I believe you have me confused with someone else."

Sam grabbed her arm, stopping her with an emphatic grip. "I need to know, doctor, who's doing this?"

The doctor leaned in close. Then, in a whisper, she said, "I have no idea what you're talking about, but if you don't let go, I'll call security to restrain you and then will wait here until the police come to lock you up."

Sam let go.

The doctor turned and walked out quickly.

Sam was about to leave, but then thought of Maricris – the triage nurse. He knew she wasn't involved in this, but someone had gotten to her. When she first called the police, they had told her something that had made her frightened.

He needed to speak with her.

She must have the answers.

Sam walked up to the triage nurse now in charge. "Excuse me, I was here earlier, I spoke with the triage nurse before you... the one you must have taken over for when you came onto your shift."

"Okay," she said, noncommittally. "What's this about? What's your name? Do you want me to check when you're likely to be seen by a doctor?"

"No, I'm not a patient. My friend came in earlier. She was really helpful. I just wanted to thank her personally. I'd like to bring her flowers."

Realization dawned on the triage nurse, and she met him with a conspiratorial gaze and laugh in her voice. "You liked her. You want me to find out if she's single?"

Sam spread his hands. "You got me. I don't want to pry. If she's got a boyfriend, she won't ever hear from me again."

The nurse gave him an unabashed elevator glance. She grinned. "You're pretty good looking. I'm sure she won't mind. Hell, if she's not interested, I'll give you my number. Do you remember her name?"

"Yes. It was unique. Her name was Maricris."

The triage nurse frowned. "Who?"

"She told me her name was Maricris."

"Maricris..." the nurse repeated the name, playing it in her head, as though searching to see if it sounded familiar. It must have drawn something from her memories because she looked up, smiled, and said, "Really pretty. Asian background. Very senior nurse. Australian accent?"

"Yes! That's the one!" Sam said, visibly relieved that someone finally remembered something about his earlier experience there. "Please, I need to speak to her!"

The nurse frowned. "Sir, that's not possible."

"Why not?"

The nurse gave an apologetic smile. The sort of look a lot of people had been giving him lately. "I'm afraid Maricris returned to Australia six months ago."

Chapter Thirteen

Sam left the hospital.

He got into the Bricklin, where Caliburn was dozing in the front passenger seat, and drove off, not wanting to draw any more attention to himself. He kept driving, heading toward Québec. Worried that he was being followed, his eyes kept darting toward the rearview mirror, but it didn't show any headlights on his tail.

On the way he called Elise, filling her in on everything.

When he was finished with the entire bizarre story, he pulled over and uploaded the data from the USB stick to the cloud so that she could work her magic. As soon as the upload was complete, he checked again for anyone following him – which there didn't seem to be – and then turned out onto the main road again, still heading to Québec. He had Elise on speaker, and wished he'd gotten around to installing a custom blue tooth car connection for his phone.

In the background, he could hear her hammering away at her keyboard. The steady staccato almost sounded violent and definitely angry. Sometimes, he wondered whether or not she needed to hit so many keys whenever he sent her a computer problem, or whether she simply had a program running in the background and pounded the keys to make him think she was working hard.

He kept driving in silence for several minutes.

Before Elise broke it. "I'm sorry, I can't help you with this."

"Really?" Sam frowned. "I seem to keep hearing that a lot tonight. I was hoping you would be the one to change my losing streak."

"Sorry. It won't be me."

"How come?" Sam asked, curiosity rising. "You're probably the smartest cryptographer on the planet, if you can't solve my problem, who can?"

"Whoever owns the second half of this cipher, I suppose."

"Come again?"

Elise said, "This is only half of a cipher."

"The entire thing is just a secret key?"

"Yes."

Sam's eyes narrowed. "Any idea what it unlocks?"

"Yes and no."

That seemed unusually vague for Elise. Sam asked, "Which is it?"

"Both. I know it leads to a website on the Dark Net, but what data is stored on that website is anyone's guess."

"Right, so how do we reach that website."

"You can't."

Elise appeared surprisingly pessimistic on the topic. Sam said, "No chance you can hack into it or something?"

"None."

"Why?"

Elise said, "The USB contains only half of a Dark Net hyperlink. Someone else has the second half, and without that, it's going to be impossible, or at least take about a million years to guess it."

Sam persisted. "Can't you work some sort of magic?"

"No. It's not a matter of hacking. I need the second part of the cipher to open the key."

"Which means?"

Elise said, "If you want answers, and considering what Godkin said about the USB, I'd recommend you had better pay his brother a visit."

"All right, thanks for your help."

"Hey, no problem. Anything else I can do for you while I'm at the computer?"

"Yeah, as a matter of fact, can you make a booking for a train trip from Québec to Minnesota for the car, Caliburn and myself."

"Sure. I'll arrange it for you and email the tickets. When do you want to leave?"

"On the next train. I can be there in an hour."

He heard that staccato again on the keyboard and a few seconds later, she said, "There's an Amtrak leaving Québec for Minneapolis at 3:45 a.m. you should make it easily."

"Perfect. Book it."

Elise said, "I'll send you an email with the confirmation." She paused a beat. "Sam…"

"Yes?"

"Have you contacted Tom about this yet?"

"About what?"

"The fact that you nearly got yourself killed and are now most likely to be targeted by a biker gang who like to associate themselves with violent Vikings."

Sam grinned. He was flattered that Elise cared about him so much, before admitting, "Not yet."

"Why not?"

"He's on the first real vacation he's had in years. Let him and Genevieve enjoy it."

"What about you?"

"What about me?" Sam grinned. "I'm almost done with this thing. I'll find Godkin's brother, hand over the USB and let it be. This isn't my battle."

"Really?" Elise didn't bother to hide her skepticism. "Just like that, you're going to let this one go?"

The outer edges of his lips curled into a grin. "Is that so unbelievable."

Elise replied with an emphatic, "Yes."

"All right. I might stick around long enough to find out what was on that USB. But Miles said his brother could handle it – whatever it is. If he can, I'll leave him be and continue my own vacation... it's been years since I've had time off, too."

"Even if it means letting a violent biker gang get away?"

Sam said, "Even if it means letting them slip through my fingers. I'm not the police. This isn't my area of expertise and I'm not planning on going on a personal vendetta just because I got caught up in the middle of some sort of in-house biker gang turf war."

"Really?"

"Is that so surprising to you?"

"That you're going to let something like this go?" Elise laughed out loud. "Yeah."

"Why?"

"Because if it is, it will be the first time I've ever seen you let anything go."

Sam grinned. "This might just be the first."

"I hope so. Good luck."

"I'll let you know what I find in Minnesota."

Elise said, "Get some rest on the train."

Chapter Fourteen

Caves of Balankanche – Mexico Yucatán Peninsula

Dr. Pablo Veracruz was breathing heavily from exhaustion.

He was a small man. Just five foot, with a lithe and wiry frame, almost like a bantamweight boxer. His skin was olive-toned and he had intense, piercing dark eyes and a thick shadow of a beard that women had often found attractive. Not that he'd ever been that interested in relationships. He was dedicated to his life's ambition, searching for a hidden chamber, sealed by the Mayan to protect their greatest artifacts from the invading Spanish so many centuries ago. It was this obsession that had led him to this dark, almost vile, and previously undiscovered tunnel deep beneath the earth in the ancient Caves of Balankanche.

On his belly, and stretched outward – making his body as flat as possible – he stared at the narrow limestone constriction ahead known as a choke point. The beam of his headlamp flickered across the white limestone, so ubiquitous throughout the Yucatán, before landing on the constriction.

It looked impossibly narrow.

But then, so did most things when you were buried this far beneath the earth. In caving terms, it was without a doubt the crux of his problem.

A second later, the beam's flickering light faded sharply. The batteries were getting low. He had spares, but to reach them, he would need to find a larger space, an alcove or somewhere big enough to move his arms behind his back and access the bag that trailed behind his feet attached to a thin rope.

He took a couple of deep breaths. Veracruz considered turning around, but the thought of trying to negotiate nearly three hundred feet of intense cave, as it hugged and squeezed him tight, backward, seemed too painful to contemplate.

Better to keep going or turn around?

Both included significant risks. Potentially life ending risks if he were honest. A few seconds later, the light of his headlamp flickered, dimmed, and eventually ceased to exist, leaving him in complete darkness. He cursed. That did it. He needed to change the batteries on his headlamp and the only way to do that was to go forward.

He shifted his body weight from his hands to his elbows, to his hips, knees, and finally his feet, making a strange, shuffling progress akin to a worm.

It was slow going.

He was breathing hard.

Small. Shallow breaths. It was all he could do. Until he could no longer even do that. Worried that he would become completely stuck, Dr. Pablo Veracruz stopped in the darkness.

He could feel the shadow of fear sneaking up on him. Its deceitful tendrils catching his mind. The walls of the ancient limestone closed in on him. It wasn't simply metaphorical. The tunnels had narrowed to the point that the constriction had trapped him. He fought to suppress the terror that rose in his chest like bile.

Part of him still considered trying to back up, but it was nearly impossible. No, he needed to keep going. Pablo exhaled through pursed lips, deflating his chest as much as possible, and pulled himself a little farther.

Making tiny movements by opening and closing his fingers, he tried to create enough friction to pull his languid frame through. It was slow and painful work and his entire body was being torn by shards of limestone as it was compressed through the constriction. But at least he was moving again. He kept at it, making modest progress at best for some time… maybe another twenty minutes or so…

And then stopped.

Because he was now properly trapped. He knew it in an instant. This was every caver – hell every person's – worst nightmare. He was bound by the earth, deep underground, in a tomb that no person might ever discover. His heart was hammering in his chest now. He struggled to move, but couldn't. Exhaustion bled out of him like a balloon. He tried to breathe out but his chest was already deflated.

Panic set in quickly.

He couldn't move. Couldn't breathe. The blood had frozen in his veins. His lungs stopped. He could hear his pulse, his heartbeat growing impossibly loud until it was the only sound he could hear echoing in his ears.

If he could scream, he would have.

A guttural cry filled his throat.

But almost as soon as it had manifested, the sound had been stifled by the pressure on his chest from the walls, that now felt like they had completely closed on him like a vise.

His mind was filled with the realization that he might be permanently stuck far beneath the earth, trapped in a narrow constriction not seen by living humans for more than a millennium. It was up to him to free himself and failure to do so would result in his bodily remains most likely lying there for another millennium before being found.

With his chest constricted between the two pieces of smooth limestone, he could barely breathe. His lungs were unable to fully expand with each breath. Instead, he took fast, shallow breaths, which in turn, caused him to panic further. But the more he tried to slow his breathing, the dizzier he became, and he feared that he was on the verge of passing out – where he would never again awaken.

Struggling, tenuously, to remain conscious and focused, he turned his mind to the feelings of elation that had come just hours before.

He couldn't go forward.

He couldn't go backward.

Trapped.

Pablo needed to rest and regather his strength before trying again. But to do that, he would need to stop his mind from descending into the depths of insanity.

He tried to focus, concentrating on the long road he'd taken to reach this point, and the elation that he'd felt just hours earlier, as he made the discovery of the sealed tunnel. As with so much in life, a series of seemingly random events, left entirely to chance, led to this very moment.

Pablo cast his mind back to where it all began…

Chapter Fifteen

In 1969 archaeologists hunting for a sacred well beneath the ancient Maya city of Chichén Itzá on Mexico's Yucatán Peninsula accidentally discovered a trove of more than 150 ritual objects –untouched for more than a thousand years – in a series of cave chambers that may have held clues to the rise and fall of the ancient Maya.

After its initial discovery by farmers, Balamku was visited by archaeologist Víctor Segovia Pinto, who wrote up a report noting the presence of an extensive amount of archaeological material. One in particular, referenced a Mayan story about a treasure trove being buried, in a nearby and extensive cave system, long ago, before the Spanish invasion. But instead of excavating the site, Segovia then directed the farmers to seal up the entrance, and all records of the discovery of the cave seemed to vanish.

For years, people have searched for this vast treasure trove.

And in his research as a Mexican archeologist, Dr. Pablo Veracruz had become certain that the nearby Caves of Balankanche were the extensive system referenced. Not just certain. Obsessed. It was the most famous Maya cave site near Chichén Itzá, in Mexico. The name translated to "the cave of the sacred jaguar throne." It was, Veracruz knew, a reference to the Mayan leaders, not the animal jaguar.

The cave was approximately 2.5 miles southeast of the Chichén Itzá archaeological zone and formed a network of sacred caves. The caves themselves were now well-known tourist sites. Inside, a large selection of ancient pottery and idols may still be seen in the positions where they were left in pre-Columbian times.

Going back even further, on 15 September 1959, José Humberto Gómez, a local guide, discovered a false wall in the cave. Behind it he found an extended network of caves with significant quantities of undisturbed archaeological remains, including pottery and stone-carved censers, stone implements and jewelry. The Instituto Nacional de Antropología e Historia converted the cave into an underground museum, and the objects after being catalogued were returned to their original place so visitors can see them in situ.

In more recent times, Veracruz was part of a team of archeologists who used a composite laser scan to map Chichén Itzá's Cave of Balankanche. It showed that the shape of its great limestone column is strongly evocative of the World Tree in Maya mythological belief systems.

The information was published in an article he wrote for National Geographic, an article that garnered him some accolades within the archeological community, as well as with the wider support of various wealthy donors who were happy to support him in some of his future projects.

What wasn't ever published was the fact the limestone column was just the beginning. If one took the map of the Maya mythological tree of life, and superimposed it upon that of the limestone column, the known map of the Cave of Balankanche, and then extended the imaginary tree to encompass the Chichén Itzá archeological site, including the Cenote Sagrado, the entire map linked up.

Once visually seen, it was impossible to forget.

The squiggly lines of the tree's mythological roots were so perfectly set, that it became impossible to imagine people discovering the image of the tree of life by chance. Instead, it was more likely, Veracruz concluded that the entire tree had been carved out of the limestone or that the ancient pyramid of Chichén Itzá had been built to match perfectly with the Cenote Sagrado to recreate the World Tree.

World trees were a prevalent motif occurring in the mythical cosmologies, creation accounts, and iconographies of the pre-Columbian cultures of Mesoamerica. In the Mesoamerican context, world trees embodied the four cardinal directions, which also served to represent the fourfold nature of a central world tree, a symbolic axis mundi which connects the planes of the Underworld and the sky with that of the terrestrial realm.

Depictions of world trees, both in their directional and central aspects, are found in the art and mythological traditions of cultures such as the Maya, Aztec, Izapan, Mixtec, Olmec, and others, dating to at least the Mid to Late Formative periods of Mesoamerican chronology.

The Yucatán Peninsula was a limestone plain, with no rivers or streams. The region was pockmarked with natural sinkholes, called cenotes, which exposed the water table to the surface. One of the most impressive of these is the Cenote Sagrado, which is 200 feet in diameter and surrounded by sheer cliffs that drop to the water table some 90 feet below.

The Cenote Sagrado was a place of pilgrimage for ancient Maya people who, according to ethnohistoric sources, would conduct sacrifices during times of drought. Archaeological investigations support this as thousands of objects have been removed from the bottom of the cenote, including material such as gold, carved jade, copal, pottery, flint, obsidian, shell, wood, rubber, cloth, as well as skeletons of children and men.

All this led to his belief that a second, larger passageway had been long since cemented shut... But after nearly twenty years of research and thousands of hours of on site, actual archeology, Veracruz had never been able to locate any evidence of another such tunnel or of a secret passageway long since buried or sealed.

That was until recently when he got lucky...

Double lucky in fact.

It had been an unnaturally wet season this year. Now, after the rain, came the heat of summer with equal fervor. If that wasn't enough, the Yucatán Peninsula, which was not as seismically active as the area close to the boundary between the North American and Cocos plates, experienced one of its largest earthquakes in more than a century. Probably more than five centuries.

And for the first time in nearly a millennium, the ancient pyramid of Chichén Itzá shifted. From the outside, it had left no noticeable differences, but inside, faint lines had started to show, revealing hidden passages.

Chichén Itzá became off limits to tourists as archeologists filled the ancient pyramid like ants swarming to protect their queen. The entire pyramid became filled with high-tech archeological equipment, ground penetrating LIDAR, laser mapping devices, and other measuring devices. It was one of the biggest things to hit the Mexican archeological world in decades.

But while archeologists flocked to Chichén Itzá, Dr. Pablo Veracruz headed to Balankanche. For the past two weeks, he'd worked using an extensive array of LIDAR scanners. LIDAR, which stood for light detecting and ranging, used lasers to shine on the area to be mapped, before emitting brief pulses of light.

The amount of time it takes for those pulses to reflect back to the instrument is measured, and each measurement is plotted using GPS. Computers then use that data to construct a 3-D map of the area. It was the same technology he'd used for years within the cave of Balankanche to no avail.

Only this time was different.

This time, it identified a crack in an otherwise solid wall of limestone. The ancient Maya were master craftsmen and had developed a unique way of mixing limestone to seal hidden passages and protect treasure troves for the ages.

To Veracruz, it all made sense.

Maya architecture spans several thousands of years, several eras of political change, and architectural innovation before the Spanish colonization of the Americas. Often, the buildings most dramatic and easily recognizable as creations of the Maya peoples, are the step pyramids of the Terminal Pre-classic Maya period and beyond. Any civilization capable of building such marvels, were surely capable of sealing a hidden chamber forever.

Veracruz had broken through the fragmented pieces of limestone with a pickaxe and within the better part of an hour had crawled through and into the narrow passageway. At the time, his elation had prevented him from thinking things through any further. He hadn't considered the fact that the region of the Balankanche Cave where he had been working was off-limits to tourists, and only accessible to archeologists – all of which would most likely be working at Chichén Itzá for months to come – or the fact that as a self-avowed loner, nobody knew where he was working or would think to notify the authorities if he went missing.

Instead, like a fool rushing toward gold… he had entered the ancient Maya tunnel that had been sealed for centuries…

Chapter Sixteen

Dr. Pablo Veracruz opened his eyes.

Only absolute darkness stared back at him. He blinked away the fog, and the nightmare in which he'd become trapped flooded back like an evil shroud, wrapping its deadly fingers over him. He squeezed his eyes shut and suppressed the terror that he felt rise, and, if released, would end up exploding, leaving his mental faculties permanently destroyed.

Instead, it made him wet himself.

Putting the smell and the hygiene issues aside as the least of his problems, he felt the warm liquid slide along his torso. The slight reduction to his bladder size wasn't going to help him squeeze through the narrow constriction – after all, it was his shoulders that were stuck, not his hips – but the liquid might. Veracruz allowed the liquid to find its way through the invisible gaps in his body spacing by adjusting his breathing and concurrently tensing and relaxing various muscles. By the time it reached his face, he knew he'd done as much as could be physically done.

It was now or never.

Time to give it everything, and when his energy failed him, he would either be free of his nightmarish bindings, or rot in his subterranean hell for all of eternity.

Veracruz took a couple breaths, collecting his thoughts and planning the not-so-intricate steps to achieve his freedom. He produced a mental image of himself achieving the goal and then he rolled the dice, and gambled with his life.

He took a breath in as deep as it could go, and then exhaled everything, until he could no longer breathe out any more, and his chest was as small as it would ever be. This was the most dangerous move yet.

And it all depended entirely on luck.

If he moved forward and the space opened up, Veracruz would have won his freedom and the ability to breathe again. But, if he moved forward and the constriction worsened, he might find himself in a position where he could no longer move and at the same time, there was no longer enough space to breathe – at all.

Better to die quick, than to rot away entombed in hell.

With that thought in the back of his mind, Veracruz began to move. Fingers, elbows, chest, hips, legs, feet… he shifted the weight from one to the next and back again.

Like a heavy cargo ship leaving port, it was slow to overcome the resistance and begin to move, but soon, he felt his stomach, followed by parts of his back, scrape across the limestone walls. He dared not breathe in until he was certain. Like the gambler, who doesn't want to look at his cards until all the final hands had been played, he postponed the truth until the end.

His lungs burned and finally, he couldn't resist that primal urge to breathe.

Veracruz breathed in.

The muscles of his diaphragm moved downward, his chest wall expanded, and sweet, precious air was sucked into his desperate lungs.

Euphoria followed.

He pulled himself just that little deeper and stopped. Around him, he found himself inside a void. He tentatively felt with his outstretched hands for the nearest wall, but instead discovered only emptiness.

Veracruz wanted to cry with happiness.

In disbelief, he shifted his other hand outward. Still nothing. He slowly extended his legs and arms like one would when trying to make a snow angel. There was just a void. It felt magical. Better than anything else he'd ever experienced in his life.

Veracruz tried to reach the ceiling, but his arms couldn't extend far enough. That was almost too much for him to bear and his brain, having mentally cracked during his period of entrapment, feared that he was still unconscious, still trapped in the horrific constriction.

He stood up, feeling surreal. His cramped legs, arms, and back feeling a strange mixture of pain – like someone who'd just gotten out of bed after sleeping too long and feeling a bit stiff – and exhilarated at his freedom. He stretched up and tried to reach the ceiling. Still just nothingness. He rationalized that he must be awake, and that he'd managed to make it through.

Slowly, and feeling more certain about his luck with every passing second, Veracruz bent down and reached for the bag he'd been towing which included a few supplies. There was some food – a sandwich and a couple of muesli bars, a bottle of water, a digital camera, a most important of all, a hand-held flashlight and spare batteries.

Veracruz fumbled with the switch of the flashlight. He held his breath and flicked it to the on position. The glow of the LED light began to fill the room. It was massive. The biggest by far within the entire system of caves within Balankanche. The beam of the flashlight disappeared into the distant walls of the cathedral. He wanted to scream with joy.

He was inside a massive cathedral shaped cavern.

It was big enough to play a game of football, a stark contrast to the tight hell in which he'd been confined only minutes earlier. More than that, the cavern was filled with artifacts and images painted onto the walls. His beam landed on a cascade of offerings left by the ancient residents of Chichén Itzá, so perfectly preserved and untouched that stalagmites had formed around the incense burners, vases, decorated plates, and other objects in the cavern.

At a glance, he imagined that the cavern contained a veritable treasure trove of ancient Mayan history, with all of the images on the walls predating the Spanish invasion. Without question, this was what he'd spent the majority of his adult life searching for – the greatest treasure of the Mayans – sealed to protect their vast wealth from the invading Spanish.

Veracruz walked along the edge of the cavern and reflected how quickly despondency had been replaced by utter mesmerized glee, his light swaying side to side as it searched the new cavern. He stopped, and fixed the beam of his flashlight on an image to his left, something that really caught his eye.

It was a large painting…

Probably spanning more than thirty feet in total.

It depicted dozens of ships. They looked grand by comparison to the other primitive boats seen in the rest of the photos.

He studied the ship at the head of the fleet. It had three decks of oars, and a large sail. The sail appeared white, with the exception of a large insignia of a butterfly stitched into its middle. The color had faded, but the butterfly was royal purple with a double set of eyes on the back of its wings. The startling effect made it look like the butterfly tracked his movement no matter where he positioned himself within the cave.

Veracruz took a step back. It wasn't exactly what he was looking for… instead, the discovery was far more valuable than anything he could have ever imagined. It confirmed that a Hellenistic fleet of triremes, powered by sail and oar, crossed the Atlantic nearly 2,000 years ago.

Over the next few hours, he took more than a hundred photos of the stunning image of the Hellenistic fleet across the backdrop of the Yucatán Peninsula.

Afterward, he mentally prepared himself for the grueling reality that he needed to pass through the choke point to reach the outside world where he could reveal his discovery. The prospect of facing that nightmare again terrified him, but he knew that if he fit through it once, he could do it a second time.

In the end, the entire thing was a lot easier going out than going in. Caves were like that. Everything had to do with the way your body naturally adjusted to the contours of a narrow passageway. What might be easy to enter, could be impossible going the other direction and vice versa. In this case, Veracruz negotiated the deadly choke point with surprising ease. It took nearly three hours of standard caving to fight his way out of the system.

By the time he passed the giant limestone column at the entrance of the cave, known as the tree of life, and clambered up the steep set of steps, into the paved entrance to Balankanche. It was late in the day. The sun was in its death throes, bruising the sky a coiling purple and orange, making the tops of the jungle trees appear to be on fire.

As soon as he'd cleared the jungle canopy Veracruz withdrew his cell phone and called a number from speed dial.

A man answered the call almost right away. "Hello Pablo. What can I do for you?"

Without preamble, he said, "Sam Reilly… I think I just found what you've been looking for."

"Come again?" came Sam's deep, and level voice on the other end. "What have you found?"

Pablo exhaled a deep breath. "I just found evidence that a Hellenistic fleet once sailed the waters of the Yucatán Peninsula."

Chapter Seventeen

The Blue Mountains, Alpine Resort – Ontario, Canada.
Tom Bower stood next to his downhill mountain bike.

There was something amusing about the sight of his massive frame straddling the *Specialized Pro* mountain bike. It was one of those bikes with a large forked front suspension and a triangular shaped aluminum alloy frame mounted on a heavy-duty rear suspension system. To Tom, it felt more like a motorcycle, despite Genevieve assuring him that it would be very different to riding one. It didn't feel different. Much lighter, maybe? Possibly more maneuverable. But it had all the normal things that a motorcycle had – forked front suspension, rear suspension, and hydraulic brakes.

He even argued to Genevieve that, given they'd just taken one of the ski-lifts to the top and gravity was going to do all the effort in bringing him back down again, he didn't even really need to peddle it to make it go. Ergo, the thing was virtually a motorcycle.

She laughed and dismissed his sentiment with the simple response, "We'll see."

"Yeah, we'll see," Tom said, a mixture of laughter and genuine pleasure on his parted lips.

At the start of the conflux of trails, he glanced back at the spectacular vista beneath a summer's sky of cerulean blue. He could have been in the Swiss Alps for all he knew looking at it. Winding trails scarred the lush forest of pines that encased the steep slopes of the resort. Several ski-lifts operated, catering to the summer adventurers who reveled in the Blue Mountains' rugged beauty, mountain bike riding, hiking, and wildlife spotting benefits.

The nearby villages of the Blue Mountains and Tyrolean resorts stood out in the distance before a backdrop of green and turquoise waters of the Georgian Bay, the northeastern arm of Lake Huron, surrounded by rugged bedrock and white pine forests.

Genevieve glanced at him. Realizing he was lost in its beauty, she asked, "Are you ready?"

Tom shook his head. "Just a sec…"

"What is it?" she asked, bringing her bike closer in to meet him.

When she was close enough to reach, he grabbed her – moving quickly – pulling her in toward him with both arms, until their eyes were level – and stopped. Genevieve had deep blue eyes, short brown hair, tied back. A single strand had come free, and she wiped it back behind her ear. She stared back at him, and smiled, restraint registering across her face.

After a few seconds, restraint gave way to desire, and she wrapped her arms around his neck. An impish and lascivious grin spread out across her parted lips, the tip of her tongue just touching the spacing between her white teeth, teasing him. "Yes?"

Tom closed the gap and kissed her. She opened her mouth in response, kissing him back. It was gentle, but full of passion.

After thirty seconds, he pulled away. "Now I'm ready."

"No, you're not," she said, grabbing Tom by his neck and pulling him in tight. She kissed him again. It was a long, soft kiss, their lips exploring gently. She stroked his cheeks and his hair, and he found himself wrapping his hands around her waist.

After a long minute she broke the kiss, panting. "Now we're good to ride. See if you can keep up."

Tom watched as she slid her full-faced helmet onto her head, and kicked off, pedaling her Trek mountain bike along the start of a green run.

He popped his own helmet on and followed her. They were both fit and the trail was graded as easy, so he found they moved quickly. It had been a long time since he'd ridden a bike and he felt a little rusty, while Genevieve appeared to be an expert. They rode along the green trail, meandering to the east of the mountain, while Tom got the handle of things.

It wasn't hard. Just like… riding a bike, he guessed.

After twenty or so minutes, she stopped, pulling up at another conflux of trails. They both pulled out a drink. Despite being early spring, it felt like a summer's day, and he noticed through her helmet's protective goggles, Genevieve's face was flushed, and there were tiny beads of sweat on her forehead.

Tom asked, "Where to?"

She gave a non-committal shrug. "You pick. Wherever you like."

"Okay," he said, running his eyes across some of the signs of upcoming trails.

They had various names that looked like something a bunch of teenagers high on one of those modern energy drinks like Red Bull or Monster had come up with. There were Shot Glass, Big Squeeze, Embryo, and Minion's Rush.

Tom was about to pick something when Genevieve said, "Hey, what do you think that guy wants?"

He turned and looked over his shoulder, farther up the hill, to where a man was waving his arms together, as though he was trying to get their attention. Tom frowned. "No idea. I mean, we're on vacation and Sam's not around, we left our phones back at the lodge, so we should be safe. Right?"

"Right…" Her eyes narrowed, and the guy kept on shouting something while swinging his arms. "He knows we can't hear him, right?"

"Yeah… he's seems really intent on getting our attention. Maybe we should ride up to him? Maybe someone's hurt?"

"Yeah, you're right. We'd better do that."

They turned around and Tom swore.

Behind them, a large black bear and two cubs wandered toward them.

Genevieve yelled, "Go!"

Tom didn't need to be told twice. He stepped on his pedals and began to ride, taking the first turn-off he could, a really steep one called *Big Sleeze* – a double black diamond run. It crossed a wooden bridge then began to turn, before dipping straight down like a damned rollercoaster.

The trail swerved around a series of near vertical berms, allowing them to squeeze ever tighter through the banked corners. The entire run felt like he was on a luge racing down a bobsleigh track.

The Specialized Pro picked up speed.

Within seconds, he no longer worried about the bears. Instead, every cell in his body worked at trying to stay upright on his bike. The ground leveled out for a few seconds before offering two options. One that went up and one that went down.

Tom took the trail heading up – thinking it might slow him down – what he didn't realize was that it was leading to a jump. By the time he'd clicked, it was too late to do anything about it. He set up for the jump, leveled the bike mid-air, and landed perfectly on the down ramp.

He jammed on the brakes, taking the bike to a complete stop another hundred feet down the track. Putting his feet down to stand, he glanced over his shoulder and spotted Genevieve flying through the air doing tricks that clearly belonged on the X-Games.

Tom waited for her to land.

She came to a skidding stop next to him. He said, "Hey, you can ride!"

"I told you I can ride!" she said. "You told me you'd never been on a mountain bike before!"

Tom grinned. "I might have understated my experience…"

"I'll say… you just carved up a double black run at the Blue Mountains like a pro!"

Behind them, the guy who had been waving at them earlier came racing along the trail. He looked serious. Like an Olympian having the ride of his life. He cleared the jump, jammed on his brakes, and pulled up right next to the two of them.

The guy removed his helmet. "I don't suppose you're Tom Bower?"

"That's me," Tom replied, a lilt in his voice, like, *how the hell do they find me?* "What's up?"

The guy handed him a cell phone. "I've been asked to give this to you."

"Who asked you?"

A second later the cell phone began to ring.

Tom could see he wasn't going to get much in the way of answers from the messenger. So instead of trying, he hit the answer button. "Hello?"

"Tom," it was Elise who spoke. "Vacation's over… Sam's in trouble."

His heart skipped a beat. "What's happened? What sort of trouble?"

"The sort of trouble he's good at finding himself in when you're not around…" Elise paused a beat, letting those words sink in. "And I'm afraid I believe he's going to need you and Genevieve's help to get him out of it."

Chapter Eighteen

Paul M. Tellier Tunnel, Sarnia – Canada

The Amtrak cross country train raced quietly across the spectacular countryside of lush green trees, hills, and the distant turquoise waters of Lake Huron. It was powered by four GE P42DC passenger diesel locomotives, capable of producing a combined output in excess of 16,000 horse power. The four powerhouses pulled a long line of cars that snaked back along the iron tracks for the better part of a mile. In the front, and closest to the noisy engines, were the coach cars, followed by business and first class, two sets of dining cars, two glass domed observational cars, one baggage car, and a series of trailing flatbed vehicular cars.

Inside a first-class sleeper suite, Sam Reilly woke up to the gentle shifting sound of the steel wheels rocking along the tracks creating an almost hypnotizing, yet constant, rhythm of a *thud-thud*, *thud-thud*.

He stared out the window, taking in the serene landscape. Sam checked his watch. It was midday. Mentally, he tried to picture the outline of the rail line from Québec to Minneapolis, and then calculate his probable position based on the time. His mind was sluggish, and the landscape – although beautiful – too monotonous and without any specific identifying landmarks in which to orient himself.

They had passed Lake Ontario and Toronto hours ago…

Right as he was considering the possibilities, the train began its descent into a long tunnel. It was just the right amount of imagery, or lack of it in this case, to jog Sam's memories and place the train on his mental map.

On the other end of the bed, Caliburn seemed to sleep on, oblivious to the fact they were leaving Canada and entering the US.

They had entered the Paul M. Tellier tunnel, linking Sarnia Ontario to Port Huron Michigan, and running parallel to St. Clair tunnel, the world's first international rail tunnel, as well as the first railway tunnel built under a river in North America. The tunnel was over six thousand feet long, with more than 2300 feet lying under the St. Clair River.

They came out the other end and darkness gave way to daylight and crystal-clear skies of blue. The train slowed, and fifteen minutes later, it came to a stop at Port Huron Station.

The train seemed delayed for a while, but that didn't bother Sam. He was in no rush for anything. Despite getting involved in some strange biker gang-cum-Viking group, Sam wasn't prepared for it to ruin his first real vacation in years. The way he looked at it, he'd always wanted to take a rail trip across the Great Lakes. No reason not to enjoy it.

Caliburn, as though hearing his internal voice, sat up on his paws, his head tilting to the left, and his big eyes meeting Sam's with a mixture of love and curiosity.

Sam held his gaze. "Good morning."

The golden retriever tilted its head and mewled.

The train released its brakes, and Sam felt the gentle jolt as the train began its slow process of picking up speed once more. He turned to Caliburn. "We're just leaving Port Huron Station."

Caliburn, upon realizing they had a long way to go, turned his head, somehow burying it beneath both his paws, and after doing a funny little shuffle with his hind legs and tail until all was set in a new comfortable position, dozed off to sleep almost instantaneously.

"I wish to hell I could get back to sleep that easily." Sam shook his head and grinned. "I'm going to order some lunch."

Caliburn's ears cocked, and an instant later, the large dog was upright.

He gave a stifled bark.

Sam grinned, giving the dog a gentle pat beneath its mane. "Yeah, I thought you might like to join me."

Just in case there was any previous misunderstanding, Caliburn gave another three sharp barks.

Sam hushed him with a gentle pat and said, "Okay, okay... but no more barking, you're not even supposed to be up here with me."

Caliburn leveled his dark brown eyes on him. If a dog was ever capable of rolling its eyes and gazing with piercing scrutiny, it was Caliburn.

Sam turned away, giving Caliburn a firm pat. "Hey, I don't make the rules about dogs and passenger trains!"

The dog's tail wagged incessantly, and he barked again, as though this was a fun game.

"Hey," Sam said, his voice rising a notch. "I'm serious... it's all fun and games now until someone catches you and you end up spending the next thirty-two hours riding in the baggage car inside some tiny cage!"

Caliburn's tail lowered between his legs, he bared his teeth in a guttural and reproachful growl.

You wouldn't dare!

Sam had had enough of the game. "All right, forget it. If they kick us off the train, we'll drive. Agreed?"

The dog barked again.

His tail wagging happily once more.

Sam called the car attendant, and ordered two meals. After a moment of confusion, he confirmed his order and that he did, indeed, want two full meals for himself. He was famished. Hell, if Caliburn didn't stop playing, Sam was half tempted to eat both meals himself!

Twenty minutes later, the car attendant knocked on the door.

"Just a minute," Sam said. Turning to Caliburn, he mouthed the words, "Hide..."

The dog turned around, burying its head beneath a crumpled mess of blankets at the end of the bed, and stretching out long. The dog's golden hair forming a dark contrast with the blue upholstery and blankets.

Sam whispered, "Caliburn! The bed's blue!"

A split second later, the dog's golden hair turned a matching shade of blue.

Sam stared at the image for a moment. The scattered mess of blankets at the end of the bed looked unusual, but it looked more like he was lazy rather than that he'd smuggled a dog on board. No, Caliburn had done a perfect job of camouflaging himself. The sight never ceased to amaze him.

Caliburn was a rescue dog.

But not a regular one. He had once been a highly classified, secret military experiment, to genetically develop the perfect soldier. The program failed miserably with its human trials, but the initial attempt with a dog had worked wonders.

Caliburn had been the recipient of such fantastical science.

Engineered with a mixture of DNA extracted from an octopus, among other things. He inherited from the octopus DNA a unique ability to camouflage its skin. The concept wasn't entirely rare in nature – albeit a little unusual for a dog – the defensive mechanism worked with chromatophores, or little sacs in an animal's skin and hair follicles, filled with pigmentation, that erupt in response to external impulses in its nervous system. This allowed its hair follicles to alter color as part of its intrinsic camouflage defense. The dog was highly intelligent, although naturally a little lazy, and could transform its entire coat to match anything he wanted.

Sam opened the door and greeted the car attendant, a fifty-something year old gentleman who reminded him of that butler from Downton Abbey. The man placed the two plates of food covered with a silver cloche on the table at the middle of the room.

"Thank you," Sam said.

The car attendant turned to leave. Then, with a suppressed grin, he said, "You must be very hungry sir."

"Famished," Sam agreed, and then closed the door behind him.

He removed the cloche and stared at the food.

For himself, there was grilled Atlantic salmon with asparagus, mushrooms, and roast squash in some sort of French buttery sauce that Sam couldn't quite pronounce. He breathed in, his mouth salivating as he savored the scent. His eyes then drifted to Caliburn's meal – spaghetti bolognaise. Behind him, Sam could hear the dog's tail wagging like the arm of an over-excited grandfather clock.

Sam licked his lips. "He's gone, Caliburn."

The dog jumped up, its thick carpet of hair turned gold once more.

Despite holding the enviable accolade of smartest dog on the planet, Caliburn looked just like every other dog Sam had met, as soon as food was placed within reach. The dog mowed down the enormous bowl of spaghetti Bolognese within seconds.

Sam smiled, picked up his fork, glanced at the dog, and took his first bite. *"Bon Appetit."*

Chapter Nineteen

The Amtrak train kept up its steady chatter as it made its way uphill toward Flint, Michigan. Sam perched himself along the window seat with his legs crossed, like some sort of Zen yoga master. A dense forest of red maple, white cedar, quaking aspen, black cherry and hemlock rushed by the window in a blur.

He thought about the email Pablo Veracruz had sent him and particularly about the ancient image he'd found on the newly discovered cavern. It depicted a 1st Century Hellenistic fleet sailing across the Yucatán Peninsula.

A smile creased his lips.

It was nearly impossible to believe that Cleopatra VII had been right.

He thought about what she had written…

A fleet of Hellenistic Greeks in triremes, powered by sail and oar, sailed across an icy sea to reach a distant land. Far beyond anywhere in the known world. They set colonies and mined gold, which appeared to be plentiful. Some made recurrent trips, while others stayed to live out their lives, trading the warm Aegean for the cold waters of the Distant Land.

Sam remembered reading her notes, his eyes wide with rapt attention.

Of the great fleet, two people were continuously referenced for their valor. Their names were Odin and Thor. They had fiery red beards and led their fleet of triremes, filled with warriors, to the distant lands, returning with gold and stories of easy conquests of the foreign lands. Odin and Thor became legendary. They ransacked distant villages, and built a sacred grotto and filled it with their treasures as a reward and testament to their dead who perished valiantly in battle. The two men drove fear into the hearts of their enemies.

Sam shook his head.

What was the chance that someone would find archeological evidence of Thor and Odin being Hellenistic sailors? More importantly, what was the likelihood that such information would come out less than twenty-four hours after he'd been attacked by wannabe Vikings, who called themselves Berserkers?

It almost seemed too unlikely a coincidence.

Sam decided that as soon as he'd found Godkin's brother and delivered the USB stick, along with his condolences over the death of Miles, he would head to the Yucatán Peninsula with Tom to determine the veracity of the archeological discovery.

Until then, he was still on vacation...

Caliburn resumed his sleeping position and Sam kept reading his book. It was *Every Breath*, by Nicholas Sparks. Not his usual read, he had to admit. But he was enjoying it. A guilty pleasure. A love story so fantastical and heartbreaking that it couldn't be any further removed from his regular life. It was a little unbelievable. But that's not so bad. After all, we all read to escape the world in which we live – even if that world happened to already be perfectly delightful.

On the bed, Caliburn's ears pricked up. The hair on his back suddenly spiking upward, his eyes watchful and intent. Sam put the book down. His eyes narrowed, darting from the door back to Caliburn.

What is it?

A crisp knock rasped at the door.

It was followed by a polite voice. "Service, please."

Sam glanced at Caliburn who had already camouflaged himself at the head of the bed. Sam sat up, feeling the slight tightness in his joints after sitting for too long, and wandered over to the door.

He unlocked the latch and opened it himself. "Hello."

"Good afternoon," the car attendant said. He was much younger than the previous one – probably early to mid-twenties if Sam had to guess – but every bit as well dressed and politely spoken. "I'm just here for the trays."

"Thank you," Sam said, gesturing to where they were left on the table. "You can tell the chef I enjoyed the meals very much."

"That's so nice to hear. I'll pass it on."

The attendant stepped forward to collect the trays and the door's natural closing mechanism forced the door shut. He leaned down and reached for the tray. In the process, part of his sleeve pulled back.

Sam's eyes locked onto a tattoo on his forearm.

The car attendant noticed Sam's gaze. He put the trays back down, and immediately rolled down his sleeves again. The kid set his jaw. There were tiny tremors in his face, but he stood rigid. His face turned scarlet and the vein in his forehead was pulsing. An assorted mixture of embarrassment and under riding fear appeared to surface that seemed at odds with the situation. Suddenly the tension in the room was taut as razor wire.

Sam felt it too.

What's more, he knew exactly why. He'd seen that tattoo before. Different anatomical location, but same undeniable image. It depicted the face of a Viking warrior, protected by a steel helmet with horns. Beside which, were five filled in tear drops. It was identical to the one he'd seen on Miles Godkin's arm the day he pulled him from the water at St. Martins. Only this one had two more tear drops.

Had this meant he'd murdered two more people?

Sam had no intention of making it three.

He made a disarming smile. "Nice tattoo. What is that?"

The car attendant swallowed hard, feigning embarrassment, and said, "I'm sorry, I'm not supposed to have tattoos."

Sam waved him away with a placating hand. "Is that some sort of cute little munchkin?"

The attendant turned away. "No..."

"Sure it is... what is it?" Sam persisted. "Some sort of miniature Viking? Except Vikings never wore horned helmets. The only authentic Viking helmet ever discovered is decidedly horn-free. The horned trend was fabricated during the 19th century, perhaps inspired by descriptions of northern Europeans by ancient Greek and Roman chroniclers. Long before the Vikings' time, Norse and Germanic priests did indeed wear horned helmets for ceremonial purposes."

Stunned, the man was taken aback.

Sam said, "And that tattoo looks like it's laughing. Are those tears of laughter running down its cheeks?"

The car attendant's façade disappeared like the drapes at a theatre.

Sam readied himself to launch at the Berserker, but the kid had drawn his weapon already. It was a pistol. A Beretta 9mm. Attached to its barrel was a silencer. Despite the kid's youth, there was a hard set to his jaw, and defiant glare in his eyes. This wasn't going to be his first murder, and probably not his last, if Sam didn't do something to stop it.

Sam turned the palms of his hands outward in a placating gesture. "Hey, I'm just here to enjoy a vacation."

"Really?" The man locked eyes with him. "Because what I've heard Mr. Reilly, you're responsible for the deaths of five of our members... and that kind of thing's unforgivable."

Sam shrugged. "So what are we doing chatting?"

The Berserker raised an eyebrow. "Why haven't I killed you yet?"

"The thought did enter my mind." Sam gave an ambivalent shrug of his shoulder. It kind of suggested that he was okay to be killed, but could he decide whether or not to do it, so he could get back to the book he was reading?

The barrel was aimed at Sam's head. From this distance, there was no way in the world he could miss. "I need to know who sent you?"

Sam's lips twisted into a puzzled grin. "Sent me? I just came for a driving vacation... thought I'd see the countryside in Canada and now I'm enjoying a cross country train ride."

The kid shook his head. "You think we're stupid? Okay, tell me this... how much do you know about Berserker."

"I know it's the name you've been calling yourselves. Someone grew up watching too many Viking shows I assume?"

"I'm talking about RX16SF."

This time, Sam didn't even have to feign ignorance. He had no idea what the man was talking about. "Come again?"

"Don't try and hide the fact you know about RX16SF. I mean, if you didn't, why would you bother going to all that trouble to kick over an ant's nest, and really upset us?" The kid's eyes narrowed. "No. You've come here to find out about RX16SF – AKA Berserker."

Sam could see he wasn't going to get anywhere denying things. "Okay. Yes, I came here because of RX16SF. Now what?"

"Who wants it?" The kid shook his head and started naming a series of biker gangs Sam had heard of but had no idea what they actually did. "You can tell your boss we got it first, and no one's going to take it off us."

Sam shrugged. Without having a clue what else to say, he said, "Okay."

"Good," the kid seemed relieved by what he'd said.

Sam asked, "Now what?"

"Now, because you were honest, I'll let you pick… where do you want it? In the head or the chest?"

Sam said, "I'll take… now Caliburn!"

The blue blanket on the bed suddenly erupted. Teeth flashing, the apparition attacked with the ferocity and unexpectedness of a Stephen King horror film. It dived from the top of the bed, across the room, landing on the kid's forearm.

The Berserker fired a shot.

There was a crisp, rasping sound, as the silencer did its job. The 9 mm parabellum landed somewhere on the bedframe.

Caliburn's teeth gnawed at the Berserker's arm.

The kid's eyes went wide. Terror was written across his face. It was easy to see why. *A fucking blanket just leaped across the room and bit me!*

Caliburn kept up his deadly grip. He was slow to anger, but when he did – or when someone threatened someone close to him – Caliburn was lethal. He opened his mouth for a split second. The relief suddenly spreading across the kid's face, before Caliburn latched on a second time – this time with much greater force. The Beretta fell free from the kid's hands.

Sam didn't wait.

Most people go straight for the gun. That's their mistake. People are so afraid of death that they intrinsically developed narrow vision, focusing on the weapon. Sam was just about as far from most people as anyone can get.

He jumped toward the kid.

Without making any attempt for the weapon, he grabbed the kid by his shoulders, pulling the Berserker toward him. The kid had expected to be struck, and so had pushed forward. As a consequence, both motions were in alignment and the Berserker fell to the ground.

Standing above him, Sam drove his foot toward the kid's head. He rolled like a fireman, and Sam's foot hit the ground instead.

The Berserker then swung his hand down with an open palm, using it like a scythe.

The blow landed on the back of Sam's knee.

Pain like fire, shot through his leg and Sam dropped to the ground.

On the floor, the Berserker regained his composure. No longer racing for the pistol, he turned to Sam, swinging a second blow – this time at Sam's neck. It was Sam's turn to move quickly. He blocked with his forearm and moved with his left arm to punch his attacker.

The kid didn't try to block it.

Instead, he moved in close – engaging Sam in a grappling hook and hugging him tight. The two wrestled on the floor, struggling to gain some semblance of power over the other person. The Berserker obviously knew Brazilian Jiu Jitsu. Sam had studied a variety of martial arts, but there was no doubt in his mind, the kid was better at wrestling.

Within seconds, the Berserker had gained the dominant position on top, and was rapidly applying pressure. It was a lethal choke hold to Sam's neck. In a competition, he would have already tapped out and accepted defeat. Hell, he would have given most of his fortune to be able to tap out now, but the only form of submission his opponent would accept would be his death.

And that wasn't going to do for Sam.

He fought with every ounce of strength, just to stay conscious. But with every second, his mind would wonder, his thoughts more difficult, and his sight darkened.

He was losing it.

Everything.

Where the hell was Caliburn?

With his one free hand, Sam kept trying to strike his opponent in his head. But it's hard from down below to derive enough force to inflict any real damage to the person on top.

It didn't stop him trying.

On the third attempt, he heard Caliburn give a curt bark. It wasn't a threatening growl like a predator. This was a message.

What the hell was he trying to say?

Sam moved his hand out and found Caliburn's fur coat. The dog moved in to nudge him with his wet nose. He ran his hand down the dog's mane, toward his mouth. Inside, Caliburn gripped the barrel of the Beretta. Sam grabbed the handle, rotated the gun so that it pointed at the Berserker's head, and squeezed the trigger.

Another rasping sound filled the suite.

The 9 mm parabellum struck the man's jaw at point blank range. The bullet tore away the guy's jaw and part of his face, but missed the brain. The kid released his tension on Sam's throat.

Sam rolled backward, putting as much space as he could between the two of them. The kid's eyes filled with terror, but he was still conscious. More than that. He went Berserk. He launched himself at Sam, as though he might still complete his mission during his final death throes.

Sam squeezed off another two rounds.

The bullets landed right at the center of the kid's chest. His momentum carried him forward, but the kid fell to the floor, his body, lifeless and still.

Sam took a couple deep breaths and then turned to Caliburn. "You took your damned time!"

Caliburn wasn't buying into the guilt thing. He looked up at him with piercing eyes and gave another bark. The meaning of this one was clear – *I'm glad you're alive. You can thank me later.*

Sam got it.

He patted the dog's mane. "Thanks, Caliburn for saving my life."

Chapter Twenty

Sam went into survival mode.

He locked the cabin door and moved quickly. He searched the Berserker for any sort of ID or anything he could use to get Elise to track him. There wasn't anything. He pocketed the Beretta. It was a standard issue military pistol with a 15-round magazine. By his count four had been fired, meaning he still had eleven to play with. He had no intention of waiting around long enough to find out whether or not that would be enough.

Sam grabbed his backpack and started to fill it with his laptop, book, and few personal items, before slipping his arms through the straps. It wasn't much. He traveled light and a lot of his personal things were still in the car which was parked on one of the last flatbed vehicular carriages. All told, he was ready to go within a space of a minute. He needed to disappear, but first he had to get rid of the body. The last thing he wanted right now was an investigation into someone murdered in his own sleeper suite.

He searched the room, looking for somewhere – anywhere – to hide the body. He could deal with the authorities later. Right now, he needed to get off the train before someone finished the job and Sam had no intention of becoming the cause of another added tear to someone's Viking tattoo in some sort of brazen and ritualistic gang tattoo ceremony. If he could hide the body, they might stop coming after him in the immediate future. It would buy some time.

That was, if they thought he was already dead.

He turned around in the small suite, opened the clothes locker, but shut the door immediately. It was too small. The kid would never fit. He considered the shower, but it would be the first place the next people they sent for Sam would most likely look. No, he needed to do a better job of it than that.

Caliburn made a stifled bark.

Sam turned to see him staring at the window. They were coming up to a bridge across a river. His heart was racing, pounding in his chest. He needed to move quickly if he wanted to make it. He nodded, in affirmation of Caliburn's idea.

He slid the large window all the way open.

Air whistled as it blew into the sleeping suite. Sam squatted down and gripped the kid's dead hand in one of his, and pulled the body over his shoulder in the classic fireman lift. The kid was a big guy. Plenty of time wasted in the gym. Probably a little over two hundred pounds. Sam gritted his teeth, and heaved to lift him up to the open window. The train blew its horn, and raced across the bridge, passing an unnamed river far below.

Now or never…

Sam stood up onto the chair, giving himself the last bit of clearance needed to push the body through the open window. It lingered there for a split second, caught somehow by the weight toward the hips and the torso in a delicate balance like a pendulum. A moment later, Sam changed his grip and lifted both legs, until the body slid free. He glanced out the window and watched as the body fell all the way to the fast-flowing river far below.

Sam closed the window again. Wiping away any blood and tidying up. He turned to Caliburn and said, "It's time to go."

He stepped out the door into the main thoroughfare.

Sam's eyes darted left and right.

To the left, heading toward the trailing carriage – and where Sam wanted to go – he spotted two men leaning against a wall at the end of the carriage. Their eyes were glued to their phones, their fingers dancing away at the screen, their minds absorbed by whatever games they were playing. They might have been passengers. Or they might have been security for the Berserkers, guarding Sam's door until the original hitman came out and confirmed the task had been done. To the right, there was nothing but an empty carriageway. He considered going right first, until he knew what the guys were doing, and then tracking back afterward.

A split second later, one of the men looked up from his phone. Something in his face shifted. The easygoing and relaxed expression gave way to shock and dismay. Sam thought about how to play the next few seconds – ambivalent, going to the bathroom, or aggressive and violent – in the end, the two goons made the decision for him.

They reached for their handguns. But neither got the chance to remove them from their holsters. Sam, already gripping the silenced Beretta, aimed and fired two shots in quick succession. Both head shots.

Two more Berserkers dead.

The body count was building up in an unimaginable way. Strangely, his mind wondered how the gang would manage to cover up these deaths. He dismissed the thought a second later. Not his problem. He didn't bother to search these two for IDs. No reason to expect to find them any different than the first one. He knelt down and retrieved their guns. Removed their full magazines, pocketing them in his backpack, and then dropped the unloaded pistols in the bin. He stepped past the two dead Berserkers and headed toward the trailing cars.

He patted Caliburn. "You'd better go first."

Caliburn barked, his eyes giving him a forlorn look like a forgotten soldier.

Sam nodded. "It's not for long. There's nothing you can do, and I'd rather you not get shot. Besides, if you do spot anymore trouble, they're not likely to attack you, but you can forewarn me. If we get separated, wait for me near the Bricklin. We're getting off at the next stop. Okay?"

Caliburn gave an affirmative bark – *agreed.*

Sam watched as Caliburn began to head off. He would no doubt create a stir with anyone who spotted him along the way, but Caliburn could play the friendly family dog if he needed, getting out of most anything by being cute and affectionate. Failing that, he was quick, agile, and damned smart.

He would make it back to the car and wait for him.

He gave Caliburn a couple minute's head start and then began to follow, passing through both sets of dining carts. He entered the first observational carriage. It was completely empty. That struck him as odd. Not that it was filled throughout the entire trip. After all, there's only so much observing anyone can do during a 48- or 72-hour train journey, but still, it seemed unusual for no one to be around during the middle of the day.

Sam moved through the carriage and then stopped. Because up ahead, Caliburn gave a series of sharp barks.

He knew exactly what it meant.

Trouble.

Chapter Twenty-One

Someone opened fire.

It wasn't with a silenced pistol. Apparently, all bets were off and the Berserkers were no longer taking any chances or cared about collateral damage or hiding themselves. A sharp barrage of *rat-a-tat-tats* filled the observational carriage, as someone kept their finger depressing the trigger of a machinegun.

The enormous glass dome shattered.

Sam hit the deck, taking cover behind a steel bulkhead before the stairs. He shielded his head with his backpack as glass rained down on him.

Silence followed.

He held his breath and listened.

All he could hear was the sound of the Amtrak cross country train making its way along the steel tracks. Its driver, nearly a quarter of a mile away, remained oblivious to the war-like conditions rapidly erupting toward the trailing carriages.

Sam gripped the handle of his Beretta ready to make his next move. From the other end of the carriage, he heard the sound of multiple footsteps crunching on the glass as they approached.

One of the attackers spoke into a cell phone. "This guy's like a rat. Let's not take any more chances. Divert the boys from Fort Gratiot."

There was a slight pause, and then one guy said, "Yes, all of them. We're gonna need their help to clean up this fucking mess by the time we're done."

Sam didn't wait any longer.

He stood up and dived toward the stairwell.

Multiple shots followed him, but he was outside the observational carriage, and sliding through the narrow doorway between carriages seconds later.

He was running hard.

Moving like his life depended upon it. Which it did. He entered the dining carriage and knocked over a waiter who was balancing four plates on his arms as he prepared to serve lunch.

"Stay down!" Sam shouted and kept running.

Behind him, the waiter swore, and scrambled to his feet. A few seconds later, more shots began to fire and the dining carriage turned to pandemonium. Sam pushed his way through, shouting and telling everyone to, "Get down and stay down!"

He kept going, heading for the driver's carriage.

Twice he paused long enough to fire a shot at his attackers. They didn't land anywhere near them, but were close enough to make them pause – forcing them to take valuable seconds to clear out each carriage before continuing on.

It bought him time.

He passed through the business, first class, and coach carriage, and then opened the door that separated the passenger carriages from the driver and engine cars. Sam looked down. It was one of those open gaps between the two carriages, completely exposed to the elements. Below, Sam spotted an array of fine sparks, flickering across the tracks, where the wheels clipped the track as the train rounded a slight bend.

Sam reached for the door to the first engine car.

It was locked.

Sam turned around, like a mouse caught. His eyes sweeping his environment for somewhere to hide or at least take defensive cover. There wasn't any. The train was traveling at nearly 90 miles an hour. The rails were built up on a bed of stones roughly ten feet high. Trees whirred by far below, thoroughly dissuading any thoughts of jumping.

He was trapped.

There was no way he could head back inside the coach carriage. There, he would be even more exposed. He glanced around the engine carriage, seeing if there was some way he could climb above it or along the side of it.

There was no chance.

Unlike the great Western movies of yesterday, where people clamber onto the roofs of old steam trains only to have the classic shoot-out unfold, these trains had been built with a protective wall of steel around both ends of the carriages. Designed to have nothing to grip onto, it prohibited adrenaline freaks, and wannabe social media stars from turning viral by joyriding or surfing on the roof of the train.

Sam eyed the spacing beneath the train. A single glance destroyed any thought that he might have of climbing underneath the train. The modern train was built with a low center of gravity. Even a small child would struggle to squeeze into the spacing, and he had no doubt that if he hit anything it would kill him instantly.

Out of options, he turned around and entered the coach class carriage. There was a toilet to the right. He opened the door. A man in his forties was cowering inside.

Sam waved his handgun. "I'm sorry, I'm going to have to ask you to move."

The man's brows furrowed. "When you gotta go…"

"Yeah, something like that."

Sam slid past the man, closing the door behind him and locking it. He shut the toilet seat and stood on top of it. A large glass window was slightly ajar above the toilet. It was designed to allow ventilation, but not to be fully opened. There wasn't time to work on the mechanism anyway. Sam grabbed the hilt of the Beretta and smashed the window. He quickly swept away the rest of the glass that splintered and remained.

Standing on top of the toilet lid he reached up through the window. There wasn't anything to grip. He leaned outside the train, looking back toward the top of the train carriage. A steel rod rose vertically six inches above the roof. Sam had no idea what it was for, but it looked like it might be strong enough to hold his weight – if he could just reach it.

Sam clambered back into the train and removed his backpack. He lengthened the shoulder straps as far as they could go. They would do the job. So long as they held. He glanced at the locking mechanism on the strap. A mental image of its theoretical strength playing out in his head. A second later, someone knocked at the door.

Time's up.

Sam clambered out the window, throwing his pack like a mini-lasso over the rod. The first attempt missed. But the second one caught and held. Sam gripped the opposite shoulder strap, slowly increasing his weight, and praying it would hold. Behind him, he heard the rasping sound of someone shooting at the door lock.

Doubt and fear gave way to necessity.

He pulled on the strap and in one quick movement heaved himself on to the roof of the train. The wind rushed past. He removed the bag to stop anyone following. The carriage shifted, jolting side to side, and in an instant, Sam fell sideways. He grabbed hold of the steel rod with his right hand, clasping it just before he slid off the opposite side of the train to the one he'd just climbed up.

The train made its way along a valley, where it hugged the rocky edge, leaving a sheer drop, where a river flowed with a series of tempestuous rapids some two hundred feet below. With the sound of his heart hammering in his ears, Sam breathed a sigh of relief.

And a moment later, his backpack began to roll toward the edge of the train.

He stretched out, trying to catch it, but his reach was just too short. He swore silently, and a moment later the backpack fell past him. He watched it almost disappear as it fell far below, before landing on a rocky outcrop at the bank of the river – the laptop and cell phone inside smashing on impact.

Sam decided he'd seen enough.

He had no intention of his life following the same fate as his backpack. He pulled on the rod and climbed onto the roof of the train. Squatting down low, he gathered his wits about him, finding his balance, while still hanging onto the rod for support.

It wasn't hard, but the consequence of falling was death.

The train was wide, but on the roof any movement at the base of the train was amplified like a pendulum. To make matters worse, it was almost entirely flat, with places to hold onto few and far between.

He scanned the trainline, trying to decide what his next play might be.

His eyes landed on the space between the passenger carriage and the diesel engine. It was roughly 6 feet across. It was a challenge, but hardly an Olympic long-jump. No, he could manage it. The question was, whether he could stomach the risk.

From the window through which he'd climbed out, someone leaned out and started shooting at him. The trajectory was all wrong, and the rounds went over his head, but in a flash, it made the decision for him.

He would take the risk and jump the damned gap.

Sam didn't have the time or the desire to over think it. He stood up and started moving along the top of the train's roof, heading toward the gap. He stopped just short of the space, trying to get a better mental image of the distance.

A bullet whizzed past his head.

He swore loudly, shuffling backward on his belly. Someone was guarding the gap, too. That removed any chance of escaping that way. He was now in real trouble. He couldn't go any farther forward and he knew that the rear carriages were already riddled with Berserkers. He was down to just six shots too and no spare magazines – they were lost along with his laptop and cell, when his backpack went over the side of the train.

His eyes darted toward the rod.

Someone threw a rope – an actual lasso by the looks of it – landing it on the first try. God these guys moved quick. The lasso was immediately followed by a set of hands. The Berserker climbed hand over hand.

Sam drew his Beretta and shot him.

The bullet landed on his chest, providing a fatal wound.

The Berserker, true to his gang's namesake, went crazy with bloodlust, and with his right hand reached into his holster and withdrew a handgun.

Sam didn't let him fire.

He squeezed off two more rounds in rapid succession.

The Berserker fell backward, his body landing between the rocky mountainside and the train, before being pulverized by the train's wheels.

Four bullets left… Sam thought with a somber sense of fatality.

Another set of hands climbed onto the rope.

Sam squeezed off a single round.

The bullet struck the man in the forehead and he fell backward, disappearing between the train and the mountain with a horrible sound of bones being crunched.

Three rounds to go…

Sam moved forward and tried to remove the lasso.

He couldn't.

The downward pressure from someone holding onto it inside was too great. If he had a knife, he could cut it, but he didn't. He found the irony that because he was on an international train trip, anti-terrorist laws prevented him from carrying anything that could be used as a weapon, such as a knife, and yet, the train now seemed to be crawling with gun-wielding thugs.

Another Berserker began to climb.

Sam shot him dead.

Two rounds left…

Sam said, "I can do this all day. How many people do you want to lose?"

That made them pause for a few minutes.

Sam caught his breath.

Then, above him, he heard the distant whirr of an approaching helicopter.

In the back of his mind, he remembered the call one of the Berserkers had made from inside the observation carriage – *Divert the boys from Fort Gratiot* – and the most horrible realization came to fruition.

His day was just about to get much worse.

Chapter Twenty-Two

The situation reached critical.

Sam threw all caution to the wind. Like the classic gambler who had risked everything, he no longer had anything left to lose. Jumping up, he ran across the train carriage, heading toward the trailing cars. Forgetting about the cliff on one side and the crunching wheels of the train on the other, he ran toward the first gap between carriages and jumped it. He made the landing easily and kept going without looking back. He jumped the next one, followed by the next.

Bolstered by the sight of their reinforcements, Berserkers began to scale the rope, and driven with the madness of those in a drug induced psychosis, they began their chase. Someone fired a couple shots. Sam had no idea where they landed, but was thankful it wasn't on him. After the third barrage of shots, Sam turned, aimed, and squeezed off a single round. The shot missed. And the Berserkers kept running at him.

He planted his feet firm, narrowed his gaze, zeroed in on his target, and fired off another single shot. It struck the Berserker closest to him, who kept running for another few feet, before tripping and falling.

One shot left.

Sam kept running.

Past the observation carriages.

The helicopter was now overhead. It was smaller than he expected. A Robinson 44. He could tell just by the sound having flown one for a mustering season in the Australian outback in his youth. For a second he thought he might have a reprieve. Perhaps this wasn't the Berserker's back up from *Fort Gratiot* after all? His eyes narrowed on the chopper. Through the narrow window on the side of the helicopter, he spotted the long barrel of a machinegun.

Sam swallowed.

Then again, maybe he was all out of luck.

The Berserker inside the helicopter opened fire.

Bullets raked the length of the carriage Sam was on top of.

Sprinting he reached the end of the car and instead of jumping the gap, he dropped down into the traveling space between the observational and luggage carriage. The bullets continued to rake the rooftop of the train and the helicopter banked, ready to go around for another run.

Sam wasn't planning on waiting around.

He opened the door to the luggage car and entered.

Behind him, a Berserker fired at him from the roof. Acting on impulse, Sam fired back. The shot struck his target and the man fell all the way through the gap between the carriage, disappearing underneath.

Zero shots left.

The thought terrified Sam. His only hope now was to reach the Bricklin which was parked on the very last railway carriage. If he could get there, he could retrieve the contents of his armory, and finish this fight once and for all.

But first he had to reach it.

He stepped through the luggage carriage. It was basically an open rectangular box with a thoroughfare that split the carriage in two, straight down the middle. On either side, were rows upon rows of luggage. At the far end was another set of toilets. Male and female. Sam raced by them all, taking little notice of anything. The car opened up to the first of the vehicular flatbed carriages.

At the far end of the first one, there were two Berserkers coming his way.

Sam turned.

But there was already another Berserker coming his way.

Sam locked both toilet doors, and slid into a gap between the luggage directly opposite the toilet. It wouldn't hold out against anything but the most cursory glance, but it would have to do. Right now, hiding was his only hope.

And without his cell phone, no one was coming to his aid.

Chapter Twenty-Three

Tom withdrew the barrel of his Heckler and Koch MP5 submachinegun.

Turning to Genevieve who was at the controls of the Robinson 44, he said, "Did you see that! It was almost too easy. It felt like cheating. We just had them all line up along the top of the train, and I got to pick them off one after the next."

Genevieve banked, taking them around to line up with the train again. "I don't care if you did cheat. Did you see how close they were to killing Sam."

Tom shrugged. "Ah, Sam can take care of himself. He has more lives than a cat."

"Really?" Genevieve looked serious. "You're going to play that game again?"

"Hey, you don't think Sam had that situation under control?" Tom grinned. "I feel like if we'd given Sam another few minutes, he would have totally had it all sorted."

"I'm not so convinced we have this situation sorted," Genevieve said, pointing at the two Berserkers who were heading toward the luggage carriage.

"Ah shit…" Tom swore, his jaw suddenly becoming taut, his eyes focused. "Can you put us down?"

Genevieve stared at the train. She banked again, coming a full circle and lining up behind the train. She slowed her speed to keep up with the train, but slow enough to make sure she didn't overshoot it. "There's not a lot of room here, but I'll give it a shot."

Tom stared at the train snaking its way across the mountain range. "Where are you aiming for?"

"The second to last flatbed."

Tom scanned the area, looking at the spot she was landing. There was only one car on it. A bright yellow Lamborghini. It was small enough, and low enough to the ground, that one could probably land in front of it, without damaging the Lamborghini. Not many people could. But Genevieve was outside the one percent of pilots when it came to her capabilities. Tom knew for a fact that she was extraordinary at two things. Flying helicopters and killing people. Not necessarily in that order. For a moment, he recalled how he'd spent the night in bed with her and decided to make that three things in which she excelled.

Genevieve took the helicopter down to land on the back of an open tray carriage somewhere in the middle of the train.

Tom grinned. "You're aren't really doing what I think you're planning on doing?"

"Sure. Why not?"

"Why don't you just drop me off…"

"Because there are several people on that train who want Sam dead."

"You don't think I can handle them?"

"Tom… you realize that to me, you're like you are to Sam… do you know what I mean?"

Tom grinned. "Yes. When I'm away, Sam gets into trouble. When you're away, I get into trouble."

"That's right. And all being said and done, I think while the bad people with pop-guns are after Sam, it's probably a good idea if we stick together, deal?"

"Deal…"

She began to lower the helicopter…

Tom's eyes narrowed. The distance between the Lamborghini and the end of the platform seemed just shy of long enough to place the Robinson 44's skids. "On second thoughts, there's probably not enough room…"

"Watch me," Genevieve said, her face set with determination.

Her tongue curled out to the side of her mouth with concentration, as she juggled the array of helicopter controls in a delicate balancing act. She pulled back on the joystick known as the cyclic collective, raising the nose a fraction, while reducing power on the collective to prevent the helicopter from gaining altitude. She held her right foot on the pedal to prevent the helicopter from spinning while she reduced power – setting the helicopter into a gradual flare – she set the skids down between the Lamborghini and the front of the vehicular carriage.

As soon the helicopter was down, she pushed the cyclic all the way forward, so that the pitch of the main rotor blade was altered in such a way as to force the helicopter downward, instead of it trying to lift off.

Tom clasped her on her shoulder. "Okay, I'm impressed."

She shrugged. "Plenty of room…"

"Maybe for a quarter, between us and that Lamborghini, but nothing else."

She left the engine running, the main rotor-blade spinning, and climbed out. It was something that would horrify any flight instructor, but hey, she was already breaking any number of civil aviation laws by doing what she was doing, so why stop there? Besides, she had a fair idea that when it came time to leave, they were probably going to need to do so in a hurry.

Tom glanced at the Lamborghini. The slightest of scratches was visible across its yellow hood, where the helicopter's skids must have just scratched the car. He frowned, shouting above the noise of the beating rotor blades, "Should we leave the owner an IOU?"

"Grab the license plate and we'll send the owner a check…" Her lips parted into a mischievous grin. "Depending on how badly I scratch it on our way out."

Tom's eyes glanced toward the rotor blades. "You think there's enough room?"

She locked a full magazine into her Heckler and Koch MP5 submachinegun. Gave an indifferent shrug. "I don't know. We're probably going to clip any incoming trains, but I didn't see any in the distance when we landed, so if we go quickly, we might just get lucky."

"Agreed." Tom said, "What about tunnels?"

She gave a half-shrug. "We might fit… then again, we might not. We'll just have to be quick."

Chapter Twenty-Four

Sam listened to the gunshots.

One, two, three.

All short bursts of machinegun fire. It was like listening to the sound of his death. Only death didn't quite know where he was. He imagined the remaining Berserkers walking around the luggage car, indiscriminately firing pot shots into the luggage, hoping to get lucky. Maybe expecting him to panic and run out into the open with his hands up.

That sure as hell wasn't how he was going out.

No, he would go out fighting all the way to the end. There was no way he was giving up. Despite the odds. He considered his odds, which he placed somewhere approximately in the range of zilch and no chance, and realized the sound of shooting had turned silent.

His ears pricked as he tried to listen.

There were footsteps on the floor. Big steps. Whoever it was wasn't trying to conceal their presence. It was classically the overconfidence of the Berserkers. And why shouldn't they be? After all, they had plenty of gang members and all the firearms. While Sam had the butt of a pistol to use as a weapon.

Sam receded as far back into the luggage compartment as he could. He was almost completely buried by the luggage. Someone opened the toilet doors. There was a second set of feet moving. They belonged to someone lighter, or better at concealing the sound of their steps at any rate. The bigger steps turned from where they were coming near the toilets and stopped.

Sam imagined someone looking back at the rows of luggage, squinting, and trying to see where a grown man might hide. In front of him, Sam heard bags being pulled away, as though someone had begun the inevitable, yet tedious task of searching the entire luggage carriage.

The person was getting closer.

Sam turned the pistol around so that he could grip the back of the Beretta. It wasn't going to do much good. The weapon used a carbon slide and alloy frame. Not a lot of weight there. Sam tucked the weapon into the back of his pants – not yet willing to relinquish it in the off chance he was able to find some more bullets – and prepared to use his fists.

It was dark in the luggage carriage and difficult to make out anything more than the most basic shapes. But even in the dark, he could tell the Berserker closest to him was a giant, with a great barrel chest and shoulders that made him look like a small mountain. It had to be the big guy who found him, not the small person with the gentle steps.

The luggage just in front of him was pulled free.

Now or never…

Sam squatted down and launched himself at his attacker. His only hope was to take the Berserker by surprise, disarm him, and then continue shooting his way out of hell.

His fist struck the side of something big.

The giant moved with surprising speed and agility. He whipped around, slamming his arms into Sam's in a movement that crossed between a hacking motion and blocking one. The Berserker's elbow connected with Sam's forearm. It felt like sudden shards of pain shot up his arm that tested Sam's bones not to break.

"Sam!" Came a voice he recognized. "It's me!"

Sam rubbed his arm, checking that it wasn't broken. "Tom?"

"Woah! What is it with you and attacking me on trains?"

"Sorry." Sam frowned. "I assume Genevieve's with you?"

"Sure am," she said, her voice coming from the back of the carriage. "And we've got to go. I don't know how long we've got."

"Sounds good," Sam said, clambering out from underneath a pile of strewn baggage. "These guys seem to keep multiplying."

Tom helped him up. "Where's Caliburn?"

"He's waiting by the car," Sam said. "It's on the last vehicle carriage. You get the helicopter ready, and I'll meet you there."

Tom's phone rang.

He answered it. Listened. And swore. "Come on, we've really gotta go!"

Sam asked, "What now?"

"That was Elise. She's got real-time satellite surveillance of the train line... and what she's seen is not good."

Sam asked, "What have we got?"

Tom said, "There's half a dozen motorcycles riding along the tracks, soon to catch up to us."

Sam remembered the Berserker's words.

Divert the boys from Fort Gratiot...

Genevieve said, "Then we'd better make sure we're nowhere to be found when they get here."

A moment later the entire carriage went dark as the train entered a tunnel.

Tom and Genevieve swore.

And a split-second later, there was a thunderous cacophony of metal grinding on stone, followed by an explosion. Sam instinctively ducked down, as a fireball ripped through the edge of the carriage, before the blast in the narrow tunnel, starved of oxygen, finally dissipated.

With his ears still ringing, Sam asked, "What the hell was that?"

Genevieve swallowed. "That would be our ride being a combination of too tall and wide to fit inside the tunnel."

Chapter Twenty-Five

The emergency brakes locked.

The luggage, along with everyone and everything else, slid forward as the Amtrak GEP42DC came to a stop some 1.2 miles after the engineer slammed on the emergency brakes. The train was stopped in a slightly upward gradient two thirds of the way up a mountain pass, with a vertical cliff on one side that would take an expert rock climber to scale, and a river far below.

Sam stepped out of the luggage carriage and took stock of the situation. The train was through the tunnel, and warm sunlight glared down on the wreckage. The flatbed vehicle carriage – which was almost entirely steel – appeared unscathed. Most likely disintegrated Robinson 44 was nowhere to be seen, having probably been knocked off the train entirely after the collision. At the back of the carriage were the remains of a once bright yellow Lamborghini. It had been compressed into the steel flatbed, taking a whole new meaning to the car term, *being lowered*. The next cars on the next carriage were damaged but not completely destroyed, with the blast radius lessening the farther back.

Sam said, "We still need to get going."

Genevieve agreed. "I saw a rocky outcrop back there that we could defend all day. I just don't know if we'll reach it in time."

Sam shook his head. "I have a better idea."

She said, "I'm listening."

"We need to get to the Bricklin and retrieve Caliburn. Then we're going to bring the fight to them."

"How are you planning on doing that?"

"I'll show you."

They raced across the two vehicle flatbed carriages, meeting up with an excited Caliburn, who appeared to have come out of the whole experience unharmed. Sometimes you just get lucky. Sam gave him a quick pat.

Sam's Bricklin appeared entirely unscathed. Behind it were a pair of Harley Davidson motorcycles. The keys were still in their ignitions as though the riders had expected to need to leave before the train came to a stop.

Sam threw the keys to Genevieve, and said, "There's a heavy machinegun inside the trunk. We're gonna need it."

"I'm on it," she said, catching the keys.

"Tom," Sam said, jumping down the gap between carriages. "You're with me."

Together, they stared at the coupling system.

The coupling mechanism was used to connect rolling stock in a train. The design of the coupler is standard, and is almost as important as the track gauge, since flexibility and convenience are maximized if all rolling stock can be coupled together.

In most trains, the equipment that connects the couplings to the rolling stock was known as the draft gear or draw gear. The Amtrak cross country train used H-Tightlock couplers, a variety of Janney couplers, that were typically used on North American mainline passenger rail cars. They were designed with mechanical features which reduced slack in normal operation and prevented telescoping in derailments, yet remained compatible with other Janney types used by North American freight railroads.

Sam studied the locking mechanism. He tapped on its marking, as though it somehow meant something to him. "Like all Janney couplers, the Tightlock is 'semi-automatic' with the couplers on cars or locomotives automatically locking when cars are pushed together. However, most tightlock couplers are not fully automatic, as workers still need to go between cars to hook up the air lines for the pneumatic brakes, and connect cables for head-end power and other communications. Also, to separate cars, a worker needs to use a lever to move the locking pin that keeps the coupler closed."

Tom looked at him like he was talking another language. "Right."

Sam said, "Can you pass me that lever over there?"

Tom withdrew a large steel lever, that looked like a prybar, and had been attached to the side of the train.

Sam took it, and gently nudged the locking pin until it came free.

Nothing happened.

Tom frowned. "Are you forgetting something?"

"Yeah, the brakes now need to be disconnected if we're going to get this thing moving."

The braking system used a pneumatic pipe that clasped the disc brakes in place. The compressor on the locomotive charges the main reservoir with air at 125–140 psi. The train brakes are released by admitting air to the train pipe through the engineer's brake valve.

A fully charged brake pipe is typically 70–90 psi for freight trains and 110 psi for passenger trains. The brakes are applied when the engineer moves the brake handle to the "service" position, which causes a reduction in pressure in the train pipe. In normal braking, the pressure in the train pipe does not reduce to zero. If it does fall to zero – because of a broken brake hose – an emergency brake application will be made.

Sam stared at the pneumatic pipe, trying to work out what went where. His brow furrowed as he tried to track the piping, before deciding none of it really mattered, and – using the lever prybar – smashed the main connector.

On the third strike, the nozzle snapped in two, and Sam was rewarded with the *hiss* of air, releasing the pressure on the carriage's disc brakes until they came free.

And the trailing flatbed carriage began rolling downhill…

Chapter Twenty-Six

The flatbed carriage rolled toward the tunnel.

It started slow, but picked up speed as it approached the tunnel. It was moving at just five to ten miles an hour. At more than 40 tons, the carriage was a lethal weapon, its kinetic energy enough to go through just about anything and anyone in its way.

On the steel flatbed Genevieve set up the Browning .50 caliber heavy machine gun on its M3 tripod, while Tom rolled out and attached its linked ammunition belt.

Sam opened the door to the Bricklin. "You'd better get inside Caliburn."

Caliburn's gaze drifted to Genevieve and Tom, before landing on Sam. His eyes were forlorn and full of concern.

"We'll be all right," Sam said, gripping the Heckler and Koch MP7 he'd retrieved from the Bricklin's secret armament safe. "They're not expecting us. They won't even know what hit them."

Caliburn gave a short bark.

I hope so.

Sam closed the door.

The free-running flatbed carriage entered the tunnel. Without any power, it moved silently like a wraith in the darkness.

Up ahead, six small beams of light flickered.

Genevieve lined up the barrel of the Browning .50 caliber with the riders, and said, "Wait for it…"

The flatbed rolled on.

The riders rode in three uneven rows of two along the track.

Sam said, "Hold on to something…"

But the words weren't necessary.

If a glass of water had been placed on the flatbed it wouldn't have even registered a ripple as the steel blade of the carriage's ramp slammed into the first two riders, rolling straight over them as though they didn't even exist.

The next two rows of Harley Davidsons spilled off onto the second train track.

Genevieve opened fire.

The dark tunnel turned to daylight as the heavy machinegun began its destruction. The tunnel began to flicker with the flashes of gunfire.

In a split second it was all over.

Genevieve picked up the heavy machinegun and moved it to the front of the flatbed, setting up the tripod so that she could pick up any survivors. But she didn't have to. The Berserkers never stood a chance.

They were safe.

The flatbed kept rolling out toward the daylight at the other end of the tunnel. Outside the tunnel, the burned remains of the Robinson 44 blocked the tracks. The carriage struck it without a jolt and kept going, knocking the helicopter off the track down to the river far below. Sam pulled on the carriage's individual emergency brakes. The flatbed slowed gradually to a complete stop. Genevieve released the loading tray, and it lowered to the tracks below.

Tom glanced at the carnage they'd left. "Now what?"

Sam grinned, his eyes looking at the road crossing up ahead. "Now I'd say we get out of here before anyone knows what's going on."

"Where are we heading?"

"Minnesota," Sam answered without hesitation.

"Why?" Tom asked, climbing onto the motorcycle next to Genevieve.

Sam drew out a long breath. "Answers."

Chapter Twenty-Seven

Omnia Nightclub – Caesars Palace, Las Vegas

Alana Wilson stepped into the opulent lobby of Caesars Palace.

Positioned on the west side of the Las Vegas Strip between Bellagio and The Mirage, it boasted a facility that gave guests a sense of decadence from life during the height of the Roman Empire. She followed the large marbled steps into Omnia, the tri-level night club.

Several pairs of eyes glanced at her, tracking her movements as she walked. It was like that in most places, and with the sort of body that most women would die for, she was used to the attention. Tonight, it was particularly bad. Normally, she dressed down, but tonight was different. She was dressed to impress.

It didn't take much.

She had red-gold hair and sea-green eyes. Her full lips were cast in a red Chanel lipstick, giving her porcelain face a particularly sexy appearance. At six foot, with a slim, full figure she was striking. Still in her mid-twenties, she wore a red tight fitting backless Haute Couture midi dress and matching Christian Louboutin high heels. To say she was spectacular was an understatement. She simply oozed sex appeal.

A casual observer might assume that she could have any guy, and probably most girls, at the click of her finger. And they would probably be right. What they might be surprised to discover was that she had been single for precisely a year, after her last breakup, leaving her simply uninterested in the whole dating thing.

A good friend of hers had just gotten married, and it had triggered something inside of her that hadn't stirred for some time. An innate desire. Despite her looks, she'd never felt the need to get married, or that desire for intimacy, but something about the wedding had stirred it and for the first time in more than a year, she had decided to go out and pick up. Maybe it was the fact that the wedding fell on the anniversary of her breakup with Oliver Klein – no relation to Calvin but equally as hot – or simply the fact that she'd had her fair share of bubbling wines at the wedding, or simply because her friends had been persistent...

She didn't know.

But whatever it was, she agreed to go to Omnia, and now that she was here, she'd made the decision that she wanted to get laid. And why not? After all, if you couldn't have a one-night stand in Las Vegas, when could you?

Something about the idea thrilled and scared the hell out of her.

She felt nervous just stepping into the place. Much more than she expected. It wasn't like she'd even picked a guy she liked yet, and there was plenty of time to back down on her decision. Besides, she liked to drink and she liked to dance. So who cares? Right? Only there was a niggling anxiety that kept rising up in her chest, despite her best efforts to suppress it.

One of her friends noticed it and offered her a drink.

She took it, drinking it down in one go. Her friend watched her and laughed. She smiled, feeling a little better, revealing an equally perfect set of white, even teeth. "Thank you... I needed that!"

"You're welcome..." her friend ran her tongue across her lower lip. "You wanna try something... different?"

Alana laughed. "Wow... thanks Jess... I'm flattered, but I'm not sure you're quite what I'm looking for tonight."

Jess placed an affectionate arm on her shoulder. There was something playful about it. Sexy. But also, friendly. She suppressed a grin. Her piercing blue eyes narrowed in on her. "That's not what I was thinking."

"What did you have in mind?"

"This," Jess said, opening a mini compartment from inside her purse, that revealed three individual tablets.

Alana swore. "Are those drugs!"

"Shush!" Jess said, closing the lid. "Do you want to get us arrested?"

"Sorry. I just wasn't expecting it… that's all."

Jess shook her head. "You really missed out on all of it, didn't you?"

"Me? No. I've tried pot…"

"Really?"

"Sure. Once. Technically, my friend had the joint and I breathed in a little bit of the smoke."

"Wow, Alana… you are bad ass! You've tried second-hand marijuana smoke. You know that's now legal in most states these days, don't you?"

"Whatever…"

Jess grabbed her hand. "So, do you wanna try it tonight? It might just give you that edge you need to feel… a little more confident and then," she stared her up and down in one slow elevator glance, "I guarantee you can have the best night of your life with any man you choose in this whole damned place."

Alana laughed. "Is it safe?"

"Sure. I mean, probably."

"Will I get addicted? You know, become a junkie or something?"

Jess rolled her eyes. "Are you kidding me? It's one pill!"

"Okay, okay…" Alana wasn't one to be pushed into anything.

Despite her glamorous appearance and her unusual decision to have her first and probably only one-night stand, she was highly intelligent. So smart that she skipped three grades, graduating school early, and entering university when she was fourteen. She studied law at Harvard on a full scholarship and by the age of nineteen had passed the bar in New York, where she wasn't legally allowed to drink alcohol for two more years.

Against her normal behavior, she said, "Sure. What have you got?"

Jess opened up her secret compartment revealing three little tablets. They looked so innocuous one might mistake them for a Tylenol or maybe a Vitamin C tablet. "Take anything that jumps out at you."

Alana stared at them, quickly picking out a cute one shaped just like a little Viking wielding an axe. She held it up close to her face so she could see it better. "Hello little guy…"

Jess nudged her. "Unless you want to lose that classy license to practice law, I suggest you swallow it quick."

"Okay," Alana said, taking the tablet in her mouth and washing it down with another glass of wine.

Jess gave her a big hug, still laughing. "Congratulations… you're now an adult… let's go find you the hottest guy in this place."

Alana followed her deeper onto the dance floor. She still felt nervous. After a few minutes, she said, "I don't feel anything."

"Give it time."

Her friend Danielle caught up with them and the three girls danced in a circle, each cutting a striking figure in their own right. Together, they made for the sort of eye candy that seemed out of reach to everyone. Soon Alana began to feel the effects of the drug – whatever it was she had taken – and started to feel a little more relaxed.

In fact, she was certain the drug was starting to work its magic. After all, she no longer felt guilty that she took an illegal drug without even asking what it was she had taken. Heck, she picked it out because there was a cute little Viking on the tablet. It was probably the most stupid thing she'd ever done.

But it didn't matter.

It hadn't killed her and she felt great.

Not just great. Better than that. She was confident. Uninhibited. And in the mood for dancing and maybe even a little bit of seduction. Her eyes scanned the sea of people. They were all dressed to the nines. She knew she could have anyone she wanted. She knew that was different too. Alana wasn't one of those people who didn't realize she was good-looking. She knew it. But despite that, she'd actually always had difficulties picking up. Maybe it was because men were awkward around her, or maybe because, she just never got how to play the game. Either way, she normally had difficulties with the whole dating thing altogether. But tonight was different. Suddenly, she could see everything clearly.

She really was the most beautiful, sexiest woman on the entire dance floor. That wasn't bravado, or vanity speaking. It was just fact. And for the first time in her life, she really knew it. She ran her eyes across the dance floor, deciding that she didn't just want to pick up a one-night stand, she wanted to pick up the most gorgeous man in the nightclub. Her eyes finally landed on a person sitting next to the bar, in some sort of high-end Italian tailored suit, talking to some other men, who were also good looking.

An Italian guy. Her male equivalent she figured.

Alana drifted away from her friends without saying goodbye. Danielle started to follow, but Jess held her hand and mouthed something to her which sounded like, *Just watch her.* Alana heard them giggle, but didn't care.

So what if they wanted to watch her put on a show?

She stepped up to the Italian. Any semblance of anxiety, now a distant memory. She leaned in close, wrapping her arm around his neck. The man seemed taken aback at first, expecting to find some intoxicated fool to scold, but a glance at her, prevented him from doing so.

She leaned in close and said, "I'm going to make tonight the luckiest night of your life."

"Is that so?" He asked, standing up. He smiled. It was a nice smile. Boyish and cute, yet somehow strong and assertive too. Lots of teeth. He was clean shaven, but he was one of those men whose face always sported the dark appeal of someone with a five-o-clock shadow – no matter what time it was.

"Yes," she shot him a lascivious smile, licked her lips provocatively, and wrapped her arms around his neck. Her sea green eyes stared at him. She breathed in deeply. He even smelled good.

The stranger grinned. His piercing hazel eyes meeting hers with a mixture of hope and mistrust, but behind that, there was a whole bucket load of desire. "Did someone put you up to this?"

She laughed. "No."

"Okay, because I don't care if they did…" Another boyish grin formed on his parted lips. He looked like the sort of man she would have ordinarily found over-confident. The kind of guy who knew he was really good looking. But something about her had caused him to take a tumble with that confidence, and he was starting to cover it with a joke. He was really cute. "I mean, even if this is a joke at my expense, my goodness, it's completely worth it. Damn, you are beautiful."

She leaned in before he could say another word and kissed him.

He hesitated for a moment. Not withdrawing, but resisting his obvious desire. It lasted just seconds, before he submitted. His mouth parted and she explored his taste eagerly with her tongue. She kissed him back, passionately.

It felt good.

Better than good.

It was the nicest kiss she'd ever had.

And she was the one in control. She sensed his curiosity and hesitancy, and she disregarded it, taking exactly what she wanted. It was so outside her normal emotional response that it simultaneously amazed and excited her, triggering some sort of primal urge.

He pulled away.

She tried to hold him, but he was too strong for her.

He smiled and ran his tongue across his upper lip. "That was nice."

"Yeah…" she leaned in and whispered in his ear, "I have a suite upstairs. How about we skip the rest of the formalities, and I take you to bed right now."

He paused for a beat, his eyes meeting hers, trying to see if she was serious. Recognizing that she was, he exhaled a long breath and said, "Okay." He drew a breath and swallowed. "I mean, I'm not going to end up in a bath of ice with my kidneys missing or something, am I?"

"No." She shook her head. Playful. Seductive. "It's not that."

A wry grin formed on his lips. "What is it then?"

Alana held his gaze. "The truth?"

His eyes looked at her in wonder and his grin said, *this ought to be good*. "Sure."

"I haven't been laid in over a year, my best friend just got married, and I just took some sort of drug my friend offered me – the first time in my life I've taken drugs by the way – and apparently it's removed any inhibitions I might have otherwise had." She kissed him playfully again. Enjoying herself. "So, like I said, tonight's your lucky night."

Desire flashed across his face. "Yeah, I'll say… tonight's my lucky night."

"Yeah, your lucky night," she said, laughing.

He matched her laugh. A sparkling glint like diamond in his hazel eyes. His laughter segued into a chuckle and then the smile slipped away and he pulled back from her. "I'm sorry… I don't even know your name."

"Alana," she said, already impatiently getting out her keycard for the hotel. "And you are?"

"Alessandro."

"Alessandro," she tried the name out, liking the way it played on her lips. "Of course, even your name is sexy."

"Thank you," he said, his tone suddenly serious. He took her hand in his and gave it an affectionate squeeze. "I'm really glad to have met you Alana, but I'm not going to sleep with you tonight."

She felt her heart jolt.

Adrenaline and rage began to swell up throughout her whole body. She'd never felt herself so angry. She tried to control it, but the lure of the emotion was too strong for her to resist. "What do you mean? I throw myself at you, and you're what, turning me down?"

Alessandro took a step back. "Look, Alana, I was serious when I said it was my lucky night that I met you. You are absolutely stunning. Not just stunning, strikingly beautiful. You're not just the best-looking person who's ever taken an interest in me, you're the best-looking person I've ever seen in real life, or on TV. And from what you tell me, you're actually a nice person. Someone I'd love to get to know. So, if given the chance to go to bed with you or do anything with you ever again, I will gladly take it."

"But you won't tonight," she said, shoving him in the chest with both her hands.

He looked startled, but maintained a steady tone and even temper. His voice betrayed a sense of empathy and was apologetic when he spoke. "Alana, the only reason you're even talking to me tonight is because your stupid friend drugged you and, as much as every cell in my body wants to go to bed with you, I won't do something that I'm certain you will regret in the morning."

She pushed him again. "Typical... I had to pick the one and only truly decent and honorable man in the damned club!"

"I'm sorry." He spread his hands out. "I'll tell you what... I'll give you my number. If you have any interest in calling me tomorrow, I'll gladly pick up where we left off, or even go back a little earlier and maybe go for a coffee or something and get to know you. What do you say?"

Any sense of control that she might have once had over her emotions disintegrated. She stared at him. Her otherwise beautiful face now filled with rage and vitriolic hatred. She shoved him hard enough to knock him onto the ground. "Fuck you!"

He fell backward and dropped his glass, which shattered on the ground.

The Italian picked himself up and raised a hand in a placating gesture. A crowd started to form. People were looking at him, their eyes darting toward her, and it was clear from everyone's faces that they assumed he'd done something to wrong her.

Security approached. "Are you all right, ma'am?"

She didn't know what to say. Her brain misfired. She knew there was something she was supposed to do, but the rage clouded over, shrouding every semblance of reasonable mental function.

Alessandro spoke for her. "She's all right. Just a little drunk. That's all. Let's go find your friends."

His voice made her snap out of it.

It was his fault.

Everything was his fault.

She bent down and picked up a couple of the bulky pieces of his broken glass, holding the shards tight in each hand.

Alessandro tried to take them from her. "It's okay, I'll sort this mess out. How about you point out your friends and we'll get you back to your room. What do you say?"

It was the last thing she heard.

Whatever was holding her rage back, finally snapped.

She spun around, using the shards of glass like razor blades. They sliced at Alessandro's throat, severing tissue, tendons, and the large blood vessels that fed his brain. His eyes, so intensely serene just a moment before, now read abject horror. His once proud and sexy demeanor, now weak and terrified as blood gushed out of his throat. He gurgled and fell to the floor, his hands frantically gripping his throat in a vain attempt to survive.

It took a few seconds for anyone to realize what she'd done.

Someone saw all that blood and screamed. In the back of her mind, she heard a little voice that said, *I did that!* And then, a bigger voice this time… *I liked it… and can do it some more!*

A couple of security guards approached her. Their hands were held outward in a placating gesture. "Are you all right, ma'am?"

She didn't answer.

Instead, she moved forward, swinging her arms wildly. The shards of glass sliced at the security guards who jumped back. She didn't even know where the glass struck, but she kept moving, going in for the kill.

It didn't take long.

Now that she knew exactly where to aim.

She was getting better! Alana sliced at their throats, and before she even knew it, she inflicted mortal wounds to both of them. Adrenaline rushed through her body, while dopamine and serotonin – known as the feel-good brain chemicals – flooded her brain, rewarding her for her behavior.

In that instant, she felt almost certain this was what she really needed. She felt a more innate freedom than any sort of orgasm Alessandro might have provided. People kept trying to subdue her, but she moved too quickly, and in each hand, she still held shards of glass like deadly weapons.

The bloodbath continued.

Her friends tried to intervene. A small part of her, somewhere in the back of her brain, tried to answer – but her arms did all the talking.

She didn't remember killing either of them, but she recalled the look on their faces when they were dead.

Somewhere… she had no idea how long, some people arrived with guns. Maybe they were police or security… or maybe just concerned citizens with guns, who knows? But somewhere in the process, they started shouting at her to put the glass down or they would shoot.

She didn't.

Shots were fired.

There was a searing pain in her chest and abdomen.

She'd taken three rounds.

Even in her euphoric state, she understood that those, too, were mortal wounds. But it didn't stop the killing. Hell, it didn't even stop the deluge of dopamine and serotonin. Driven on by some sort of boosted up fight or flight system, she bounced back up like a freak out of a horror movie, and sliced at the people with guns.

And it felt amazing!

Alana didn't know how many more of them she killed.

But somewhere along the lines, she felt the cold barrel of a gun placed right at the back of her head. The game was over and she knew it. It was fun while it lasted. She spun around with her glorious shards of glass. The barrel exploded and a shot struck her in the back of her head, severing her brainstem, and destroying any sign of her once beautiful face. Behind her, the man who had killed her gripped his throat.

He was the last person she killed.

Chapter Twenty-Eight

DARPA Oversight Committee – Pentagon

Doug Jones, Senator for Minnesota was proud of his involvement with DARPA. He was currently the chairman of its oversight committee. The committee included four senators, two scientists, and two senior military officers – making up just eight people who held the fate of the future US military power in their grasp.

The Defense Advanced Research Projects Agency had a long and sometimes disturbing history that everyday citizens might find troubling to accept. It was because of people like him, and the role DARPA played, that those very same everyday citizens who might object to some of the projects that he had personally helped authorize, were able to sleep a little better and a little safer at night. Jones was good with it. He slept fine. Guilt, never nagging at his moral compass.

The ends justify the means.

The creation of the Advanced Research Projects Agency – ARPA – was authorized by President Dwight D. Eisenhower in 1958 for the purpose of forming and executing research and development projects to expand the frontiers of technology and science, and able to reach far beyond immediate military requirements. It was first established in February 1958. Its creation was directly attributed to the launching of Sputnik and to U.S. realization that the Soviet Union had developed the capacity to rapidly exploit military technology.

It originally worked on space projects, but when NASA was formed later that same year, all space projects, and the majority of ARPA's funding were transferred to it. ARPA was repurposed to do "high-risk," "high-gain," "far out" military research, a posture that was enthusiastically embraced by the nation's scientists and research universities.

This allowed ARPA to concentrate its efforts on the Project Defender – defense against ballistic missiles – Project Vela – nuclear test detection – and Project AGILE – counterinsurgency R&D programs – and to begin work on computer processing, behavioral sciences, and materials sciences. The DEFENDER and AGILE programs formed the foundation of DARPA's sensor, surveillance, and directed energy R&D, particularly in the study of radar, infrared sensing, and x-ray/gamma ray detection.

And now, the project worked on RX16SF.

He was damned proud of what his people had achieved. Better it should belong to them and not some other hostile nation. God forbid if it were to end up in the hands of any other nation – who cares whether they were hostile or not? No, if such a horrible thing should exist at all, it should be in their power.

He waited and watched as the rest of the committee members took their seats. The meeting took place behind closed doors. Minutes were kept, but most of those were buried in so much bureaucratic red-tape that even if someone had the guts to subpoena it, the final document would come out with so much redaction to render it entirely unreadable and worthless. The last member took a seat, and someone closed the door, where two armed military personnel stood guard.

Senator Jones began without preamble. "We all know why this meeting was called today. We have a serious problem with RX16SF." He paused a beat, handing out the current report on the trial. "I'm sure you're all aware of its success, as well as its limitations. I suppose what we have to decide is, are we going to persist, or do we need to shut the program down? Can we start with you, Professor Reed? Can you talk us through what the trial has found?"

"Yes, of course." Professor Rebecca Reed led the advanced behavioral science labs at Berkeley, and had joined the committee for her scientific background. "As you're all aware, the program has tested RX16SF on sixteen volunteers gathered from a variety of background in special forces, including four from the Navy SEALS, Green Berets, Rangers, Marine Raiders, to make a total of sixteen test subjects." She paused a beat, looked at the chairman.

Senator Jones said, "Go on."

"In all sixteen cases, we found that RX16SF heightened the senses of the test subjects remarkably. Their sight improved, their hearing improved beyond the range of what is deemed possible for the human ear to achieve, their sense of smell became closer to canine olfactory, even touch became noticeably better." Reed paused. The lines around her face somehow deepened with regret as she continued. "The test subjects reacted faster, and achieved better scores in every skill test while taking the drug. Their aggression in hand-to-hand combat nearly tripled. But, with the large doses of adrenaline and nor-adrenaline being released by their own bodies in response to the drug, they started to develop behavioral issues."

Fleet Admiral Gordon Smith interrupted. "We knew this at the start and that's why we chose to trial the drug on special forces, who are adept at controlling their emotions in the most heated of situations."

Professor Reed held up a hand in a gesture that made it clear she wasn't going down the path of special forces propaganda. This was a real scientific test, and the results were facts, not fiction. "Four of the initial sixteen test subjects are dead now because they were unable to control their emotions."

Senator Jones said, "We've discussed that risk at the last meeting and the physicians assured us that they could overcome those outbursts with the use of mediated anti-anxiety medications and muscle relaxants."

Professor Reed suppressed a thinly veiled smile. "Chairman Jones, with all due respect, we don't want our soldiers subdued. What's the point of giving our soldiers super powers if we're going to have to sedate them to harness it?"

"All right," Jones said, looking at the two scientists. "So, the question is, can we harness the awesome powers of RX16SF?"

Professor Reed shook her head.

Jones said, "Professor Rhinehart?"

Sarah Rhinehart was a leading researcher at Harvard's biochemistry faculty. She frowned. "It's possible we just don't have the solution yet."

Professor Reed grimaced. "That's because there isn't one. It's a classic catch twenty-two. Illogical and senseless. At the end of the day, we can't use its benefits because it makes our soldiers too dangerous unless we sedate them, rendering them not dangerous enough."

Rhinehart persisted. "It's a game of titration. We need to find the right balance and the right concoction of drugs. But it is still possible."

Chairman Jones said, "So, scientifically, it's in the realm of possible, although far-fetched. That's not altogether so bad. I mean, DARPA was built to work outside the constrictions of what was believed to be accepted." He turned to the two military members. Fleet Admiral Gordon Smith and Frank Meyers, a Four-Star General. "What do you think? Do the benefits outweigh the risks?"

Both men said, "Absolutely."

General Meyers then clarified further. "This substance is out there. From what I'm told, it occurs naturally. If we don't work out something to do with it, eventually, someone else will."

Chairman Jones turned to the senators. "What do you think?"

Althea Hammond, Senator for Vermont shook her head. "Do we have a timeline for coming up with a solution?"

"No," Professor Rhinehart answered, "But I would suggest that within two years if we don't have a solution, then no one else is going to ever find one."

Denis Yago, Senator for California said, "I don't think people will be happy when the news of what we're playing with gets out."

"Gets out!" Chairman Jones shook his head, barely containing his underlying fury. "Since when has the public ever been happy about any of the projects DARPA's been working on until they're proven. Hell, DARPA produced the first technology that led to the creation of GPS. Tell me anyone who isn't thankful that they no longer need to fight over directions and take the time to learn how to read a damned map! Besides, who said anything about telling the general public anything?"

Amanda Hearten, originally a cop-turned-lawyer, who went on to become a county prosecutor, before serving eight years as the Attorney General, before eventually being elected Senator of Texas, spoke emphatically. "We need to shut this thing down and bury it for good."

Chairman Jones was shocked. He knew and respected Senator Hearten very much and knew that she was too old, and too intelligent to dismiss her opinion out of hand. "Let's hear what you have, Senator Hearten."

"Let's start with the lesser of the two problems," Senator Hearten said. "In the Yucatán Peninsula a Mexican archeologist has just discovered an ancient image of a Hellenistic fleet that sailed into the region nearly two thousand years ago."

There was a quiet collective gasp at the revelation.

Chairman Jones said, "Even so, it's hard to imagine someone putting that sort of archeological discovery together with the discovery of RX16SF. Is it really that bad?"

She nodded. "All it takes is for someone to discover that a Hellenistic fleet reached the Americas for someone to put two and two together and then they'll do what we did, and go in search of what we now call RX16SF."

General Meyers said, "We can put people in place to shut down archeological evidence. We could even plant counterespionage propaganda to show that the original discovery was a hoax."

"Maybe," Senator Hearten conceded, although the hard set of her jaw suggested she was about to do anything but concede. "If it was just that, I'd probably say the potential benefits justify the risks…"

Chairman Jones was getting impatient. "What else have you got for us?"

She threw a single enlarged image from the New York Times on the table. "What about this?"

Chairman Jones stared at the image and all his hopes and dreams for RX16SF collapsed in an instant.

It depicted a beautiful woman at a nightclub with red-gold hair and striking sea green eyes. Next to it, was a note about an up and coming lawyer going berserk at a nightclub in Las Vegas and killing 23 people with a couple shards of glass.

There was only one explanation for it.
RX16SF

Chairman Jones said, "Ah Christ! Someone leaked the drug onto the street market?"

Senator Yago said, "We've known there's been a leak for a few months now. But we hoped it was just one of the test subjects taking the stuff home just in case we closed the program."

The Chairman didn't need to see any more. He knew there was a problem as soon as Senator Hearten opened her mouth. She wouldn't have gone to bat for the "no team" unless she had damning evidence. And this, was the most damning of all.

"Okay," he said, "Let's shut the program down."

Professor Reed said, "All of it?

He nodded. "Every last bit of it."

"What about the test subjects?"

"What about them?" General Meyer asked. "Tell them we're shutting it down. They're special forces. They'll understand."

Professor Rhinehart was emphatic. "No, they won't."

Jones asked, "Why not?"

"Have you ever tried to take away a drug from an addict?" Rhinehart countered.

"It's that bad?"

"Worse."

Jones asked, "How so?"

Rhinehart spoke in a slow, deliberate tone. Her voice melancholy. "Imagine your worst meth or heroin addict... now picture what they would do to keep feeding their addiction... and now, imagine that drug makes them highly intelligent, increasingly volatile, and extremely strong?"

The senator gasped.

Rhinehart continued. "And now, picture all those drug addicts being special forces, part of America's greatest fighting men."

Chairman Jones said, "Does anyone here believe the program can be salvaged?"

He looked around the room. All he could see were people shaking their heads.

"All right, everyone agrees RX16SF needs to be shut down?"

There was an all-round nod of agreement.

It was a unanimous decision.

And with that, the DARPA Oversight Committee signed the death sentence for the remaining twelve test subjects.

Chapter Twenty-Nine

Secret Military Experimental Base – Seattle.

Dean had never felt stronger.

At five foot-eight he was considered an average height by American standards. With 180 pounds of solid muscle, he was anything but. The very epitome of usable strength. He was fast, lithe, flexible, and capable of making his body do things that bordered on the impossible side of the line of human capabilities.

For the past two years, he'd been part of a secret military experiment. Only part of his former self remained, while RX16SF had removed the rest of it. His surname and family connections had been wiped. Along with the rest of his team of test subjects, they all only used their first names, to protect the program from ever being traced.

One of the reasons why he was selected in the first place was his naturally reclusive tendency. His parents died when he was still in grade school. He didn't generally play well with others. He was a poor student and quick to violence, which meant that he got expelled often. Which meant the state, who was responsible for him, moved him around a lot.

Never once had he felt strongly enough about any friendship to warrant keeping in touch with them after he moved. When he finished school, he had no support and little family to fall back on, and somehow, somewhere along the line, he sort of fell into the Army. Strangely enough, it was here that his life turned around. He excelled at the physical challenges the Army provided, as well as those that were mentally taxing. His initial Armed Services Vocational Aptitude Battery score was high and he was recommended for Special Forces. Where he'd never really had family, his platoon became the closest thing to one he'd ever known.

Now, nearly ten years on, he had spent the last two years away from just about everyone and everything he'd ever known. With the exception of some short leave times – which he suspected were also part of the testing process – he hadn't been out of the base in nearly two years.

Nestled in the mountain ranges of the Olympic National Park in the Pacific Northwest, their training camp looked like anything but a secret military base. They lived in makeshift lodges they had built by themselves using material taken right out of the lush forest. They hunted for their food and survived like their ancestors, using only weapons they made by themselves.

It was deemed that RX16SF made them more akin to a hunter gatherer lifestyle, and that the test subjects would never survive in a civilian context. The park was a perfect training ground, with its luminous peaks, lush rain forests, and a stretch of wild beaches, all contained on a peninsula across the water from Seattle.

For safety measures, the test subjects were always unarmed.

When they hunted, they produced their own weapons from materials found on site. They were already experts in hand-to-hand warfare and firearms. When the tests needed to include shooting the subjects would be retrieved and taken to a military base. Otherwise, they could make their own.

Even those bright people at DARPA weren't stupid enough to allow them to carry loaded weapons when they weren't in the middle of battle.

Dean's life had just gotten better and better since he arrived in the military.

That was, until the experiment.

RX16SF had changed all that.

It was an incredible drug. Legend had it that they weren't the first to use the drug for this purpose. Apparently, its history went back, a long way back. Far enough that its secrets had been long forgotten. But from the way the Professor had spoken about the drug, he was starting to wonder if the drug had been around since antiquity, before being lost during the Dark Ages.

Not that it mattered much to him.

History was never his strong point. Sad as it was to admit, even to himself, killing and violence were.

And RX16SF sure as hell made him better at it.

The drug had made him sharper, faster, stronger, and more capable in every single way measurable. He had been tested in every simulated military scenario applied to Special Forces, and achieved scores off every chart.

The program wasn't just hypothetical.

He and the small group of specialist soldiers who were part of the test group, had been exposed to actual warfare. Over the past two years they had been inserted into several actual warzones. They had provided covert ops in Russia, Ukraine, Iran, Iraq, the Middle East, and Africa.

All of them had excelled when they were over there fighting.

It was what they were built for.

And RX16SF made them do it better.

Problems only occurred when they weren't allowed to fight. The drug made them… more susceptible to their innate violence. It removed mental barriers that affect all civilized people and differentiates them from wild animals. Four people from his platoon of test subjects had killed each other during R and R time because of this. In fact, it took all of his self-control to keep the urges at bay whenever he wasn't training or actively fighting.

It was only in a warzone that he could relax his guard and feel safe.

Despite all that, he loved the drug. He would never recommend it to anyone and he definitely hoped the program was mothballed for the obvious dangers it provided. It needed doing, but he for one would do everything in his power to keep using the drug.

It made him think about the one piece of Shakespeare that he always remembered from school, because of the intrinsic truth it spoke.

This above all: to thine own self be true, And it must follow, as the night the day, Thou canst not then be false to any man.

It was a small part in a longer speech in Hamlet. The words spoken by King Claudius' chief minister, Polonius, where he is giving his son, Laertes, his blessing and advice on how to behave while at the university. For some strange reason, Dean thought of the quote now…

Because, if he was honest to himself, he was absolutely addicted to RX16SF.

It was because of this addiction, that he felt his anxiety levels continuously rise over the past few weeks. At first, he wasn't certain, and he wondered whether it was the side-effect of the drug leading to a little paranoia, but the more he watched the base, the more he became certain that someone was going to try and take RX16SF away from him. From all of them. The DARPA Oversight Committee, he knew, couldn't sit back and idly watch four of its sixteen test subjects kill each other without questioning the reliability of the project.

No, they would need to shut it down.

Over the past couple of weeks something had definitely changed. The Professor – or what people called him because he too, no longer had a real name – had begun organizing all the records and data connected to the project, setting it up at the centralized lab, affectionately known as the Meth Lab – for the fact that it produced and housed their drugs.

The Professor worked out of the largest building on the compound. From the outside it looked just like the other makeshift log houses, only a little bigger. But it was just a façade. Inside, it was a state of the art, biochemical lab, in which RX16SF could be synthesized – or at least its raw material – could be worked, and tests on the subjects could be scrutinized.

Dean knew everything about the Professor.

He'd been watching the man, scrutinizing him like a scientist might a lab rat, as much as the Professor had been studying him. It was a two-way system. Only Dean had no intention of ever letting anyone know about it.

That's what would keep him alive.

They were fools to think that they could introduce men like himself to RX16SF and then take it away from them. No, he needed to know its formula and for that he needed to watch the Professor. He'd started on the process as soon as they arrived in the Olympic National Park. The log cabin was built into the side of the mountain, with a series of logs, lined up to form the walls with a thatched roof. On the inside of course, it was every bit as modern as a commercial drug lab.

What the rest of the team didn't realize was, that from the very first day when work commenced on the project, he'd discovered that the back of the lab could be accessed through a nearby cave. If he chiseled away at a stone that blocked his progress, he would be capable of slipping through. He worked the project in the night time when others were sleeping. The US Army's Special Forces are known to the public as Green Berets — but they call themselves *the quiet professionals*. And Dean lived up to this name as he worked tirelessly. It was long, and slow, work, but he needed to burn the energy anyway and concentrating on such a mindless task helped him keep his sanity despite being on RX16SF.

By the time he was finished, he could swivel the boulder, and slip in through the narrow opening and insert himself into a secret compartment directly behind the Meth Lab. From there he drilled tiny holes and installed surveillance cameras inside. In doing so, he'd learned and made secondary documents for everything. He knew the chemical composition for RX16SF and the formula to synthetically reproduce it. Although he would never have the scientific knowhow to actually do so, he knew that if he got desperate, he would be able to find someone who could take the recipe and make it for him. And nearly a decade as a Green Beret had taught him how to be persuasive, even to the most determined.

During his overseas insertions, he'd slowly smuggled back large amounts of C4 and over the past two years had wired the entire Meth Lab to explode. At the time, he wasn't even sure why he'd done it. Perhaps he was just bored and needed to do something he wasn't supposed to, just like a kid acting out his emotions. He definitely knew that having a secret operation that he was running on his own kept him focused and probably kept him alive, while the other men in his platoon were beginning to go crazy as RX16SF rewired and took over their brains.

Either way, as time went on, Dean became more and more certain that the program wasn't going to be viable for the masses, and if that was the case, then everything needed to go. DARPA had specialized in the "high-risk," "high-gain," "far out" type of research, and the consequence of such, was that they had gotten into trouble multiple times for what might have been considered overstepping the boundaries of ethical research.

In his mind, there was no way DARPA could risk a program like RX16SF getting out. No, when they shut the program down, they would wipe it away clean, destroying all traces that it ever existed – and he was one of those traces.

Overhead, he heard the *thump, thump* of powerful rotor-blades. He knew that sound, recognized it in an instant, better than anyone else.

And why shouldn't he?

They were the sounds Black Hawk helicopters made.

Two of them.

And they most likely formed an assault team – coming for him.

Chapter Thirty

Dean's heart raced.

He made his way to the secret hiding spot behind the Meth Lab. Like all good soldiers, he knew he was in the fight of his life. He wished he could have reached the rest of his platoon. After all, they were in the fight of their lives, too. But the base at the Olympic National Park didn't work that way. For safety measures, the test subjects were encouraged to hunt on their own. At any one time, they could be spread out over more than twenty miles of mountain range – dense and impossibly difficult, isolated terrain.

No, he needed to save himself.

Dean reached the inner cave, sliding the rock back into place. It formed a small bunker. Still, he felt intensely vulnerable. In his belt he carried a stone carved into a razor-sharp edge to form a stone-age knife, and a wooden spear, while his attackers would be carrying Heckler and Koch HK 280 sniper rifles.

Hidden inside the cave, Dean watched a live video feed of the inside of the Meth Lab.

He watched, as the leader of what he could only assume to be the clean up team approach the Professor. The Professor, apparently aware of what was about to take place, handed over a large pile of folders containing all the data associated with RX16SF.

When the Professor was finished, he said, "Is that everything?"

"Yes, sir. That's every last piece of data regarding RX16SF."

"Very good."

The soldier then withdrew his service pistol and shot the Professor dead.

Dean had seen enough. He was expecting it, but still the betrayal rocked him mentally. He backed away from the Meth Lab – heading silently out into the woods. When he'd reached a relatively safe distance, he flicked the switch, and the Meth Lab exploded, killing the head of the ghosts – an elite team of ex-Special Forces, the government sometimes used when they wanted to wipe the slate clean.

In the confusion of the unexpected explosion, Dean – true to his service motto – silently walked away into the darkness of the night.

Chapter Thirty-One

The Sanctuary, Minnesota

Sam Reilly stared at the house.

It was one of those tiny houses like you see scattered on the internet, described as one of an actual movement. There were lots of viral feeds about living a simpler life in a smaller space, after having the realization that the big houses are stupid and that the large cost of living that comes with it, is both unnecessary and a detriment to their happiness. Everyone he knew had seen the articles and thought it made plenty of sense, but no one he knew ever actually did it. Yet, here he was, staring at a tiny house.

The little dwelling looked like a miniature two story log-house, with the second story appearing as a gabled annex and a single window. It probably allowed just enough space for two people to sleep together – so long as they were happy being really close all night. The entire thing was somewhere in the vicinity of 300 square feet. There was a small deck with a single chair in the front. It kind of looked cute.

Sam ran his eyes across the neighboring houses in the village. It turned out Godkin's brother lived in what appeared to be some sort of commune, or idyllic community of tiny houses. Every one of them completely different, as though the owners took a unique attention to detail in shrinking what would otherwise have been houses that constituted the American Dream.

Next to him, in the Bricklin, Tom gripped his Heckler and Koch MP5 submachinegun. He wore an almost embarrassed grin as he stared at the tiny house. "You know, when Genevieve originally wanted to join us, warning that it could be a big house and we don't know what sort of trap we'd find inside, a part of me was tempted to say I agreed… but I think we'll be all right. I mean, you could only fit one, possibly two of those Berserkers inside the entire house."

"I agree," Sam said, glancing back around at the open fields that surrounded the tiny house, leaving little in the way of concealment for any would-be attackers. The place somehow reminded him of a classier version of a campground. He pressed the door open button, and the gull-winged doors opened simultaneously with a slow hum of the motor working the hydraulics. "Shall we?"

Caliburn, sitting in the empty space behind the twin-seats, barked and was the first out the doors, his tail wagging incessantly. Sam picked up his own MP5. Despite the quaint and surreal appearances, he'd been attacked relentlessly in the past few days by Berserkers, and the last thing he needed was to become complacent.

Tom concurred. "Let's."

They walked around the tiny house, double checking that no-one was waiting for them inside. Caliburn, with his canine heightened sense of smell, wandered around the premises, but appeared unfazed. Apart from being highly intelligent, the golden retriever had an uncanny sixth sense when it came to danger.

"All good, Caliburn?" Sam asked.

Caliburn barked. His happily wagging tail signifying there was nothing untoward.

Sam took one last sweep of the village, deciding that the name, Sanctuary seemed well placed. He met Tom's eye, who nodded and covered him. Sam stepped up to the door and knocked. There was no answer. He grabbed the door handle. It was unlocked. He turned it and stepped in.

Inside was a stark contrast from the near perfect, almost manicured image of a tiny house from the outside. If its interior had once matched, it sure as hell didn't anymore. Someone had obviously ransacked the place. Everything that could be opened had been, and everything that couldn't be opened had been destroyed. Nothing had been left to chance.

Tom said, "Either Godkin's brother really had trouble finding the remote, or I'd say someone else knew that he held the other part of Miles Godkin's USB."

"It looks like it," Sam said.

He picked up a single photo frame.

The glass was cracked but the picture inside was still clearly visible. It depicted a good looking, clean cut man in military dress uniform.

Sam's eyes narrowed on the green beret. "Wow... this guy's special forces."

Tom glanced around at the tiny house. "Not really the sort of house you'd expect a Green Beret to live in, is it?"

Green Berets were the US Army unconventional warfare apparatus, involved in Combat Search and Rescue, Psychological, and Peacekeeping missions. Their roles were generally classified and most civilians would have never heard of them if it weren't for the Rambo franchise.

"No, but then again, maybe it's just perfect." Sam glanced at the series of medals on the man's uniform, which indicated he'd served more than his fair share of time on overseas deployment. "He's probably not stateside very often, and so doesn't need a lot of room. Besides," Sam said, looking out at the view of the snow-capped mountains in the distance, "What a great place to unwind!"

Sam stepped out of the tiny house and looked around.

Tom asked, "What are you thinking?"

"I'm not sure. I still don't have a clue what sort of mess I've stumbled across. I mean, I thought Godkin was a low-level wannabe gang member involved in drugs. Then, when he was dying, he tells me he was actually undercover – although for who, he didn't say – and that the USB had all the proof he needed to bring something big down, and to get it to his brother. He gave me his brother's address and said that he'd know what to do."

"And now we find his brother's house has been ransacked, and his brother also, just so happened to be a Green Beret."

Sam nodded. "Yeah, I watched the Rambo franchise, too. He's not the sort of guy one would expect a low-level biker gang to get the better of."

"No. I'd like to assume they don't know about his background and they're probably going to regret ever getting involved in drugs, or whatever it is they're involved in, when they do."

"Which brings me to my next thought… who is Miles Godkin's brother."

"You didn't get a name."

"No. Miles never told me. I probably should have given Elise the address and had her look him up."

Tom closed the door. "Come on, let's get a coffee. I'll message Elise on the way and see what she can find."

"Agreed."

Sam drove twenty minutes back to a diner on the highway.

He parked the Bricklin, switched off the car, and his cell phone began to ring. He answered it and listened as Elise filled him in on everything she'd learned. He thanked her, asked her to find out everything she could on the Berserker gang, and then hung up.

Tom met his eye. "Find anything?"

Sam said, "She says his name's Dean Godkin. The guy was a real hero. Served overseas in every hotspot you could imagine. Far more tours of duty than anyone is ever forced to do."

"You mean he kept volunteering?"

"Looks like it. This guy is your real life, bigger than life, military deal. Served three tours in Afghanistan and two in Iraq. Those are just the ones on his regular file."

"There's more?"

"Most of what he's done is classified. Elise said it took some serious hacking to find any traces of it. But he's been everywhere, serving in a long list of covert missions around the globe, until recently."

Tom licked his lips. "What happened recently?"

Sam said, "That's just it. Recently, he went AWOL and the military police in combination with the civilian police have issued an APB. The APB – All Points Bulletin – identified him as special forces, most likely armed and extremely well trained in an array of weapons and hand-to-hand combat, highly dangerous. But as of today, no one has seen any sign of him."

"Which means he's really good at his job, or he's dead."

"Exactly," Sam admitted.

Tom folded his arms across his chest. "So, we're at the end of the line."

"It would appear so."

Tom said, "What do you want to do?"

Sam looked up at the diner. "Well, first, let's gets some lunch. I'm famished."

"And then?"

"How do you feel about a trip to the Yucatán Peninsula?"

Tom laughed. "Great. What did you have in mind?"

Sam took a seat at a booth. "An archeologist friend of mine has discovered an old cave painting depicting a Hellenistic fleet in the Yucatán."

"No way. Cleopatra was right. The Hellenistic fleet actually managed to cross the Atlantic?"

Sam laughed. "Yeah, and I want to see it for myself, and decide if its real."

Chapter Thirty-Two

Xcalacoop – Yucatán Peninsula

Dr. Pablo Veracruz opened the door to his apartment.

Technically, it was a motel in downtown Xcalacoop, some five minutes' drive south of Chichén Itzá along highway 180. It might as well have been his home. He'd lived there for nearly three years now as he researched the nearby Caves of Balankanche, driven well past the point of obsession, in the search for its hidden passageway. Even now, it surprised him how the story had turned out. After all these years, he had begun to doubt if he was even right and never in his wildest dreams, did he believe the discovery of the sealed chamber would divulge so many secrets and so much treasure.

It was because of this wild success that Veracruz had needed to employ Rafael Vargis, a retired once semi-successful MMA fighter. The kid – not that you could call him that judging by his size – was 25 years old and if the scars and mangled shape of his nose, forehead, and jaw structure were anything to go off, he was never the best fighter. Still, the kid was at least three hundred pounds and although apathy and retirement from MMA had turned some of that weight to fat, there was still a hell of a lot of muscle. With that mixed in with his almost disturbing facial injuries, Veracruz deemed the kid to be enough of a deterrent to any would-be attackers.

After his recent discovery at Balankanche, Veracruz had been approached by several archeologists who tried to bribe – and failing that, hurt – their way onto his team to investigate the find. As news got out, and the enormity of the discovery and its valuable treasures became the stories of legends, the thinly veiled threats had worsened. Now, he employed a small team of archeologists, kept 24 hours armed guards at the entrance to Balankanche, and used Vargis as a driver and de-facto bodyguard when he traveled from home to the caves and vice versa.

"Everything okay, boss?" the kid asked, looking down at him, like a big, friendly giant… or given the shape of his head, ogre might be a better description.

"Very good," Veracruz replied, still feeling somewhat anxious about dawdling in the open. "I'll see you in the morning."

"Yes, sir," Vargis agreed. "Good night."

Veracruz closed the door, quickly securing a series of oversized security locks afterward. He placed his laptop bag on a small table and removed his shoes.

Thirty seconds later, there was a knock at the door. It was soft, almost apologetic.

Veracruz stepped toward the door. He opened it a few inches, leaving the door chain attached. He asked, "What did you forget, Vargis?"

Only Vargis didn't answer.

Through the narrow gap in the ajar door, he spotted two men. In a split-second glance, Veracruz took the whole scene in. They were white. Possibly Americans. They wore denim jeans and polo shirts that squeezed like torniquets around their muscular arms. Both men had tattoos. They could have been professional soldiers, or special forces, or mercenaries sent there to find out the location of the long sealed ancient Mayan treasure trove. One thing was certain, they sure as hell weren't on vacation, here to ask him about sightseeing recommendations.

Veracruz kept his wits. "I'll just be a minute. Let me throw some clothes on."

He tried to shut the door.

But they didn't let him.

Not even close.

They kicked the door in before he had a chance to slide the deadbolts into place. Veracruz tried to hold it together, but realized in seconds that the whole process was futile. With each kick, the door splintered like a shipwreck on a reef turning to flotsam.

On the third kick, Veracruz turned and ran.

He lived on the third story of the motel. There was a balcony at the back and a small table and chairs on which he sometimes worked in the afternoons. He raced through the back door and out on to the balcony. The ancient pyramid of Chichén Itzá rose majestically out from the jungle in the distance. The sun was setting, coloring the sky a rich purple.

Veracruz stopped and stared at the ground far below. It was somewhere in the vicinity of twenty-five feet. There was no grass, just a thick pile of leaves fallen from nearby trees. The ground looked soft. At a guess, he figured he'd probably survive the fall, but his bones might end up thoroughly broken.

His eyes darted across the other balconies, looking for an alternative solution. In the movies, people were always climbing from one balcony down to the next. This wasn't going to be like that. There was no way he was going to reach the second and first level balconies.

Behind him, the two strangers were through the door, racing to him.

Veracruz swallowed, took a deep breath.

This is gonna hurt…

He glanced over his shoulder.

Both men had their guns drawn. At the end of the barrels they seemed to have additional short attachments that if those spy novels were anything to go off, meant they were silenced. Not good. Any fear he had of jumping disappeared with that sight.

Veracruz clambered over the balcony, lowered himself as far as he could, and in one quick movement, swung out from the building and let go.

He hit the ground and rolled.

The pain was less than he imagined. Or was it just the adrenaline keeping him going? He didn't know. Either way, he knew that if he didn't keep moving, he was dead. He forced himself to stand. Searing pain raced through his legs, but they took his weight, which meant nothing – important – was broken.

Veracruz began running into the jungle. Functioning on pure survival mode, he hoped to hell the dense forest might offer some protection. Behind him, he heard the loud sounds of crunching leaves, where his two pursuers followed at a run.

He moved quickly.

There was a time, long ago, when he was a long distance runner. His height made him far from competitive, but it hadn't stopped him competing in several marathons over the years. The unique combination of adrenaline and muscle memory, allowed him to move fast in the jungle. After ten minutes, he knew he was pulling away from his attackers. Veracruz kept running. Like all good marathon runners, he was able to set a fast pace, and then keep it there, while his attackers had most likely begun to run out of energy.

Mentally, he tried to picture the surrounding topography. Ten miles to the south was another road. If he kept heading that way, he might reach it in time to flag down a driver, and escape. He cursed himself for not having the foresight to grab his phone before he'd left. He picked up a stick. It was about the length of his arm and thick. The thing would work as a weapon, but would be a poor choice against two pistols. Still, without any other options, he kept it in his hands for safe keeping.

Veracruz reached the road.

It wasn't a main road, and this time of night, it could be barren.

He headed south.

A few minutes later, he saw the distant glow of headlights coming over the horizon. It was an old Mercedes Benz. He tried to flag the driver down, waving his arms. The car slowed. He locked eyes, pleadingly with the driver, a woman in her sixties or seventies, and then moved toward the passenger's side door.

The driver gunned the engine, and the Mercedes Benz drove off.

Veracruz swore.

In his hand, he was still holding the stick like a giant club. He grimaced. That was stupid. Of course, no one was going to stop for him on a dark road, looking like that. He glanced behind him. There were no longer any signs of his pursuers. It confirmed that he'd lost them back in the jungle when he outran them.

A couple minutes later, another car approach.

This one was a green Jeep. It looked dated and heavily beat up. Veracruz waved his arms and tried to flag it down.

The man driving the Jeep spotted him, and pulled up next to him.

Veracruz quickly moved to open the passenger door. "Thank you so much for stopping. Quick… I've been attacked."

"You're welcome," the driver said, a bemused smile on his lips. Then, leveling the barrel of his gun at him, he said, "You'd better get in, Veracruz."

Chapter Thirty-Three

A few minutes later, Dr. Pablo Veracruz was sitting at the desk of his study.

The driver hadn't told him anything. The man, a Jarhead undoubtedly from someone's military, radioed in to his partner, but that was it. There was no explanation about what was expected of him, but Veracruz knew what they wanted.

They wanted to know the exact location of his discovery. It might seem crazy, given that everyone who might have heard about it by now, knew that it must have occurred in Balankanche. And why wouldn't they? He'd spent the last twenty years of his life trying to find it. Yet, Balankanche was a labyrinthian maze of secret tunnels. If he walked away tomorrow, it might take people who knew about his discovery months just to locate the grand cathedral which housed the prized Mayan artifacts and drawings.

But strangely, they didn't care about the location of the prize. In fact, they didn't care about it at all. Instead, they focused on who he employed, where they lived, who knew about the project, and where he kept all his photos of the inside. After twenty minutes, the second man turned up, along with a third. The third person was balding, with a heavy combover and thick glasses, he looked like every stereotypical computer geek.

The driver asked Veracruz to turn his laptop on and put in the password. Veracruz paused, trying to work out how to possibly drag out the inevitable any longer. He could see where this was leading and didn't like the end scenario. They wanted all the information he had, and when they had it, they would most likely kill him.

The driver punched him hard. "We really don't have all day."

The blow hit him in the solar plexus, sucking the wind out of his lungs. For an agonizing full minute, his diaphragm was paralyzed and panic set in as the urge to breathe overwhelmed his mind. Finally, he drew a breath. It came out like a gasp.

The driver gestured toward the laptop. "The password."

Veracruz typed it in correctly and pressed enter.

Geek guy thanked him and plugged in an external hard drive into the laptop, as he quickly went through the process of extracting whatever data they were looking for. Veracruz imagined that they – whoever they were – wanted all of his research and data about the Mayan find. The other two thugs simply sat there and watched. No one spoke.

After several minutes, Geek guy turned the laptop over to his email account. "Password please."

Veracruz glanced at the driver, who stood up and clenched his fist, as though pre-empting any delay like last time.

Veracruz held up a placating hand. "Okay, okay. I'll do it. Don't hit me."

He typed in the password and slid the laptop back to the geek.

Ten minutes later, Geek guy closed the laptop, and packed it up.

Driver asked, "You got all of it?"

The Geek nodded. "Yeah, I've got the list."

Driver turned to Veracruz. "Did you tell anyone else about your discovery?"

"No," Veracruz said, forgetting about his phone call to Sam Reilly. "That's it. That's everything and everyone."

"Good," Driver said, standing up. "We're done here."

A second later, Driver put the barrel of his silenced handgun to Veracruz's head and squeezed the trigger twice.

Shooting him dead.

Chapter Thirty-Four

The Gulfstream G650 landed at the Mérida International Airport.

Its pilots taxied to the private jet hangar. It slowed to a stop and two officials stepped on board to fast-track customs and quarantine. When they were done, Sam Reilly and Tom Bower stepped off the aircraft. A blue Ford Raptor was parked on the side of the taxiway. The driver got out, greeted them cordially, and handed Sam the keys.

They got in the car and began driving toward the Caves of Balankanche. On the way, Sam tried calling his friend again. It went straight to his voicemail.

He shook his head and frowned. "Still nothing."

Tom shrugged. "Maybe your friend doesn't actually like you?"

The edge of Sam's lips curved into the briefest of smiles. "Actually, you might be right there. Pablo Veracruz is the classic loner. He doesn't like anyone."

"Really?"

"Yeah. Maybe that's what drove him to a life of archeology… I don't know."

They kept driving and an hour later, Chichén Itzá came into view, rising high above the dark green jungle that shrouded most of the Yucatán Peninsula.

Tom returned to his original question. "So if your friend wants to be left alone, what are we doing here?"

"Hey, it didn't stop him calling me," Sam countered.

"Yeah, to boast that he'd found evidence of your mythical Hellenistic fleet that sailed the Americas."

"Exactly. If it turns out to be valid, this will be the greatest archeological find in more than a century. Having Hellenistic Greeks beat Christopher Columbus by nearly fifteen hundred years would be like Neil Armstrong stepping on the moon only to find a plaque from Australia."

Tom laughed. "Australians don't make good astronauts?"

"I'm sure they do," Sam admitted. "It's just they didn't even have a foot in the game in 1969."

Tom suppressed a smile, his face reading like he still wasn't quite sure if the analogy fit. "All right, so when was the last time you heard from Veracruz?"

"Two days ago. After he called me, he emailed me some photos of the grand cathedral he'd discovered."

"Which was where the Mayans housed the image of the Hellenistic fleet with the backdrop of the coast of the Yucatán Peninsula?"

"That's right."

"And since then, you've heard nothing?"

"No," Sam admitted. "I've sent him a few texts and even left a couple voicemails saying that we'd be here to have a look, but so far, haven't heard anything."

"Does that seem odd to you?"'

"Not particularly. As we discussed earlier, he's a loner and on top of that, he's spends most of his days underground – ergo, no cell phone reception."

"All right, so where are we headed?"

Sam kept driving. "Where this all began, at the Caves of Balankanche."

Tom asked, "What do we know about them?"

"The ancient Mayan cave site lies a short distance from the archaeological Maya-Toltec city of Chichén Itzá, Yucatán. For more than two thousand years, it has been the focus of rituals dedicated to the Maya rain god, Chaac, and, in the Post-Classic period, also to his Toltec counterpart, Tlaloc. Small buildings and platforms surrounded the cave's entrance; inside, stairs, walls, altars and ritual displays of ceramics and small stone implements were discovered. The site is crowded with tourists who watched too much Indiana Jones."

"Sounds like an interesting place. Shall we buy a tourist ticket?"

"Maybe," Sam said, his eyes focused on the road.

They arrived at the entrance to the Caves of Balankanche a short time later. A series of police cars and emergency vehicles filled the parking lot, and rows of warning tape cordoned off the entrance.

Sam pulled up the Ford Raptor and met Tom's eye. "What do you think?"

Tom swallowed. "I don't know. I just hope this works out better than last time."

Sam nodded. Last time they were in the Yucatán they nearly died trying to navigate the flooded passages of Xibalba.

A police officer came to greet him, and Sam had a feeling they weren't going to be so lucky.

Chapter Thirty-Five

It only took seconds for Sam's premonition to unfold into a dark reality.

After some discussion and phone calls, Sam and Tom were introduced to the lead investigator, a man named Pedro Gonzales. Gonzales was a short man with a mustache and intelligent brown eyes. What he lacked in stature, he made up for in physique. The man looked like a square. Sam was sure that once upon a time the guy just about lived at a gym, pumped iron, and took a concoction of performance enhancing drugs. Those days were long gone, and Gonzales' muscles had turned mostly to fat.

Gonzales brought them up to speed about the situation.

The Caves of Balankanche had suffered a collapse. It wasn't a natural collapse. Someone used a significant amount of dynamite to bring the roof down in the newer area, where Dr. Pablo Veracruz had recently been working. Although Veracruz hadn't been at the site at the time, several archeologists who were working on the project had been and all were presumed dead.

Sam asked, "Does Dr. Veracruz know yet?"

Gonzalez deflected the question. "How well do you know Dr. Veracruz?"

"Not very well," Sam admitted. "We've worked together on a few projects over the years. Nothing major. He's consulted for me when I need help with Mayan archeology. Why?"

"And he contacted you about his discovery?"

"That's right. I believe I was the first one he told."

Gonzalez arched an eyebrow. Something about that statement surprised him. He opened his mouth to speak, then closed it again.

Sam's eyes narrowed. "What is it?"

"Dr. Veracruz was very coy about his discovery."

"That makes sense."

Gonzales said, "Does it?"

"Yeah, something like this could be potentially filled with priceless treasures. The last thing he needs are a bunch of grave robbers breaking into the passageway that led to the grand cathedral…" Sam paused. A wry expression etched across his face. "Was that what happened here? Someone tried to break into Dr. Veracruz's archeological site?"

"No. We don't think that's the case."

"Right," Sam said, in a way that showed he really didn't understand anything about what was going on.

Gonzales persisted. "So why would Dr. Veracruz make a call to you?"

"Ah, that I can explain," Sam said. "Dr. Veracruz believed he'd discovered evidence of something that I have believed for some time, but most scholars look at as nothing more than a legend or a fanciful myth."

"And that was?"

"That Christopher Columbus wasn't the first European to step foot on the Americas."

"Who did?"

On his phone he brought up the image that Veracruz had sent him. "These people – Hellenistic Greeks."

"Interesting," Gonzales said, examining the photo. "How would such a discovery affect the world?"

"You mean, other than the scholars and historians who would have a field day debating its validity?"

"No, I'm more curious…"

Sam drew a breath. "Why someone would kill to keep it secret?"

Detective Gonzales nodded. "Yes, that's exactly what I'm interested in."

"I have no idea. I mean, it would definitely change a lot of historical claims, but realistically, I can't see why anyone would kill to protect the secret."

Gonzales continued. "You see, from the tapes we've reviewed, it appears that no one has stolen anything from the newly discovered cavern within Balankanche. Instead, some people went to great lengths to destroy it."

Sam said, "The grand cathedral's been destroyed?"

"It would appear so." The detective was grim. "Removing with it, all evidence of this so called Hellenistic fleet."

"That's not true… I'm certain Dr. Veracruz has taken photos and categorized everything. All you need to do is contact…" Sam tried to speak. Choked. His tongue, suddenly too dry to talk. Understanding suddenly striking him like the Reaper's scythe. "They got to Dr. Veracruz too, didn't they?"

Gonzales nodded. "And his bodyguard-cum-driver… a big MMA fighter named, Rafael Vargis."

Sam looked off distantly, his eyes staring at the grand entrance to Balankanche. At its ornate limestone Mayan decorations, his mind saw the place where his reclusive friend had spent the majority of his life – only to have it taken from him at what should have been the highlight. He turned to face Gonzales. "Where were they killed?"

"Vargis was executed in his car. Two shots to the back of the head. His body left in the driver's seat. It appears he dropped Veracruz off and was attacked almost immediately afterward."

"And Veracruz?"

"In his house. The place he was using as an office. Same thing. Execution style shots to the back of the head. Two. Very precise. Professional hits. I can tell you now, this wasn't drug related."

"Really?" Sam asked. He could have told Gonzales that Veracruz wasn't the type of guy involved in drug cartels, but he was interested to know why the detective was certain about it. "Why?"

"Too professional. No collateral damage and everything was done simultaneously. The cave was detonated and then anyone and everyone connected to Dr. Veracruz's project was eliminated."

Sam asked, "Everyone?"

"Yeah. We've got a list of his old emails. Everyone he contacted on that list about his project is now dead."

A shadow of fear crossed his face. "Not everyone, detective."

Gonzales frowned. "No?"

Sam exhaled a long breath. "No, I was on that list."

Chapter Thirty-Six

Sam watched the color drain from detective Gonzales's face.

Fear blended with confusion and the detective said, "We have a complete list. Your name was, fortunately for you, not on that list."

Sam nodded. "It wouldn't be, but I assure you, I received an email from Veracruz regarding his discovery of the Hellenistic fleet in the Yucatán."

Gonzales persisted, "May I ask what email you use?"

"It would be identified under the heading of Elise. All my emails go through her secure network, before being rerouted to me."

"If that is so, I might fear for the life of your friend, Elise."

"I doubt it." Sam's tone was soft, but defiant. "For starters, only the best hackers in the world would be able to identify where the user of that network exists in real life, and secondly, Elise works on board my ship – a veritable fortress I assure you."

Gonzales nodded. He feigned relief, but fear was etched in the deep lines across his face, too. The man placed his hands together, his fingers steepled, and said, "I am very sorry for your loss, Mr. Reilly. But I fear you have already taken up too much of my time. I should continue with my investigation."

"Of course," Sam said. Then, pausing just a beat, he said, "Do you mind if Tom and I go and see where Dr. Veracruz lived?"

Gonzales's face turned hard. "You realize it is an active crime scene?"

Sam nodded. "Of course."

"I've had my people do some research on you Mr. Reilly. I understand that you have an exemplary past, with many accolades to your name, but crime scene investigation, I believe, is not one of them."

"No, no. I just want to see where he lived." Sam paused, as though trying to find the right justification.

Gonzales's eyes narrowed. "Go on, Mr. Reilly, what is it you are looking for?"

"You see… Dr. Pablo Veracruz was a brilliant archeologist, the discovery that ultimately got him killed only goes to prove that." The edges of Sam's lips turned upward into the crease of a smile. "But as you know he was an antisocial recluse, who was quite paranoid. For years he's been worried about people stealing his research."

"And what, you think he left some sort of clue?"

Sam shrugged. "I realize I don't have any background in criminology or anything to do with investigating a murder scene, but I believe my unique… friendship, if you can call it that, with Veracruz, puts me in a very unusual position of being well suited to spot any clues he might have left behind."

"What aren't you telling me?"

"Nothing. I'd just like to see the motel where he lives. I'm not at all suggesting your officers overlooked anything, just that he might have left a very specific archeological clue for me."

"Why you specifically?"

"It's a long story. Just a hunch. But he and I have been discussing the possibility of this Hellenistic fleet in the Americas for some time now, and I believe he would have left me a specific note or USB or something."

"I can assure you, if he had, my people would have found it by now." Gonzales met Sam's eyes, and must have seen something there, because a moment later, he said, "I tell you what, I'll take you up to the crime scene and walk you through what we know myself. How does that sound?"

"That sounds very kind of you," Sam replied. "Are you sure your presence here can be spared for an hour or two?"

There was a twinkle in Gonzales's eye, and Sam detected something akin to a small grin forming on the man's lips. "Yes, I believe it's worth my while to see what you can find."

Chapter Thirty-Seven

The tires of the Ford Raptor crunched along the gravel driveway and came to a stop in the front of the motel that Dr. Pablo Veracruz had called home for the past three years. Sam Reilly got out the passenger side. He stopped beside the driver's side door. Tom rolled down the window. Their eyes locked with mutual understanding.

Sam said, "I'll see you soon."

Tom nodded. "I'll try not to take too long."

Sam watched Detective Gonzales pull in behind them. He got out and said, "Your friend's not staying to help with the investigation?"

"He'll be back soon. I asked him to go find some lunch for us. There's a take away place we both liked at Valladolid."

Gonzales arched an eyebrow. "Valladolid's an hour away."

Sam nodded. "I'm in no rush for lunch."

Understanding registered on the detective's face. "You think I might be more comfortable bringing you through the crime scene alone? The less people involved, the better?"

Sam raised an eyebrow and met his eye. "Something like that. Shall we?"

Over the next twenty minutes the detective brought Sam through the crime scene at the motel. He showed where the door had been kicked in by two people, how they had concluded that Veracruz had made a run for it by jumping off the three-story balcony only to be recaptured, brought back to the motel room, and his office searched before he was executed.

Sam followed him through the motel room, keeping up with the narrative of the murder. Everything seemed to make sense to him. Mentally, he tried to picture his friend's attempt to survive. There wasn't a lot of chance Veracruz was ever going to escape let alone get out alive.

Sam asked, "What do the motel's security tapes show?"

"Nothing."

Sam frowned. "Nothing?"

"No. I don't know anything about whoever put this hit out, but I can tell you, they were professionals – that's for sure. They were thorough and they sure as hell didn't leave any loose strings."

"The surveillance recordings were doctored?"

"That's right. The attack is completely missing."

Sam said, "What about Veracruz's security monitors?"

Gonzales looked blank. "Veracruz had tapes?"

"Sure did. The guy was off the charts when it came to intelligence but he was paranoid about everything. A guy like that always has a back to base security camera recording everything that's happening on the sight."

"Any idea where he'd position it?"

"The camera?" Sam shrugged. "He's probably got them hidden throughout the entire apartment, but I guarantee he'd have one in his office, where most of his research was kept."

Gonzales moved quickly through to the office. The same place where Veracruz was found dead with two bullet holes in the back of his head. Together, they ran their eyes across the room. There was nothing obvious.

Then again, why should there be?

What's the point of having a secret recording that's obvious? Sam had a look around. There was nothing he could see. Everything seemed in its right place. There was a desk – the drawers pulled out already and strewn across the floor – a wall mounted air conditioner, that had been ripped out of the wall, and nothing else. On the ceiling there was a single smoke detector. It flashed red, indicating it had power.

Sam turned and walked to the kitchen, combined with living room space. He stared at the ceiling. His lips curled into a smile. There, on the ceiling was another smoke alarm. Not just one. Six in total throughout the tiny motel apartment. Either the proprietors of the motel were the most conscientious and risk averse Sam had ever heard of, or Veracruz was positively terrified of fire – but more likely, those smoke alarms supported hidden cameras.

Sam grabbed a chair and brought it to the study. He stood on it and reached up to the smoke alarm. It didn't take much to untwist the device. It was battery operated and not connected to the power mains. At a glance it sure as hell looked like a smoke alarm. It even had one of those warnings, *Nuclear Material – Dispose of Safely*, that appeared inside most smoke alarms.

He handed it to Gonzales, who glanced at it and then handed it back to him. "It's just a smoke alarm."

Sam spread his arms out. "Maybe I was wrong."

He took the smoke alarm back and examined it once more. He pulled out the battery shaped "nuclear material" thingy that rested at the center of the smoke detector. The entire thing came free. Inside, was a small USB device.

Sam grinned. "Look at this!"

A few minutes later, Gonzales plugged the USB device into his laptop. He opened up the document which kept a rolling weekly recording of the top-down view from the smoke alarm. He quickly scrolled through until it reached the point where two men were holding Veracruz at gunpoint, and pressed the play button.

It depicted two people.

They were white. Possibly Americans. They wore denim jeans and polo shirts that squeezed like tourniquets around their muscular arms. Both men had tattoos. They could have been professional soldiers, or special forces, or mercenaries.

Sam pressed pause, freezing the video frame. "There..."

Gonzales's eyes locked onto it. "The special forces tattoo?"

"No. I hadn't noticed that." Sam's eyes narrowed on the second one.

It depicted a SEAL Trident, Anchor, Eagle, and Pistol. It was a common enough military ink. The symbols recognized Navy Seals and designated them as having completed their training. The design represented not just the Navy with its anchor, but all the areas the SEALs protect, including air – eagle – land – pistol – and trident – water.

These elements also hold secondary meanings as well. For instance, the placement of the eagle's head demonstrates its humility, while the cocked pistol shows how they must be ready at all times. The trident symbolizes the Seals' connection with the ocean – one of the most brutal terrains to fight on. This vast element commanded by the likes of Poseidon and Neptune must be mastered by the Seals.

Sam said, "The guy's retired special forces."

Gonzales said, "Retired?"

"Probably. If this was someone from my government, I'm pretty certain they wouldn't have sent someone showing off his SEAL insignia."

"They might be ghosts?"

Mentally, Sam agreed wholeheartedly. They were most likely ghosts, a part of a unique team of retired special forces who no longer existed on the books, whose job it was to go in and clean up a mess, performing dirty tasks. If something Veracruz had discovered somehow became a threat to national security, these were the people most likely to be sent in to remove it. Sam shook his head, "I doubt it."

"Okay, what about the other tattoo?" Gonzales caught his eye. "You said you recognized it?"

"Yeah…" Sam said, staring at the tattoo.

And why shouldn't he recognize it? He'd been seeing a lot of it lately. It depicted a small Viking with an axe… and more tears. The very same ink he'd seen on each of the Berserkers who kept trying to attack him.

"What does it mean?" Gonzales asked.

"I have no idea, but I intend to find out."

Sam pressed play again and the recording played out. They watched Veracruz kneel down, whisper a silent prayer, and quietly be executed. It looked almost surreal. Somehow, at the end of the day, Sam doubted very much that he would go so quietly.

Afterward, one of the men asked the other one where their local contact was. The second one told the first that he'd be there any minute.

Gonzales pressed the pause button.

Sam looked at him. His blue eyes piercing, as they held his gaze. "Why did you stop it?"

The detective shrugged. "The show's over. We're not going to get anything else from this." He cast his gaze toward the frozen image of the study. "This is exactly how the room was found."

Sam leaned forward and pressed play. "All the same, I'd like to watch this play out."

Gonzales arched an eyebrow. "Are you sure?"

"Yes."

Gonzales shrugged. "Suit yourself."

Sam watched the next few minutes play out.

In the video, a third person arrived. He was wearing a police uniform. The man told them in Spanish to leave the damned body alone, leave everything exactly where it was, so that he could deal with it. The police officer then turned to leave.

Sam pressed the pause button again.

It froze on the police officer's face.

Sam recognized the image as Gonzales.

His eyes darted toward the detective.

But already, Detective Gonzales had his weapon drawn, and was pointing it at Sam. His lips twisted into a malicious smile. "So, now you know the truth."

Chapter Thirty-Eight

Sam slowly raised his hands in a placating gesture.

Detective Gonzales shrugged. "You just couldn't let it go, could you?"

"Sorry. A friend of mine died."

"Yeah, well, now you're going to have to join him. What a waste hey? I would have expected more of you, given your reputation."

Sam suppressed a knowing grin. "Believe me, I of all people am most sorry to disappoint you."

Gonzales laughed at that. The detective seemed relaxed. And why shouldn't he be? He held all the cards being the only one armed, and right now, Sam was on the opposite side of the room. Even Usain Bolt would struggle to reach the man before he was shot. The pistol lowered just a little bit, it was held at more of a downward angle, more out of laziness on the detective's part than anything else.

"Who else knows?" Gonzales asked.

"About the discovery?"

"Yeah."

"No one... I think..." Sam's lips curled into a confident grin. "Actually, there are a few people..."

"Such as?"

"Why should I tell you?" Sam said, "Won't you just kill me anyway?"

"Sure. But you can die quickly or very, very slowly... it's your choice."

"Uh-huh..." Sam said, "Right, so you want names?"

"That would be much appreciated."

"Okay. There's Elise… she's my computer hacker who works on my ship – you might have trouble locating her, and even if you do, you'll have a hard time reaching her while she lives aboard my ship, but you're welcome to try. Then there's the rest of my crew to be honest… they probably know by now…" Sam licked his lips and grinned. "Oh, and then there's Tom… he has a fair idea I'd say."

Right on cue, Tom put the barrel of his Glock onto the side of the detective's head. The cold, hard steel, pressing into the man's skin.

Tom said, "I suggest you slowly lower the pistol."

Detective Gonzales exhaled slowly. "You never went to Valladolid, did you?"

"Nope," Tom admitted. "Been here all along."

Gonzales asked Sam, "How did you know?"

Sam held his gaze. "That you were on the take?"

"It's a bad word, but yeah, how did you know I was on the take?"

"I didn't. It was just a hunch. I couldn't see what else the lead detective of such a significant investigation would want with babysitting some interfering shmuck such as myself."

"Right…" Gonzales sighed. "Now what?"

"Now you put down the gun and tell us exactly who's involved in this thing."

Gonzales nodded.

He began to lower his pistol.

A moment later, he tried to lift it again.

Tom didn't give him another chance. He squeezed the trigger and a 9mm Parabellum left the barrel at a rate of 1,230 feet per second. At that speed the round penetrated Gonzales's skull, severing his brain stem in an instant, a fine mist of pink spraying the wall behind him, before anyone could hear the clicking sound of Tom squeezing the trigger.

Sam exchanged a glance with Tom. "Yeah, it's Xibalba all over again."

Chapter Thirty-Nine

Tom drove the Ford Raptor hard and fast.

They needed to be out of the country before anyone knew what happened. Sam picked up his cell phone and made a call to a secure number, placing the phone on speaker so that Tom could hear the conversation.

The Secretary of Defense answered on the first ring.

Without preamble, she said, "You've stumbled across something you shouldn't have. You need to leave it alone."

Sam said, "Madam Secretary, I have Tom Bower on speaker with us. I hope you don't mind. I believe he needs to be involved in this conversation too."

"Hello Tom," she said. "That's fine."

"Madam Secretary," Tom said.

Sam licked his lips, returning to the Secretary of Defense's initial statement, he asked, "What have I stumbled across?"

"This drug that's turning users into murderers... what are they calling it on the street?"

"Berserker."

"Right," the Secretary of Defense said, "You need to shut the investigation down."

Sam's eyes narrowed, still amazed by how much she already knew about his involvement. "Why?"

"I can't say."

"You don't know?"

"Not exactly. I can imagine, but as you're aware, some programs are kept secret... even from the government that's supposed to be run by the good guys."

Sam said, "It's all a part of your plausible deniability."

"Exactly."

Sam gripped the side of the door, as Tom took a corner a little too fast, and the wheels screeched. "Can you tell me who was running the program?"

The Secretary said, "DARPA."

Sam made a small curse under his breath. DARPA stood for Defense Advanced Research Projects Agency, an advanced-technology branch of the U.S. Department of Defense. He could easily imagine that they were studying the effects of a drug capable of turning its soldiers superhuman.

He drew a breath. "They were trying to make super soldiers!"

He waited for the Secretary of Defense to deny it.

She didn't.

He took her silence as confirmation.

Sam frowned. "Let me guess... The drug worked, but the side-effects started to kill people – not just the soldiers who took the experimental drugs, but also everyone around them."

"The program's been shut down by the President himself."

"And everything about it erased?"

Her voice was soft, but authoritative. "You know how these things are done."

Sam said, "Sure, and yet we're still seeing the aftermath."

He imagined her biting her tongue in frustration. "All right, so they tried to shut the program down..."

Sam asked, "What went wrong?"

"Dean Godkin went wrong."

Sam thought about what Elise had told him about Godkin, and asked, "Who's that?"

"One of the guinea pigs. Also, probably the best soldier we've ever created."

Sam exhaled deeply. "Let me guess, he didn't take too kindly to the program being shut down – particularly with him being part of it."

"No, I can't say I expect he did."

Sam let the silence linger for a while. Both of them knew the words shut down in this instance was a euphemism for erased – AKA killed or exterminated – including the lives of every experimental candidate.

Sam persisted. "What happened?"

"He killed six of our operatives. Most of the cleanup crew, brought in from an external source, to eradicate every piece of evidence of the program. By the time he was done, there were only a few survivors."

"Any idea where he went from there?"

"No… But now the drugs are coming out on the street as party drugs… all around the world…"

Sam swallowed. "He sold the recipe to the next higher bidder?"

"It would appear so, and that bidder would be an International Drug Cartel."

Sam exhaled. "The Berserkers."

"That's what they're calling themselves, although where the hell they came from is anyone's guess. There was no record of them even existing more than a year ago."

A bald-headed eagle cried in the distance. Sam looked up at the symbol so frequently associated with the US greatness, and somehow it all suddenly felt like a lie. "Those drugs are killing users and innocent bystanders."

She kept her mouth shut.

"Like Pandora's Box," Sam said, "the mysteries of this drug have been released on the world, its demons now free to run wild and wreak havoc."

"A team's been put in place to put it back in the box."

Sam drew a breath. "I'm sorry, Madam Secretary."

She made a deep sigh on the other end of the line. "You're not going to drop this thing, despite my orders?"

"That's right."

"I was afraid you were going to say that." The Secretary's tone softened. "Why?"

"We made mistakes. No one is above the law. The government was wrong. DARPA was wrong. And now a lot of people are dead. Some were archeologists, who were silenced because of what they had discovered about the Berserker drug. They were my friends. I'm going to get to the bottom of this mess. I owe it to them. You, we, DARPA, owe it to the people."

"I thought you would say that."

"I'm sorry."

"Sam…"

"Yes?"

Her voice was cold and hard, with a melancholy yet emphatic tone. "I can't protect you on this one."

Sam said, "I understand."

"Good luck. You're going to need it."

Sam caught her before she ended the call. "Oh, there's something else you're not going to like."

He heard her sigh. "What have you done now?"

"I killed a person. Technically, Tom killed a person to save my life."

Her voice was hard. "Oh, Tom! Did you have to?"

"I apologize wholeheartedly, Madam Secretary."

"That's all right," she said with surprising equanimity. "I suppose it couldn't have been helped."

"It really couldn't," Sam confirmed.

She said, "So, what does this have to do with me?"

"It might come back to bite us."

"Us?" The Secretary of Defense asked. "You mean, you and Tom, right?"

"No. I mean, you. The US government."

"Why?" She asked, her tone still curious, but becoming sharper as the severity of the event came out. "Did Tom kill someone important?"

"Yeah, the lead detective, and chief of the local police department."

"Tom… did you not think about this before you shot him!" she scolded.

"I'm sorry ma'am… he was about to shoot Sam dead."

"And you didn't stop to ask yourself how much of a mess this would be for me to clean up?"

Tom gritted his teeth. "Afraid the thought didn't even cross my mind, ma'am."

She said, "Ah, I should have expected as much damned loyalty to Sam from you, without even a passing thought about the trouble I'm now going to have to deal with."

Sam said, "Look. This is your people's mess. Someone from your department sent down this clean up team. They screwed up. I mean, they really did! When they not only killed my friend and nearly succeeded in killing me, but let me find out about it. So, yes, this is your problem. I'm washing my hands of it and getting the hell out of here before anyone manages to place us at the scene of the killing. Do you understand?"

"I do and I wish you luck in your endeavor, although I doubt it coincides very much with my own." She paused. "There is one thing you might be able to do for me if you get the chance?"

A wave of concern flashed across Sam's eyes. "What's that?"

"If you happen to run into Dean Godkin and he doesn't kill you first, do me a favor and finish what our ghost team failed to do."

"What makes you think we're going to run into him?" Sam asked. "I mean, he could be anywhere in the world by now?"

"Basic deduction, you're both looking for the same thing. You're both pretty smart people. There's a good chance both of you might actually find what you're looking for." Without trying to mince her words, and eager to receive confirmation, she said, "So, will you kill him?"

Sam bit his lower lip. "I don't know, from what you've told me, I would have thought Godkin was on our side?"

"Your side, maybe, but not ours," she countered.

"We'll see if we come across him and I'll make up my mind then."

The Secretary said, "I wouldn't advise that."

"Yeah, why is that?"

Her voice sent a cold shadow down his spine. "Because by the time you discover he's not on your side, you will already be dead."

Chapter Forty

Lake Crescent, Washington

Dean Godkin stared at the deep, freshwater lake.

At this distance, it looked so blue that it could almost be considered translucent. The water sparkled tantalizingly in the sun, his eyes were so intrinsically drawn toward it, that it might as well have been made of diamond. The unique lake owed its brilliant blue waters and exceptional clarity to a lack of nitrogen in the water, which inhibited the growth of algae.

Having allowed himself a minute reprieve to enjoy the view, he kept walking. The intermission made him feel better. The fact he could appreciate a view somehow made him feel still human. There was a long way to go.

Once he reached the lake's shore, he followed the Spruce Railroad Trail as the old logging track meandered along the shores. Keeping to the north side of the lake, he passed a popular swimming and diving area known as Devils Punch Bowl, before finally reaching the entrance to an old, dilapidated railroad tunnel that had been out of use for a very long time.

He glanced at the wooden beams that formed the vaulted ceiling of the tunnel. They were made of hardwood, but looked like they had seen better days… the tunnel had a warning about being dangerous and that people shouldn't enter it. For added measure, the bottom of the entrance had been boarded up with slats of pine. The almost ubiquitous rain, courtesy of the Pacific Ocean, which created a marine layer where clouds are frequent in the winter, spring and fall, had helped turn those slats rotten, and it didn't take much for him to work enough free that he could squeeze through.

Inside, he shined a flashlight up at the ceiling again. The workmanship had once been expert, but years of rain seeping through from the soil above had done its work to erode much of the beam's structural strength. At a glance, he spotted three separate beams that had broken free and fallen to the ground, where the track had once lay.

Dean smiled, picturing the warning sign. He decided it seemed to offer good advice, not to enter the old rail tunnel. Still, he needed to enter it, and besides, an unlikely cave-in of a railway tunnel that had lasted nearly a hundred years, seemed the least of his worries right now. He kept walking, marching by default, into the dark passageway. The beam of his flashlight flickering across the disused tracks as he went.

He startled more than a dozen sleeping bats. Spooked by his appearance they flew over his head, and into safety of the darkness beyond, deep inside. He kept walking, following the creatures of the night deeper into their lair. Roughly six hundred feet in, he stopped, having found what he was looking for.

He shined his flashlight to the left of the old rail track. An alcove nearly forty feet long by ten feet wide, appeared. The beam of his light reflected on the still water like a mirror. If the place hadn't been so dark, dilapidated, and almost certainly just about due to collapse under the weight of a million tons of mountain, Dean could have almost pictured it making a nice swimming pool. That, and if the temperature wasn't near freezing all year round.

It had once been a water stop.

In the good old days of steam locomotion, a Water Stop, also known as a Water Station, was a place where steam trains could stop to replenish water. This was back in times when the movement by steam locomotion required infinitely large amounts of water. Sometimes these stops were called Wood and Water or Coal and Water Stops, given that fuel to replenish the engines was also essential when adding water. In the very early days, trains needed Water Stops every seven to ten miles, before the introduction of a dedicated tender – or water and fuel carriage – allowed trains to run continuously without refill for up to a hundred miles at a time.

Dean imagined it must have been desperate times to need to build one midway through the mountain. But there you have it, the wonders of progress.

He stared at the Water Stop.

Dean had hoped he'd never need to return to it, and yet something about the place made him feel proud. As far as he was concerned, he'd picked the perfect place to hide it. He rolled up his sleeves, leaned over the edge, and dipped his arm, right down to his shoulder to the first ledge of the water pond. His fingers felt along the silty bottom in complete darkness. It took a while and for a moment, he was worried that someone might have found it. The thought was preposterous. He needn't have worried at all.

A few seconds later, his fingers found part of the chain.

It was coiled up in a disheveled clump that would make the laziest of sailors complain. Gripping the end of the chain, he pulled it free of the water pond, and then slowly, hand over hand, began the tedious job of pulling it in. The task took the better part of fifteen minutes, but eventually, Dean was able to heave the last of the chain out of the water…

Dean stared at the plastic container.

It was made with a thick, plastic resin, making it exceptionally strong, while remaining immune to elemental problems such as being submerged for years. He unlatched all four of its locking mechanisms and then popped the hatch open.

Inside was a spare set of civilian clothes, a wig that gave him thick, wavy brown hair, and glasses. He took his disguise and put it aside. Next there were a couple passports – they were real, obtained in the normal way, just with a fake name – a not-so-small stash of RX16SF, $50K in cash in four $10,000 bundles of $100s and five bundles of $2k in a mixture of small denominations. There was a Colt M45 semiautomatic pistol, along with a small box of magazines. There was also a Heckler and Koch HK G28 sniper rifle. Next to the sniper rifle, was a folded piece of paper. He took it out, unfolded it, and looked at it underneath the beam of his flashlight.

It was a printed copy of the DARPA Oversight Committee.

There were eight names.

He stared at the faces, memorizing them on sight, and knew that in the days to come, he would come to learn everything about each and every one of them.

He had to.

It was the only way he could be sure, before he erased them all.

Chapter Forty-One

The Gulfstream G650 took off along runway 10 at Mérida International Airport. It steadily climbed to ten thousand feet, before banking to the right and setting a course on a northern vector. In the luxurious comfort of the back of the privately owned jet, Sam and Tom sat at a desk, on a speaker phone to Elise. Sam brought her up to speed about the events at the Yucatán Peninsula as well as what the Secretary of Defense had to say about it.

When he was finished, Elise said, "So the Secretary of Defense ordered you to leave it the hell alone under the guise of national security. Is that right?"

"Yeah, that just about sums it up."

Elise paused, letting those words sink in for a minute. "Let me guess, you've decided to ignore her warnings – I mean, orders – and go after this Berserker gang even though they clearly are deeply connected to a US secret military program to test drugs on members of their special forces. Did I miss anything?"

Sam exchanged a glance with Tom, who appeared to be grinning. His arms spread out in a gesture of, *I told you Elise would see it rather the same way I do…*

Sam bit his lower lip. "No, I'd say that just about sums things up."

She said, "Very good. I just wanted to be clear on that."

Sam suppressed a retort. "What made you think that I couldn't just let it go?"

"Sam, in all the time I've known you, I don't think I have ever seen you simply let something like this go. You're like some sort of cavalier hero, that seems in desperate need to right all the wrongs in the world."

"Hey, not just all the wrongs. In this case, I was happy having a vacation. Hell, I was happy to let it go after I saved the kid's life. Where I lost interest in letting things go was when the same Berserkers succeeded in killing the kid and tried their darnedest to kill me. Since then, they've made two more attempts on my life, and succeeded in killing one of my friends. So no, I don't care that the Secretary of Defense asked me to leave it alone, I'd say I'm now pretty much involved in this thing, and I'll see it through to its grizzly end."

"That's good. I'm glad you don't disappoint. I just won a few hundred dollars."

"Really?" Sam asked. "Who took the bet?"

"Genevieve did, but I gave her odds of 10 to 1 that you wouldn't be able to leave this alone until you found out what was really going on."

Sam said, "Hey, I hate to think I'm so transparent."

Tom said, "I hate to think Genevieve would make such a terrible bet."

"Don't worry. She didn't want to. She said it was a bad bet and then I asked her what sort of odds she'd give it. When she said 10 to 1, I told her it was a deal. She tried to take it back, but I informed her we didn't do take-backs at my bookies."

"That makes more sense," Tom said. The jet began to bank, setting up its primarily northern course, before climbing to its cruising altitude of 50,000 feet, where they soared, high above any commercial jets. Tom stood up and mouthed to Sam, "I'm just going to have a chat with the pilots."

Sam nodded.

Elise said, "Okay, so what's your next move?"

"I need to find these Berserkers." Sam said, "According to the Secretary of Defense, a man named Dean Godkin upon discovering that the secret program he was involved in to test a drug called RX16SF was being shut down, went berserk, killed the cleanup team who were supposed to neutralize him and the other test subjects, and then, sold the chemical composition of the drug to a new drug cartel."

"These are the Berserkers who keep attacking you?"

"It would appear so."

"But you don't believe Dean Godkin's the one we have to worry about?"

"I have no idea what to think of Dean Godkin. I mean, his brother seemed to think that Dean was the good guy, and that by getting his half of the USB to Dean, his brother was going to bring to light everything they had spent two years trying to prove. Either way, it doesn't really matter. Godkin is special forces, he's high on this Berserker drug – RX16SF – which allegedly makes people highly intelligent, stronger, faster, and better at fighting as far as I can tell, and is highly addictive. If Godkin doesn't want to be found we'll never find him. No, we need to go after these Berserkers."

"Okay, so if we're buying into the Secretary of Defense's narrative that Godkin was selling the drugs to this street gang called the Berserkers, what makes you think that they have anything to do with whoever went down to the Yucatán and killed your friend?"

"I have a theory about that… I've been reviewing the images that Dr. Veracruz sent me. Originally, I was only interested in the one depicting the Hellenistic fleet, and brushed over the other ones with a glance. But now that I've had the time to look at them, I spotted one that I believe the people on the DARPA Oversight Committee might be willing to kill to suppress."

"Go on."

"It depicted a large cavern. Inside, Vikings drank from goblets and were then seen to transform into giants with massive weapons. The images appeared almost comical, but now that I look at them, it's easy to accept what they mean. It means the ancient Mayans knew that these Vikings had a place where they could drink something that made them incredibly strong and powerful."

"You think someone from DARPA got a hold of a similar archeological discovery and that it led them to find Valhalla?" Elise asked. "Where they then discovered RX16SF in its natural form?"

"Hey, it's a far-fetched long shot I know, but it's all I've got."

"Okay, so, hypothetically, let's say you're right. Veracruz's discovery might have shown the location of Valhalla, where this drug was being mined or extracted somehow. That explains why the DARPA Oversight Committee might send a ghost team down to the Yucatán to destroy all evidence of its existence, but if that's the case, why go after the Berserkers at all? I mean, they're just a street gang? A minor drug cartel? It's a problem, but not for you. Leave them to the DEA who are tasked with drug trafficking and distribution within the USA."

"Because one of the clean-up crew that killed Veracruz was also a member of the Berserker gang," Sam countered.

"Which means the Secretary of Defense is lying to you," Elise said.

"Or someone's lying to her. It doesn't matter. Either way, someone from DARPA is in bed with the Berserkers – and I intend to find out who."

"Okay, so what do you want me to look for?"

Sam said, "Well… Valhalla would be nice."

"I'll try a Google search for its coordinates, but I wouldn't hold your breath." Elise laughed. "You got anything else?"

"Yeah, I'm looking for early signs of Vikings in North America – most likely Canada."

Elise said, "Have you heard of L'Anse aux Meadows?"

Sam thought about all he'd heard of the 10th century Viking settlement on what is now the modern-day northernmost tip of the Great Northern Peninsula on the island of Newfoundland in the Canadian province of Newfoundland and Labrador. He shook his head. "I'm looking for something much older… or more recent."

"Which is it?" Elise asked. "You want an older Viking or a modern one?"

"Both. I'm looking for signs of Vikings dating back to the 1st century. They would be the Hellenistic fleet. I mean, if they made it as far south as the Yucatán, there has to be some sort of evidence of them farther north, right?"

In the background Elise was already hammering away at her keys, setting up search parameters for a program that would extract data from every newspaper, archeological paper, through to historical stories that might somehow be linked to what Sam was after. "Okay, what about the more recent things? What are you looking for?"

"This Berserker gang for one thing," Sam said. He paused, drew a breath. "But there's something else too. I don't know. Just search for something unusual. I mean, maybe we're going about this all wrong. Maybe, the Berserkers found the drug first, and approached the US government with it, who handed it to DARPA to test?"

She didn't try to hide the incredulity in her voice. "You think a street gang found a new drug and DARPA had a field day testing it out on our special forces?"

"Stranger things have happened."

"Talking about stranger things. I'm not getting any hit on this Berserker gang at all."

"I know! Neither did I when I did a basic Google search. I mean, if this thing has gone global, why the hell aren't the papers full of stories about these wannabe Vikings?"

"Good question."

A few minutes went by and Elise said, "Eureka."

Sam grinned. "You found something?"

Elise said, "Uh-huh, but you're probably not going to like it."

Sam's heart began to thump in his chest. It was a good sign when Elise said that he wasn't going to like it. "What have you got?"

"A woman from the small township of Kelsey, Manitoba."

Sam looked blank. "In Canada?"

"Uh-huh, unless you know of another Manitoba I don't know about?"

Sam ignored her tease. "Yeah, yeah, tell me about this woman."

"Apparently she wrote a letter to the local paper about Viking ghosts wreaking havoc each year in spring, just after a blood red moon."

"A blood red moon?"

"It's when the Earth's moon is in a total lunar eclipse. While it has no special astronomical significance, the view in the sky is striking as the usually whitish moon becomes red or ruddy-brown. It usually happens around twice a year."

Sam said, "I know what a blood moon is."

"Okay, I just thought I'd clear that up for you."

Sam arched an eyebrow. "What did the authorities have to say about it?"

"Not much. No one was ever charged."

"What did she say they did?"

"I'll let you read the story, but basically she says that on roughly the same day every year, a group of Viking ghosts descend on the town wreaking havoc, before changing into Berserkers and destroying everything in their paths, rampaging and stealing."

Sam said, "She sounds like some kind of conspiracy nut?"

"She might be." Elise admitted. "But she's got photos of the destruction... and she said they all had matching tattoos on their arms."

Sam held his breath. "Does she describe the tattoos?"

Elise grinned. "Yeah, they have an image of a Viking, with a horned helmet. They were all identical, only some of the men had teardrops next to the Vikings."

Sam swore. "That's it!"

"It looks like it."

"Okay, tell Matthew to set a course with the *Tahila* for the Hudson Bay!"

Tom finished chatting to the pilots and returned to the main lounge. He glanced at Sam. "You've got a plan?"

Sam nodded. "We're going to Kelsey, Manitoba..."

"Okay... and why are we going there?"

Sam grinned. "To chase Viking ghosts."

Chapter Forty-Two

Hudson Bay, Canada

The midnight sun dipped low on the horizon, casting a warm glow across the pristine shores of the Hudson Bay. A radiant display of green, red, and blue hues flashed across the sky, draped in a blanket of velvet blackness, pierced by the light of more than a thousand stars. The streaks of color, which danced like flames across the arctic clouds, were the northern aurora borealis, named after the Roman goddess of dawn – Aurora – and the Greek name for north wind – Borealis.

Beneath this magical display of nature, a ship motored silently.

Its dark, sharp-angled and low-lying hull gave the ship a predator like image, as though it was stalking some sort of mythical quarry beneath the sea – slicing through the darkness, leaving a white glow in its wake.

The motor yacht rounded Polar Bear Provincial Park and entered the Hudson Bay.

A black Eurocopter AS350 circled overhead, before quickly landing on the ship's helipad, despite the *Tahila* running at over sixty knots.

Sam Reilly stared at the last remnant of the sun in wonder. He'd seen the aurora borealis before, and the aurora australis in the southern hemisphere. But this was the first time he'd witnessed it above a midnight sky.

The midnight sun is a natural phenomenon that occurs in the summer months in places north of the Arctic Circle or south of the Antarctic Circle, when the sun remains visible at the local midnight. In the Arctic, the sun appears to move from left to right, but in Antarctica the equivalent apparent motion is from right to left. This occurs at latitudes from 65°44' to 90° north or south, and this doesn't stop exactly at the Arctic Circle or the Antarctic Circle, due to refraction.

Sam waited until Genevieve shut down the engine, and the whir of the rotor blades finally slowed to a complete stop, before he and Tom climbed out.

Matthew, the ship's skipper greeted Sam with a suppressed smirk on his face. "How was your vacation?"

Sam drew a deep breath. "You know damned well how my vacation went. Through no fault of my own, and simple stupid altruism, I tried to save a kid from drowning, and ever since then I've been punished for it!"

Veyron, the ship's engineer said, "And the Yucatán?"

Tom said, "He's had better trips."

Matthew said, "Was it as bad as Xibalba?"

Sam paused, thought about his earlier trip to the region with Tom. After navigating a submerged labyrinthian tunnel to reach the Mayan temple of the Death Gods, he and Tom had to battle warriors who were disguised as ancient Gods on the Xibalban ballcourt – the stakes of the game were life and death. He frowned. "I think it was worse than Xibalba."

"Wow. That bad hey?" Matthew said. "I'm sorry to hear that. Welcome back by the way."

"Thank you," Sam said. "I don't plan on being here too long. Genevieve's going to refuel the Eurocopter and I'll be flying out to meet someone in the morning."

"So I hear," Matthew suppressed a grin. "Something about chasing Viking ghosts?"

"Yeah, something like that... although I suspect these apparitions have a decidedly more mortal grounding and that there's a perfectly reasonably scientific explanation for her stories."

"Probably, either way, I suspect you and Tom will work it out."

"Actually, I'm going on my own."

Matthew's thin brows drew together. "You're not taking Tom with you?"

Sam exhaled a long breath. "No. This woman only wants to talk to me."

"You? Why?" Matthew asked. Then, before Sam could answer, he said, "How does she even know who you are?"

Sam spread his arms. "Apparently she's read my book and is interested in meeting me."

Matthew's face twisted into a mask of incredulity. "That biography you managed to pen in your spare time, detailing your bizarre archeological discoveries?"

"That's the one."

Matthew laughed. "I thought no one liked your book?"

"Some people liked it, but it mostly missed the mark. Everyone seemed to assume it was full of fictional tales and gross hyperbole of our sea adventures. The reviews suggest people liked the writing."

Matthew grinned. "If I recall correctly, those same people also argued that it was probably ghost written..."

Sam laughed, his face set with feigned indifference. "I don't care what they think."

"And the important thing is it was entertaining enough that some crazy woman from Manitoba – who thinks she's been seeing Viking ghosts – is willing to take you into her confidence."

"That's right."

Matthew said, "Do you think she's crazy?"

"Maybe, but from what I've read about her complaints, I think her troublesome ghosts are real."

Matthew placed a reassuring hand on his shoulder. "Get some rest."

"I will," Sam promised, "And in the morning, I'm going to find these Viking ghosts."

Chapter Forty-Three

Churchill, Manitoba

The *Tahila* dropped her anchor off the coast of Churchill.

Located on the western coast of the Hudson Bay, at the mouth of the Churchill River on the 58th parallel north, far above most Canadian populated areas, it was one of the most remote cities in Canada. Sam found himself naturally drawn to the place. Despite being modernized, it still held the romantic appeal of an old western outcrop, surrounded by true wilderness.

Sam and Tom loaded up the Eurocopter 350 Squirrel with arctic dive gear, along with an array of search equipment, including ground penetrating radar, sonar buoys, and bathymetric computers – just in the off chance he got lucky, and this woman from Kelsey led him to Valhalla. He threw in his diver propulsion vehicle for good measure.

Confident that he had all that he might need, Sam worked through the pre-flight checklist for the Eurocopter with Genevieve, pre-programming the GPS coordinates for Kelsey, and calculated the fuel requirements and potential flight range if he got his wish to scout the region where these Vikings had been sighted. Last, in a compartment in the cockpit, he secured a Mossberg 500 pump action shotgun. It was loaded with special 3 inch "Magnum" shells, with one in the chamber and five in the magazine. He threw in an additional box of shot-gun shells. Not because he was worried about fighting off Viking ghosts – or Berserkers for that matter – but because he was heading into the wild, where bears and other predator wildlife ruled supreme.

Sam sat in the cockpit, clasped the seatbelt across his waist and chest, switched on the aircraft's electrical system, and started the engine. The Turbomeca Arriel powerplant began to slowly turn the three-blade main rotor, which picked up speed until it became little more than a blur overhead.

Standing at the side of the open cockpit door, Tom asked, "Are you sure you'll be okay?"

"Yeah, I'll be fine." Sam licked his lips, a mischievous grin forming. He glanced out at the calm sea, toward Churchill. With a teasing lilt to his voice, he said, "Watch out for polar bears while you're waiting! I hear this entire region is riddled with them… I read something about Churchill having the highest number of polar bears of any region on earth. Apparently, they can swim pretty well, and climb onto boats."

"If they can board the *Tahila*, they're welcome to her," Tom said, refusing to take the bait. After all, the *Tahila* had more than eight feet of freeboard, that would stop any bears from boarding her. Instead, he returned to Sam. "Make sure you give me a call before you approach any Berserkers. Don't leave anything to chance with these people."

"I will," Sam promised, "But I'm doubting we'll see any today. According to the letter this woman wrote regarding Viking ghosts, they only came once a year during a blood moon, so I think we'll be safe. Besides, that was nearly two years ago and they haven't been around since."

Tom's brown eyes hardened. "All the same, trouble seems to follow you."

Sam suppressed a smile. "I'll have to admit, you might be right there. I'll be careful."

"All right, good luck," Tom said, closing the cockpit door and giving the side of the aircraft a reassuring rasp with his hand, to indicate it was good to go.

Sam glanced at the flight instruments. He confirmed that the engine oil was warm and the rotors had reached their desired RPM, and then began to perform the delicate balancing act between the collective pitch control, the cyclic pitch control, and the antitorque pedals developed through a lifetime at the controls, to take the Eurocopter 350 Squirrel to the sky.

The tri-blades changed their pitch, and with a violent thumping sound, the rotors began to produce more than three tons of downward pressure, whipping the placid sea below into a white frenzy beneath its downwash. At an altitude of fifty feet, Sam banked the helicopter into a southwestern direction, and began to pick up speed.

He tracked the Churchill River, where a pod of beluga whales joined thousands of other beluga whales, as they moved into the warmer waters of the Churchill River estuary to calf. The creatures were easily recognizable, even from the Eurocopter's altitude, thanks to their stark white coloring and globular head on the background of the almost turquoise river that snaked southwest.

After nearly twenty minutes, he banked to the south, leaving his view of the river behind in exchange for the verdant-blue of a dense forest, before eventually opening up across Split Lake, and finally landing in the front of a large rural estate on the southern edge of Kelsey – where a woman who might be a crazy conspiracy theorist, was waiting to greet him.

Chapter Forty-Four

Kelsey, Manitoba

The hum of the helicopter turned to silence, and the blades eventually slowed to a stop. Sam opened the cockpit door and stepped out.

A woman working on a blue BMW800ST touring motorcycle, stood up to greet him. There was an oily rag in her hand, which she used to wipe away the grease that covered her hands, as she walked.

Sam stepped forward to meet her, taking her in with a glance.

She was just a little shorter than him, with an athletic figure and determined stride, that suggested she'd spent a great deal of her life in the outdoors. She had jeans, leather boots, and a white T-shirt, over which she wore a leather jacket, proudly sporting the Toronto's Blue Jays. She had brown hair with blonde highlights, casually pulled back in a braid, intelligent brown eyes, and a mischievous smile. A black and white fox terrier followed obediently at her side.

"Sam Reilly?" she asked, shaking his hand.

"Yes. You must be Suttie," he said.

"That's me."

"Nice to meet you Suttie," Sam said, noting her firm handshake. He considered her name. The letter didn't include a surname, and he wondered whether she had intentionally done so to maintain her anonymity. "What's your surname? Or should I be asking what's your first name?"

She laughed, revealing a nice set of big white teeth. "Just Suttie is fine."

Sam didn't push it. "Okay."

He squatted down and patted the dog, who responded happily.

Suttie asked, "Do you want to come inside where we can chat?"

"Sure."

Sam followed her into a large kitchen. She put the kettle on and asked, "Can I offer you a drink?"

"Sure. Whatever you're having."

"Coffee. Full strength. Is that all right?"

Sam nodded. "Yes, thank you."

Suttie's eyes darted out the window, glancing toward the Eurocopter now parked on her front lawn. "Where have you come from? I assumed you would have taken a commercial flight to Kelsey airport."

"No, we were kind of in the area already."

"Oh yeah?" she asked. "Where's the *Tahila*?"

He paused, wondering how much she knew about him and the ship. "It's at anchor off the coast of Churchill."

"Really?" She smiled, her voice taking on a teasing lilt. "I hope they don't get attacked from polar bears."

Sam laughed for a few seconds, before it segued into genuine concern. "Wait… is that really a thing?'

"You want to know if you need to be careful of polar bears in Churchill?" She met his eye. "Yeah, of course it's a real thing."

"Oh… sorry, I just thought it was one of those things people joked about… like being careful of grizzly bears in Alaska, even though moose are responsible for far more deaths each year."

Her face flashed with genuine concern, and her tone turned serious. "You should really watch out for grizzly bears in Alaska, too."

Returning to Churchill, Sam said, "How worried should I be about my friends on the coast of Churchill?"

"Not too much. From what I've read, the *Tahila's* a pretty big ship. It's unlikely a polar bear's going to be able to climb on board. They should be fine."

"And when they go into town to kill time or have a drink?"

"Yeah, they should watch out for polar bears." She handed him a coffee.

"Thank you," Sam said, taking a sip.

Suttie went on, pleasure at his discomfort plastered across her face. "The Churchill region has one of the biggest polar bear denning areas in the world. The ice throughout Hudson Bay melts completely by the end of July or early August and does not refreeze until approximately early November. This means that all bears must come ashore for about 3-4 months. Polar bears were once thought to be solitary animals that would avoid contact with other bears except for mating. In the Churchill region, however, many alliances between bears are made in the fall. These friendships last only until the ice forms, then it is every bear for itself to hunt ringed seals."

"Do you get many tourists up here sightseeing?"

"To see Polar Bears?"

"Yeah."

"Starting in the 1980s, the town developed a sizable tourism industry focused on the migration habits of the polar bear. Tourists can safely view polar bears from specially modified vehicles built to navigate the tundra terrain. Utilizing a set of trails created by the Canadian and US military, responsible tour operators are granted permits to access these trails for wildlife viewing. Staying on these established trails ensures no further damage is done to the tundra ecosystem. October and early November are the most feasible times to see polar bears, thousands of which wait on the vast peninsula until the water freezes on Hudson Bay so they can return to hunt their primary food source, ringed seals. There are also opportunities to see polar bears in the non-winter months, with tours via boat visiting the coastal areas where polar bears can be found both on land and swimming in the sea."

Sam was intrigued, more than concerned. "How do the locals deal with the polar bears?"

She licked her lips. Her eyes flashing amusement. "To be honest, it just becomes a way of life. Many locals even leave their cars unlocked in case someone needs to make a quick escape from the polar bears in the area."

"You're kidding me?"

"No, I promise it's true!" She laughed. "In fact, the authorities maintain a so-called 'polar bear jail' where bears, generally adolescent males, who persistently loiter in or close to town, are held after being tranquilized, pending release back into the wild when the bay freezes over."

"Amazing," Sam said. "I love it."

A few minutes later, an older woman entered the kitchen. She glanced at Sam, back to Suttie. "Who's your friend, dear?"

"This is Sam Reilly, mom," Suttie said. Then, turning to Sam, she said, "This is my mom, Valerie."

Sam looked up, meeting her weathered, but intelligent gaze. "Pleased to meet you, ma'am."

Her mom nodded, but said nothing. Instead, she looked blank, as though the name didn't mean anything to her. Her eyes turned politely to Suttie, a wry smile plastered across her face, in a gesture that Sam couldn't quite make out.

Suttie appeared to get it, and said, "He wrote a book on ancient maritime archeology that I liked. I gave it to you to read. You said you liked it."

Her mom shrugged as though she either couldn't remember the book, or having read it, didn't care. Either way, she seemed too polite to say so. She whispered, "What's he doing here?"

Suttie smiled. "He's here to investigate our Viking ghosts."

"Ah," her mother smiled kindly with a newfound respect for him. "Bless your cotton socks! Those Viking ghosts have been driving us crazy for years. In fact, I think they've been getting worse."

Chapter Forty-Five

Sam said, "So tell me about the Vikings."

Suttie held her breath, indecision appeared to flash across her eyes, as though she wasn't sure how much to tell him or where to begin. If Sam had to guess, he figured she'd tried to tell the story to other people before, and had been told she was crazy. She let out a long exhale and said, "It happens only once a year in spring, during a blood-moon, the Vikings turn into Berserkers and raid the village."

"Interesting, how long has this been going on for?"

"This isn't just a recent thing. Stories about Viking ghosts raiding the region goes back centuries."

Sam suppressed his outward incredulity. "Centuries?"

"No kidding. This has been going on since my mom's grandmother was a little girl."

Sam studied her. He had no idea what to make of her story, or its veracity, but one thing was certain, she believed it. "You're serious, aren't you?"

"I sure am," she replied. "I can prove it to you…"

"Okay, prove it."

Suttie retrieved a family history book. It showed photos and drawings dating back more than a hundred years, when her great grandparents had taken on a large estate to try cattle farming in the region back in 1890. "Here, have a look at these."

Sam began to slowly flip through her family journal cum-photo album. A lot of the images depicted typical scenes of everyday farming life, including tractors and plows, while the rest of it showed family portraits ranging from current color photos, through to black and white, sepia, and some hand-drawn sketches. There were various images of some ancient clay pots that were purportedly found on the property and some weapons.

Still, nothing that explicitly cried out Viking encounter.

Sam asked, "How much land did your original family's property entail?"

"The original land rights were for some twenty thousand hectares and stretched from present day Kelsey, down the Nelson River to Sipiwesk Lake and Bear Island and all the land surrounding by roughly fifty miles."

"Wow, that's a lot of land!"

"It was a long time ago. Land was cheaper back then. The farm has been carved up and sold plenty of times since then, and now days, we just run a hobby farm."

Sam nodded, still flicking through her photo album. "There's some interesting artifacts here but I don't see anything that confirms your theory about Viking raiders?"

Suttie brought up a page which showed a series of artifacts found on the property over the years. There were clay pots, swords, knives, and other such images, but nothing that spelled Viking. Sam studied the images. "I've heard about L'Anse aux Meadows, but didn't realize any Vikings made it this far southwest?"

"Uh-huh…" she confirmed. "I'm certain of it. The rumors are that the Viking ghosts come out when there is a blood moon, and raid the village."

Sam wasn't buying any of it. "It's just legends."

"The best legends are based on just a little bit of truth."

Sam smiled, handing her his empty cup. "Who said that?"

Suttie laughed. "You did."

Sam grinned. "In my book?"

"Yeah, don't you remember?" She met his eye. "Maybe there's something to those whole ghostwriter rumors?"

Sam ignored the tease. "Did you like my book?"

"Ah… it was okay. Kind of amateurish, but a fun read. I wouldn't believe any of those things really happened."

Sam bit his lower lip. "Really?"

"Sure, hey… if half those stories are true, you've lived an amazing life."

"Thanks." Sam returned to their earlier conversation. "You said something about the best legends being based on just a little bit of truth?"

"Uh-huh."

His eyes narrowed, landing heavily on hers. "So what's the truth here?"

Suttie held his gaze, her voice solemn. "The ghosts came from that shipwreck."

"What shipwreck?"

"The Viking one."

"Wait, there's a Viking shipwreck nearby?"

"Yeah. It's at the bottom of Sipiwesk Lake, just off Black Bear Island."

"No kidding. How come I've never heard of it?"

"Not many people have. There's not a lot to look at. Viking ships, as you know, are basic and centuries of exposure to the harsh Manitoba elements have left this one particularly barren. I suppose no archeologist has ever taken the time to look at it."

Sam's eyes narrowed. "But you've seen it? Are you sure it's a Viking ship?"

"Yeah. I've SCUBA dived it plenty of times. I'm certain it's a Viking ship."

"What makes you so sure?"

"I'm sure."

Sam persisted. "It could be Dutch or French… or even British. I mean, an early settlers' shipwreck that's a few hundred years old tends to look just like a dilapidated Viking shipwreck once it's been under water long enough."

Suttie wouldn't give an inch. "Not this one. This one's a Viking shipwreck."

"Why?" Sam asked. "What makes you so sure?"

"Because once, when I was still young, I dived it and found a Viking sword."

Sam frowned. She looked a lot younger than him. Still, his heart lurched at the thought that she might have found a Viking sword. "Do you still have the sword?"

"Yeah," she went into a room at the back of the house and retrieved it, handing it to him to look at.

Sam stared at the sword.

Suttie asked, "What do you think?"

Sam drew an astonished breath. "I think it's a beautiful Viking sword."

Chapter Forty-Six

Sam examined the weapon.

At a glance he could tell it was Viking in origin. The hilt was ornate and decorated lavishly with gold and silver. The blade had been rusted through, but professionally repaired. A name was carved into the blade.

Gunnlogi.

Sam said, "Any idea what that means?"

"Uh-huh," she said, nodding to him. "I had someone translate it for me years ago. It means, *Battle Flame.*"

"A good name for a Viking sword."

He looked at the metal closer. Even though he wasn't a metallurgist, Sam could see the teardrop swirls. The sight made his throat go dry.

He frowned. "This is made of Damascus steel."

Even as he said it, his heart plummeted. If it was Damascus steel, that removed all chance of it being a Hellenistic shipwreck. How could it be, the Hellenistic fleet crossed the Atlantic during the 1st century, while Damascus steel only began to turn up during the 9th and 10th Century – placing the sword's origins as most likely part of the 10th Century exploration of North America by Vikings.

Suttie nodded. "Yeah, that's what the man said…"

"What man?"

"The metallurgist. I took it to a place in Toronto. There was a guy specializing in ancient antiques and I paid him to have a look at the sword."

Sam laughed. "Did you tell him where you found it?"

"No. Of course not!"

"Why not?"

"I didn't need every wannabe treasure hunter and adventurer coming up here and destroying our little part of the woods, while they searched for Viking treasure."

Sam considered that for a moment. "That's reasonable."

He thought about the sword's possible and yet unlikely origins. The remarkable characteristics of Damascus steel became known to Europe when the Crusaders reached the Middle East, beginning in the 11th century. They discovered that swords of this metal could split a feather in midair, yet retain their edge through many a battle with the Saracens. The swords were easily recognized by a characteristic watery or 'damask' pattern on their blades. Damascus steel was the forged steel of the blades of swords smithed in the Near East from ingots of Wootz steel imported from Southern India. These swords are characterized by distinctive patterns of banding and mottling reminiscent of flowing water, or in a 'ladder' or 'teardrop' pattern.

The sight suddenly made him realize the swirling teardrop pattern matched the image on the Berserker's tattoos. They weren't just signs or records of the Berserker's kills, but a tribute to the swords found nearby. It made him suddenly wonder, did the Berserkers find this Viking ship first, and develop their tattoos based on the images?

Suttie said, "You look disappointed?"

Sam shook his head. "No, it's just I was hoping the metal might indicate it came from even earlier."

Her eyes narrowed. "As in from the North American First People's metal work?"

"No, not quite that early," Sam said, thinking about the Old Copper culture that appeared more than 3,000 years BC – long before the Hellenistic fleet that sailed across eh Atlantic in the 1st Century. "Besides, as far as I know, Canada's First People never reached a point of actual metal work?"

"That's mostly true," Suttie admitted, "but that's not to say there were no metal works in pre-Columbian North America."

Sam said, "I've heard about the Old Copper culture. Where copper, found freely throughout the Great Lakes region, was used to make tools and weapons, particularly adzes, gouges, and axes."

"That's right," she said. "Native copper was relatively abundant, particularly in the Great Lakes region. The latest glacial period resulted in the scouring of copper bearing rocks. Once the ice retreated, these were readily available for use in a variety of sizes. Copper was shaped via cold hammering into objects from very early dates – as early as the Archaic period in the Great Lakes region – 8000–1000 BCE."

Sam frowned. "But no mining of copper?"

"There is some evidence of actual mining of copper veins, but disagreement exists as to the dates." She sighed, as though taking her time to recall her high school history lessons. "Extraction would have been extremely difficult. Hammerstones may have been used to break off pieces small enough to be worked. This labor-intensive process might have been eased by building a fire on top of the deposit, then quickly dousing the hot rock with water, creating small cracks. This process could be repeated to create more small cracks. The copper could then be cold-hammered into shape, which would make it brittle, or hammered and heated in an annealing process to avoid this. The final object would then have to be ground and sharpened using local sandstone. Numerous bars have also been found, possibly indicative of trade for which their shaping into a bar would also serve as proof of quality."

"Interesting," Sam said. "But their technology never progressed?"

Suttie's eyes stared off in the distance. "This Old Copper Culture never became particularly advanced, and never discovered the principal of creating alloys. This means that many, though they could make metal objects and weapons, continued to use their flint tools, which could maintain a sharper edge for much longer. The unalloyed copper could simply not compete, and in the later days of the Old Copper Culture the metal was almost exclusively used for ceremonial items."

Sam said, "They never worked iron?"

Suttie smiled. "From what archeologists have discovered, the North American First People worked extensively with iron in the Pacific Northwest."

"Really?" Sam asked. "I never knew that."

"Not many people do, but it's true." Suttie paused, thinking where to start. "Traditional ironwork in the Northwest Coast has been found in places like the Ozette Indian Village Archeological Site, where iron chisels and knives were discovered. These artifacts seem to have been crafted around 1613, based on the dendrochronological analysis of associated pieces of wood in the site, and were made out of drift iron from Asian – specifically Japanese – shipwrecks, which were swept by the Kuroshio Current towards the coast of North America."

"You're kidding," Sam said, thinking back to the wreckage of the *Hoshi Maru*, a Japanese trawler, damaged during the 2011 tsunami, only to be washed up on the coast of Oregon, nearly a decade later, after the Kuroshio Current had slowly dragged it across the North Pacific. "How often did Japanese shipwrecks land on the North American Coast?"

"A fair bit, I'd imagine." Suttie thought about it some more. "The tradition of working with Asian drift iron was well-developed in the Northwest before European contact, and was present among several native peoples from the region, including the Chinookan peoples and the Tlingit, who seem to have had their own specific word for the metallic material. The wrecking of Japanese vessels in the North Pacific basin was fairly common, and the iron tools and weaponry they carried provided the necessary materials for the development of the local ironwork traditions among the Northwestern Pacific Coast peoples, although there were also other sources of iron, like that from meteorites, which was occasionally worked using stone anvils."

"Interesting," Sam said, his mind returning to the Viking ship she'd originally started talking about. He held his breath. "Would you still know where that shipwreck is?"

"The Viking one?"

"Yeah," Sam confirmed.

She nodded. "Uh-huh. Why, do you want me to show you?"

His voice betrayed a sudden interest. "Can you?"

"That depends, did you happen to bring your SCUBA gear?"

"Yeah. It's in the helicopter."

"Then I would love to show you the Viking shipwreck."

Sam's lips curled into a grin. "That, Suttie, makes you my new found best friend."

Chapter Forty-Seven

Sipiwesk Lake, Manitoba

The Eurocopter 350 Squirrel flew south above Nelson River.

Sam carefully scanned the flight instruments, before gazing across the pristine landscape that fell beneath them. He and Suttie had remained mostly silent since taking off, with both of them lost in their own thoughts.

Suttie finally broke the silence. "You mentioned yesterday that you were in Nova Scotia recently on a driving vacation?"

Sam nodded. "Uh-huh."

"Where were you headed?"

"Nowhere in particular. Just enjoying the sights. I was planning on slowly driving across Canada from the east coast to the west. Why, have you got any recommendations?"

She arched an eyebrow. "Of sights to see in Canada?"

"Sure."

"How long do you have?" A pleasant smile flickered across her face. "It would take a lifetime to see Canada's natural wonders."

"Okay, my life's fairly full already. I don't know if I could add an additional one to it. How about an abridged version?"

"Well," Suttie paused, closing her eyes, as though mentally picturing her favorite places. When she opened them again, she said, "From National Parks – Banff, Jasper, Waterton, Elk Island and Wood Buffalo – through to the Hot Springs, and spring break up of the ice on the Saskatchewan River Alberta is a treasure trove."

"Those are your favorites?"

"Just in Alberta…"

Sam suppressed a grin. "Okay, that's not really narrowing it down much. What are your best memories when it comes to personal road trips?"

She paused a beat. Really giving it some thought. "My fondest memories still are the Northern lights farther north in Slave Lake as they were in vivid colors. They looked like they belonged on National Geographic or something David Attenborough might narrate. What else is there? I'd recommend heading to the south of Calgary to stop in at the Tyrell Museum of Paleontology where dinosaur bones and extinct shell fossils are prolific. The land is clay so when it rains the hills are mud slides. To my grief, my children found this out before me. If I had put them out to dry instead of washing them in the showers, they would have hardened into little statues, clothes and all."

Sam laughed at the description of her children, and despite not being a parent he could imagine children taking to the clay mud slides in an instant. "I'll have to remember to shower after playing in the clay."

"Be sure that you do," she said, her voice a little too serious. "I remember driving from Saskatchewan through to Manitoba… It was usually just a route on the Trans-Canada Highway while going to other places of interest. It is flat prairie for the most part. In saying that, we drove it at night during the Christmas season once. The moon cast a blue glow on the white fields, accentuated often with Christmas lights from sparsely spaced farmhouses. Another time, my daughter and I traveled by train through the night. There was a lightning storm across the prairie. Watching it was spectacular as you could see for unquestionable miles of flat prairie."

Sam smiled. "It's sounds like a nice trip to do with your daughter."

Suttie smiled, evidently lost in fond memories. "It was, I assure you."

Sam reached the end of the river, and at a hundred and twenty knots, the helicopter raced across the waters of Sipiwesk Lake, revealing the dark blue and turquoise waters. They passed a shallow section of the lake, where some beavers had damned an otherwise small estuary.

He slowed the helicopter to a hover, just long enough to cast his eyes along a large beaver dam. There were two of them, paddling on their backs, dragging a large log to add to the base of their dam. The creatures looked adorable without any stretch of one's imagination. Despite their razor-sharp teeth, one couldn't help but want to go and cuddle them.

There were hundreds upon hundreds of fallen trees scattered across the edge of the lake. The place was scarred with the jagged remains of tree stumps where beavers had gnawed their way through the main trunks of fully grown trees.

A wry smile crossed Sam's face. "What the hell are they doing?"

Suttie glanced at him, her face a mask of surprise, as though he'd asked a question akin to, *Why does the sun come up in the morning?* When she realized he was serious, she said, "They're building a dam."

Sam suppressed a retort. "Yeah, I do get that… I mean, why are they building a dam? What are they trying to achieve?"

"Oh… you're serious."

"Yeah!"

"Oh, right. I'll bring it back to the basics. A beaver dam is made of logs and mud, which blocks or slows down the flow of water in a river or stream. It raises the level of the stream it plans to live on and the increased water area becomes a new wetland and home to fish, turtles, frogs, birds and ducks."

"For the beavers to eat?"

Suttie shook her head. "No. Beavers are strict herbivores – AKA – vegetarians."

"So why do they dam the creeks and streams?"

She shrugged. "To make a bigger space to live."

Sam glanced at the miles upon miles of lakes. "Does this region have enough natural habitats for beavers?"

"Sure, but there are a lot of beavers."

"That sounds like it could be a real problem."

"It is," she said. "Beaver have also become problematic in other areas. In the Interlake farming region of Manitoba, about 120 miles north of Winnipeg, people have been complaining about the pesky rodents flooding pasture land. Last year the provincial government spent about $160,000 removing dams along with some 5,600 nuisance beavers."

"Wow. I had no idea it was that bad," he said, banking the helicopter, and continuing along their original course.

Suttie said, "It's worse in Argentina."

Sam frowned. "Argentina. What are beavers doing in South America?

"It's the usual sort of mistake humans tend to make. Nothing quite like landing in hell for all one's good intentions."

"What happened?"

"Beavers were supposed to "enrich" Patagonia, economically and ecologically. At least that was the ambition of Argentina's military when it flew 10 pairs of Canadian beavers from Manitoba to Tierra Del Fuego, Argentina's southernmost province, in 1946. The soldiers set the beavers loose on the shores of Lake Fagnano in hopes of spurring a fur trade and attracting more residents to the sparsely populated area."

"Just ten beavers. It's a wonder they survived the harsh conditions."

"There was some concern about the fragility of the experiment. Beavers are monogamous. If one of the animals were to die, its mate would be unlikely to reproduce. But such worry was misplaced. While the fur trade never materialized, what did explode were beaver numbers."

"What did that do to their local ecology?"

"In their wake they left phantom forests. North American trees have evolved over millions of years to survive beavers' industrious chewing. Trees like willow, cottonwood, American beech, and alder have all evolved responses to beaver chewing and flooding. They re-sprout when you cut them down, produce defensive chemicals, and tolerate wet soils. But because beavers are not native to South America, the continent's trees have not developed the same defenses."

"What are they doing about it?"

"The government's spent a fortune combating the problem, but a number of wildlife volunteers are spending months there hunting and culling the creatures."

"The poor beavers," Sam said. "I realize it's not to kill animals. It's to save the ecosystem. It's not the beavers' fault – cutting down trees is in their nature. The blame rests with humans."

"Exactly."

Up ahead, Bear Island approached to the south. Suttie pointed toward an inlet on the western side of the island. Sam flew overhead, circling around. The water was quite shallow. Probably just thirty or so feet deep. The inlet was surrounded by a steep rocky outcrop more than a hundred feet high in all directions. At the very end, a small forest of dark green tropical plants appeared out of place in the cool climate within a small rocky cavern. As with so much of Manitoba, a beaver dam blocked the entrance.

And in the middle of the bay, the remains of a shipwreck were clearly visible.

Chapter Forty-Eight

Sam brought the Eurocopter down to land on a nearby beach.

The downwash of the rotor blades whipped up the still water of the lake's edge into a frenzy of white, foamy water, and the broad leaves of nearby peachleaf willow and aspen blew and bent over in the draft. He switched off the engine, and the nearby trees righted themselves once more.

Sam stepped out of the helicopter and confirmed that the skids had found suitable perch on the gravelly shore, despite being less than a dozen feet from the inlet water's edge. The lake returned to its previous state of calm, and a casual glance across the beach showed no signs of a recent shift in the water's height, reassuring him that there was no unusual tide system like the one he'd witnessed at St. Martins in the Bay of Fundy.

He ran his eyes across the shore, up to the rocky cliffs and surrounding forest. The shore was a sea of white stones, smoothed flat through centuries of abrasion by the water. He picked up a white stone. The limestone rocks weren't simple rock, he noticed on closer inspection. They were made out of layers upon layers of sediment. Sediment packed into compact plaques of hard limestone and inside there was a fossilized fish. He lifted his gaze and realized the entire shore was filled with fossils.

Sam handed a rock to Suttie. "Any idea where these fossils came from?"

"A tropical sea during the Ordovician period," Suttie said, handing him the stone back. "You can keep it as a souvenir."

His eyes locked with hers, trying to judge if she'd just made it up. "Seriously?"

"Yeah, my dad told me when I was a kid and used to play here, and then when I was older, I went to the effort of looking it up myself. It turns out, the Ordovician Period lasted almost 45 million years, beginning 488.3 million years ago and ending 443.7 million years ago."

"There you go," Sam said, placing the stone in one of the lockers at the rear of the helicopter.

Suttie stretched her legs. Her eyes swept the turquoise waters toward the entrance to the inlet. It was still a couple hundred feet across the lake, and the wreck site was at least another five hundred feet from the entrance to the inlet.

She met his eye, and, as though reading his thoughts, she said, "I hope you've got a boat in the back of that helicopter, or we're going to have one heck of a long surface swim."

He nodded. "Yeah, a small inflatable Zodiac."

They quickly unloaded the boat first. Sam snapped open the inbuilt carbon dioxide canister, and the boat inflated in a matter of seconds to the sudden sound of high-pressured gas finding its freedom, the same way many lifejackets and lifeboats inflate. He retrieved the Honda 10 horsepower motor and attached it to the back of the boat, before pulling the Zodiac to the edge of the water.

Next, they donned their dry suits and dive equipment. After checking each other over, they were in the Zodiac heading out to the wreck site. All in total, it was just under half an hour, between landing the helicopter, anchoring at the wreck, and entering the water.

The water was shallow. Not much more than thirty feet at the bottom and they were SCUBA diving with single tanks of air, which, for that depth, would provide them ample bottom time with no decompression stops.

Suttie was first in the water. A moment later, Sam attached his fins, adjusted his facemask, placed the regulator in his mouth, before rolling backward into the water. On the surface Sam exchanged a glance with Suttie who confirmed she was good to go, making the okay signal with her thumb and index finger joined, and her remaining three fingers pointed up. Sam pointed his thumb down, confirming he was going to commence his descent.

Sam dipped his head into the water. The visibility was excellent. Somewhere in the vicinity of a hundred feet. From the surface, he could clearly make out the entire shape of the shipwreck. The combination of freshwater, protected and still water within the end of inlet, along with coldness, made the water quality perfect for diving.

A moment later, he released air from his buoyancy control device, sending a small burst of bubbles to the surface, and immediately began his descent, following the rope anchor all the way to the bottom, where it rested just west of the shipwreck.

He swallowed, equalizing the pressure in his ears, and followed as Suttie led the way to the wreck site. Even as he approached, Sam was certain that the ship had once been a Viking longboat. Only the skeletal shell remained intact and sticking above the sandy bottom of the lake, with much of the hull hidden beneath centuries of silt deposits.

Sam made a lap around the exterior of the shipwreck, before entering from above. There wasn't much to see, or do. In fact, on closer inspection, only the exterior of the hull was fully buried in silt. The internal hull – if you could call it that – was actually completely exposed. A small school of mature sturgeon fish swam by.

He recalled that sturgeons were primarily benthic feeders, which meant they ate everything and anything that might lay on the bottom layer, such as shells, crustaceans, and small fish. Fundamentally, they were ground suckers. And having taken a liking for whatever barnacles had once inhabited the hull, the creatures had done Sam's job for him, by clearing everything out far better than he could have after a week with a suction dredge.

Sam met Suttie's eye.

She gave a kind of shrug, that said, *well, what do you think?* Sam gave the all-good signal with his hand, and a smile that well reflected that he was enjoying the dive. She smiled back at him and then pointed enthusiastically toward the aft of the wreck, as though there was something way more interesting to see back there. Something he had to see.

Sam happily followed her.

Despite there being nothing in the way of Viking artifacts, the fact remained, he was staring at a 10th century Viking ship, deep within Manitoba – somewhere no other archeologists had found verifiable evidence of Viking travel.

Suttie stopped and pointed to a large clay pot resting on the bottom of the hull.

Sam froze. His heart thumping against his ribcage. Suddenly everything had changed. His interesting, yet uneventful dive of the remains of a 10th century shipwreck instantly became the most interesting thing he'd seen in a very long time.

Because, there, in front him…

Lay something that didn't belong.

Certainly not on board a 10th century Viking ship. The pot, came from an entirely different period of time, altogether.

Chapter Forty-Nine

Sam pulled the Zodiac up onto the shore.

Suttie began doffing her SCUBA gear, laying it all out on an outstretched tarpaulin. She studied him, as he removed his gear without saying anything. He had a big grin on his face, and his heart still hammered in his chest at the implications of the clay pot, but he wanted to clean it first, just to be sure.

Sam worked in silence, driven by some sort of innate desire to prove a point to himself, before revealing it to his host. He retrieved a small electrically powered water pump from the trunk of the helicopter, attaching a small hose from it to the lake's edge, using it to hose away the centuries of dirt on the pot. His eyes critically examined the structure, like an art dealer might study a masterpiece.

The single clay pot had two handles and a neck that was considerably narrower than the body. Painted on the side of the pot was a depiction of two warriors fighting. One with a hammer the other with a spear. Something about the decorations made him think of the weapons of the great Viking gods – the Hammer of Thor, and the Spear of Odin – even that seemed highly out of place, unless the timeline of the Viking gods needed to be significantly readjusted.

He turned it over.

Painted on the side of the pot was a butterfly. The color had faded, but it might have once been dark blue, or even purple. The creature seemed to have a double set of eyes on the back of its wings, which played the illusion of appearing to track his movements as he turned the jar around. The lid had long ago decayed or been broken, and inside he was rewarded with nothing but murky water.

Finally, unable to take it any longer, Suttie asked, "So, what do you think?"

The crease of a smile teased his lips. His voice and tone, appearing to hide some sort of secret disappointment. "Well, it's a 10th century Viking ship."

"Definitely 10th century?"

"Yeah, most likely. We'd have to organize carbon dating of the hull to be precise, but it will most likely come up somewhere around there. Dendrological studies of the wood might even be able to identify the location of the forest where the trees were felled that made up the ship. I'd be willing to bet it didn't come from nearby forests in Canada. Most likely, the wood is pine from Norway and Sweden, or oak from Denmark."

She pulled back a whisp of brown-blonde hair from her eyes, tucking in behind her ear. "But I thought the Norsemen who discovered North America came from Greenland?"

He looked at her and said, "They did – or at least that's what archeologists believe – yet that doesn't mean their ships did. I don't know if you've ever been to Greenland, but forests of tall hardwood trees don't exist there. In fact, the only forest they have on the island is contained within a small valley, called Qinngua – where a tiny thicket, consisting mainly of downy birch and gray-leaf willow grow."

She held his gaze. "I take it those sorts of trees weren't very good for shipbuilding?"

"Not even close. Trade was highly important to the Greenland Norse and they relied on imports of lumber due to the barrenness of their homeland. In turn they exported goods such as walrus ivory and hide, live polar bears, and narwhal tusks." He drew a breath. "Sorry, I'm getting sidetracked. The upshot is, yes... I believe you're right, this is a 10th Century Viking shipwreck."

Suttie pushed his arm, playfully. "I told you so... you look surprised!"

"Not surprised. Just disappointed."

Her eyes narrowed. "Why?"

"A friend of mine, an archeologist in Mexico recently found evidence that a 1st Century Hellenistic fleet was the first Europeans to explore North America. And I was hoping this was that place…"

"And now you're certain it isn't?"

"No."

"Why?"

"That Viking sword for one thing. It was made from Damascus steel which we know for a fact wasn't developed until the 10th Century at the very earliest…"

He stopped and Suttie sensed he was holding back on something. "What is it?"

Sam grinned. "Well, the thing is… that ship's somewhat of an anomaly now… in fact, it's an anachronism by definition – a chronological inconsistency and mismatch of persons, events, objects, language terms and customs from different time periods."

Suttie's eyes widened, flashing interest. There was a mocking laughter hidden behind them. She smiled. Great smile. Lots of teeth. She opened her mouth to ask something, then closed it again, as though not quite sure where even to begin, before finally settling with, simply asking, "Why?"

"The Viking sword is distinctly 10th Century, minimum, but this clay pot…" Sam said, looking at the innocuous looking clay pot as though it were priceless. "This clay pot is something entirely different."

"Yes?" She asked, "What about the clay pot?"

"It's classic 1st Century Hellenistic pottery called amphorae. As you can see, the two-handled pot has a neck that is considerably narrower than the body."

She nodded. "I can see the shape. Why? What was it used for?"

"It was used for the storage of liquids and solids such as grain. The containers had a pointed bottom and characteristic shape and size which fit tightly against each other in storage rooms and packages, tied together with rope and delivered by land or sea. The size and shape have been determined from at least as early as the Neolithic Period."

Suttie drew a breath. "Sam... What are you saying?"

He exhaled slowly. "I'm saying that I believe that this is a 10th Century Viking ship, that found the remains of the 1st Century Hellenistic fleet... that this ship is the last link to one of the greatest archeological treasures of North America – something I've been trying to find for a very long time."

She placed her hands akimbo and laughed. "And what's that?"

Sam beamed with excitement. "A place called Valhalla."

Chapter Fifty

They made a second dive an hour later.

Sam stared at the wreck site from directly above for several minutes, just taking in the image of the longship. His mind, mentally filling in the gaps, trying to picture the original Viking ship. Longships were characterized as graceful, long, wide and light, with a hull designed for speed. The ship's shallow draft allowed navigation in waters only three feet deep and permitted arbitrary beach landings, while its light weight enabled it to be carried over portages or used bottom-up for shelter in camps. They were also double-ended, the symmetrical bow and stern allowing the ship to reverse direction quickly without a turnaround. This trait proved particularly useful at northern latitudes, where icebergs and sea ice posed hazards to navigation.

Somewhere, in the recess of his mind, Sam thought he saw something that didn't belong. An outpoint, or visual oddity to the fundamental structure of the ship. He slowly circled the outline of the wreck, confident that the fault would eventually seep from his subconscious mind into his more useful consciousness.

As he swam, he considered the normal construction of a Viking ship.

The Viking shipbuilders had no written diagrams or standard design plan. The shipbuilder pictured the longship before its construction, based on previous builds, and the ship was then constructed from the keel up. The keel and stems were made first. The shape of the stem was based on segments of circles of varying sizes. The keel was an inverted T shape to accept the garboard planks. In the longships the keel was made up of several sections spliced together and fastened with treenails.

The next step was building the strakes – the lines of planks joined endwise from stem to stern. Nearly all longships were clinker – also known as lapstrake – built, meaning that each hull plank overlapped the next. Each plank was hewn from an oak tree so that the finished timber was about 0.98 inches thick and tapered along each edge to a thickness of about 0.79 inches. The planks were radially hewn so that the grain was approximately at right angles to the surface of the plank. This provided maximum strength, an even bend and an even rate of expansion and contraction in water. This is called in modern terms quartersawn, and has the least natural shrinkage of any cut section of wood.

The plank above the turn of the bilge, the meginhufr, was about 1.5 inches thick on very long ships, but narrower to take the strain of the crossbeams. This was also the area subject to collisions. The planks overlapped and were joined by iron rivets. Each overlap was stuffed with wool or animal hair or sometimes hemp soaked in pine tar to ensure water tightness.

Amidships, where the slats were straight, the rivets are about 6 inches apart, but they were closer together as the planks swept up to the curved bow and stern. There was considerable twist and bend in the end ones. This was achieved by use of both thinner and narrower planks. In more sophisticated builds, forward planks were cut from natural curved trees called reaction wood. Planks were installed unseasoned or wet.

Partly worked stems and sterns have been located in bogs. It has been suggested that they were stored there over winter to stop the wood from drying and cracking. The moisture in wet planks allowed the builder to force the planks into a more acute bend, if need be; once dry it would stay in the forced position. At the bow and the stern builders were able to create hollow sections, or compound bends, at the waterline, making the entry point very fine.

In less sophisticated ships short and nearly straight planks were used at the bow and stern. Where long timber was not available or the ship was very long, the planks were butt-joined, although overlapping scarf joints fixed with nails were also used.

As the planks reached the desired height, the interior frame – known as futtocks – and cross beams were added. Frames were placed close together, which was an enduring feature of thin planked ships. Viking boat builders used a spacing of about 33 inches. Part of the reason for this spacing was to achieve the correct distance between rowing stations and to create space for the chests used by Norse sailors as seats called thwarts.

The bottom futtocks next to the keel were made from natural L-shaped crooks. The upper futtocks were usually not attached to the lower futtocks to allow some hull twist. The parts were held together with iron rivets, hammered in from the outside of the hull and fastened from the inside with a rove – also known as a washer. The surplus rivet was then cut off. A ship normally used about 1,500 pounds of iron nails.

In some ships the gap between the lower uneven futtock and the lapstrake planks was filled with a spacer block roughly 8 inches long. In later ships spruce stringers were fastened lengthwise to the futtocks roughly parallel to the keel. Longships had about five rivets for each yard of plank. In many early ships treenails were used to fasten large timbers. First, a hole was drilled through two adjoining timbers, a wooden peg inserted which was split and a thin wedge inserted to expand the peg. Some treenails have been found with traces of linseed oil suggesting that treenails were soaked before the pegs were inserted. When dried the oil would act as a semi-waterproof weak filler or glue.

It was thinking about the thwarts that made Sam pause. Something about the seats-cum-chests used by Vikings at their rowing stations, that made him finally see it. There appeared to be a disparity between the length of the exterior hull and the internal hull. Specifically, there was an additional spacing of roughly two feet at one end of the hull. Something, that, like the ancient Greek amphorae, was an anachronism.

In later years, ship builders went on to incorporate such gaps as a safety measure in the case of a seagoing collision. But Vikings did not. In fact, it was a classic design of a longboat that a clean hull ran the length of the ship. Vikings stored their treasure in thwarts, which were connected straight to the main hull and used as rowing benches.

Sam considered that.

It wasn't inconceivable that the shipwright or possibly even the owner might have built a secret hold in which to store his most valuable treasures, such as gold trinkets and whatnot. The owner, like so many sailors throughout history, would most naturally have wanted to build a secret locker.

Sam ran his eyes across the shipwreck again.

If the ancient Viking owner had desired such a thing, it could only have ever been at that specific point toward the very end of the aft section of the hull.

There was only one way to find out.

He drew his dive knife from its sheath across his lower calf and used the blunt tip of the blade to chip away at the edge of the wood. The ancient grain gave way, revealing a hidden opening. He peeled back the wood to reveal the remains of a hidden storage compartment. Suttie stopped next to him, her eyes wide and luminous at the discovery.

Sam shined the beam of his flashlight into the dark abyss.

Only the outline of a wooden box glowed back at him. He and Suttie used their hands to pull away more of the storage compartment's façade, until he was able to retrieve the entire box. It was quite large. Roughly four feet wide, two long, by one deep. Sam tried to pull it free, but the entire side wall of the box, still visible, came free.

Centuries of silt parted, and the visibility inside reduced to near zero.

Sam fixed the beam of his flashlight inside, trying to penetrate the haze. At first, he was rewarded by only darkness, but as he circled the arc around, he was greeted by something... something entirely unexpected.

A sharp glow, pierced the debris, and glared back at him.

For a second, Sam thought he was witnessing a strange, luminous sea creature because it seemed so intensely bright. He stared at it, his eyes narrowing, as he tried to make sense of his discovery. It appeared to be a small stone. Some sort of crystal by the looks of things. Shaped like a rhombohedron, the three-dimensional figure was like a cuboid, except its faces were formed in the shape of a rhombi instead of rectangles. He reached in, extending his arm all the way inside, up until his shoulder prevented him from going any deeper, and grabbed the stone in his left hand.

It was smaller than he expected, fitting neatly in the palm of his hand.

He quickly withdrew it, placing it in a small dive bag Suttie held open for him, zipping the bag up afterward to be certain he didn't lose his find. Sam carefully reached inside and, using only his fingers and sense of touch, searched for anything else of value that might have been secured all these years. His hands landed on a small stone tablet. Excited, he quickly pulled it free. At a glance, he could tell there had once been writing on the stone, but centuries worth of silt and debris had stained it, rendering it unreadable without proper cleaning. He stored it with the crystal and continued searching the secret compartment.

His next two attempts proved fruitless.

On his very last one, his fingers touched something flat. He carefully gripped it in his fingers, and withdrew it slowly, not quite sure what it was he even had.

Sam placed it in his hand and fixed his flashlight on the strange device.

It was circular, like a disc, and made of some sort of ancient hardwood. He secured the device in his dive bag, made a final sweep of the hidden compartment with his right hand in the off chance he'd overlooked something.

Suttie fixed her flashlight on the device. Beneath her dive mask, her lips curled with curiosity, and she turned the palms of her gloved hands outward, as if to say, *what is it?*

Sam turned his thumb upward, indicating they should surface, and find out.

They surfaced quickly, Suttie climbing on board the Zodiac first, with Sam passing up the dive bag with their assorted goodies, before following her on board.

He stared at the three items, now clearly visible in the daylight.

Sam ran his eyes across the artifacts. "A crystal rhombohedron, a stone tablet with some sort of writing, and a wooden disc. Not bad for a day's work?"

"Not bad at all," Suttie agreed.

Sam picked up the tablet first, running his eyes across the indecipherable markings etched into its face.

Suttie asked, "Any idea what it is?"

"I think… that is to say, I hope it's a navigational rune stone. The Vikings themselves wrote short messages in runes on wood and stone when they sailed so that they could retrace their journeys if need be."

She glanced at the strange markings. "What language is that?"

"Runic," Sam said without hesitation.

Suttie's eyes locked on the runic script. "What does it say?"

Sam shook his head. "I have no idea. I'll have to get it translated, but I'm hoping it will have various navigational notes about the voyage they had undertaken. If we're lucky, and I mean, really lucky, they will have made reference to Valhalla or wherever they found this amphorae pot. Surely wherever they found it would have been note-worthy enough to mark in the rune stone."

Suttie turned her gaze toward the second stone. The strange shaped crystal. "What about the other one?"

Sam's eyes lit up in awe. "That... Suttie, is called a sunstone."

She held her breath for a second. "I thought Viking sunstones were a myth?"

"So did I. Even though Norse sagas are filled with tales of navigating through deadly clouds with the use of a sunstone, no one has ever discovered a sunstone at a Viking archeological site, or longboat shipwreck."

Suttie grinned. "Until now."

Sam nodded. His eyes wide. "Until now."

Chapter Fifty-One

On the beach Sam studied the three devices.

Sam said, "Vikings could read and write quite well for the time. They used a non-standardized alphabet, called runor, built upon sound values. While there are few remains of runic writing on paper from the Viking era, thousands of stones with runic inscriptions have been found where Vikings lived."

Suttie said, "And you're hoping this runic stone, holds the secret location of Valhalla?"

"That would be nice." Sam drew a breath. "Realistically, once these artifacts are on board the *Tahila* where they can be photographed and studied properly, we should be able to get a good idea where your Viking ship has traveled. We know it reached some location where the 1st Century Hellenistic fleet had once existed because of the amphorae we found. Ergo, the navigator must have made a note of it… and hopefully that note is in the runic stone. In all reality, we'll probably find a series of locations along a certain latitude. Then, we can backtrack, and try and re-discover what they found."

"Sounds complicated."

"Not so much complicated as time consuming. Marine archeology, you'll find is an art as much as a science, and then again, sometimes you just have to get lucky."

Suttie smiled wistfully. "Tell me about the Sunstone."

"What do you want to know?"

"Everything."

Sam grinned. "I'm not sure I can tell you all that much."

"Do you know how it worked?"

"Uh-huh…" Sam paused, thinking about what he'd read years ago about the unique device. "Viking seafarers knew how to use the altitude of the sun at midday and the stars to estimate latitude which was helpful when sailing to a destination of known latitude. Depth sounding was probably used in the Baltic Sea, but not in the deeper waters of the Atlantic.

"Viking navigators were close observers of sea and weather conditions. The behavior of sea birds could indicate the presence of land nearby, and cloud formations in an otherwise cloudless sky could suggest land just over the horizon." Sam turned the palms of his hands outward, in a gesture resonating the simple fact of life for the Viking seafarers. "You must remember that the Vikings were often at the mercy of the weather and shipwrecks were common. The discoveries of Iceland, Greenland and Vinland were all made when Viking ships were blown off course during extreme weather conditions."

"To avoid getting lost on their voyages across the North Atlantic 1000 years ago, Vikings relied on the sun to determine their heading. This was long before magnetic compasses were available in Europe by the way. But cloudy days could have sent their ships dangerously off course, especially during the all-day summer sun at those far-north latitudes. The Norse sagas mention a mysterious sunstone used for navigation. It is believed that these sunstones could have been calcite crystals and that Vikings could have used them to get highly accurate compass readings even when the sun was hidden."

"That much I kinda know, but how do they work?"

Sam said, "The trick for locating the position of the hidden sun is to detect polarization, the orientation of light waves along their path. Even on a cloudy day, the sky still forms a pattern of concentric rings of polarized light with the sun at its center. If you have a crystal that depolarizes light, you can determine the location of the rings around the hidden sun."

Suttie said, "That sounds pretty smart for people going back to the 10th Century."

"Like I said, Vikings were no dummies. Despite what modern TV shows might have us believe about their brutality, they were scholars and highly intelligent people."

"So what sort of crystal did they use to depolarize the sun?"

Sam said, "Calcite is such a crystal. It has a property called birefringence."

"Bio... what?"

"Birefringence. It basically means that light passing through calcite is split along two paths, forming a double image on the far side. The brightness of the two images relative to each other depends on the polarization of the light. By passing light from the sky through calcite and changing the crystal's orientation until the projections of the split beams are equally bright, allowing them to take a sun reading even when cloud cover would otherwise have prevented it."

"So what... did they just hold the crystal up against the sky?"

"No. That's where the Uunartoq disc comes in," Sam said, holding up the wooden disc they'd found. "They used a chunk of calcite from Iceland spar, a rock familiar to the Vikings, and locked it into a wooden device that beams light from the sky onto the crystal through a hole and projects the double image onto a surface for comparison. They then used it over the course of a completely overcast day. They took the measurements from a point on land where they knew the sun's exact trajectory."

Sam paused, waiting for any questions. When Suttie simply nodded, he kept going.

"Like a sundial, a sun compass features a vertical pin. The sun's rays cause the pin to cast a shadow which is longer in the morning and late afternoon and shortest at solar high-noon, and this shadow is used to create gnomonic lines. The disc is placed in a fixed level position and an observer regularly marks the shifting position of the pin tip's shadow across the disc during the course of the day. When these position marks are connected, the result is a west-to-east gnomonic line that comes closest to the vertical pin at high-noon. In the northern hemisphere, a straight line drawn from the base of the pin to that closest high-noon position will point directly to true north, which will then serve as the compass' north index mark. The gnomonic line will be essentially straight during the vernal and autumnal equinoxes, and downward concave at the summer solstice."

Suttie stared at the Uunartoq disc. There were dozens of small grooves marked into the disc. "Any idea what these are?"

"I'd have to look at some charts and find an expert on the subject, but I have a fair guess what they might represent."

"Well... go on, don't keep me guessing."

"All right. One theory is that a Uunartoq disc, used in conjunction with a sunstone allowed the user to determine their latitude as well as a compass heading. A number of researchers from the University of Hungary, pointed to a series of very short inscribed lines stacked atop one another on the disc's north index mark, whereas gnomonic lines by necessity run from west to east across the sun compass's face. Under this theory, the disc's user would have made a reference point at the north index mark at high-noon just prior to departure and then made subsequent high-noon marks during the course of the journey, and compared these against their home's reference point. If the journey's marks were in the same position as the home reference point, it meant that the user had been maintaining a consistent latitude. A high-noon mark coming in below the home reference meant that one was further south."

Sam said, "A modern replica showing how a course of Northwest by West may have been plotted by the Uunartoq disc's user around the time of the summer solstice. The traveler rotates the disc while keeping it level until the vertical gnomonic pin tip's shadow touches the summer solstice gnomonic line, which reveals the direction of true north. The traveler then turns the horizontal directional pin five compass points to the west for NWbW, and adjusts course to match the direction of the pin."

"Sounds amazingly complicated," Suttie said. "Now what?"

Sam thought about it for a moment. He was keen to get his finding back on board the *Tahila* where they could be better examined. They might still return to the wreck site with a metal detector, but he doubted it would help him find anything – certainly nothing as valuable as the sunstone and navigational runestone, which might open the door to Valhalla. Still there was one thing that he'd like to still see before leaving the area.

He said, "I saw a cave at the end of the inlet. I wouldn't mind checking it out."

"Sure. What do you expect to find?"

"Nothing to be honest. Some artifacts might have washed ashore, but if they had and they've been exposed to the elements above water, all evidence of them have probably been destroyed centuries ago."

"So why do you want to go there?"

Sam shrugged. "No reason, really. I just need to rule out missing something obvious."

Chapter Fifty-Two

Sam motored the Zodiac round the bend and entered the inlet for the third time that day. This time, as he cruised toward the Viking wreck, he didn't slow to a stop. Instead, he kept going, motoring all the way up to the very end of the inlet. His eyes ran across the jagged and vertical cliffs, a mixture of limestone and granite, polished smooth by millions of years of being weather beaten.

"There must have been no survivors," Suttie said, her words wistful.

Sam frowned. "Survivors?"

"From the Viking ship," she explained. "I know that it was many centuries ago, but it's still a shame to think that those brave explorers simply perished on the far side of the world, away from everything they had ever known."

He thought about that for a second. "What makes you say there weren't?"

"Well, if there were, you would think that they would have inevitably intermingled with the North American First Peoples of the region, and their descendants would have ended up with blond hair, generally being the more dominant genetic trait."

"There aren't any blond haired First People in Manitoba?"

"Not that I've heard of. Ergo, I'm guessing the Vikings must have died."

"Not necessarily," Sam said. "Viking gentlemen preferred being blond. Brunette Vikings –usually men – would use a strong soap with a high lye content to bleach their hair. In some regions, beards were lightened as well. As a bonus, these treatments likely helped to thwart head lice. So maybe it was more about killing pests."

Suttie laughed.

"Vikings were also known to be clean freaks," Sam added. "Excavations of Viking sites have turned up tweezers, razors, combs and ear cleaners made from animal bones and antlers. They bathed at least once a week – much more frequently than other Europeans of their day. But they were also gifted with natural hot springs. So maybe it was more about enjoying a hot bath in a cold climate than being clean."

"Sadly, we know some things, but we can't always understand why. Not unless we could get into a time machine to live there and learn their culture." Suttie grinned, not to be outdone by Sam's knowledge of Vikings. "Did you know, clean freaks though they were, the Vikings had no qualms about harnessing the power of one human waste product. Want to take a guess which one?"

Sam frowned. "Not really. What?"

She said, "They would collect a fungus called touchwood from tree bark and boil it for several days in urine before pounding it into something akin to felt. The sodium nitrate found in urine would allow the material to smolder rather than burn, so Vikings could take fire with them on the go."

"You're kidding!"

"I'm not! I promise!"

A few seconds later, they reached the end of the inlet and Sam gave the engine a sharp burst, and motored the Zodiac onto the rocky beach. He tilted the outboard motor, lifting the propeller out of the water, and the inflatable coasted up on to the shore. Sam and Suttie jumped out and pulled it a few feet farther up, just to be safe.

Confident that their ride wasn't going to accidentally get caught in a wave and drift back into the inlet, Sam allowed his eyes to wander, taking in the entire place at a glance. It was a landscape photographer's paradise. The crystal-clear water, white polished stone beach, leading to limestone and granite cliffs rising majestically from the edge of the shore. The white stone a stark contrast to the deep greens and yellows of the willow, aspen, and poplar trees.

At the end of the rocky beach, time had eroded two large limestone boulders that leaned in on each other, creating an opening large enough for an adult to walk through – revealing a moderate sized cave.

Sam glanced at Suttie. "Have you ever been inside?"

She smiled. "Of course."

"Is there anything worth seeing?"

She made a mischievous grin. "You'll just have to go see for yourself."

Sam suppressed a smile. "Really?"

She shrugged. "Sure, why not? There's nothing Viking related, but I promise you it will be worth your effort."

"Okay," Sam said, taking the bait.

He walked through the opening, wishing he'd brought a flashlight.

The tunnel was roughly twenty feet long, and fairly narrow – more like a slot canyon than a cave – before opening up to a large cathedral cavern.

He smiled as he stared at the wonder before him...

The grotto was vaulted by giant walls of limestone. Millennia of erosion in the soft, porous limestone high above resulted in multiple openings, which allowed beams of sunlight to illuminate the cavern like an array of spotlights.

Sam's eyes followed the beams, tracing their origins, before landing on a forest of dark leafed plants. With the exception of the raised section where the strange plants grew fiercely, the entire grotto was flooded with a lagoon. The water was still, but Sam guessed in a region with so much porous limestone, it wouldn't take much for the water to seep in during one of Sipiwesk Lake's king tides. Or even, an underground stream? Not that it mattered.

His eyes returned to the plants. He wasn't much of a botanist, but he was certain he'd never seen anything like the strange plants in all his – veritably wide – travels. His eyes narrowed as he studied the plants. There was something almost distinctively Jurassic about their appearance. They had big leaves. They were nearly six feet wide, oval shaped and a dark seaweed green. At the center of the plant was a single stalk, with what appeared to be the giant bud of an unopened flower.

Half a dozen butterflies appeared to be lingering beneath the unopened bud.

Like the plants, these looked like they had been beefed up on steroids or something, with the smallest one being at least the size of his fully outstretched hand. They were beautiful to look at, with a purple velvety color on one side of their wings, and an almost rainbow prismatic glow on the other. They appeared to be fluttering in the beam of light, warming themselves in the rays.

Sam watched one in particular as it landed on an enormous leaf. It stayed still just long enough for him to capture a good quality photo. Not just one, but several photos. All from different angles. Hopefully, someone would be able to use it to identify the creature and possibly the plants as well. The butterfly took off and joined the rest of the group.

He stared at them in wonder for a few minutes with rapt pleasure, giving them his undivided and muted attention, captured by their spell. His ocean blue eyes wide, taking in the sight almost reverently, he felt his heart begin to race, as though there was something almost spiritual about them.

Suttie was the first to break the silence. "They're called a kaleidoscope."

Sam turned to face her. The spell broken. "Sorry, what?"

"A group of butterflies... they're called a kaleidoscope."

He considered that and smiled. "Good name."

Sam brought up the photos he'd taken on his cell phone.

He studied the large wings. They were royal purple with a double set of eyes on the back of its wings. Up close, he could just make out the four individual images that looked like eyes, but from any distance, they looked like a pair of eyes. The double set of eyes gave the butterfly's wings the unique effect that no matter where you were, the eyes appeared to be tracking you, following his movements.

He said, "I don't suppose you know their name?"

"The butterflies?" she asked.

He nodded.

She shook her head. "No. But they seem to like those plants. Every time I've been here, they always appear to linger in this cavern."

"I wonder if anyone's ever studied them?" Sam asked, his voice wistful.

A shadow of fear crossed Suttie's face. "Actually, it's funny you should mention that..."

"Why?"

"Two years ago, this whole place was cordoned off. There was a big gate... barbed wire fence. The whole lot. Lots of security guards."

Sam furrowed his brow. "Did they say why?"

"No. And when I tried to ask what was going on, I was told under no uncertain circumstances that I wasn't to ask any more questions…"

"What did you do?"

She bit back a mischievous grin on her parted lips. "I couldn't help myself."

"Oh, tell me!"

"I assumed someone had finally come to look into the Viking ship."

"And?"

She clasped her hands together. "I had a look."

"How?"

"There's a secret tunnel. Its underwater. I dived it and surfaced inside the grotto, just over there. I surfaced… just for a few seconds and took a peek."

Intrigued, Sam asked, "What did you see?"

"There were men in protective coveralls… you know like the sort of PPE you see in those horror movies with the yellow biosecurity symbol on them."

Sam frowned. "A trefoil?"

"A what?" she asked.

"You know, the sign for nuclear radiation?"

"No, this was the other one… the biological hazard one…"

Sam finished it for her, drawing it with his finger in the sand. "With three black circles forming a triangular shape, with a single interlapping one at the center, on a bright yellow background?"

"That's it!" she said, "That's what I saw on their suits."

"What were they doing?"

"I don't know. But they were taking samples of the plants."

Sam stared at the plants…

And wondered…

Who the hell was coming for it?

Suttie said, "There's something else you should know."

"What?"

"I watched a couple of them remove their biosecurity suits…" She paused a beat. Her eyes darted furtively, as though checking that no one else was around the cavern to overhear what she had to say. Then, with a determined voice, she whispered, "They wore military uniforms underneath. I didn't recognize the uniforms at first. I mean, camouflage is camouflage right… no matter what the country of origin?"

"Right," Sam agreed.

Suttie said, "But then I saw it."

"Saw what?" Sam asked, no longer able to hide his impatience.

"A flag. It was on the soldiers right upper arm." She expelled a long sigh, as though there was no coming back. "The patch bore the image of the flag of the United States of America."

Sam shook his head. "What the hell were American soldiers doing on Canadian soil, secretly studying ancient plants?"

Chapter Fifty-Three

Doug Jones was deeply satisfied.

The Senator for Minnesota, leaned back in his office chair, behind a solid desk made of mahogany, chestnut and tulip poplar that had been in his family for nearly two centuries. Outside his window, the sun was beginning its descent, turning the sky a wash of purple, pink, and blue.

It was Friday afternoon and he was feeling good about the world as he poured himself a glass of Glenfiddich 23, a particularly good year. Some mistakes had been made earlier in the week regarding the whole DARPA fiasco. Decisions were made – hard ones – but the right ones, and the problem seemed to have been dealt with expediently and definitively. Now, to even things up, a bill he'd been working for nearly two years finally passed in the Senate.

His secretary stepped into his office. "There's a gentleman here to see you, sir."

The Senator frowned. "Didn't I tell you to clear my afternoon schedule, Mary?"

"You did, sir..." She waited for him. A coquettish and easily persuasive smile formed on her lips. He knew that smile, it meant she wanted him to hear her out, or give her a favor in something. She was older than him by nearly a decade, but she had even white teeth and ringlets of gray hair that framed an altogether still beautiful and endearing face. She had intensely blue eyes, behind which was a mind as smart as any he'd ever met. He easily imagined that smile had granted her many wishes throughout the years.

The edge of his lips curled upward. His momentary hostility naturally segueing toward his default personality of amiability, well-practiced after 26 years in Office. "I'm sorry, Mary... who is he?"

"The gentleman had an appointment and I tried to cancel it, but I couldn't reach him, and now he's turned up. I feel bad to send him away. He said he wouldn't take more than about ten minutes of your valuable time." She paused a beat, and then, knowing that the men and women of the military held a special place in his heart, she said, "He's from the Army – retired – but I thought you might make an exception for him."

The Senator nodded. He glanced at his wristwatch. His wife was hosting a party in his honor for succeeding in passing the bill, but he had time. "Sure, send him in."

"Thank you, sir."

She stepped out of his office and returned thirty seconds later, with the gentleman. The Senator stood up out of respect, his eyes appraising the man in a split second with the capability of a seasoned politician, who needed to place everyone with precision – as a *potential donor, rival, problem*, or *vote*. This man was clearly military or ex-military. He was short, yet somehow looked large. His posture ramrod straight. His physique filled with muscles.

The stranger handed the Senator's secretary a red pen, thanked her for the borrow, and offered him a warm handshake. "Thank you so much for getting me in to see you today Senator Jones."

The Senator took his hand, shaking it warmly. *Definitely a vote*. He smiled. It came off as affable instead of obsequious. "Call me Doug."

"Thank you, Doug. That's very kind of you."

"No problem. Have a seat," The Senator gestured toward the leather chair opposite his table, and reached for the bottle of Glenfiddich 23 and a second glass. "Can I offer you a drink?"

The stranger nodded. "Sure."

"I don't normally drink in the office," the Senator said, his voice conspiratorial, as though he was taking the man into his confidence. "But I passed a defense bill today that I'm awfully proud of… so I'm kind of celebrating."

"Congratulations," the stranger said.

The Senator poured some scotch. "Do you want it straight or on the rocks?"

"Straight, please."

The Senator passed the glass to the stranger.

The stranger lifted his glass. "To your defense bill passing."

"Thank you," The Senator said. "Now, what can I do for you, sir?"

The stranger unfolded an A4 sized piece of paper and handed it to him. "I wondered whether you could take a look at this for me?"

The Senator took the paper, unfolded it. He ran his eyes across the page. There were the faces of eight people. Each one had a name below to identify them, as well as their designation – not that he needed their names, he knew each and every one of them very well – and why shouldn't he? He'd met them once a month for nearly four years as part of the DARPA Oversight Committee. Four senators, two scientists, and two senior military officers – making up just eight people who held the fate of the future US military power in their grasp.

His face had been casually crossed out with a red pen.

A shadow of fear passed over the Senator, and something caught in his throat. "I'm sorry, I didn't catch your name?"

The stranger smiled. There was something disturbing about it. "Dean Godkin."

The Senator's eyes narrowed looking at the ghost before him.

The name didn't mean anything right away, but when it clicked, it struck him like a sledgehammer. When he had authorized the cleaning team to wipe out everything attached to the RX16SF program, he'd insisted on seeing the names of all sixteen test subjects – after all, it was the very least he could do to the noble Americans who had sacrificed their lives for their nation.

He shook his head. He'd been told the slate had been wiped clean. He smiled. This time it came off as obsequious, not affable. His tone firm, but gentle. "What can I do for you, son?"

Dean Godkin smiled. "Nothing. Absolutely nothing."

Senator Jones spread his arms, stepping back from his desk. "Now, don't do anything rash… we can come up with a compromise somehow. What is it you want me to do?"

"Absolutely nothing." Godkin laughed sardonically. "I already have every name and their addresses."

"Every name you want?" The fog lifted and the Senator, thinking of the other names on the list of people who worked on the DARPA Oversight Committee, and the complete realization of his situation manifested. "You don't have to do this!"

The Senator turned and ran.

But he never even made it to the door.

Dean Godkin, the fingers of his left hand affectionately nursing his glass of Glenfiddich 23, withdrew a service issued pistol with his right, and shot the Senator in the head twice.

He drank the last of his Glenfiddich 23.

Chapter Fifty-Four

Sam Reilly flew the Eurocopter 350 Squirrel across Lake Sipiwesk. Its tri-rotor blades making a constant *thump, thump* sound, as it churned up the crisp spring air on their way northeast back to Kelsey.

Beside him, Suttie listened as he ran through his theory about her mysterious ghosts.

"These Vikings who rise up from Valhalla and trouble you once a year…" he paused, trying but stumbling to find the right direction or place to begin. "They only rise up from the dead during a blood moon?"

She nodded. "That's right."

"There's never been an anomaly, where they come another day?"

"No, never." She smiled, defiantly meeting his gaze. "Not even once."

Sam's eyes narrowed. "And when they do come, what sort of things do they do?"

"A whole bunch of things…" she said, her eyes locked on a forest of willow trees swaying in the distance, but her mind witnessing things that had happened in the distant past. "Animals are slaughtered. At least a few cattle die, but sometimes a pig, a couple chickens – the acts almost seem too random to be poachers. I mean, we have more than three thousand head of cattle, and yet they slaughter one or two, butchering them on the spot and leaving the carcass for wild animals to feast."

"It couldn't have just been a polar bear or something?"

"No. Maybe if it was just one, but not three. Besides, even if we could justify that, it still doesn't explain how it happens every time there's a blood moon."

Sam nodded. "No, it doesn't. Anything else they do?"

"They generally steal things. Sometimes they damage cars, property, even fences – the destruction is widespread, but seemingly senseless, serving no purpose."

"How many times did this happen?"

"Once a year, every year during a blood moon."

"And when did it start?"

"I have no idea. All I can tell you is that it's been going on longer than our family has been farming in the region – so more than a hundred years."

Sam said, "That's so bizarre."

"So what's your theory?"

Sam grinned. "Who said I had one?"

"I do." She laughed. "Besides, I can tell you've been holding out on me, trying to figure things out for yourself before you give it to me. Am I right?"

Sam let himself laugh out loud. "You're right."

"Okay, so out with it. What have you got?"

"It's not a full theory and I suppose we'd need to wait until the next blood moon to test it out, but I'm willing to let you have the disconnected strings that I've got if you're interested?"

"Sure. I'll take them. Let me hear it."

"All right." Sam paused, trying to think where to start. "Those Jurassic plants inside the cavern… Have you ever seen their flowers?"

"No. But the butterflies go berserk just after a blood moon."

"Right. Only ever after a blood moon."

"That's right."

Sam drew a breath. "I'll bet you a botanist would be hard pressed to name them. I've taken some photos of the plants and the butterflies and messaged them to a friend of mine, and we'll find out soon whether my hunch holds any merit. Either way, my guess is that they certainly don't belong in Manitoba!"

"Where do you think they came from?"

"A Hellenistic fleet that first sailed to the Americas sometime during the 1st century."

Suttie's eyes widened in wonder. "The same place where that clay pot – what did you call it, an amphora – came from?"

"That's right," Sam confirmed. "My guess is that the Vikings who once sailed that longboat came across a place I suspect accounts for the origins of Valhalla, known in Viking lore as the place where valiant warriors feast. You see, as with some legends, the story changes with time and so does its truth. Although I still don't know what Valhalla holds, my guess is it won't be the remains of Viking warriors."

"So what do you think Valhalla actually is?"

"I don't know," Sam admitted. "But I'll tell you what I do know. In the 1st Century a Hellenistic fleet sailed from Ancient Greece, led by two warriors known as Thor and Odin. They made multiple trips across the Atlantic, each time sailors returned with tales more and more fantastical about their victories. Their fellow raiders becoming increasingly violent in their conquests. The stories turned to legends, and the legends eventually lost into the mythology of Viking lore."

"But somewhere, buried beneath nearly two millennia, there was a plant that looked like it came straight out of the set for Jurassic Park?" Suttie was smiling as she talked, the words sounding ridiculous when they were spoken out loud, and yet as Sam listened, he knew with a growing certainty that they were equally correct. "And it was the seeds of those plants that were probably stored within the amphorae, which washed up onto the shore, eventually taking hold inside that cavern on Black Bear Island. And those plants flower just once a year, releasing some sort of toxin that sends people crazy – turning them into Berserkers – who run wild, ravaging my family's land."

Sam nodded. "And that means, whoever's been harvesting these flowers has lived in the area for generations."

Suttie's eyes went wide. She drew a sharp breath. "This explains the Battle of Fish Creek!"

Sam looked at her, a wry grin forming on his parted lips. "Fish Creek?"

"Uh-huh," she nodded. "On a cold April morning in 1885 some 200 Canadian forces clashed with just 40 Métis rebels at a coulee in a place called Fish Creek – Saskatchewan."

"Go on."

"The Canadian forces were expected to quell the North-West Rebellion. It was meant to be a decisive victory. Major General Frederick Middleton, who had taken a hot air balloon to scout the landscape of the battlefield, watched on in horror as more than 200 well-equipped Canadian soldiers were overrun by just 40 poorly armed and ill-equipped Métis rebels."

Sam said, "That's five to one and yet they lost the battle?"

"Google it," Suttie said, with a smile that betrayed her obvious respect for the David versus Goliath type victory. "The Battle of Fish Creek has gone down in history as one of the worst military defeats of all time, and historians to this day can't seem to agree how the Métis rebels won the battle. It just seemed like the rebels simply went on a rampage, driven by some mysterious power, and conquered their enemy."

Sam grinned. "As though they were all high on some sort of berserker drug."

Chapter Fifty-Five

Sam explained to Suttie that he planned to return to the *Tahila* to get the Viking Sunstone, Navigation Runestone, and Uunartoq disc examined, and hopefully interpreted. He was about to climb into the Eurocopter and had promised her that he'd keep in touch and update her with any discoveries they might find, when his cell phone rang.

He retrieved it from his cargo pocket, glanced at the name next to the incoming call.

It read, *Margaret.*

No surname. There didn't have to be. That name alone meant the world to him.

Sam hit the green accept button, and said, "Madam Secretary."

The Secretary of Defense's voice was cold and hard. "Sam, we need your help."

"As always, I'm at your service, ma'am." Sam's gaze turned toward the distant forest, as he took a few steps to take him out of Suttie's earshot. "What do you need?"

"It has to do with what you're investigating."

Ice poured into his veins. "I told you I'm not going to stop until I find out who's responsible."

"I'm not asking you to stop."

Sam arched an eyebrow. "You're not?"

"No. Things have changed which have made much of the original risks moot."

"How?"

The Secretary said, "The DARPA Oversight Committee recently shut down a secret program that tested drugs designed to make super soldiers."

She let that acknowledgement sit there for a moment, waiting for him to make a comment. When he didn't, she continued.

"It was shut down because some of the test subjects inadvertently killed each other and in Las Vegas, an otherwise normal and respectable woman, killed more than a dozen people at a nightclub with a couple shards of broken glass."

Sam drew a breath. "The experimental drug came from an ancient plant used by a Hellenistic fleet that arrived in the Americas during the 1st Century, and created a concoction used to turn its soldiers into Berserkers…"

She didn't agree or deny the concept.

He took it as a yes. "That's why when a friend of mine discovered an image in a cave of the ancient fleet sailing into the Yucatán and some reference to Valhalla… the DARPA Oversight Committee knew they needed to take action and eliminate all evidence of the cave in case someone was to find the location in which the drugs had been harvested. Do I have it about right?"

"Close enough." The Secretary of Defense said, "Dean Godkin, one of the test subjects and also the brother of a man whose life you tried to save in Canada, sold the formula for the drugs to a drug cartel – now known colloquially as the Berserkers – an offshoot of an international drug cartel – with seriously deep pockets."

"I've met some of the Berserkers," Sam admitted. "They weren't the friendliest people I've had to deal with for a while. But I'm confused… why are you coming to me with all this now? I thought the DARPA Oversight Committee had put an airtight lid on this thing?"

"They had."

"And you tried to make me promise to stay out of it, because even you couldn't protect me from the powerful members of the committee?"

"I did."

Sam frowned. "So why are you coming to me now?"

"Because Dean Godkin went after each member of the DARPA Oversight Committee."

Sam pictured the Green Beret, driven mad by the Berserker drug. Simultaneously increasing his mental and physical strength while filling him with rage, as he targeted each and every member of the committee that signed his death warrant. It wouldn't be pretty. "How many did he get?"

"As of six hours ago... seven."

"Seven!" Sam cursed. "How many were on the damned committee?"

She answered without hesitation. Her voice cold and mechanical. "Eight."

"There's only one person left alive?" Sam asked. "Who?"

"Sarah Rhinehart, a leading researcher of Harvard's biochemistry faculty."

"Where's she staying?" Sam asked.

"She's bunkered down at her family's estate... a castle on Vancouver Island. It's naturally well protected by the elements, but she has her own private security team there."

"I hope she's hired best security team."

"I believe she does," she said. "I'm flying out there today."

"You?" Sam asked, incredulously. "Why you?"

"I know her personally and as a biochemist and only person left alive from the original oversight committee that dealt with the program, Sarah offers the best insight into this drug. I want her opinion on it, and how much of a threat this thing is going to be to national security."

Sam could already imagine how much of a threat this thing offered national security. If Dean Godkin was selling the drug to a street gang, it was only a matter of time before terrorists, or other militaries around the world got their hands on it.

He said, "Okay, what do you need from me?"

"We need you to help find Dean Godkin."

"How would I do that?"

"We believe you have something that he was after. Something his brother left you… a USB stick…"

Sam grinned. Glad that he was on his cell phone and that she couldn't see his face in person. If she had, he never would have been able to keep a poker face. It amazed him how much information naturally drifted her way. She must have been fed intel from every direction and her mind worked like a computer, naturally sifting through what was relevant and what wasn't, instinctively linking several chains of data together to make sense out of a seemingly disjointed bundle of data. "All right. I'll do it, but I have no idea where we're going to find him."

She paused. "To be honest, we believe he will come to you."

"Me?" Sam asked. "I'm in Manitoba currently. I can't imagine he's going to show up here."

"No. We'd like you to catch the next flight to Vancouver Island."

The truth hit him like a shard of glass. "You want to use me as bait, to bring Godkin out of hiding?"

"Yes. If I'm right, all you have to do is step foot on that island, and Godkin will find you."

Sam laughed uncomfortably. "Let's say that he does find me. What's to stop him putting two bullets in my head?"

"Nothing… everything…"

"What does that even mean?"

"It means that this man's military record is impeccable. He is the epitome of duty and honor."

Sam didn't buy it. "Yet he's killed seven members of DARPA's Oversight Committee?"

"He sees those as honorable kills. The committee authorized the death of him and the rest of the test subjects – his platoon, so to speak – and so his honor system has authorized the killings."

Sam arched an eyebrow. "But not mine?"

She said, "We're pretty certain that's his line of thinking."

Sam swallowed hard. "It's only my life if you get this thing wrong."

"Right." She spoke matter-of-factly. "Will you do it?"

He considered his options, and answered what he knew he must. "Yes. I'll need to contact Tom and bring in some of my people for the project."

"You can't do that."

"Why not?"

"Dean's an expert. If he sees you with other people, he'll leave you alone. We can't risk it. This is our one chance to bring him in."

"How?"

"Just arrive on the island, make contact, and I'll organize a clean-up team to take care of the rest."

Sam felt his anger boil. "The same team that killed my friend in the Yucatán?"

"Probably," she admitted.

"I hope I'm not the one about to be cleaned up in the process."

"No. I give you my word, you're to walk away from this. You're not to be touched by our people. I didn't spend more than a decade grooming you to become one of our nation's best weapons, only to have some secret clean up team eradicate you."

Sam smiled. "Your sentimentality is touching, Madam Secretary."

"Hey, I just wanted you to know I was telling the truth. You will be protected."

"All right, I'll do it. But I still doubt there's any chance in the world that Dean Godkin is going to find me just because I catch a flight into Vancouver Island."

"We'll see," she said, ending the call.

A moment later, his cell rang again.

It was still in his hand.

He glanced at the screen expecting to see Margaret's name on the display. It wasn't. Sam didn't recognize the number.

He answered it. "Hello?"

"Mr. Sam Reilly?"

"Yes?"

"My name's Dean Godkin… I believe you were looking for me."

Chapter Fifty-Six

Sam listened in silence.

He'd learned long ago that the best way to interrogate someone was to keep your mouth shut and let the other person do the talking. Secrets were beasts unto themselves and took effort to restrain. He didn't need to wait long. Once Godkin got talking, it was as if a spigot had been turned, and now the secrets flowed like water from a faucet.

Godkin confirmed the Secretary of Defense's story about DARPA running a secret program to test a drug that turned soldiers into super soldiers. He didn't know where the drug originated, but doubted it was developed in a lab, because part of the team of people working on the program included an archeologist and a historian. He went on to confirm that he'd set about to systematically kill every member of the oversight committee who had signed the order to shut down the program and wipe all evidence of its existence from the face of the earth.

When he was finished, Godkin said, "Do you have any questions?"

Sam asked, "Why me?"

"You're asking why I'm talking to you?"

"It did cross my mind."

"My brother, Miles Godkin, worked under cover for the CIA and believed someone from the DARPA Oversight Committee was selling the secret formula to a drug cartel. It was this evidence that I believe my brother gave to you."

Sam said, "I was told you were the sellout. That you were the one who leaked the formula to a global drug cartel."

"You've been told wrong. I didn't have anything to do with it. And what's more, ten to one, whatever's on that USB stick my brother gave you, will prove it."

"Do you know who's responsible for the leak?"

"No. But if you bring me that USB stick, I can connect it to my half of the cipher, and together we learn the truth." Dean said, "We need to meet."

Sam said, "Sure. What do you have in mind?"

"You can come to me."

"All right. Where are you?"

"No. That's not going to work for me."

"Why not?"

"If I tell you, you'll just contact the authorities, and right now, at least until we find the contents of that USB stick my brother gave to you, I have no idea who to trust."

Sam smiled. "Okay. What do you have in mind?"

Godkin said, "Where are you?"

Sam looked around, a cold shiver passing over his head. Dean Godkin was a deadly Green Beret, hyped up on Berserker drugs. The last thing he needed was to have someone like that looking over his shoulder.

He glanced at his surroundings, reassuring himself that he was safe. Suttie lived on hundreds of hectares. A forest of black spruce – ubiquitous throughout so much of Manitoba – lined the end of the property, some five hundred feet away. It was unlikely Godkin was waiting inside the forest with a sniper rifle.

He drew a breath. "I'm in Manitoba."

"Where?" Godkin persisted.

"I'm not sure I want to tell you."

"I get that. I'll make it easier for you. Where's your nearest airport?"

That seemed safe. "Kelsey."

"All right. Just give me a minute." In the background, Godkin was typing on a keyboard. "How long will it take you to reach the airport?"

"I can be there in fifteen minutes."

"Good. In thirty there's a flight to Toronto with your name on it."

"Wait..." Sam said, "Where am I headed?"

"You'll find out when you get there."

"Wait!" Sam protested. "Thirty minutes isn't enough to get through airport security!"

"Then I suggest you get going, because your aircraft isn't going to wait and neither am I."

Sam pocketed his cell phone. His heart racing, a million thoughts charging through his mind, as he considered his priorities.

Suttie exchanged a glance with him. Her face registered that a tempest was brewing. "Is everything all right?"

"Not really." Sam said, "I need to get to the airport as quick as I can. I'll explain what's happening on the way."

"Okay. I'll drive," she said without hesitation.

She pulled out a Subaru Outback. He climbed in and as soon as the door was shut, she had her foot down, and the AWD began churning up the gravel as she raced toward the airport.

In the end, it took less than five minutes.

Just before they arrived, she asked, "What about your helicopter?"

"Do you mind picking up my friend, Tom from Churchill?"

"Sure. You want him to pick up the Eurocopter?"

"Him or someone else. If you show them the Viking Navigational Runestone, Sunstone, and Disc, they will be able to find someone who can translate the runic script, and hopefully we can reverse engineer their voyage."

A suppressed smile flickered across Suttie's lips. "You want to go after it, don't you?"

Sam met her eye. "Valhalla?"

"Yeah. That's what hoping to find, isn't it?"

Sam nodded. "You're right. I am. Do you want to come with me?"

Suttie grinned. "You bet I do!"

Chapter Fifty-Seven

Comox Airport – Vancouver Island, Canada

Over the course of the next sixteen hours, Sam made a number of flights in the most indirect route anyone had ever taken between Kelsey and Vancouver Island. From Kelsey he boarded a plane to Toronto, whereupon he was greeted by a member of the flight crew, who handed him tickets for his next flight and ushered him to a flight leaving immediately for Montreal. The same charade continued throughout the night until he eventually landed at Saskatchewan, followed by Vancouver, and eventually landing at Comox Airport on Vancouver Island. Throughout each of the flights, he had been prevented from making any phone calls.

Sam stepped out of the 737 and switched his cell phone back on.

As soon as the phone linked with a local cell tower, it updated with a message from Elise. He called her back.

"Where have you been?" Elise asked.

"I've been in the air."

"For sixteen hours?"

Sam sighed. "It was a scenic flight."

"Sure." Elise returned to the reason for her call. "I showed those images to a Lepidopterologist..."

"What images?" Sam asked, and then before she could answer, he said, "And what's a..."

Elise said, "Lepidopterology is a branch of entomology concerning the scientific study of moths and the three superfamilies of butterflies."

"Oh, right," Sam said, suddenly remembering that he'd sent her the photos of the plants and butterflies found near Black Bear Island. "Of course. Go on, what did he or she say?"

"He believes your mysterious butterfly came from Ancient Greece."

"Strange it should find itself in a cave off Black Bear Island, Manitoba."

"Even stranger still, he says that the butterfly was thought to have become extinct somewhere around the 1st century."

"You're kidding."

"No. That's the last anyone heard or seen of it since then."

Sam said, "Thank you, Elise."

"No problem. Anything else I can help you with?"

"Yeah, I need you to look into someone for me…"

"Sure. Who?"

"Sarah Rhinehart. She's currently a professor at Harvard, working in their biochemistry faculty. Apparently, her family owns property on Vancouver Island. That's all I know."

"Okay, I'll fill in the gaps." She paused a beat. "Sam… what's this about?"

"I don't know yet. All I know is that she was originally part of DARPA's Oversight Committee. And now, everyone else on that committee is dead."

"Everyone else?"

"Afraid so. Dean Godkin who I'm about to meet with, systematically tracked each and every one of them down and killed them."

Her voice was stern, yet sympathetic, like a parent grilling a child for being stupid. "And you're meeting up with him."

Sam suppressed a grin. "The Secretary of Defense thinks I'll be okay."

"It wouldn't be the first time she's put you in harm's way."

"That's true."

"Sam…"

"Yeah?"

"Have you got this thing under control?"

Sam swallowed hard. "Not even close."

A moment later, he was greeted by a man at the gate who informed him that a float plane was waiting to take him to his final destination.

Sam asked the stranger where he was headed. The man simply shook his head and shrugged, informing him that he was just the messenger. A few minutes later, they had exited the airport and headed down through a dense trail, before the forest gave way to the rocky shore of Kye Bay – where a blue de Havilland Canada DHC-2 Beaver waited for him.

The seaplane rested idly at its anchor in the tranquil water, its pontoons drifting against the beach. There was no pilot nearby. The messenger gestured for him to take a seat inside. Sam stepped across the starboard pontoon, opened the door and climbed in.

Sam turned his gaze to the messenger. "No pilot?"

The man shrugged. "I was told you could fly just about anything." It was a statement, not a question.

Sam expelled a breath, taking a seat in the cockpit. "Okay. Where am I headed?"

"I don't know. Honestly, I have no idea."

The edges of Sam's lips curled upward. "So, you don't know where I'm headed, and I don't know where I'm headed, and yet, I'm to pilot this seaplane there. Does that make sense to you?"

The guy shrugged again as though it was not his problem. "The coordinates have been pre-programmed into the Navionics. The fuel tank's full and I've been assured that it will be ample fuel to go where you're heading. The radio has been disabled, so I suggest you don't deviate from your flight path, or you might just find yourself getting shot down by Canada's Air Force."

Sam nodded. "Okay."

He switched on the electronic master switch.

Running his eyes across the avionics, he frowned. "There's nothing programmed into the GPS?"

The messenger nodded, as though expecting the question. "It's pre-programmed to display the coordinates, including your flight vectors and paths once you reach an altitude of 1,000 feet."

"Right," Sam said, and sighed heavily.

He couldn't help but smile. There was a certain level of genius in Dean Godkin's plan. By sending him by commercial aircraft and by ensuring that he didn't take any checked in luggage, Godkin had been able to make certain Sam hadn't been able to carry a weapon with him. Throughout the flights his cell phone had been disabled under federal aviation laws, and so he hadn't been able to contact his people for help, and now, he was about to fly to a remote location somewhere within the isolated lands of Vancouver Island.

Even if he wanted to message someone about his destination, he wouldn't know it until he was in the air, by which time it would probably take too long for anyone to reach the location before him – and besides, without the radio, it wasn't like he could contact anyone from the air, anyway. His cell phone could be used as a satellite phone, but to do so he needed a direct line of sight to the sky – something fairly difficult to achieve during flight, especially with him at the controls.

Sam thought about his next move and Godkin's warning that if he deviated from the travel plans, the one-time only deal was permanently off. Torn, he hoped to hell that his instincts about Godkin had been right, and that the truth would be revealed within the contents of the USB stick that Miles had left him.

And with that, he switched the engine on, and began his pre-flight takeoff checks.

Chapter Fifty-Eight

The de Havilland Canada DHC-2 Beaver was a single-engine, high-wing, propeller-driven short takeoff and landing bush plane. It was perfectly designed for the remote environments of Canada's labyrinth of ubiquitous waterways, lakes, rivers, and bays.

Sam turned the key, and the Pratt & Whitney Canada PT6 turboprop engine kicked over. The propeller began to turn with a little sputter, before roaring to life, disappearing into an invisible whir as it picked up speed. He ran his eyes across the instruments. The aircraft was well maintained and in good condition. His ears pricked, and he instinctively listened to the engine, which sounded like it was running well.

He adjusted the rudder, turning the nose to port, and gave the propeller a sharp burst of power. The de Havilland Canada DHC-2 turned into the wind. A moment later, Sam glanced up at the open horizon to confirm that his runway was free of traffic, and pushed the throttle all the way forward.

The propeller raced toward its maximum RPM and the de Havilland DHC-2 crept forward. Sluggish at first, until it had picked up enough speed that the pontoons began to skim the surface of the water, and the aircraft quickly became lithe and maneuverable.

Soon, Sam needed to work to restrain the seaplane from taking off on its own. He applied just a little bit of forward pressure on the wheel to keep him on the water. When he couldn't keep the aircraft grounded any longer, he gently brought the wheel toward his chest, and the Seaplane happily relinquished its earthly restraints, taking to the skies.

Sam steadily climbed until he reached 1,000 feet. He leveled off and a few seconds later the Navionics flashed with a new pre-programmed route. He clicked to accept the route and began scrolling through the map.

It turned out he was now heading to a place called Hot Springs Cove.

The cove was on the west coast of Vancouver Island, in a southwestern direction of Comox. Despite its location, the flight route had planned to take him north until the Campbell River, before following the valley across the island, avoiding the highs of the mountains that adorned the central dividing peaks of Vancouver Island.

Sam followed the vectors set on the Navionics, heading north until he reached the Campbell River, before banking to the southeast, and eventually setting up in a valley that carved its way across the island. Etched out by Gold River over the eons, he flew in the middle of the valley, while 7,000-foot mountain peaks hugged him from either side of the valley, where pine trees rose like the ramparts of a medieval fortress. Above him, bald-headed eagles soared, while below him, a couple grizzlies plucked at the salmon.

The valley opened up, Gold River, widening into a Bay. A black steamboat ushered adventurous tourists through the island's wild west. Sam eased the seaplane around Bligh Island, past Yuquot, before briefly taking the aircraft into the North Pacific Ocean, and back on a southerly direction, rounding the twin Mate Islands, before setting up in a due north direction, into Hot Springs Cove.

He banked north and got his first glimpse of the shallow beach at the end of the basin, where several boats and another floatplane were tied to a dock. It was summer, and despite the remoteness, the entire region welcomed throngs of adventurers and fishermen who vacationed there. A small colony of sea lions guarded the entrance to the cove, as they lazily soaked in the warm water and adjacent rocks.

Hot Springs Cove is a splendid hot spring still enjoyable in its natural state, located in Maquinna Provincial Park in the remote northern end of Clayoquot Sound. The boiling spring water bubbles up from deep in the earth and cascades down a small cliff into a series of natural layered rock pools, cooled by the incoming Pacific Ocean surf. Giant Douglas firs lined the rocky coast.

Sam set up for a reconnaissance fly-over and possible landing into the bay, taking the de Havilland Beaver down low, just fifty feet above the water. Holding her level, as he searched for logs and any other impediments that might make for a horrible landing.

The water was calm, almost glassy.

He brought the seaplane in low, ready to make an easy landing.

Sam set the flaps to full and reduced speed. His gaze ran across the bay, where he had a clear run all the way to the end of the bay.

He reduced power, and the aircraft began its final few feet of descent.

30 feet…

20 feet…

10 feet…

The ocean rose to greet him.

Suddenly the water itself jumped out at him.

Dead ahead of him, a gray whale breached, rising at least 10 feet out of the water in the process.

Sam swore.

He pushed the throttle in full, and pulled back on the wheel.

The seaplane climbed, but nothing worked fast enough. He knew, instinctively, that it would be close. He grimaced, holding the wheel to his chest, as hard as he dared. Up ahead, he spotted the massive tail coming out of the water, ready to slam down upon him, like a giant flyswatter.

They were too close.

He would never make it in time. Not going over the whale.

Sam banked the seaplane, its starboard wingtips dipping low – no more than a few feet out of the water – as he swung around the whale, before gently easing the aircraft back into a straight-climb position. His heart pounded in his chest, as the threat disappeared with the bay, far below. Sam made another circuit and spotted his unintended foe.

Two gray whales – a mother and her calf – were making their way back out to sea. Sam's gaze traced their movements, and spotted a large pod of orcas swimming just outside of the cove, like a lethal barricade. The killer whales, Sam knew, were the gray whales only predator.

He watched as the two grays began to make an attempt to escape through the deadly barricade. Sam tracked them as the orcas began to give chase. It was like watching one of those wildlife docos, where you want to cry out to the cameraperson, to do something, before that lion eats the helpless springbok… only even that would be stupid given that's what the lion eats. It was just nature. But, still, Sam couldn't look away and he found the sight surprisingly disturbing.

The gray whales moved quickly, and it looked like they were going to escape. If it had been just the mom, he was sure she would have made it out into the deep ocean without too much trouble, but with her young calf, it might be a different story. The orcas closed in on them, and before they reached the kill, the two gray whales dived, disappearing into the waters far below.

Sam watched for another couple minutes, trying to find the outcome, but the two grays seemed to disappear. He wished them good luck, circled around, and set up for another attempt to land at the Hot Springs Cove.

He banked to the left, setting up to do a reconnaissance fly-past to rule out any floating logs, small boats, sand bars, or surface debris. He flew over a long distance, making sure his waterway was clear and long enough. The surface of the lake wasn't rough, a condition that would make it hazardous to land. Worse, though, the water was now dead calm.

Sam shook his head, surprised by how much the water conditions can change in such a short time. A glassy, flat surface reflects like a mirror – one of the most dangerous conditions a seaplane pilot can face. This made it extremely difficult for Sam to judge actual height. When landing on water, one can't rely on an altimeter. The difference between one foot and ten was a thin line between a safe landing, or flying your plane with power straight into the water and sinking.

When he was ready, Sam opened his side window, making a sharp bank to the left. He wasn't wearing a cap to drop out the window, so instead searched for something else to use to cause ripples. There wasn't anything. He looked at the avionics display and thought seriously of throwing the damned thing overboard.

Then, far below, a jet ski raced along the glassy waters of the bay, leaving a series of ripples in its wake.

It was just what Sam needed.

He flew a sharp, 180 degrees turn and set up for his final approach. With the flaps still set at full, he reduced power, and brought the seaplane into a glide. Using peripheral vision for cues, he observed the height of trees on shore, his eyes carefully observing the ripples on the water.

Just above the surface, he raised the nose. This made the aircraft flare, meaning to lose lift and stall, slowing its descent, causing its twin pontoons to softly hydroplane for a moment before it sank gently into the water.

Sam taxied the seaplane in toward the jetty.

He found a yellow, temporary visitors mooring, slowing the de-Havilland to a complete stop right next to it. Unclipping his belt, he opened the door, and climbed down the ladder. Holding onto the wing support, he reached down and picked the mooring line floating on the surface of the water, tying it off on the cleat at the front of the pontoon. Confident the seaplane was secure, he stepped back into the cockpit, reduced the engine to an idle, before powering off completely. The engine coughed and the propeller stopped spinning.

A man with a rowboat tied to the jetty kindly came to greet him and offered him a ride to shore. Sam took it with his gratitude. He made his way along the jetty to the main boardwalk that headed into the forest.

Sam took in the splendor of Hot Springs Cove. Despite its adventurous tourists, the place hadn't yet been bought up by the big names and made into an elite resort for the rich or for the masses. It brought a smile to Sam's face. He walked on a little and spotted the boiling spring water bubbles as they rose up from deep in the earth and cascaded down a small cliff into a series of natural layered rock pools, cooled by the incoming Pacific Ocean surf, sending steam into the air. The spring water appeared wickedly hot, and was clear like a distillery, with just a faint smell and taste of Sulphur.

He didn't get much farther, before he was greeted by a ghost...

"Hello," Dean Godkin said, wearing nothing more than a pair of board shorts, stepping out of the warm waters.

"Godkin?" Sam asked.

Dean smiled at him. "Welcome to The Island, Sam Reilly."

Chapter Fifty-Nine

Sam stared at Dean Godkin.

The brotherly resemblance to Miles was indisputable. Where Miles was muscular, Dean was next level. The man looked like he belonged on the front cover of a Men's Health magazine… or possibly a Hitachi Bulldozer magazine, for that matter? The man was roughly five foot-eight. But despite his average height, he looked formidable by any measure. At a guess, he was 180 pounds without an ounce of fat on him.

Sam locked eyes with Godkin. He had dark gray eyes. There was something pensive and intelligent in his gaze. The subtle power of absolute authority that came with holding one's life in his hands, appeared to be etched in the lines on his face. A moment later, he lowered his gaze, really seeing Godkin for the first time. The edges of Sam's lips curled into a grin.

Dean was wearing nothing but a pair of board shorts. They were decorated with the images of pink frangipanis and looked decidedly Hawaiian, forming a jarring contrast to his weapon-like physique, and deadly reputation. He was still wet from the nearby hot spring in which he'd been bathing, and steam rose from his muscular body. He had broad shoulders that tapered into a narrow waist, where his abdominal muscles appeared to have been chiseled by Michelangelo himself. From his shoulders casually hung arms as thick as a man's thighs, with triceps and biceps so sharp they appeared almost cartoonish in nature.

Sam began to laugh. He was expecting to find a gun pointed in his direction, but instead found a younger looking Arnold Schwarzenegger, dressed for a Hawaiian vacation. "You look comfy."

Dean shrugged. "Hey, it took you long enough to reach me. Besides, this was my show of faith to you."

Sam rolled his eyes. "Come again?"

Dean clarified. "I'm not carrying a weapon."

"I can tell."

"I meant for you to see." Dean, registering the blank expression on Sam's face, turned his palms outward in a placating gesture. "That way you know I'm on your side."

Sam wasn't convinced. Besides, Godkin was a Green Beret hyped up on Berserker drugs. Both of them knew that Dean could probably kill Sam in a hand-to-hand fight without breaking a sweat, so the whole not carrying a weapon thing appeared moot, and far from reassuring.

Unsure where else to go, Sam got to the point of his trip. "I brought the USB stick, do you have somewhere for us to go find the truth?"

"Yeah. I've rented a cabin. It's nearby. We'll go there and put it into my laptop."

Sam followed Dean along the well-maintained cedar boardwalk as it meandered through an enchanting rainforest. Giant Douglas firs framed the majestic coastline, rising some 250 feet into the air, like ancient sentinels guarding the source of the hot spring. Ten minutes later, Godkin stopped, gesturing with his right hand toward a small log cabin.

Sam arched an eyebrow. "Yours?"

"My humble abode for the past two days."

Not really sure what words seemed appropriate, Sam said, "It looks nice."

"It is," Dean said, opening the door. "Come in, let's go find some answers."

Sam stepped through the door, studying the place as he walked, looking for hidden weapons or anything else that Godkin might be capable of using to attack him. Inside, the cabin was spartan. There were several bunkbeds. There were no mattresses or sheeting. At the end of the one farthest away, a single sleeping bag – already folded into its bag – rested on its own. Next to the door, there was a small backpack. Otherwise, the cabin was empty.

Godkin grabbed a towel from the bag, dried himself, and threw a shirt on. He removed his laptop and took a seat on the floor – looking surprisingly limber and comfortable there, more like a yogi expert, than a muscle-bound jarhead. He opened the screen, and pressed the on button. The computer was solid, covered in what appeared to be a hardened shell of metal, the sort the military used for its soldiers throughout the world during deployment. At a guess, given his history, it was issued to him by the US Army.

A photograph proudly adorned the desktop's wallpaper.

It depicted two brothers. Sam recognized a younger Dean and Miles Godkin. Even at a glance, Sam realized that they were twins. Somehow it shocked him. Since the photo had been taken, Dean had obviously gained muscle – perhaps the Berserker drug had aided him in that endeavor? – while Miles had somehow lost some of his size and Sam began to mentally question whether or not the kid could have intentionally done so for his secret mission? Then again, maybe both Godkin brothers were lying to him.

Sam's eyes narrowed in on the image.

Suddenly, he recognized where they were standing when the photo had been taken. It was the entrance to a large government building, with a marbled floor. At their feet, was an American Eagle above a shield with a compass rose at the center. Sam knew the symbol well, along with its meaning. The American Eagle is the national bird and is a symbol of strength and alertness. The shield is the standard symbol of defense. Intelligence provided to our policymakers is to help defend our country. The radiating spokes of the compass rose depict the convergence of intelligence data from all areas of the world to a central point.

It was the CIA Seal.

The two Godkin brothers were at the CIA headquarters, in Langley, Virginia.

Sam drew a breath. "Your brother really did work for the CIA?"

Godkin opened his mouth to speak, then closed it again. Either he didn't want to try and explain the truth or justify himself, or he decided they no longer had the time for such petty arguments, about what his brother was really doing that day he was nearly killed at the St. Martins Sea Caves in the Bay of Fundy, before successfully being killed that night.

Sam studied the image. Both faces. Then, suddenly everything clicked. "Miles wasn't the only one who was CIA?"

"No," Dean confirmed.

"You spent your entire life in the US Army, but when you were selected for this program, you... what, decided to join the CIA?"

Dean shook his head. "No."

Sam closed his eyes, picturing what would have caused him to spy on his own people. "Miles recruited you!"

"Bingo," Dean said. "Come on, I'm hoping he came through with the goods. If not, all has been for nothing, and I'm likely to get permanently wiped from the face of the earth."

He clicked on a document still open on the desktop.

It was labeled, Berserker Investigation.

Looking over Godkin's shoulder, Sam spotted several files pertaining to an investigation. At the end of the third row, was a document labeled, *Brother Cipher*. He clicked open, and another obscure hypertext link came up.

Sam's eyes narrowed. "What was your brother doing?"

Dean held his hand out. "Pass me your USB stick and we'll find out together."

Sam retrieved the stick from a zippered pocket on his right thigh and handed it to Godkin. "You don't know at all?"

"Thanks," Dean said, inserting the USB stick into the computer. He withdrew a satellite phone attached to the laptop case, and set it up so the laptop could connect to the internet. On the phone, an image of three satellites circling the globe appeared, indicating the phone was searching for its connection. While he waited, Dean said, "Look… the CIA got wind of a new super drug being developed through DARPA. There were some talks about whether or not the drug was ethical, but that wasn't really their concern."

Sam frowned. "It wasn't?"

Godkin almost laughed. "Of course, it wasn't. The moral and ethical debate about performance enhancing drugs on the battlefield was lost decades ago. Hell, the military is constantly using technology to build better warships, aircraft, weapons, and armor – why shouldn't they give soldiers the pharmacological edge of performance enhancing drugs?"

"I don't know, the same reason it's frowned on in competitive sports, I guess?"

Godkin shook his head. "This isn't about being a good sport and not cheating. In battle, drugs can save lives. They can make soldiers stronger, faster, while increasing their mental acuity, which all in turn, work to allow them to complete their missions better, faster, and without as much loss of life. Hell, soldiers have long taken drugs to help them fight."

"They have?" Sam asked, a little tone of surprise in his voice.

"They sure have. Amphetamines like Dexedrine were distributed widely to American, German, British and other forces during World War II and to U.S. service members in Korea, Vietnam, Kuwait, Iraq and Afghanistan. In 1991, the Air Force chief-of-staff stopped the practice because, in his words, "Jedi knights don't need them." But the ban lasted only five years. DARPA, an agency that does cutting-edge research for the U.S. Department of Defense, is trying to make soldiers "kill-proof" by developing super-nutrition pills and substances to make them smarter and stronger. New drugs that reduce the need for sleep, such as modafinil, are being tested. Researchers are even looking into modifying soldiers' genes."

"All right," Sam said, "So, if the CIA weren't worried about the ethics of this Berserker drug, what were they concerned about?"

Godkin leveled his gaze on Sam. His tone was cold and hard. "Where the drug came from and more importantly, where it was going."

Sam paused a beat, not sure he'd heard right. "Come again?"

"No one knows where these drugs came from. In fact, talking to the pharmacologist who worked on the program, the drug – RX16SF – can't be produced synthetically. That means they've sourced the bio compounds from a plant somewhere – and given the secrecy on its location, I'll bet you my retirement fund wherever those plants are found, they're sure as shit not stateside."

"Let me guess," Sam said, "They're found in Manitoba, Canada?"

"Maybe. That I don't know."

"But your brother was in Canada, trying to infiltrate the Berserker gang?"

The satellite phone turned green to indicate it had secured a connection. Godkin clicked synchronize, and the laptop paired with the satellite phone for some lightning-fast Wi-Fi. "Yeah, the CIA believed that the Berserker gang had bought the drug from someone within the RX16SF program."

"I was told by the Secretary of Defense that you were the one selling the drug."

He shook his head. "It wasn't me. That's for damned sure."

And with that, he opened the data in his brother's USB stick – linking the two ciphers together – and the computer began to link up to a data storage cache, buried deep within the dark net.

Chapter Sixty

Sam stared at the secret website.

It appeared to have been hundreds of hours of CIA surveillance and research on the Berserker gang, who had only seemed to come into existence roughly two years earlier – the same time the RX16SF program began. Godkin skipped the videos, and kept scrolling, until he came to his brother's report.

There were hours of data to review, but both their sets of eyes landed on the most important statement in the whole report...

It was a single name and it purported who the leak was within the RX16SF program. The person making a fortune selling US military secrets.

Sarah Rhinehart.

Sam and Dean exchanged a glance.

It provided some answers, while asking a whole new set of questions.

The biggest, and first one to come to Sam's mind, was...

Was this why, of the entire list of people involved in the program, only Sarah Rhinehart was still alive?

Did Dean Godkin leave her to last, because he suspected her as being the guiltiest of betrayals to his country?

Or, had he left Sarah Rhinehart alive, because the two of them were in this thing together?

Sam considered how to play his hand. The last thing he wanted to do was confront Godkin on his own turf. No, he was better off waiting this out, seeing how it played out.

A minute later, Sam's cell phone rang.

He glanced at the screen. It showed the incoming call was from Elise.

Sam answered it without preamble. "What have you got?"

"Sarah Rhinehart is a leading biochemistry lecturer at Harvard university. She's also rich. I mean, rich enough that she has a small castle – AKA private citadel – on the banks of the Seymour Narrows."

"That's right here on Vancouver Island?"

"Yes, somewhere up north. It's meant to be set on a particularly dangerous part of the river, where the current acts as a natural deterrent, let's call it, elemental protection, for her family's estate."

"They're that rich?"

"Yes, but she wasn't always rich. In fact, her bank account has – and I say this with all pun intended – recently gone Berserk in the past two years."

"She's the one who sold out RX16SF to a drug cartel?"

"It would look like it." Elise's tone had an almost laughing lilt to it. "It gets better."

"Do tell."

"Even though Sarah Rhinehart works in the US, her permanent residency is her homeland, Canada. Want to guess where she grew up?"

"I have no idea."

"A small town to the west of Black Bear Island, Manitoba."

"Good God!" Sam said, "She knew about the Berserker drug long before DARPA started investigating it."

"Not only did she know it, she owns the company that first sold the rights to DARPA to investigate."

Chapter Sixty-One

Comox, Vancouver Island

The de Havilland Canada DHC-2 Beaver banked to the right, before settling into a glide just over the crystal clear, calm waters of the Kye Bay. Sam eased back on the throttle until the little aircraft flared, and a few seconds later, its pontoons gracefully sank into the bay.

It was an easy landing in a highly forgiving plane.

Sam motored toward the shore, until the twin pontoons touched the rocky beach. He then swung the rudder around full, and gave the propeller one short burst. The seaplane turned on its axis, finishing with its nose pointed out toward the bay.

Sam cut the engine. The prop coughed, slowed, and eventually came to a complete stop. He opened the door and dropped a small anchor. The same messenger who had picked Sam up from the airport met them on the shore, taking the keys and what appeared to be a large tip from Dean. They began walking up the trail.

Halfway up the trail, Sam stopped Dean. "How do you really want to handle this?"

Dean got straight to the point. "You mean, how are we going to get Sarah Rhinehart?"

"Yeah, I mean, you looked at those satellite images of her estate. It would be a nightmare for the Canadian Mounties to raid, the place is so well defended naturally it would take a small army to storm the citadel."

"That's what I was thinking..." Dean said wistfully.

Sam said, "You want to take it by force with a private army?"

"No. Nothing so ridiculous. Besides, time is a matter of essence, we need to capture her now, before she has time to prepare."

"Well what else are you suggesting?"

Dean Godkin said, "A small… covert operation. You and myself. We go in via boat, and capture Sarah Rhinehart and bring her to trial."

Sam met his eye. "You sure you don't mean execute without a jury?"

"No. This needs to be public. I want this to come out."

"You want her dead."

"Of course I do. She's responsible for the deaths of a lot of good people – my people, including my brother. But the best way to get revenge is to bring her in and shut down her entire operation. So I'll swallow my pride and bring her in for a trial."

"Do you promise you're not going to go in there and shoot her dead?"

"The thought did cross my mind, but no, that won't shut down the program. Someone else will take her place. The only way to bring this thing forward, is to bring Rhinehart in for a trial."

"All right, then we stick to the plan… if we're going to do this, we're going to need all the help we can get."

"What did you have in mind?"

"There's a woman, Deborah Easley. She helped save your brother from drowning at St. Martins Sea Caves. She actually lives at the point, just overlooking the main runway at Comox. She's organized to bring in two friends of hers who might be able to help us out."

"Help?" Dean's brow furrowed with confusion. "I thought you didn't want to make this a personal army thing?"

"I don't. These two people are here to provide some expert local advice about the region. One is named Mark. He's a third-generation logger, who has worked on the Island all his life. If anyone knows something about the Seymour Narrows, its him."

"And the other guy?"

"He's named Doug. A real wild man, Deb tells me. He goes out and hunts in the dangerous wilderness at the north of the island. She says, if we want to talk about access and things, he's the guy to talk to."

"Can we trust them?"

"Yeah." Sam shrugged. "Deb says we can. Besides, I'm not telling them we want to kidnap a rich woman who lives there. We just want to find out how to beat the river. From what I've read, it takes serious local knowledge to reach it."

"You sure we can't fly?"

"No. I've looked at the maps. The river is deadly to land on. We're just as likely to get sucked up into some sort of whirlpool when we land. No, we'll have to take a small powerboat."

"All right, let's go meet your friend."

They walked up to the airport, following the route around Kye Road, before stopping at the gate of a large house right on the point overlooking the bay. The house was surrounded by a manicured garden with verdant grass, where two deer – a mother and her fawn – nibbled happily. They stopped, looked up at Sam and Dean, saw that they meant them no harm, and went back to nibbling.

Sam knocked on Deb's door.

She opened it a few seconds later. "Hello Sam."

"Hi Deb," Sam said. "Thanks for helping us out. I really appreciate it."

"No problem," she said, her eyes landing on Dean. "You look almost exactly like your brother."

Chapter Sixty-Two

They followed Deb through her house to a small table and chairs out the back that overlooked the bay all the way out to the mainland. Sam's eyes swept the spectacular vista. Her property was roughly thirty feet above the bay, giving her an excellent vantage point. The yard was spartan, with a few manicured plants surrounding a grassed area, where a single spruce tree dominated the vista, upon which, a large bald-headed eagle stood perched upon its massive nest.

The tide was out, and the dark stones that lined the shore stretched nearly two hundred feet out into the bay, where a couple of grown women and a whole bunch of kids collected seashells. Deb pointed them out, proudly telling Sam that they were her daughters, and grandkids.

At the table, Sam and Dean were introduced to Mark and Doug. They sat down and Deb offered some coffee straight from the pot. Sam accepted the offer and Dean knocked it back, asking for some water instead.

A few minutes later, after some basic civilities were met, Mark said, "I hear you need to reach a property along the Seymour Narrows?"

"That's right. It's a long story, but we'd rather not be seen in the process."

Doug said, "Why not go in overland then?"

Dean shook his head. "We're fairly certain the owner of the house in question has a high-tech security surveillance system in place through the woods. We might get lucky, but we're most likely to be caught."

"Whereas, coming by the water you can come straight up through the front door," Mark said. "I mean there's much less risk of people coming in through the Narrow, but the fact is, people do take their boats there. So what's to stop you being spotted even via the water?"

"Nothing," Sam admitted. "But at least we'll have their security down to a smaller area. If she's going to be tipped off that we're coming, the less time we can make it between finding out and us actually being there, the better."

"Okay." Mark suppressed a grin. "Tell me, what do you know about the Seymour Narrows?"

"Not much. I've looked at them on a map and I can see that there's a hell of a lot of ocean water being squeezed between a lethal narrow point. I know they have a reputation of creating a fairly dangerous environment for boating."

Mark genuinely laughed at that. "Dangerous might be the understatement."

Sam sighed. "All right, so tell us about the Seymour Narrows."

Mark drew a breath, trying to consider where to begin. "Seymour Narrows is a three-mile section of the Discovery Passage in British Columbia known for strong tidal currents. Discovery Passage lies between Vancouver Island at Menzies Bay, British Columbia and Quadra Island except at its northern end where the eastern shoreline is Sonora Island. The section known as Seymour Narrows begins about eleven miles from the south end of Discovery Passage where it enters the Georgia Strait near Campbell River. For most of the length of the narrows, the channel is about half a mile wide. Through this narrow channel, currents regularly reach fifteen knots."

"That's where Ripple Rock once existed?"

"Yeah, Ripple Rock was a submerged twin-peak mountain that lay just nine feet beneath the surface of Seymour Narrows. It was a serious hazard to shipping, sinking 119 vessels and taking 114 lives. The gunboat *USS Saranac* was one of the rock's first recorded victims. On April 5, 1958, after twenty-seven months of tunneling and engineering work, Ripple Rock was blown up with 1,375 tons of Nitramex 2H explosive making it the largest commercial, non-nuclear blast in North America. The Halifax Explosion in 1917 was larger but it was not a deliberate act."

"So how dangerous are the narrows these days?"

"The Seymour Narrows is part of a maze-like series of small channels and cuts stretching between Seattle and Alaska known as the Inside Passage. It's often frequented by cruise ships today, but the spectacular coastal views and protection from open ocean come at a price. The areas are made dangerous by tidal currents. These oceanic capillaries are where the sea breathes in and out in the form of tides. Ocean rapids like Seymour's are the result of a differential between tidal elevations at either end. These differentials essentially create bi-directional ocean-rivers. Add a large, jagged underwater rock to the already difficult-to-steer passage and you have a recipe for shipwrecks."

The ground shook suddenly with the might of an earthquake, filled by a terrible roar like thunder splitting the clouds, before the sky above turned dark with the roar of a squadron of fighter jets, taking off just above Deb's house.

It was so loud, Sam had to cover his ears.

When the jets began to disappear beyond the horizon, Sam asked, "What was that?"

Deb smiled. "That's the Canadian Forces Base Comox 19 Wing. They're flying McDonnell Douglas CF-18 Hornet fighter-interceptors."

Sam watched them as they banked, simultaneously in perfect formation and headed north. "Do they do that often?"

"Not too often, just a couple times a day. You get used to it really... living underneath a RCAF base."

"I guess so."

Over the next twenty or so minutes, Doug and Mark debated about the best times to approach the Seymour Narrows and how to do so. It was decided that slack tide was the only time to even attempt it, and a jetboat, like a large inflatable Zodiac with twin or even quad outboard motors designed to overcome the ocean rapids, which flowed at more than 15 knots, was the only vessel to use.

When they were finished, Sam asked, "Anything else we should know?"

Doug folded his arms across his chest. "Yeah, watch out for the grizzlies up there."

Sam frowned. "Grizzlies... I didn't think they made it out to the island?"

"Oh... they do," Mark backed Doug up.

Doug said, "They generally swim across the channel from the mainland, although there have been some reports over the past few years of them actually hibernating on the island. They're particularly common on the Campbell River where you're going."

Dean said, "I don't think they'll be a problem. I assure you we'll be the deadliest species on the island."

Doug laughed at that. "Oh yeah, what sort of weapons are you packing?"

Dean wasn't planning on being forthcoming on his not so small arsenal he had in storage just for this specific trip.

Watching Dean for a response, and being met with only silence, Doug patted him on the shoulders and said, "Good luck with it. Because, just so you know, unless you're armed for an African safari, with the sort of caliber weapon needed to take down an elephant, the grizzlies will make short work of you."

Sam didn't want the bravado to get out of hand. Instead, he changed the topic, drawing it back to the interesting fact that grizzlies were living on Vancouver Island. "That must be a nightmare having the grizzlies permanently on the island?"

"Not really," Doug replied. "From the top of the mountain to the valley bottom and estuaries, they are a keystone species for biodiversity."

"Really?" Sam asked, surprised to find Doug so much of an environmentalist.

Doug smiled. "Grizzlies play a huge role in nature, particularly in coastal ecosystems. Salmon carcasses they discard fuel tree and plant growth, and in the alpine, they cultivate the soil by digging up squirrel holes and bulbs."

"What about the black bears?" Sam asked.

"What about them?" Doug replied.

"I thought Vancouver Island had the densest population of black bears in the world?"

"Uh-huh. There's about 7,000 living on the island. Plenty of them up there along the Campbell River, but they won't cause you much trouble."

Sam asked, "Do the grizzlies and the black bears get along?"

"I think they're mostly indifferent to each other," Doug said. "That is, unless they're short of food or territory."

Sam suppressed a grin. "Then what happens."

Doug turned to Mark. "You want to tell him what you found in your backyard?"

Mark shrugged. "I was out walking with my dog a couple years ago and came across a black bear completely gutted."

Sam's eyes narrowed. "You think a grizzly bear did it?"

"Well, I can tell you now, there's no other animal on Vancouver Island capable of doing that."

Dean gritted his teeth, smiling maliciously. "I could name at least one other animal."

Sam stood up. "All right, it's been interesting hearing about your take on navigating the Seymour Narrows, and about the grizzly bears, but we'd better get going."

"You're welcome," Mark said.

Doug said, "If you head up to the township of Campbell River, there's a marina there. I believe there's a tour company that offers ocean rapid tours. I doubt they will be interested in renting out one of their craft, but you never know."

Sam said, "Thanks, that's a good idea. We'll look into it."

Sam and Dean thanked Deb for her help, and Sam promised to tell her how everything panned out in the end.

They left and walked back to the long-term parking where Dean had left his rental car, along with the arsenal he planned to use to assault Sarah Rhinehart's citadel.

It would take planning, and preparation, but Sam was beginning to see that it would be possible to capture Rhinehart.

The question remained, whether that was the best course of action?

As he pondered this, his cell phone rang.

And suddenly, everything had changed.

Chapter Sixty-Three

Sam glanced at his cell phone.

The incoming call was from Margaret. AKA the US Secretary of Defense.

He answered it immediately. "Madam Secretary?"

"I'm afraid she's a little busy right now," came an unfamiliar woman's voice. "May I take a message?"

Sam thought back to Margaret's last message – she was on her way to meet Sarah Rhinehart now – and a cold shadow crept down his spine.

Sam felt his heart skip a beat. "Who are you?"

"My name is Sarah Rhinehart."

"Rhinehart?" Sam said the name slowly, as though it seemed unfamiliar to him. "I'm sorry you have me at a loss. How do I know you? And why do you have the Secretary of Defense's cell phone?"

She laughed. "Let's not play games. You know who I am and I know who you are. What's more, you and I both need each other."

"Okay, I'm listening."

Rhinehart said, "I have Margaret. People believe she's here as my guest, but if you were to send in an assault team, I assure you she wouldn't come out of the attack alive."

Sam drew a breath. "All right. What do you suggest?"

"An exchange. The USB and Dean Godkin for her."

"I don't even know what's on it."

She said, "Ah, but I do. And I assure you, I want to keep it that way."

"You're proposing a trade?"

"Yes."

Sam's eyes met Godkin's in the distance. "All right. I'll do it."

"And, Sam… I don't want to have half the bloody US Navy coming in on me. I'm giving you this one chance. It's just you and Godkin coming in via boat. If I spot anyone else, I'll kill her myself. Do I make myself clear?"

Sam gritted his teeth. "Crystal."

Godkin looked at him. His piercing gray eyes landing on him like the inquisitor. "She knows we're coming, doesn't she?"

Sam shrugged. "She's got an idea."

"She might be expecting us, but not this quickly."

Sam nodded. "No, she's not expecting us, not like this."

Chapter Sixty-Four

Campbell River Marina

Sam stepped into what appeared to be a red, floating barn house.

It was the main office of the adventure sightseeing tour company. Behind the counter a twenty-something year old woman with long blonde hair, a big smile, and thick ski jacket booked an older couple in for a guided tour of the ocean rapids.

When she was finished, Sam introduced himself, and asked if she had any vessel for rent. She apologized, and informed him that the company didn't rent any of their fleet out, but that he could hire a guide and a boat for a private adventure. After some discussions, and eventually managing to get through to the owner of the company, Sam handed down one hell of a deposit, and paid an exorbitant fee to hire a vessel for 24 hours. The guide, a woman named Bec, brought him and Dean out to the last finger of the marina, which housed a large Zodiac.

She said, "This is *Roxy*, our newest Zodiac, built by Victorian based builders Titan Boats. She has been custom designed to meet the unique environment found along the Campbell River and Seymour Narrows. She has twin 300 hp Yamaha outboards, which will allow you to churn your way through the worst of the ocean rapids found anywhere along the Vancouver Isles."

Sam ran his eyes across the vessel. It looked like one of those jetboats you see taking tourists up rivers, trying to scare them by getting dangerously close to rocks as they scream along. It was basically an oversized Zodiac inflatable. It had a standing pilot-house with a wheel toward the back of the boat, and about a dozen seats up front in the complete open. They would be sitting ducks as they approached Rhinehart's estate.

He didn't trust her, but he hoped to hell that she would keep her word to avoid the wrath of the US Department of Defense. All she had to do was keep her cool long enough for Sam to make the exchange. After that, it was anyone's guess what would happen.

Sam studied the pilot house. It was standing with a small cover for sun protection over a small framework of aluminum. At the back of which, was a rescue buoy and what appeared to be an oversized sea scooter.

Sam looked at the saleswoman. "What's the story with the diver propulsion vehicle?"

"Oh, that's for use in the case of a person overboard."

Sam frowned. "Come again?"

Bec said, "The whirlpools along the Seymour Narrows are so powerful that it would be impossible to swim against them to escape their deadly clutches. Thus, for safety each of our Zodiacs have a highly powerful DPV. There are two breathing regulators, but just enough air for roughly five minutes of consumption by two people in shallow depths."

Sam looked at her, a wry and incredulous grin plastered across his lips. "You're kidding, right?"

"No, I'm deadly serious."

"Has it ever been used?"

"No, not yet. And I hope it will never have to."

"I'm not sure it's the best solution?"

"Really, what do you know about these things?" she asked, her voice dubious, but polite.

"I've had a little bit of experience recently with whirlpools and DPVs. I think you'd be hard pressed to rescue someone using one – especially with just five minutes' supply of air."

She shrugged. "I don't know, but all the more reason to be careful out there."

Sam nodded. "Okay, we will be."

Sam thanked her, and she wished them well.

A few minutes later, Dean turned up with his goodies in their military box on top of a wheel barrow. They loaded the box onto the boat and a few minutes later, Sam turned the ignition and the twin 300 hp Yamaha outboards roared to life with a throaty growl. Dean untied the lines, climbed on board, and Sam motored *Roxy* out into the river. They headed north for about fifteen minutes before pulling into the calm waters of a nearby estuary to gear up.

Godkin opened his storage box.

It looked like something that would have made Rambo proud. There were grenades, pistols, a sniper rifle, and a couple submachineguns.

Godkin handed Sam a Kevlar bullet proof vest. "It probably won't do you much good. Anyone worth anything will put bullets in your head as soon as we step off the boat, but… hey, no reason not to protect yourself where you can."

Sam took it, placing the vest over his shirt. "Thanks."

It looked more than a little obvious, but what did that matter? Rhinehart must know that he wasn't going to walk into a trap completely defenseless? He looked at Godkin. His vest looked different somehow. It had places for weapons and all sort of things.

His eyes narrowed on Godkin's chest. "What are those?"

Godkin pulled back the Velcro covers, revealing six grenades. "I know how this is going to go… and I have no intention of going quietly."

Sam said, "You don't know that…"

Godkin stopped him with the wave of his hand. "You and I both know Rhinehart needs me and the USB stick. You and the Secretary of Defense might get lucky, but that's not on the cards for me."

Sam was going to try and say something in Godkin's defense, but stopped himself. Godkin was speaking the truth. Rhinehart needed him. If they had more time to go in with a Special Forces assault team, they might be able to save the Secretary of Defense and still walk away, but as it was, with the time constraints, it was unlikely any of them were getting out alive, and even less likely that Godkin was.

Sam said, "All right. But if we're going to do this, I think I have a better idea of how we're going to win. And also, there's one thing we have going for us."

Godkin said, "Oh yeah, what's that?"

Sam's voice was cold and unbroken. "Rhinehart knows all about you, but she has no idea who she's picked a fight with, when she came after me."

Chapter Sixty-Five

Roxy, the over-powered jetboat raced north along the Campbell River.

It was midday. The sky was a regal blue brindle, with the softest accents of white. The crisp air was warmed by the beams of sun, making the river sparkle like diamonds, in nature's paradise. Sam motored past Menzies Bay, the one just before the narrows. Up ahead, he got his first glimpse of Seymour Narrows, connecting the Johnstone Strait in the north to the Strait of Georgia in the south.

The water looked deceptively calm.

It was a deep, sapphire blue, with shades of viridian nearer to the jagged rocky shore. There were a series of white and disturbed water up ahead, indicating highly aerated sections of the river. The tide had just turned, so the greatest amounts of water were about to be forced through the narrowest point in the river, where two oceans of water met.

Sam motored slowly, trying to get a feel for the river, before he upped the throttle and tried to escape its lethal tendrils. In the back of his mind he recalled what Deb's friend, Mark, had said regarding the strange water system.

There's no certainty where a whirlpool will form, and even on a perfectly still river, they have the ability to appear out of nowhere. Still, there are things to remember, that help you increase your odds of predicting their occurrence.

They tend to appear just downstream of areas where the water gets funneled into a constricted area. Where the waterway opens up again, you'll probably get an eddy – localized back-current – and there will be a line where the two opposing currents cross known as an eddy line. If the strength of these currents is high enough, a whirlpool can appear. Of course, there can also be considerations underneath the water, such as shelves that can contribute, so whirlpools are not always easy to predict.

Sam looked at Dean, who was holding onto the side rail with a single hand. His expression was unperturbed. Even relaxed. As though the elemental dangers were nothing to him, more than that, they only reinforced his belief that he was the most dangerous thing for a hundred miles. Given what they were up against, Sam was glad that the man felt that way.

He eased the throttles forward, and *Roxy* motored against the strong current, barely keeping pace. He didn't gun it. Not yet. He wanted to get a feel for the extreme power of mother nature. He was tiptoeing his way along.

A small maelstrom opened up nearby.

It was probably only three or four feet across, but it was deep – Sam couldn't see its bottom. In his jittery state, it appeared to run to the ocean floor. Fueled by fear, he increased the throttle probably a little more than he needed, and nudged the Zodiac out of its pull. A passing log about half the size of a telegraph pole, was not so lucky. Sam watched in awe, as it was sucked down the vortex and out of sight, before the whirlpool closed over it like a giant mouth, clamping shut.

What seemed like minutes later, but was probably only seconds, the log's buoyancy triumphed over the dissipated current – shooting upright out of the water like a breaching whale some fifty or more feet away.

Sam knew that whirlpools in this area varied from the thousands of insignificant – harmless although they will still change your course – to hundreds of open whirlpools several feet across and which are steep sloped and several feet deep – capable of grabbing and capsizing small boats – to a few huge and stationery pools 30 to 40 feet across, capable of sinking even large boats.

Up ahead, two opposing currents began to meet, forming a large, stationary ocean rapid – of which the Seymour Narrows and Skookumchuck rapids were notorious. Sam reduced power, until *Roxy* became stationary against the 15-knot current, as he considered the best way to approach it. The ocean rapid looked like one of those stationary waves at a mechanical surf park. The water itself was glossy, instead of foamy, almost surreal. Two kayakers, wearing double life-jackets, crested the wave and began screaming with joy as they rode the unbelievable rapid.

Sam and Dean exchanged a glance. Sam said, "Now those people are nuts!"

Dean checked his weapons. The two of them were about to take on an entire drug cartel on their own, at the Boss's home turf. He made a wistful smile. "Yeah, completely crazy."

Sam pushed the twin-throttles all the way forward, and *Roxy's* powerful outboard whined, as her strength began to overcome the current.

Sam said, "Hold on!"

Godkin gave a half-shrug, as though there was nothing nature could throw at him anything that he couldn't handle.

The Zodiac hit the wave slowly.

Her bow simply rode the base of the ocean rapid. For a few seconds they were stationary. Trapped in the grip of its awesome power.

The engines' pitch edged closer to a scream.

And *Roxy's* bow finally broached the crest of the wave, with a giant splash.

The boat dropped down into another world.

Sam felt like they were edging through a battle zone. A strange cross between no-man's land on the Western Front and some sort of utopic paradise best left to the Discovery Channel. Small whirlpools, known as piglets, began erupting all over the place, their small but powerful current sending the Zodiac every which direction, as he fought to escape their pull. Above them, a convocation of more than a hundred bald-headed eagles filled the sky, temporarily darkening the sun. The apex predators, seemingly flying and diving and reaping the easy rewards of the battleground, as nature turned to pandemonium.

A few seconds later, Sam's eyes spotted the cause of the strange sight about a hundred feet upriver, where a giant maelstrom had opened up. Its vortex running at least twenty or possibly even thirty feet deep. All that water being sucked down into the spiraling whirlpool had to go somewhere, and it began gushing out, like a subdued geyser – where salmon, by the hundreds, were inadvertently thrown into the sky – and predators gorged on the plentiful fish with indulgence. Three grizzly bears climbed down a large tree that jutted out from a rocky outcrop to the west bank, taking their share of the helpless fish.

Somewhere toward the eastern bank, several sea lions lazed with indifference on a small island. And beside the island, jutting out along a point on Quadra Island directly opposite the Ripple Rock lookout, a citadel made of locally quarried granite rose majestically from the water's edge, perched up high, like the greatest predator of them all.

Sam turned *Roxy* into a small inlet carved into the edge of the river, where some massive boulders, where more than a dozen sealions lazed, formed a natural shelter. Behind which, a narrow channel had been carved into the stone's edge, leaving enough room for him to pilot the Zodiac up into a protected harbor that appeared more like one hell of a garage for the ultra-rich than anything else.

It tunneled through the rocky mountain, and revealed an inner, protected harbor. There was just enough room to turn the jetboat around and tie up against a wooden jetty that seemed oddly out of place. A single floatplane was tied off at the end of the jetty. Sam pictured its pilot trying to build up enough speed through the channel-cum-tunnel, before taking off into the Seymour Narrows. As a pilot, he couldn't imagine a worse place to try and takeoff or land, but whoever the pilot was, had probably managed to do it a number of times.

Above them, Sarah Rhinehart held a pistol to the back of the Secretary of Defense's head, and said, "Sam Reilly, welcome to my fortress."

Chapter Sixty-Six

Ripple Rock Lookout

Genevieve set up the Barrett M107 Sniper Rifle.

The weapon was a recoil-operated, semi-automatic anti-materiel precision rifle developed by the American Barrett Firearms Manufacturing company. Despite its designation as an anti-materiel rifle, it was used by some armed forces as an anti-personnel system. The M107 variant is also called the Light Fifty for its .50 BMG chambering. This variant had a muzzle brake designed to accept a suppressor and made out of titanium instead of steel.

She attached the suppressor.

Beside her, Tom stared at the granite citadel through a pair of binoculars. She said, "How many have you got?"

Tom said, "I count eight, plus Rhinehart and the Secretary of Defense."

Genevieve nodded. "And that's why, when Sam Reilly says he's got things under control, we still need to come and save his ass."

"I know, and that's why I listened to you."

Genevieve got comfortable, lying in a prone shooting position. She brought the scope to her eye. They had a good view of the river, and a reasonable view of the citadel. The river was 2,460 feet wide and had a depth of 330 feet. From their vantage point, the entire thing looked deadly. Some of those vortexes seemed to reach all the way to the bottom of those 330 feet.

She scanned the citadel.

There were four people on the main rampart, each with rifles. Another two on the tower at the back of the main castle wall, and two more guards who were heading toward the secured section, that led down to the castle's private harbor. There was no way to tell how many others were still inside the building. She had a good visual on most of it, with the exception of the private harbor – in which she could only just see the tops of a floatplane and Sam's Zodiac.

She aimed toward the open space between the harbor and the main castle. A place that looked every bit like a miniaturized rolling grass lawn of an English manor. She began to prepare mentally for the kill shot. Snipers typically operate at ranges between 1000 and 3000 feet, and occasionally take an enemy out from much farther away. A Canadian special forces sniper, for instance, shattered the world record for longest confirmed kill shot in 2017, shooting an ISIS fighter dead in Iraq from over two miles away. Then again, Genevieve was a good marksperson, but a long way off from a professional sniper.

The big question was, could Sam draw Rhinehart out into the open long enough for her to take a shot?

Genevieve locked onto Sam and Dean, tracking their movements up toward the open green space. She drew a breath. Because there, in front of them, she could see the Secretary of Defense and Sarah Rhinehart.

She closed her left eye, and exhaled slowly. The slightest of smiles crept across her lips.

Because she had a clear sight on Sarah Rhinehart.

Chapter Sixty-Seven

Sam Reilly stepped off the Zodiac.

He pointed his Glock at Godkin and gestured for the man to walk ahead. Godkin appeared to have his wrists bound behind his back. His hands appeared to be balled into angry fists, surrounding something.

Sarah Rhinehart held a pistol to the Secretary of Defense's head. She glanced at Sam, then at his prisoner, and smiled. "Mr. Reilly, it is so good to see a man who delivers as good as his word."

"I try, ma'am."

His eyes swept the compound, taking in the two security guards closest to them – each carrying submachineguns – the six shooters stationed on the rampart and tower, before finally landing on the Secretary of Defense. She was tall, with short-cropped, dark red hair. Despite her position, the hardened bony features of her face betrayed no fear, and only the arrogant confidence of someone accustomed to power. She wore confident smile and the regal air of a person who knew exactly how the next few minutes were going to play out.

Sam said, "Madam Secretary."

She suppressed a grin. "Sam. You took your time. I expected you an hour ago."

"I'm sorry ma'am. The Campbell River can be a tad challenging at times, but we'll have you out of here any minute."

Rhinehart kept her arm around the Secretary's neck, using her as a shield from any would-be snipers waiting on the opposite side of the Seymour Narrows. Her pistol – something old that looked like it belonged in a Dirty Harry movie with Clint Eastwood – aimed at the Secretary's head. Behind them, the two guards looked edgy. This was probably the closest either of them had ever come to using their weapons.

Sam kept his Glock leveled at Godkin. His eyes met Rhinehart. "So, how do you want to do this thing?"

"A simple exchange."

"Go on?"

Rhinehart shrugged. "You send Godkin to me, and when he gets half way, I'll send your Secretary of Defense."

"No. Why should I let you have the advantage? Why don't we send both prisoners across no-man's land together?"

"Do you play chess, Mr. Reilly?"

Sam smiled, taken aback by her strange segue. "Excuse me?"

"Chess. You know the little game children and kings alike have been playing for centuries? The one with the little horses, the king, the queen, some religious thingy…"

"I know chess…" Sam said, still holding his pistol aimed at Godkin. "I just don't know what this has to do with the game?"

"Well, in this analogy, I have the Secretary of Defense – AKA the queen in chess – and you have a soldier – a mere pawn."

Sam arched an eyebrow. "You think your chess piece is worth more than mine?"

"Bingo."

Sam shrugged. "All right… count of three. I tell my chess piece to walk forward. When he gets to that midway point, you release the Secretary of Defense. Agreed?"

"Agreed."

Sam said, "Off you go Godkin."

Godkin stepped forward. His hooded eyes, somber, weary lines etched into his hard face, like a man resigned to death.

At the midway point, Godkin stopped.

His eyes fixed toward the rampart and tower.

Sam said, "Let the Secretary go, Rhinehart."

"I don't think so." Rhinehart turned her pistol toward him. "It appears you carelessly no longer have anything to trade."

Sam didn't wait for Rhinehart to take the first shot.

He aimed for the guard closest to him, and squeezed off two shots. The 9mm parabellums landed on his chest and neck. The guard fell to the ground and made no sign of getting up again. A third shot fired from the other side of the river, and the second guard died instantly. The sniper from the other side of the river now focused on the marksmen on the ramparts.

Shots rained down from the tower and the rampart.

Sam dived to the ground, and began returning fire.

Godkin uncrossed his wrists, the small nylon band, having never been attached. In his hands, he gripped two grenades. He threw them one after the other. One landed on the ramparts, closest to them, and the other inside the tower.

Four…

Three…

Two…

One…

The grenades exploded.

The rampart shook violently, like an earthquake had taken hold of its weary foundations. Its granite walls shook, and began to tumble, sending shards of splintered stone in all directions. The tower was tall and narrow, built for its noble looks instead of purpose, and the explosion was too much for it to take. The tower swayed, before giving out, and crumbling down in an earth-shattering display of destruction.

Rhinehart, like the best of gamblers, withdrew and regained control of the situation. She pushed the barrel of her pistol into the back of the Secretary's head, holding her in close like a shield. "Everyone stop!"

Sam and Godkin both aimed their handguns at Rhinehart. It might be possible to take her out, but the shot would be extremely difficult under the best of circumstances, and any mistake and the Secretary would get killed.

Sam, keeping up with the whole chess analogy, said, "What's the next move for a queen without the rest of her army?"

Rhinehart made a wry smile. "Mr. Reilly, don't you realize the queen controls the whole board?"

Sam said, "All right, so what are you going to do?"

"Not me, you."

"Okay. Go on, what am I going to do?"

"Nothing. You and Godkin are going to wait here. A queen can get to any point on the board she chooses. I choose to get on my floatplane and get out of here." She leveled her gaze at Sam. "If I see you or Godkin try and follow me, I'll kill the bitch."

The Secretary drew a breath, but there was no fear in her face. As with the rest of her life, she was the most valuable piece in the game. Everyone wanted to keep her alive. She was either a bargaining chip or a boss. Either way, they all needed her. With equanimity, she said, "Let us go, Sam."

Sam lowered his head. "Yes, ma'am."

He watched as Rhinehart and the Secretary descended the stairs down to the floatplane, below the line of sight of Genevieve's shot. She started the ignition. The little Cessna 172's propeller began to turn, quickly disappearing into a whir. Rhinehart threw off the mooring lines, and powered up. A couple of seconds later, Sam watched at the Cessna disappeared down through the tunnel, and out into the Seymour Narrows.

The floatplane engine rose a pitch, and the floatplane, broke free from its earthly restraints, beginning to climb like the bald-headed eagles that soared nearby.

Sam heard the report of several shots being fired. One, if not more, of the rounds struck the nose of the floatplane, ripping the propeller from its engine cowling, as a series of sparks flew from the nose of the aircraft.

Rhinehart, proving herself to be a good pilot, dropped the nose to maintain airspeed, and set up for an immediate landing. She pulled back, slowed her airspeed and flared directly above the calmest section of the Seymour Narrows, her pontoons barely creating a splash.

Without a propeller to maintain any forward movement, the floatplane was at the mercy of the currents – and almost immediately, it was caught, and drawn toward the large maelstrom.

Chapter Sixty-Eight

Sam and Godkin climbed onto the Zodiac, threw off the lines, and raced through the tunnel and out into the Seymour Narrows.

The tide had now fully changed its course, and the river had turned deadlier.

He looked at Godkin. "Can you see it?"

Godkin's eyes narrowed. "Over there!"

Sam squinted. Then he saw it.

The floatplane, without a propeller, had begun to drift… and had been swept up into the violent current. It was being quickly drawn toward the largest maelstrom. The sort of thing that had sunk countless vessels over the years. Not just small runabouts, but large ships, and even a ferry. For the floatplane, delicately resting on its twin pontoons, the whirlpool would crush it in an instant, before swallowing it whole, and digesting its remains in the rocky seabed far below.

Godkin exchanged a glance with Sam. Without hesitation, or thought of his own safety, he said, "Quick, you know what you have to do!"

Sam pushed the throttles all the way forward, racing toward the maelstrom.

The aircraft seemed to hang in there longer than he expected. Caught up in the current, the floatplane drifted aimlessly in large circles, with each revolution, being drawn closer to the eye of the vortex.

On the outside of the floatplane, both Rhinehart and the Secretary of Defense stood on the pontoons, gripping the wing arches for support. Rhinehart no longer appeared to be wielding a pistol at the Secretary. Given the likely outcome of the floatplane, trapped in the whirlpool, the win was probably moot.

Sam threw all caution to the wind, and instead of trying to enter the outer edge of the maelstrom, he turned the Zodiac straight for the eye of the vortex, and accelerated fully.

Roxy whined as she skipped over the outer waves of the whirlpool, before quickly becoming caught inside the narrowing eye at the center.

One after the other, the floatplane and the Zodiac spun around, slowly being sucked deeper into the vortex. The vertical walls of water now a deadly cliff some thirty feet, Sam knew it would be impossible for either vessel to climb out. After several loops around the spinning whirlpool, the vortex narrowed until both the floatplane and the Zodiac locked together.

Sam recalled the log he'd seen enter a small maelstrom earlier in the day, and pictured the water above closing in on them, sealing them like a giant mouth, thirty or more feet beneath the surface. A split second later, both vessels were drawn under, and the maelstrom closed up – burying them beneath more than a million gallons of water…

Chapter Sixty-Nine

The last thing Sam Reilly did before his world turned to darkness, was grab hold of the rescue DPV, placing the first regulator he could get his hands on, into his mouth. He pressed the start button, and the twin electric propellers whirred into life.

Sam didn't have a mask on, and the entire environment appeared like an obtuse blur. He could make out shapes and not much more. The highly buoyant Zodiac, ripped free from the dying maelstrom, and disappeared downriver. The floatplane tumbled along into the seemingly bottomless abyss.

He opened the electric throttle, and gripped the DPV with all his might, chasing after the sinking floatplane. His ears hurt, indicating he was descending faster than he could naturally equalize the pressure in his ears. He had no idea how deep they had dropped, but nor did he care. There was nothing he could do about that.

When he reached it, he realized that the Secretary and Rhinehart were nowhere to be seen. Their bodies, likely to have been knocked off, and separated from the aircraft as the vortex dragged them under.

He turned around, and spotted Rhinehart, as her body was flung helplessly around, like a ragdoll in a washing machine. Their eyes locked together for an instant, and Sam saw the abject terror in Rhinehart's face, and then she was gone.

A split second later, the Secretary came into view.

Sam mentally calculated a projection between where the Secretary was being dragged by the current and then aimed the DPV in a diagonal line toward her.

The seconds passed slowly, but his mental calculations proved accurate.

He grabbed hold of her waist with his left hand, locking in tight, to make sure he didn't lose her. With his right hand, he fed her the secondary regulator. The Secretary didn't need any more help than that. She took the regulator, placed it in her mouth and drew a deep breath. A second later she wrapped her arms around him, locking her fingers together in a vice like grip, that indicated if she was going to drown, she would be taking him with her.

It meant he could return both hands to the sea scooter.

Sam turned the DPV upward.

Roughly ten feet from the surface, their air supply ran out.

Sam slowly breathed out, kicking hard as they ascended, and the DPV whined against the discombobulated current.

They surfaced in the middle of the Seymour Narrows.

It was a giant sea of disturbed water.

And Sam doubted very much that they were going to make it out alive.

Their energy was already spent, the DPV had nowhere near enough power to keep pulling them out of the entire river, and they were close to drowning. The Secretary's head kept dipping underwater, her red hair cascading across her face.

They were floating downriver.

Sam spotted a small inlet that offered some shelter.

It was roughly fifty-fifty that they would make it. If he failed, they would be caught up in the ocean rapids that formed around the point of the rocky outcrop.

He pointed the sea scooter, and told the Secretary to hold on tight.

Soon the water settled, and he motored all the way up to the jagged bank of the river. He helped the Secretary climb onto a rock at the eastern bank of the river.

Safe out of the water, they both lay on their backs, barely enough energy to breathe.

After a few minutes, the Secretary rolled over and looked at Sam. Her emerald green eyes meeting his. She smiled. "Sam…"

"Yes ma'am?"

"Thank you for saving my life."

"You're welcome."

"I never doubted you would come through for me." She smiled magnanimously, giving him the briefest kiss on his lips. "This is exactly why I didn't want to lose you."

"Thank you, ma'am," Sam said, glad to see that her near death experience hadn't chipped her steely armor.

"Sam?"

"Yes, ma'am?"

"Dean Godkin's dead, isn't he?"

Sam thought back to the ghost of a man he'd seen out the corner of his eye, walking on the other side of the beach, heading north, into Vancouver Island's great wilderness. He thought about the man who had traded his life and everything he knew for his country, for honor and duty – and even after being betrayed – had willingly sacrificed his own life to save the Secretary's.

"Sam?" she persisted, her voice suddenly crisp.

He exhaled slowly. "Godkin's dead, ma'am. No one, even hyped up on Berserker drugs could have survived being pulled into that vortex."

She smiled. "Very good. Then that's it. Everyone and everything involved in RX16SF is now dead, and the entire project can be shelved for good."

Sam said, "As you wish, Madam Secretary."

Chapter Seventy

Gros Morne, Canada – Four Weeks Later

It took 485 million years for Mother Nature to create Gros Morne National Park, a place unlike any other on earth. A UNESCO World Heritage Site covering more than a thousand square miles the park is a never-ending series of wonders and delights, and a demonstration of the spectacularly raw and enigmatic beauty of the physical world.

The *Tahila* entered the majestic fjord.

On its deck, Sam took a reading of the sun using the sunstone and Uunartoq disc. He exhaled slowly. A grin formed on his parted lips.

Suttie said, "You look happy."

"I am." Sam handed her the ancient navigational device. "Have a look at this. It's a perfect match."

Suttie shook her head in wonder. "I can't believe we're tracking the same route these Vikings once took all those centuries ago!"

"It's quite something isn't it?"

"I'll say."

Over the past two weeks, they had followed the locations marked on the Uunartoq disc and the runic stone. It had taken the *Tahila* from Greenland to Newfoundland, all the way south to Oak Island, a place that has been a subject for treasure hunters ever since the late 1700s, with rumors that Captain Kidd's treasure was buried there.

While there was never much evidence to support what went on during the early excavations, stories began to be published and documented as early as 1856. Since that time there have been many theories that extend beyond that of Captain Kidd which include among others religious artifacts, manuscripts, and Marie Antoinette's jewels. The 'treasure' has also been prone to criticism by those who have dismissed search areas as natural phenomena. Of course, now Sam could see that some of those natural phenomena may have been caused by Vikings who inhabited there for some time.

Afterward, the Uunartoq disc took them on a voyage to L'Anse aux Meadows, a French-English name which can be translated as the bay with the grasslands. From L'Anse aux Meadows, the *Tahila* headed into the Atlantic. Somewhere, along the way, something occurred to the original Viking ship – a storm or a disaster of some sort – that caused them to turn back.

The markings on the Uunartoq disc showed the longship must have been damaged, or that there was a severe and prolonged storm, because the Viking vessel kept changing its latitude, before eventually entering the fjord at Gros Morne.

Suttie stared at the markings on the Uunartoq disc. There was only one more marking and it was close to the current one, indicating the final navigational sunstone reading was taken nearby. She paused. "They never made it back to L'Anse aux Meadows."

"It doesn't look like it," Sam admitted. "Since I've been reading up on it, there seems to be a lot of debate about the origins of L'Anse aux Meadows' name. Care to offer your opinion?"

"Sure. It's fairly straight forward."

"Do tell…" Sam said, a flicker of a smile on his lips.

"What? It's been researched to death."

"Go on. These things, in my experience, are rarely simple."

She placed her hands akimbo. "How the village itself came to be named 'L'Anse aux Meadows' is debated. One possibility is that 'L'Anse aux Meadows' is a corruption of the French designation L'Anse aux Méduses, which means 'Jellyfish Cove.' The shift from Méduses to 'Meadows' may have occurred because the landscape in the area tends to be open, with meadows. A more recent supposition is that it is derived from 'L'Anse à la Médée,' or 'The Medea's Cove,' the name it bears on an 1862 French naval chart. Whether Medea or Medusa, it is possible that the name refers to a French naval vessel."

"When referring to the Medusa, you're sure it's about the French naval vessel?"

Suttie nodded. "I'm just going off what I've read, but yeah, it's meant to be about the French naval vessel. Why?"

Sam said, "And not the curse?"

"What curse?"

"There's a legend in Greek mythology about a snake haired gorgon, known as a medusa – and if you stare into its eyes, the curse will turn you to stone… it's known as the Medusa's Curse."

She shook her head. "No, I've never heard of that… and don't see how it could possibly relate to a 10th Century Viking settlement in Newfoundland."

"Neither do I, it was just a thought."

The *Tahila* continued its journey.

Soaring fjords and moody mountains towered high above them, concealing a diverse panorama of beaches and bogs, forests and barren cliffs. Shaped by colliding continents and grinding glaciers.

Sam stared at the spectacular vista. "It's beautiful, isn't it?"

Suttie agreed, her eyes locked on the distant horizon. "Did you know it was here where the theory of plate tectonics was confirmed. You can actually walk over ancient sea floor and preserved ocean avalanches. It's a distinctive red landscape of exposed earth's mantle, thrust up by the collision of tectonic plates millions of years ago."

"No, I didn't realize that."

"It's true," she said, an impish grin forming on her lips. "Want to guess the location of the only other place on earth where you can hike on the mantle?"

Sam said, "That would be Macquarie Island, somewhere roughly between the island of Tasmania and Antarctica – a distant part of Australia. Just one more unique thing shared between Canada and Australia."

Suttie glanced at Sam, a wry smile on her intelligent face. "You might be right there. We do tend to share a lot in common with Australia."

A couple hours later, the *Tahila* slowed to a stop. Sam checked and double checked the markings on the sunstone and Uunartoq disc. There was no doubt about it. They were at the right place. His eyes swept the towering cliffs that line the water's edge. This was the last location the ancient Viking navigator marked on the Uunartoq disc.

And yet, there was nothing to be seen. Definitely no sign of Valhalla.

Not on the surface, but possibly below...

As with so many things when it came to SCUBA diving... it might be a completely different story underwater.

Chapter Seventy-One

Sam, Tom, Genevieve, and Suttie all made the dive.

They wore dry suits with thick woolen clothing underneath. A quick reconnaissance of the seabed below, revealed a large landslide had dramatically changed the shape of the vertical cliff. Sam added some air to his BCD, finding his neutral buoyancy, as he explored the pile of rocky debris that now formed its own reef.

They dived around the reef, trying to find any evidence of a means through.

Sam began his ascent, and stopped.

At a depth of roughly twenty feet, two enormous boulders rested upon each other, providing an opening just large enough to swim through.

He switched on his flashlight, shining its beam into the dark abyss.

The question remained, where did it go to?

Sam got the rest of his group's attention and signaled that he was going to enter. He slowly kicked his fins, working his way gently through the small opening, while trying his best not to stir the silt below.

After twenty to thirty feet, the gap widened, before opening completely.

Sam waited for Suttie, Tom, and Genevieve to follow, and then slowly surfaced. His head broached the water. He gave a burst of air to inflate his BCD like a lifejacket. The sound echoed in the darkness, like he was in a massive chamber.

In the distance, a small beam of light radiated down from an opening high above.

It lit up an island.

They slowly swam toward the island. It was covered in strange plants, with leaves nearly seven feet wide. They reminded him of something straight out of Jurassic Park, but he'd seen them once before... in a small grotto on Black Bear Island, Manitoba.

Suttie said, "What is this place?"

Sam looked distantly around the grotto. "If I had to guess, I'd say it's Valhalla... but not as the Viking sagas would have us imagine it. Their gods, Odin and Thor, were just Hellenistic warriors who had discovered a plant that produced seeds capable of being ground up and ingested to provide super-human powers – and a tendency toward insanity – that led to the name, Berserkers, who were so prevalent in stories of ancient Viking Lore."

Epilogue

Sam Reilly read the final report from the Secretary of Defense.

A US and Canadian taskforce had raided Sarah Rhinehart's citadel on the outskirts of the Seymour Narrows shortly after the Secretary's near-death incident, shutting down a drug cartel known as The Berserkers. It revealed that Rhinehart, along with her family, had been harvesting the key ingredient of RX16SF – AKA the Berserker Drug – from a Jurassic flower found only in a small grotto near Black Bear Island, Manitoba. The grotto has been secured under Canadian National Trust, and protected so that botanists could study the unique flora. With the head of the cartel severed, the entire biker gang fell apart.

Sam was about to shut down his laptop, when another email came through, and caught his eye. It had come from an auction house associated with Christies, and had the simple heading…

Are you interested in this?

He almost deleted it out of habit, assuming that it was merely an ad for something he wasn't interested in. But for whatever reason, he clicked the document open.

The email revealed an image that took his breath away.

It was an oil painting. The quality, along with the artist's skill, wasn't anything out of the ordinary. Not that Sam cared even a little about the artistic abilities of its painter. It was the subject of the painting, and its location that suddenly caught his attention.

It depicted a Spanish slave ship high on a river's bank. The location was marked as the Save River, Africa and the date on the painting was 16th June, 1834.

There was a single note from the auctioneer.

I've had the ship checked against historical records, and it appears to match that of the Spanish Slave Ship, Midas.

I just thought you might want to know.

Regards, Edwin Young.

Tom walked into the room, and exchanged a glance with Sam. "Why do you have that grin on your face?"

"Nothing... I just found something interesting, that's all."

"Oh yeah, where are we headed?"

Sam drew a breath. "Zimbabwe."

"Really?" Tom asked. "What's in Zimbabwe?"

"Hopefully the remains of a 360-ton Spanish slave ship named, *Midas*."

"Obviously..." Tom's eyes narrowed. "And what is it about this ship that has you suddenly so animated?"

Sam said, "*Midas* left Africa in April 1829 with a cargo of hundreds of African slaves, headed for the Americas. It was bound for the Caribbean, but it never made it."

"So... there must have been thousands of slave traders that never made it across the Atlantic. What makes this one of so much particular interest to you?"

"You see, it's believed that the African slaves revolted against the Spanish traders somewhere along the arduous journey across the Atlantic. Apparently, it was a particularly hard journey, with one prolonged navigational detour after the next, leaving the Spanish as well as the African slaves, to deteriorate."

Tom smiled, starting to see what happened. "The slaves took the ship?"

"That's right. Not only did they take the ship, killing their Spanish slave traders in the process, but they didn't stop there."

"What do you mean? What did they do?"

"They set about taking other ships, pirating the highly treasured Caribbean, as other ships – Spanish, English, French, Dutch, Portuguese – you name it, passed through their waters."

"They were getting rich off the very people who had enslaved them?"

"Yes. They retook other slave ships, gaining momentum… along with gold and treasured artifacts."

Tom's face was set with curiosity. "So, what happened to them?"

"No one knows. *Midas* was last seen somewhere off the coast of Cuba, on the 2nd of October 1833. She was presumed sunk, its infinite treasures, garnered from years of piracy, lost forever."

"Until now?"

"Yeah…" Sam turned his laptop around so Tom could see the oil painting depicting the ship. "This was painted in June 1834 – along the Save River – in modern day Zimbabwe."

"Zimbabwe?" Tom asked. "What the hell was a slave trader turned pirate doing on that side of Africa? I mean, if they wanted to get home, they were a long way off course."

Sam nodded. "That, Tom… is exactly what we're heading to Zimbabwe to find out."

The End.